WHAT GOES AROUND

DAVID SIEGEL

ARCHWAY
PUBLISHING

Archway Publishing books may be ordered through booksellers or by contacting:

Archway Publishing
1663 Liberty Drive
Bloomington, IN 47403
www.archwaypublishing.com
1 (888) 242-5904

ISBN: 978-1-4808-3741-6 (sc)
ISBN: 978-1-4808-3742-3 (e)

Library of Congress Control Number: 2016915689

Print information available on the last page.

Archway Publishing rev. date: 12/9/2016

CHAPTER 1

. . . .

You can come home now

'Please be careful. And call me.'

'Don't worry, Ma. Everything will be cool.' As if Adam had a clue.

On the morning of the day after high school graduation, Baldwin High School, Class of '75, Adam Strulovitz and his friend Stevie Schecter embarked on their hitchhiking adventure across America – a pioneer's dream of discovery on the open road; manifest destiny at the tail end of the hitchhiking era. In their brand new, full-frame backpacks and Alpine hiking boots, they stuck out their thumbs, hoping their odyssey took them across the Mississippi, through the corn-belt, over the Rockies, and into the Pacific Ocean. Like so many before them; Lewis and Clark, Kerouac and Cassady, they were going to take the journey; write the next chapter in the American legacy. They felt ready for it, although they really didn't know what it was. It was a leap of faith. Jump, and the net will appear.

Part of every paycheck Adam had earned over that year, working as a delivery driver for Ocean Chemist, one of Baldwin's two family-owned pharmacies, had gone to purchase another essential survival item; a sleeping bag that could withstand temperatures of up to fifty below, powdered ice cream, water purification pills, enough snake-bite antidote to inoculate a small Peruvian village, waterproof matches, an ounce of Panama Red, three pounds of dried fruits and nuts, and more. Because this was an undertaking far greater than anything they had undertaken before, they wanted to be as prepared as they could. Adam had rarely ventured very far from his hometown. When he did it was mostly school bus rides to other Long Island towns for school sporting events, and weekend day trips into Manhattan to visit his mother's sister and her family. The only real vacation he had ever taken was when his parents drove his two brothers and him to Cape Cod when he was in seventh grade. They were supposed to take the full week right before school started but came home after four days. His older brother Charles was acting out. He wouldn't, or couldn't, be civil or non-confrontational. He was a year and four months older than Adam, about six years older than his younger brother Barry, and generally did everything he could to let them know what an impediment they were to his existence. This was more than sibling rivalry. This was open hostility – holding Adam down and giving him the spit torture, pushing him out of the hotel room when he was in his underwear and locking the door. Nothing their parents said had any effect. It seemed Charles's whole purpose that trip was to make everybody miserable. And he succeeded. They came home early. The first and last vacation they ever took as a family. But it wasn't the end of Charles's bullying. That continued until he went away to college, SUNY Brockport, near the Canadian boarder. Not that it was all bullying, all the time. Over the years, there were periods – days, weeks - of relative calm, of family harmony, although at no point did Charles do anything to promote Adam's or Barry's happiness or emotional growth. Not a single olive branch did he ever extend. He was into his own closed-off world; soccer, television, homework, one or two nerdy friends. When the darker, aggressive mood descended, he could be an unreasonable scumbag, destabilizing the whole family. More often, he was a distant yet balanced part of their family dynamic. Adam never felt loved by him. But there were periods he felt less threatened by him, and him by Adam. Adam did his best to avoid trouble. If Charles wanted to watch something different on television from what Adam was watching, even if he had been watching for a while, it was generally a good idea to let him watch what he wanted. He had never been one to back down or concede. It would have been better if they had more televisions, but they didn't. Money was always an issue in their house. If Charles didn't want Adam touching any of his possessions, he didn't, other than Charles's drums, when he wasn't home. And their parents did what they could to keep them out of each other's way, although family dinners sometimes got pretty tense. During one memorable meal Charles kept pushing Adam's arm as he was about to put a forkful of food in his mouth, causing him to jam the fork in his face. It wasn't funny the first time.

'That's enough!' their mother screamed, again. 'How many times do I have to tell you to stop!'

'I hate him,' Charles said, with an angry sneer. 'I hope he dies.'

Enraged that her son had just wished another son dead, their mother got up, rushed over to him, went to grab him by the shirt; not to hit him. She rarely hit Charles. He needed to be talked down. She had no problem smacking Barry and Adam in the face to get her point across. Their older brother fought fire with fire. Hitting him always escalated the problem.

She went to grab him by the scruff of his shirt, get in his face and let him know how fucked up what he had just said was. But he leaned back to avoid her grip, causing her to fall into him, hand-first, breaking her wrist against his chest. It was an ugly, crunching sound. It stopped them in their tracks – like they were a still image. She still screamed at him that he was never to wish his brother dead again, her face incredibly pale.

'You better straighten out,' their father angrily insisted to Charles. He drove their mother to the hospital to get a cast on her arm that she wore for six weeks, during which time the emotions in their house were relatively calm.

Adam believed his brother's dark behavior was rooted in depression, something their parents didn't know about or made the conscious decision not to deal with. Either way, without any kind of intervention, they were powerless to stop it. So they lived with it. Even when things started to get more serious. During Charles's freshman year in college he got into bodybuilding, and all the steroids that went with it. And that combination of steroids and depression was toxic in terms of his social and emotional stability. Not only did he gain a hundred and ten pounds in six months - some muscle, mostly bulk - but he had developed an obsession with sleeping, in the morning, afternoon, evening, it didn't matter. It seemed like all he wanted to do was sleep, eat, and workout. If there was unwanted noise he would become irrational, screaming to let him sleep, sometimes punching holes in the wall in his anger, and then storming back into his room, slamming the door until shocked silence once again descended.

'Let him be,' their mother would say. 'He's going back to school in a couple of days. Just try to live with it until then.'

If Adam's parents couldn't do anything about it, what could Adam do, other than walk on eggshells when Charles was around, and avoid him as much as possible, which wasn't that hard because Charles wanted as little to do with Adam as Adam wanted to do with Charles. The only time it got really tense and threatening was when Adam didn't know Charles was in his room sleeping at three o'clock in the afternoon, and he started playing his drums, something he had started doing regularly when Charles went to college and left his drumset home. Adam had always wanted to play drums, ever since the third grade. Stevie Shecter had a drumset growing up, and the few times Adam had gone over to his house when he was younger, he loved banging on them. It felt natural. But his parents weren't into it. To them drums wasn't really an instrument. So he blew a clarinet for less than a year. That was the sum total of his elementary school musical education. Then, for Charles's fourteenth birthday, their parents bought him a drumset. Some of their neighbors started playing drums, and Charles wanted to be a part of that neighborhood vibe. It was good to get Charles involved in something, especially something that channeled his aggression, and had possible social applications. But it was weird that they had been so dismissive when Adam asked, and then they went ahead and bought Charles a set. And of course, Adam wasn't allowed to touch them, although he did sit down and play from time to time when he knew it was safe. And every time he did, it felt right. Except when he started playing when Charles was home from college, and Adam didn't know he was sleeping in the next room. Looking up from his paradiddles, Charles stood looming in the doorframe, in his underwear, still a strange sight because of the hundred and ten pounds he had gained – Adam's brother, but also a stranger - with a look of such hatred on his face that Adam froze, a deer in the headlights, waiting to see if things were going to turn violent. If they did, he was going to do everything he could to get the fuck out of there, as opposed to fight. Not only did Charles have him by more than a hundred and twenty pound, but he had been lifting weights obsessively almost every day for months and was much stronger than Adam would ever be. In the back of Adam's mind he was hoping his brother hadn't turned the corner of becoming a violent psycho. He had always been a bully. He had always been uncool and distant. But more than anything, he had been a non-entity in Adam's life, adding nothing, but not having too much of a negative impact. To have that turn violent would have been an irrecoverable change. It would have realized the worst Adam had ever thought of him. In his heart, Adam was hoping Charles hadn't taken that step. He was his brother. To know he was so far gone would have been terrible. That's why he waited it out, even though he was scared shitless.

Without saying a word, Charles walked up to Adam, grabbed his face with his right hand, mostly around his jaw. And still Adam waited, ready to defend himself, or run if he had to, but not moving until he knew where things was going.

'Are you crazy?' Charles growled, the pressure on Adam's jaw increasing to the point where he was going to have to make a move if it got any tighter.

'I didn't know you were home,' Adam said, angrily, honestly. 'It's three o'clock in the afternoon.'

That woke Charles up a little, the fact that it was late in the afternoon, and he was still sleeping. Within his steroid rage, he recognized Adam had a valid point. Adam also thought he sensed his brother could never have justified real violence against him to their mother, who was out at the time. If Charles went off on him, for so meaningless a reason, his life in their family would be forever changed. Adam felt the pressure on his jaw loosen.

'Wake me up again and I'll destroy you, understand?' Charles said, teeth clenched, pushing Adam's head back fairly hard, knocking him backwards off the drum stool and into the wall behind him. At least he hadn't attacked him. And he didn't say anything about the fact that Adam was playing his drums. He just stormed back into his room and slammed the door shut, shaking their whole house. What a relief when he went back to school two days later.

His sophomore year, not only did Charles get even more into bodybuilding and steroids, he also got into hunting and guns, which Adam found out about when Charles showed him his shotgun, and a thirty-two caliber handgun, which he proceeded to point in Adam's face, like he was joking around. Adam had no idea if it was loaded.

'Don't tell mommy or daddy that I have this,' Charles said, with this commiserating look in his eyes. Adam felt it was insane to have a gun pointed at him: undeniably real. It felt like the world was out of balance. It also felt like a power-play on his brother's part, a threat, wrapped in a joke.

'Okay,' Adam said, and got the fuck away from Charles as quickly as he could.

Over that Christmas break Charles's behavior became more erratic – still the obsession with sleep, plus a new sense of disregard, even to his parents, who he avoided as much as he could, and was generally disrespectful to when he had to deal with them, like when he needed something. Ultimately, they stopped giving him money or lending him their car. So he took Adam's without asking – stealing money from him, and waiting until he was indisposed so he could take the keys to his Dodge Coronet 440, which Adam had bought with the money he had saved working the entire previous year at Uncle Burt's Popcorn Factory; bagging industrial-sized bags of popcorn for delivery to the Tri-Cities movie theaters. Adam had been working since he was nine years old. He was the kid with the paper route.

Adam was shocked and angry when he realized Charles took his car, and planned on confronting him as soon as he got home. He had made plans to drive his friends to the movies. Since he was the only one who owned a car, he had to cancel those plans, and ended up walking over to Stevie's house and getting high with him in his garage.

'He just took it?' Stevie asked.

'Yeah. Again'

'Don't sweat it. We're gonna have the greatest summer. Check out these hiking boots.'

Not a day had gone by since committing to their cross-country adventure that they hadn't discussed some aspect of it. Stevie and Adam had known each other since kindergarten. The few play-dates they had early on had created a friendly bond between them. But they only started hanging out as friends at the beginning of their senior year in high school when, at a party, they started talking about hitchhiking around the country. Once that became a real concept, and then an actual, parent-approved plan, they started hanging out pretty regularly.

When Adam got back to his house, his brother had still not returned his car. He also realized Charles had gone into his sock draw where he kept the money he planned on taking with him that summer, and had stolen twenty dollars, a whole day's wages.

'You just took my car? Again?' he angrily said to Charles as soon as he walked into the house later that evening. 'Are you kidding me?'

'I guess so,' Charles said, with a look of utter disregard and disgust, then a little aggression. 'Watch who you're talking too.'

Their exchange got pretty heated, to the point where their mother had to intervene, screaming, 'Both of you stop it. I can't take this anymore,' which Adam thought upset his brother a little bit. Charles knew he had been pushing his mother, who he loved in his selfish raging way, a little too far.

'Go smoke your pot,' Charles said, after their mother was able to bring the decibel level down. 'I don't need you.' Essentially, he was ratting Adam out to their parents, who, Adam believed, knew he had started smoking pot that year, his incense cover-up not being very effective, especially to a woman as perceptive as his mother. The worst part of it, though, was that, not only did his brother steal money from him and take his car without asking, but he also stole pot from him. Then he told his parents he smoked pot.

'He's going back to school in a couple of days,' his mother said, when Charles was back in his room.

Adam recognized how powerless his parents were to deal with his brother. How discouraging it was to see Charles push them around the way he did, as if they were just biding their time until he was gone. But he was coming home again for the summer. He had done well as a lifeguard, a job, his first, he had gotten previous summer. That was one of the reasons Adam's trip across country was so important. The thought of living in the same house with his brother for a whole summer was impossible. That wasn't the main reason he couldn't wait to have that adventure. The adventure itself was the thing. But not having to deal with his brother was also a thing, especially after their neighbor Kenny Sackler, who was Charles's only friend at the time had to find out where Adam was so he could get in touch with him to tell him not to come home because Charles was threatening to shoot him with the handgun Adam knew he had. The tone of Kenny's voice was matter-of-fact and highly concerned.

'I'm telling you, Adam,' Kenny said, 'he's crazed. I've never seen him like this.'

The day after he took Adam's car, the day before he was supposed to take a bus back to school, Charles and Kenny went to work-out together at a local gym. Charles injected a large amount of steroids into his upper thigh, close to his scrotum, and went into an uncontrollable 'roid rage', in which Adam became the object of his extreme prejudice. Adam immediately called his mother to tell her what Kenny had just told him.

'Shit,' she said. Adam heard the exhaustion, confusion, concern, determination in her voice. 'Can you stay at Stevie's for a while?'

Kenny had once dated Stevie's sister, and knew Stevie and Adam had become good friends. The three of them had gotten stoned together a few times when Stevie had gone over to Adam's house after school or on the weekend. Stevie's had been the first place Kenny called. A lucky deduction.

'You can come home now,' Adam's mother said over the phone a few hours later. She sounded tired, but less stressed.

'Is he there?' Adam wasn't sure he wanted to be in the same house as his brother. Charles was leaving the next day. Adam had already asked Stevie's mother if he could sleep over if he needed to.

'No, Daddy's driving him back tonight.'

'Is everything okay?'

'He's gotta get off that shit. It's making him crazy. He knows it.'

'What he say about the guns?'

'I made him give me the small one, and I threw it in the creek. End of story.'

'What about the shotgun?'

'I'm not worried about that. If he wants to hunt, that's fine.'

'Really?'

'Do me a favor. Don't make this anymore than it is.'

'But he…'

'Adam, I threw the gun in the creek. That's all.'

'Okay.' Adam trusted his mother. He was proud of her for making his brother give her the gun, and then going to the creek at the end of their block and getting rid of it.

'That's it,' she said. 'I don't wanna talk about it anymore. Come home for dinner.'

Adam hoped, on the way to Brockport, his father would try to talk some sense into his brother – get through to him. His father needed to get involved in the welfare of his family. He rarely did. Usually, he let the situation control him instead of controlling the situation. As a result it had gotten out of hand. As difficult as the task of loving his brother as he got older was, Adam had always hoped his father would have found a way. His father had stopped communicating with his own brother and sisters decades before. Adam never met his father's two sisters, and had only met his brother twice, when he was much younger. His father had begun to manifest that same type of detachment with Charles. Adam never knew why his father never spoke to his family – something about they were disrespectful to his mother when they first met. That's about as far as the explanation went, although it seemed only part of the story. Adam didn't really care about his father's brother and sisters – he didn't know them. But his own son. That was a little too close to home; a very dysfunctional family dynamic.

Adam's father was a salesman by trade, selling hats for his father-in-law right after he got married. After the millenary business went the way of whale oil, he sold industrial chemicals, mostly cleaning products around New York and New Jersey's lower-rent industrial parks, requiring him to be away three or four nights a week. As the years went by, him being away so often became unworkable for their mother, who was having an increasingly difficult time raising her three sons alone. A good night was when nothing got broken, and no voices were raised. Their mother kept control as best she could, with a stern, 'quick to squash anything that could escalate' kind of love. So his father got a job in New York City's garment center, selling piece-goods, the business he had gone to college for, and one, after serving in the navy during World War II, he hoped to pursue. Hands down, active military service was the most memorable thing he ever did. He was an ensign on a ship that picked up the marines who had fought on the island of Okinawa. He was part of the Pacific armada. PT 450. Even though he never saw combat, he was in the thick of it. His duties were logistics, helping get the ship where it needed to go. He always spoke about the look in the marines' eyes when they had just come off-island. That, and just having been there were his go-to story-lines for whatever point he wanted to make; the nature of the world, his knowledge of the American psyche, or simply as a tool to engage others, as salesmen are hard-wired to do.

As the years went by, and his father's dreams started to fade – dreams of financial comfort and his sons' solidarity - he went from being an ensign to a lieutenant when speaking to other people about his war experiences. Adam knew he did it to make himself feel better about himself – the higher the rank, the greater the respect. Adam didn't think his father fully understood that most people struggle. He thought his father believed the world had singled him out for persecution. One of his father's biggest struggles was that he never made a lot of money. For the last thirty years of his professional career, which lasted until he was eighty, he complained how nobody bought domestic piece-goods anymore. The whole market had moved to Asia because of cheap labor. He would pound the pavement for eight hours a day hoping things would change, but they never did. Then he would take the LIRR home, make himself one or two martinis, have dinner with his family, and settle in from of the TV, being joined by his wife only after she finished cleaning up and making sure her children had done all of their homework or whatever needed to be done. Not once did Adam's father get involved with his children's scholastic activities. Not once did he make dinner, or do the laundry, or clean the house, or go grocery shopping. He was as old-school, old-world 'men make the money, women do everything else' as they get. Except he didn't make very much money, and their mother worked as well, starting when Adam was roughly eleven years old. She was the Administrative Assistant of the Middle School in Baldwin for thirty-five years, and if she didn't work, Adam didn't know how they would have gotten by. But for whatever reason his mother let his father get away with not doing anything except going into the City and then coming home and complaining how fucked up his business was, until the first martini kicked in and his mood started to soften. Not that he was an alcoholic, which he wasn't. Nor was life in their house unbearable. Sometimes, maybe. Adam knew his parents loved his brothers and him deeply, which was their most enduring legacy, the capacity to love unconditionally. And that's probably the most important lesson a parent can instill in a child. But that hadn't stopped his brother from threatening to shoot him. By his father not taking an active role in his own self and family interest and improvement, those interests had stopped developing. Atrophy had set in, compounded by regret over not having done the things he knew he could have done or should have done or wanted to do that would have helped him realize his family's potential. As Adam ate a subdued dinner with his mother, he hoped his father would shake off the atrophy and rise to the occasion. He had almost eight uninterrupted hours with Charles in the passenger seat, a captive audience.

'You think he'll get through to him?' Adam asked.

'I hope so, sweetheart,' his mother said. 'Eat your green beans.'

'I hate green beans.'

'Good. Eat 'em anyway.

CHAPTER 2

And then it wasn't

The rest of Adam's senior year was about working at Ocean Chemist, saving money, buying camping supplies, playing Charles's drums, seeing Led Zepplin and The Grateful Dead at Nassau Coliseum, and waiting to see which colleges he got into. Adam picked Stevie up every morning on the way to school, and they talked about the trip – possible sites they might want to see, possible routes they might want to take, supplies they still needed to buy. The only specific destinations they had were Anaheim, California, home of both Disneyland and Stevie's brother-in-law's brother Stuart, and his wife Irene, and Nederland, Colorado, home of Scott Cohen, an old neighbor of Stevie's who had gone to college in Boulder, Colorado and stayed. Fate would determine the rest. Wherever their thumbs took them, that's where they were going.

But first they had to start. So, on the morning of the day after graduation, they walked over to Long Beach Rd., Baldwin's main thoroughfare, which lead to the Long Island Expressway, eventually leading to Interstate 80 and all points west. As they hiked through familiar streets, visions of snow-capped peaks danced in their minds. Their hometown was already behind them, and they hadn't even passed the McDonalds on the corner of Long Beach Rd. and Grand Ave. But both of them had read 'Vagabonding In America' by Ed Burns, which taught them everything from sleeping on gravel, to hopping a freight train and riding the rails, so they were able to project their vague intellectual comprehension onto the unknown.

By the end of the first day, they found themselves along Interstate 80, somewhere in the middle of Pennsylvania, a great first surge. The several people who had picked them up were generally local, twenty to thirty year old guys either working or on their way to work – not the cars filled with horny women traveling to where inspiration lead, as they had fantasized about. But that didn't matter. They were glad to be on the move.

Since there were no campgrounds within a reasonable distance, and it was getting dark, they pitched their tent in a field down the embankment from the highway and spent the remainder of the evening getting high, watching the trucks roll by, waiting for shooting stars, and feasting on dried fruits, nuts and Tang.

At around three o'clock in the morning Adam awoke inside the tent with rolling stomach cramps. Apparently, large quantities of dried fruits, nuts and Tang caused diarrhea, at least for him. He spent the rest of the night shitting fire 'til dawn. But squatting in an open field, in another state, under the stars, with eighteen-wheelers whizzing by in varying patterns of silence and sound wasn't as bad as he thought it was going to be when he realized that was his only option. There was still an element of freedom and adventure about it, although bare-assed, chicken-legged squat, sweatpants around his ankles, holding the bottom of his sweatshirt forward with his left hand to keep it away from any potential mess he had no facility to clean, a wad of toilet paper in his right hand was not the image he wanted to project.

Stevie slept through it all. Adam felt secure traveling with Stevie - six-four, two-hundred-twenty pounds, captain of the football and basketball team, only son, youngest of three, almost the golden child. Was, until his mother, who was the cantor at the reformed temple they both belonged to, passed away from cancer when he was thirteen, leaving a pronounced void. But Stevie was strong enough to work his way through it. Some of his early blossoming artistic talents may have lost their inspiration. But as he grew into a very handsome, very tall, athletically gifted young man, he adjusted to life in a motherless home. His oldest sister was eleven years older than him. Essentially, she helped guide him, along with his steadfast and loving father through his adolescence. In high school he found his stride – decent student, very popular, always going out with a beautiful girl; cheerleader, hippie, goddess. Adam was definitely jealous. He had broken up with the one serious girlfriend he had in high school earlier in his senior year when she asked him if it was all right to see another guy she had met the previous summer at sleep-away camp. Stephanie Millman. She was fifteen and Adam had just turned seventeen when they both made love for the first time, in a sleeping bag in the dunes in Long Beach, Long Island away from where anyone was likely to be walking. It was one of those very starry Atlantic Ocean nights, the sound of the waves breaking twenty-thirty yards from them, when everything was in harmony. It was pure and it was eternal. And then it wasn't.

'The softest lips,' Adam recalled, bearing down in a field near exit 34 off of Interstate 80, like he was giving birth, the lonely nighttime Doppler effect of the trucks cruising by giving motion to his solitude. 'Dear Johned. In person,' he thought, still squatting. 'At least I'm here… Oh fuck. I forgot the shovel in the tent.'

Lesson learned; don't be a stoned glutton. Hitching so far from home was a serious undertaking. Give it the respect it required.

CHAPTER 3

Three thousand miles to go

The combination of inexperience, fear of the unknown, and manifest destiny lead to the first few days of an adventure experienced predominantly from the backs of flatbed trucks. Ride after uneventful ride through Ohio, Indiana, Illinois, and Iowa - through the wheat fields of Nebraska and across the Continental Divide. Nights were generally spent in desolate places near the main roads Adam and Stevie were hitching on – usually in empty fields or inside a wooded area off the highway. Twice, the police knocked on their tent to tell them they couldn't pitch it where they had.

'Pack it up. You got ten minutes,' the police insisted. They were out of there in five.

Back to the highway. They endured the rest of those nights passing time by sitting, sometimes standing, sometimes in a futile hitching pose, waiting for morning traffic to start, usually around six, six-thirty. On those occasions, Stevie and Adam took turns catching some restless sleep while the other sat in the dark unsuccessfully willing a car to pick them up, or even materialize. Those were long nights. But not overly discouraging. A little. They were making progress. By their fifth or sixth day, they had made it to Mt. Rushmore, their first big national landmark. They took pride in their accomplishment, and enjoyed the open-roof jeep tour they splurged on, which was visually beautiful and informative, containing as many angles of sight of the monument as the engineers who built the road could incorporate into their design, one through an arch cut into the trunk of a massive tree. Rather than go around the tree, the engineers decided to go through it. It was a very cool sight to see the image of Mt. Rushmore framed through that enormous tree-trunk along one of America's great scenic roads.

They camped that quiet night in a hybrid industrial/natural KIA-deluxe-style campground at the edge of the Black Hills. It was more than adequate, with its Black Hills and chaparral views. The only slight bring-down was that, because of the realities of summer travel, especially to national monuments, the campgrounds were packed. The campsites were laid out in a grid-like pattern, each campsite roughly a twentieth-of-an-acre, dozens of them, all occupied, with a shower and concession area conveniently located in the multi-acre reserve.

'I actually don't mind all the people,' Stevie said.

'Me neither.'

After all their time alone on the road, they were happy to be part of a bustling community of fellow campers, most of whom seemed like they were having a good time on their adventure. Taking advantage of the facilities, part of the not-inexpensive campground fees - supply and demand - Stevie and Adam showered for the first time since they left Baldwin, in the clean, individual, open-roof stalls with wood-slat floors. Then they pigged out on roller-heated hot dogs, French fries and soft-serve ice cream, after first smoking a joint in their tent. They had zipped up the nylon-mesh window so no other campers could smell it, forgetting that, if they wanted to get out of the tent they would have to unzip the front flap, letting out the smoke anyway, which they eventually did, laughing that they almost locked themselves in the tent. Every time they said it throughout the evening, 'We almost locked ourselves in the tent,' they started laughing hysterically. It must have been the clean, festive South Dakota air.

The next day luck was on their side. They hitched a ride all the way to The Grand Tetons for their first real night of majestic camping - their first close encounter with the enormity and grandeur of mountains. Up to that point they had been cautious, staying close to the road, no major hikes through unknown territory in search of American beauty. There was an unspoken understanding between them that their first port of call, after Mt. Rushmore, was Irene and Stuart's house in Anaheim. That was the goal. After that, the serious day-long, week-long hikes into the majestic unknown. Until then, keep doing what they had been doing; hitch all day, sometimes not getting picked up for hours, and then find a reasonably safe, reasonably legal place to pitch their tent at night. Up early, raw grains or local breakfast place, if one was in the vicinity, then back to the highway for more of the same.

Fortunately, at the Tetons, the highway passes close to the mountains – about a two-mile walk across the wooded, pastoral, postcard-perfect alpine foothills landscape. That was the kind of distance Stevie and Adam normally covered, sometime quite a bit more, looking for a campsite. How much more beautiful it was to be in the natural wonder of the Tetons than in that cornfield in Iowa.

A few mornings before, they were awakened by a German Sheppard barking right outside their tent, set up in an Iowa cornfield they couldn't have imagined anyone detecting them in, so hidden were they among the acres of stalks. They understood so little about a farmer's vigilance, they never considered it. Looking through the tent's flimsy, nylon gauze window, they could see, by the dog's teeth-baring, aggressive bark that he wasn't taking kindly to them being in his cornfield.

'What are we gonna do?' Stevie asked.

'I don't know. You're Mister Football Player.'

'I'm not going out there. Wait, listen. Did you hear that?'

They heard a whistle. Then the dog stopped barking and took off, and so did they. They felt lucky not to have been attacked.

'That wasn't the kinda luck I was hoping for, though,' Adam recalled. Stevie and Adam were sitting around their small campfire, as one with the wonders of nature as they would ever be. It was like they were in the Garden of Eden, camped on the gravelly shore of a tranquil, mountain stream-fed lake, the silhouettes of the Teton massifs right behind them. It was a landscape that elevated the soul, that hinted at the depth of creation, especially stoned on really good weed. 'I mean, at what level does it stop being luck? My younger brother actually said to me that I was lucky the poison ivy that was all over my body didn't spread to my face... I fuckin' itched like my skin was on fire, and he's telling me how lucky I am.'

'I definitely agree with Barry. You're definitely lucky you didn't get it on your face. Who'd go near ya?' He started laughing. 'I could just imagine you coming to school with poison ivy on your face. Only you.'

'Did you ever have it?'

'Nope. I've been lucky.'

'You can't believe how much it sucks. It's insane.' Adam started laughing too. 'I'm lucky 'cause I got poison ivy... Yeah, I'm lucky 'cause I lost only one arm in the corn-thrasher accident instead of both.'

'I wonder what the lowest you could go is, and still call it luck,' Stevie said. 'Like something like he's lucky to be alive.'

'He was burned over seventy percent of his body, but he's lucky it spared his face.

'Yeah, he lost both arms and a leg...'

'And his dick...'

'And an eye...'

'And his wife...'

'And his wife... Oh my God, that is so funny...'

'But he's luck to be alive.'

They could actually hear their laughter echoing off the mountains.

The Tetons renewed their faith in their excursion. Finally, camping without compromise - into the proximal Teton wilderness. It was really the first time Stevie and Adam felt their trip was what they hoped it might be – an exploration of the natural wonders of America. Mt. Rushmore was incredible, but man-made, and the camping there suburban. How peaceful and inspiring it was to commune with the infinite, the Teton peaks towering above them, on the shores of a small lake fed by the streams coming out of the highlands – smoking a joint of Panama Red in the open, with no one around, while moose grazed not a hundred yards from them.

'Whoah, look at that moose, man. Could that be a moose? I thought moose were, like, from Canada or Alaska.' Adam thought moose lived in the north country. That night in the Tetons, it was sixty-eight degrees.

'No that's definitely a moose,' Stevie said.

'Whoah, a fuckin' moose. That is so cool. Here moose.'

'What are you doing? Don't call it over.'

'Why not? That would be wild.'

''cause it's a fuckin' moose, man.'

'Yeah? So? Here moose...' The moose knew better than to engage two stoned eighteen-year-old guys, even if Adam was offering it a handful of dried fruits and nuts.

The next morning they were back on the road with their thumbs out. The road was security, and they stuck to it like a child to its mother. They both knew they were lightweights, but they didn't hold it against each other. They were making progress.

Thumbing a ride out of Reno, Nevada, they were picked up by a middle-aged Mormon proselytizer who, in exchange for listening to him preach the Mormon gospel, agreed to drive them all the way to Big Sur, where he was going to meet other Mormon preachers for an annual crawdad bake. Neither Stevie nor Adam had ever heard of any of the latter day saints that guy had rhapsodized about – Lefi, Nefi, what? - and they were more than a little shocked when he mentioned something about the Jews killing Jesus, although neither Stevie nor Adam mentioned that both of them were Jewish for fear of being dropped off in the middle of nowhere, which was where they were when the preacher made his crazy declaration. Stevie and Adam just looked at each other and kept their mouths shut.

Other than that bit of prejudicial nonsense, their night in Big Sur, their first in California, was another natural-wonder highpoint. The cliffs, rocks, redwoods, the Pacific Ocean, all of it - magic. It was everything they had hoped their trip would be. And there they were. They had made it across the country. Even learning to catch crawdads with white-bread and string was amazing, cooking them over an open fire, drinking beer with a group of men who seemed to share a strong and enduring bond.

'Imagine if they knew we were Jewish?' Adam whispered to Stevie, after one of the older, very Caucasian brothers toasted the almighty.

'I'm denying it, man. They'd kill us in our sleep. Can you believe we made it? It's so beautiful here. I wanna get married here. I love you, man.'

'I love you too, man. Wait, did you just propose to me?'

'You're such a dick.' He was smiling when he said it.

The only drawback of the evening was that Stevie and Adam couldn't get stoned, not around a group of Melchezedik priests who believed Stevie and Adam were descended from those who, they were taught, had murdered their lord and savior.

The next morning, after a breakfast of crawdads and eggs cooked over an open fire, and being blessed more than Adam ever had at any one time in his life, Stevie and Adam hitched south along the Pacific Coast Highway. Even though they had both grown up fifteen minutes from the Atlantic Ocean, where both of them spent a lot of time during their summers, the sight of the enormous west-coast cliffs descending into the Pacific was mind-blowing.

'If you look about two o'clock,' said Bill White, who had picked them up not long after bidding the Mormons farewell, 'those are blue whales. They always pass here this time of year.'

'Whales. Holy shit,' Adam said. He couldn't believe they were seeing whales in the wild. It was surreal.

Bill, a local, Hawaiian-shirt-wearing driftwood artist, spoke about other local points of interest, like the general vicinity where Jack Kerouac had stayed, and the general area where Richard Burton and Elizabeth Taylor had shot scenes from the movie 'The Sandpiper'. He told them about his wife, who was a poet, and his daughter, whose name was Snow.

'For real?' Stevie asked.

'We think it's beautiful.'

'Snow White? Okay.' Stevie must have found that funny, because after a second or two, he burst out laughing, saying 'Snow White' in the middle of his laughter.

Bill didn't think it was so funny. 'Listen, I gotta turn off here soon. Why don't I just let you guys off at this pull-over. You have a good day now.' There wasn't a turn-off for many miles.

'Good going, genius,' Adam said to Stevie as they thumbed their way along the Pacific Coast Highway.

'Snow White,' Stevie said, still laughing.

They arrived in Anaheim at four o'clock in the morning with two options; wake up Stevie's relatives, or sleep in the street.

'You guys made it,' Stuart said. 'Come in. How was your trip?'

'You guys want anything?' Irene asked, walking up behind Stuart in her nightgown, wiping sleep from her eyes,

'No thanks,' Stevie said. 'This is Adam.'

Adam was so tired, all he could do was put his hand up in the Indian 'how' sign, and let it fall back down again.

'You guys look exhausted,' Irene said. 'Why don't you get some sleep and we can catch up in the morning. And then Disneyland. Either of you ever been?' Neither of them had, although Stevie had been to Disneyworld a few years before, just after it had opened, and said it had been pretty cool, as opposed to amazing. Adam loved Irene's enthusiasm. Disneyland. If it was as good as the bed he was shown to, after having slept on the ground for a couple of weeks, it was going to be a good day.

Almost. Adam kept wanting to feel the magic of Disneyland, but it kept eluding him. He couldn't see how it was a place where dreams became real. He had never had those kinds of dreams – to ride rides you had to wait over an hour to get on, which were over in less than two minutes. Plus, he had already seen the 'It's a Small World' animated doll show at the 1964 World's Fair in Flushing, Queens, and thought it was boring then. For thirty dollars, the price of the all-day pass, and a large portion of his budget, Disneyland should have delivered on its promise. The problem was, Stevie and he were hoping to meet girls, and the only ones around were either prepubescent or walking hand-in-hand with the guys they came with.

Irene sensed Adam's disappointment. 'Not really your thing, huh Adam?' she said.

'No, it's okay.' Adam didn't want to make her feel guilty about being so enthusiastic about going. She had tried her best to make it a good day, which in terms of ice cream and weather, it was. Certainly not a total loss. And the home-made lasagna farewell dinner she made that night was delicious. Plus, they had done it. They had made it to Disneyland. As Adam thought about it, the day didn't seem as disappointing as it did just a few hours before when he was actually there. Maybe, he thought, Disneyland wasn't about actually being there, especially without a girlfriend, or some kind of reasonable female companion, to share it with. Maybe it was about the afterthought, the mantra-like quality of knowing that he had been to Disneyland.

Early the next morning, Stevie and Adam were back on the road relying on their fellow countrymen to get them from place to place. It became easy to tell who was or wasn't going to pick them up. If it wasn't in the open, utilitarian steel bed of an ageless pickup, chances were pretty small. Not out of the realm of possibility, and it was always a surprise when a regular car stopped. Sometimes a pleasant surprise, when it was a younger couple. Usually it was a thirty to fifty year old guy. But since there were a lot of thirty to fifty year old guys in pick-up trucks around, they made good progress. By day's end they had found themselves at the edge of the Barstow Desert – where rumor had it that during the heat of the day temperatures rose to over one hundred and twenty degrees, only to plummet at night to well below freezing. And they hadn't packed winter gear. They didn't even have a sweater. Rumor also had it that there was a proliferation of scorpions in the desert, and that their advancement and infiltration was undetectable. But the most unsettling piece of unconfirmed information was that they could be stranded in the desert for days without a single car driving through. But there they were, reading the inscriptions on the exit sign threatening, 'Stuck here for a week. Almost died. Good luck,' and 'Beware of the night'. The painted sky was rapidly transforming from yellows, oranges and reds, to violet and navy, the night stalking them like a panther.

'This sucks,' Stevie said.

'I know. At least we have food. You filled your water bottle at the last stop, right? Right? ... Oy.'

They were preparing to endure the demonic darkness, when, like a governor's pardon seconds before an execution, Providence shined her divine light. As the moon became visible and cast its beams over the shadowed foothills, an old, beat-up Buick Skylark drove up and stopped.

'How far you goin'?' asked a twenty-one year old, longhaired, shirtless guy who had just lit a fresh Marlboro. He looked just like Dickie Bettes from The Allman Brothers.

'We're trying to get to Nederland, Colorado,' Stevie said. 'But we'll go wherever you're going,' meaning, 'Please get us outta here.'

'I'm cruisin' to Denver, man. Nederland's only, like, fifty miles northwest. I'll drive you, if you don't mind stoppin' at Vegas for an overnight, and then the Grand Canyon. Can't miss the Grand Canyon, man.'

'No, we were hoping to get to the Grand Canyon,' Adam said. 'I can't believe it. This is amazing.'

'Well, cool. Hop in.'

The slight wrinkle, which they didn't telegraph because they needed everything to go smoothly, was that they had heard there weren't any convenient campgrounds in the Las Vegas area. So, if they had wanted to check it out, they would have had to get a hotel room. And since they couldn't afford any of the rooms on The Strip, they would have had to stay downtown, which they heard was a shit-hole, especially the types of motels they could have afforded. As a result, they had decided, when they were planning their trip, to forego Las Vegas

Bobby 'from Ventura', who was going to be a junior at the University of Denver, and was going back a little early to find living accommodations, confirmed that downtown Las Vegas was indeed a shit-hole, and offered to drive them around until they found a motel they felt was cool. Bobby was going to be staying with a girl he described as '... seriously cute – I mean like Playboy model cute.'

'Wow,' Stevie said. He was jealous, as was Adam. They hadn't spoken to a woman almost the entire trip, and this guy was gonna be banging a playboy model. But they were happy enough to have been rescued from the unknown that they both let themselves live vicariously through their cigarette-smoking savior – all of them singing along to *One Of These Nights* by The Eagles on the eight-track, the Acolyte of Barstow driving them through the beautiful desert moonscape.

Roughly four hours later, Stevie and Adam checked into the New McDonald Inn. For twelve bucks apiece, they were treated to the luxury of a Spartan, plasterboard room with no shower curtain on the stall or hot water in the bath, although there was hot water in the sink. Yet to Stevie and Adam, who could have been sleeping with scorpions, or freezing to death, it was just fine. The fact that Adam lost seventeen quarters in a row in the motel lobby's one-arm bandit, the first time he had ever gambled, kind of bummed him out. But his mood lifted the next morning as soon as Bobby picked them up.

'Next stop, Hoover Dam,' Bobby announced. He looked as content as a saint on the Sabbath - who just fucked a playboy model.

'You know, legend has it that people are buried in there,' Bobby said, as they approached the great monolith. 'Fell into the cement while they were working, and there was no way to get them out. They just had to let 'em die.'

'Whoah, bummer,' Adam said, passing him the joint.

By day's end they were camping on a wide ledge above an abandoned eagle's nest overlooking the Colorado River one hundred feet below the lip of the Grand Canyon, which spread out before them for what felt like forever.

'Oh my God,' was all Adam could say. 'Gimme the camera.'

Stevie dug into his backpack. He was the keeper of the remaining camera. Adam had left his cheap Instamatic at Mt. Rushmore - your basic stoned idiot move. At least Stevie had his.

'Come on, man. The light's almost gone.' Still no camera.

'You left it in the room,' Adam said, suddenly remembering Stevie taking everything out of his backpack so he could get a change of underwear and socks.

'Fuck. Yup. Oh well,' he said. So much for the photographic documentation of their trip.

'We'll stop off on the way out tomorrow at one of the souvenir places,' Bobby said. 'There's like a million postcards, man.'

That night they watched Sagittarius rise and fly through the velvety night sky, so luminous was his bow, the carpet of stars so vast they cast star-shadows. How easy it was to contemplate nature's vast expanse, and their place in it, overlooking the Grand Canyon.

'Neither of you sleepwalk, do ya'?' Bobby asked. 'That's a long way down.' Even though the ledge they had chosen for their campsite had over twenty feet in front of it before the drop-off, Bobby had made a good point. And even tough Adam didn't think he sleepwalked, he wasn't taking any chances. One of the more prominent realizations he had made about himself on the trip so far was how much of a pussy he was. He always erred on the side of caution, even if that meant foregoing something as exciting as sleeping under the stars on a ledge that was actually inside the Grand Canyon. He didn't hold it against himself. It was more like accepting his limited manliness with humility.

'You know what,' he said. 'I'm gonna go back up to over there,' pointing to the large, flat tract of land they had hiked prior to descending to the ledge. Stevie had already said that he planned on sleeping under the stars, something they hadn't done since they left, their tent being a place of refuge. So Adam unhooked the tent from his backpack and headed up, close enough to Bobby and Stevie to feel their presence, but far enough away that he didn't have to worry about falling off a three hundred foot cliff.

'Pussy,' Stevie said. 'Just leave us the gorp,' which Adam did. Good old raisins and peanuts.

When Adam awoke in the morning, Stevie was sleeping soundly next to him. He hadn't heard him come in.

'Pussy,' Adam whispered in his ear.

'Whatever.'

A quick breakfast of sterno-fried powered eggs and molten coffee. Then a short hike to an ancient abandoned stone community carved into the side of the canyon walls.

'Anastasi', Bobby said. 'Supposedly they knew how to party, speakin' of which...'

They had developed an unspoken, very mutual agreement. As thanks for Bobby's incredible act of picking them up and driving them to where they wanted to go, they would keep him as stoned as he wanted to be. Their pleasure. Stevie had also brought along an ounce of Panama Red –clearly, the bud of choice in Baldwin at the time - so they were good for a while.

Then the hike back to the car, a few last-minute, soul-rejuvenating mental images of the Grand Canyon, storing those away because Adam didn't know if he'd ever see anything that indescribably eternal again, and they were gone, overtaking their past on Interstate 15, steadily rolling toward the future with over six hundred miles to travel, which they planned on doing with minimal stops – a quick bite, a piss, usually next to the car on the shoulder – that was about it. The rest was a straight shot to Nederland.

Soon they were driving through the emerald pools and waterfalls and cascading cliffs of Zion National Park.

'We gotta come back here and get into that,' Adam said. The land was calling him to explore, to climb those naturally terraced, smooth, light-colored rock slopes and inclines. Even driving through it, they were captivated.

When they got to the red stone spires of Bryce Canyon, which looked like a city of sand-castle towers and church steeples, Bobby slowed down to twenty-five miles an hour so they could absorb what they were seeing, so they could feel a part of it, letting anybody pass who wanted to. 'We definitely have to come back here,' Adam said, again.

Hour upon hour of the prolific diversity of the majestic American continent. Hundreds of lakes, millions of acres of high-mountain terrain, and every color that nature can manifest, including the brightest magenta flower Adam had ever seen, with color so vivid it seemed to radiate from its petals.

'Aloinopsis,' Bobby said, 'Those are actually succulents.' Bobby was a pre-med bio major. 'I'm into flora.'

In fact, one of the reasons they were driving straight through was because Bobby was hoping to get a job at the University of Denver's horticultural lab. He had an interview in two days, and wanted to wanted to get back a day early so he could find a place to live, relax overnight, and get back into his 'Denver groove'. But as they saw the sign indicating that Canyon-lands National Park was coming up in fifty miles, Stevie and Adam appealed to Bobby's aesthetic sensibilities and suggested an overnight camp under the stars.

'Fuck it, man,' Bobby said. 'Let's do it. Why not? Hey Stevie, how's about firin' up another doober, my friend. I know a place in Canyon-lands that'll blow your mind.'

Less than an hour later, as the sky was beginning to highlight every color of the spectrum, they pulled into another other-worldly landscape so vast and serene that they stood there silent, content just to gaze across the canyons and prairies as the blood-red sun slowly descended beyond the horizon. Later, as if out of an Ansel Adams photograph, a full moon rose, illuminating the distant snow-capped peaks, giving a lunar impression to the vast expanse. Bobby directed them to a campsite near the edge of a prominent cliff eight hundred feet above a raging river, where they were lulled to sleep by the silent and unending motion of the universe. The big, open sky freed Adam's soul that night.

As the morning's first light crept over the mountains, they once again packed up their gear, making sure there were no remaining burning embers in the fire-pit. Back on Interstate 70 East for their final surge into Colorado, they crossed the boarder just in time for lunch.

'This one's on me,' Adam said, jumping out of Bobby's Buick after he had pulled into one of those combination gas station, truck-stop, convenience stores that grace the sides of rural American highways.

Walking inside, Adam gave the obligatory 'Howdy' to the proprietor and casually strolled over to the deli section, where he surreptitiously slipped a large combination package of Oscar Meyer cold cuts into his pants. His senior year of high school was the year 'Steal This Book' by Abbie Hoffman, the '60's radical, came out, and it had inspired many impressionable, ungrounded youths, Adam included, to try to get away with the petty crimes the book so aptly instructed them on how to perpetrate. It hadn't turned Adam into a hardened shoplifter, but over the course of that year, he had stolen a tennis racquet from a local sporting goods store, just walking out with it as if he had brought it with him, and other sundries, like a leather watchband and a few shirts, wearing them right out of the store. Since the proprietor of the truck stop was still at the front register reading a newspaper, Adam knew the cold cuts would be an easy lift. Once the package was securely camouflaged in his underpants, he picked up a loaf of rye bread and graciously paid for it with the innocence of a used car salesman. Back in the car, he took the lunch meat out from his lap and saw that a good portion of the salami and bologna juice from the package had leaked out, leaving a noticeable bloodstain on his crotch.

'Steal This Book, right?' Bobby said.

'Yup.'

'Just be careful around here. They'll shoot you for less.'

CHAPTER 4

Best laid plans

The faint outline of a crescent moon was floating in the evening sky when they arrived in Nederland. Although they were warned that the local rednecks were not above pumping buckshot into the backsides of the hippies who had started inhabiting their town, Stevie and Adam stood fearless in the street outside Stevie's old neighbor Scott's house as they said good-bye to their fellow journeyman Bobby, thanking him for his trust and kindness and wishing him peace and good luck.

'Take care of yourselves,' Bobby said. 'Remember, this isn't a place to get caught stealing. Especially for a couple o' freaks. And watch out who you cop your herb from. Anyway, if I don't see you in the future, I'll see you in the pasture. Dudes.' And he drove away.

'I can't believe you guys made it.' Scott said, coming out his front door, a Coors in one hand, a shotgun in the other.

'Don't shoot,' Stevie said.

'I'm tellin' ya', man. This place is like the wild west, especially with cars I don't know parking outside my front door. But then I saw your ugly face...' Adam was glad Scott recognized Stevie before he started shooting.

After Stevie and Scott finished reuniting, Stevie made the formal introductions.

'Scott this is Adam. He lives on Lexington Avenue.'

'Strulovitz, right? I think my father knew yours from the Garment Center.' Adam's father sold piece-goods. Scott's designed menswear. 'What happened to your... crotch?'

'Oh man, I ripped off a package of cold cuts and it leaked. I gotta wash it out.'

'A quick lesson in crime and punishment, huh? Steal This Book?' Apparently everyone knew about that book, at least every guy between the ages of eighteen and twenty-five. 'I'd be a little more cautious around here.' Twice warned. That was enough. 'Why don't you go inside and get yourselves cleaned up. You can borrow a pair of shorts while your pants dry. And I'll throw some burgers on the grill. You guys hungry?'

Adam washed his pants in the sink in Scott's kitchen with dish detergent, per Scott's instructions, and hung them out to dry on the clothesline out back. Scott, apparently, was living a fairly rustic life.

What a mellow, perfect summer night that was, sitting in Scott's backyard, with the streams running through it, the woods fifty yards back, the stars as clear as ever, drinking an ice cold Coors, which wasn't available back east, so its legend as one of the great domestic beers had been firmly established. It was, in fact, delicious. As was the burger, and the sense of freedom. They had made it to their second established destination. From there, they were headed wherever their thumbs took them – back to Bryce and Zion, Yellowstone, fossil hunting in Montana. Their list of possibilities was pretty untapped. Adam felt they were getting more secure within themselves and their travels to start getting into some serious hiking and camping, something they had been on the periphery of since they started their trip. At that point Adam wasn't afraid of getting lost in a national park for a few days. There was always a way out, and once out, there was a road to stick their thumbs out on.

Since Scott had only one extra room in his house, with one bed in it, Adam let Stevie have it, and unrolled his sleeping-bag on the floor next to it. His pleasure. He fell sleep with a smile on his face.

The next morning Stevie lowered the boom. After breakfast, he informed Adam he was going to take the rest of his money, buy a plane ticket, and fly home the next day. He had had enough of the hobo life, which was what hitching was, much more than the exciting camping life they thought it was going to be - not that they didn't have some spectacular nights under the stars; The Tetons, Big Sur, The Grand Canyon, just two nights before in Canyon-lands. And they had the rest of the summer to live the dream. Adam didn't care that they would have to spend more nights along the way in suburban American back-lots near the main roads they were hitching on. It came with the territory. But so did the geysers of Yellowstone, and the falls of Niagara. It was all a part of the adventure.

Not for Stevie. Not anymore.

'Come on, Adam. You gotta admit we're not exactly having the greatest time. All we do is sit in trucks and go from one place to another.'

'That's what hitching is. But what about…'

'I know, but… And I should hang out with Marcia before I leave for school.'

Stevie and Marcia had been seeing each other on and off since seventh grade, and had been hot and heavy for the last half of senior year. Marcia Hochbein: cheerleader, heartbreaker, Playboy material.

Everyone recognized Stevie and Marcia were the all-American couple – the couple on top of the wedding cake. Marcia was the eternal home-coming queen, with a body even grandfathers got tongue-tied by. And she was very sweet. When she, Stevie, and Adam talked about the trip, she was excited for it to be as exciting as they all hoped it would be. Adam was surprised Stevie had decided to spend the whole summer away from her. But once he was gone, Adam didn't think he would bail out in the middle. With a one-day notice.

'What the fuck am I gonna do now,' Adam said rhetorically. He had nothing to go back to; no girlfriend, no job, his brother. He had planned on being away long enough so that Charles would be back at school by the time he got home.

It was amazing how quickly after he told Adam he was leaving, just a minute or two, that Stevie became persona non grata. Adam would expend energy reflecting on Stevie's decision another time. Right then, it was all about figuring out what he was going to do. He was on his own facing the unknown. And it was looking right back at him, an inexperienced, Jewfro-sporting eighteen year old with limited options. He asked Scott if he could stay at his house until he figured out his next move. Scott told him he was going to see The Rolling Stones at Red Rocks the following day, and that he'd prefer not having anyone in his house when he wasn't there. So much for their fathers knowing each other. But Adam wasn't shocked. That was just another in a series of setbacks, which, two novices hitching across the country with an undeveloped itinerary were bound to run into. The law of averages. That seemed to be the way of the world – one of the things Adam had started to learn on this journey - to grab the good when he could, 'cause the not so good was coming. He thought about the night Stevie and he got picked up by the police in St. George, Utah, on their way west, day seven or eight. They didn't know hitching on the highways was illegal in Utah.

'What do you guys think you're doing?' said the officer, who scared the fuck out of them with his flashing lights, pulling up next to them on Interstate 80 with a very stern expression on his face.

'Uh, we're just trying to get to California,' Adam said, trying to quell his mounting anxiety.

'We're gonna go visit my brother-in-law and go to Disneyland,' Stevie added.

'Not tonight you're not. Get in.' They were both freaking out, on the inside.

Once they were in the back seat of the police car, the officer explained that hitchhiking was illegal on the highways of Utah, and that, ordinarily, he would drive them back over the boarder into Wyoming, but because it was night he was going to put them in their jail, not arresting them - keeping them safe until morning.

'A lot of crazy people out there,' he explained.

It could have almost been an exotic night - getting to sleep in an actual jail as a free person. The officer even told them they could use their sleeping bags. The only problem was that Stevie and Adam had enough pot between them to keep them in that Utah jail for eighteen to twenty years. It was all they could do to act cool enough so the officer didn't think they would be stupid enough to not only break the law about hitching, which the officer knew they honestly didn't know about, which was why he didn't seem that pissed off at them, hadn't searched them, and was putting them in his jail without the usual bondage – but to compound the infraction by transporting illegal drugs across state lines. Adam's stomach was in knots as he trying to stay focused. Stevie looked like a guy from the Keane paintings, of the people with big eyes. 'Please God, let this be okay,' Adam prayed. This was the most trouble he was ever in - other than the other time Stevie and he had a run-in with the police over pot, about nine months before.

Stephanie Millman, who Adam was going out with at the time, had stayed home from school with the flu that day. So Stevie and Adam decided to play a little joke on her - like they were robbers trying to break into her house. During lunch-break they drove to her neighborhood, parked around the corner so she wouldn't see Adam's car, and snuck through her neighbor's backyards, knocking lightly on her house, like they were looking for a way in.

The only thing they forgot, in their stoned juvenile comedy, was that Stephanie's neighbors, some of whom were home at the time, didn't know they were playing a joke on their neighbor. All they saw was two suspicious youths casing a house for a possible break-in. Apparently, one of them called the police, because the next thing they heard was, 'Freeze... This is the police!'

'Fuck!' Adam thought. He had a vial of pot in his pocket.

'Put your hands in the air and turn around slowly.'

'We're just playing a joke on my friend's girlfriend, officer,' Stevie said, turning around slowly with his hands in the air.

As Adam turned around he reached in his pocket and, as surreptitiously as he could, dropped the vial of pot he had on him.

'What the fuck is that?!' one of the cops asked, just as Stephanie came outside and verified they were who they said they were. It didn't matter. The cops found the pot.

'You jerk-offs are under arrest.' They handcuffed them, read them their rights, put them in the back of their police car, and told them they were in serious trouble.

They were shitting in their pants. They had just fucked up their whole lives. In his mind Adam was racing through every excuse he could think of to tell his parents, as if they could magically make everything all right. But nothing could shake the feeling of impending doom that was getting more intense every second.

'I love the police,' Stevie said, saying anything he could think of to try and minimize the trouble they were in. 'I'm the captain of the football team.'

'You should have thought of that before you fucked up,' one of the officers said. 'Now, I don't want to hear another fuckin' word out o' you jerk-offs.'

The two of them were just waiting to get to where they were going so they could call their parents. They didn't even look at each other. They were freaked out. But instead of the police station, they ended up at the police triangle across from the Dunkin' Donuts - a wooden shack-like structure that looked like an oversized bus stop where the cops hung out because there wasn't much crime in Baldwin.

'Why are we stopping here?' Adam wondered.

'Get the fuck outta the car,' one of the cops said, physically pushing them into the shack. They were shitting bricks. Were they gonna start getting physical with them? with their hands handcuffed behind their backs?

'Sit over there and don't say a fuckin' word,' one of the cops commanded. So they sat on the wooden bench across the back wall, as they were ordered to do, and awaited their fate.

'Now, if we don't got any pot, we got nothin' to bust you for, right?'

'What the fuck was he talking about,' the two of them wondered. But his premise was correct, so they nodded in unison. 'And if Mr. Captain of the football team eats the pot, we got no pot, right?' Again they nodded.

One of the cops walked over to Stevie, pulled the hair on the back of his head straight down like he was ringing a bell. 'What, are you stupid? Open your fuckin' mouth.' Stevie finally understood. Instead of getting busted, they were gonna pour the pot down Stevie's throat - make it disappear. And that's what they did. They even joked around that he'd probably get a slow gradual buzz, and that he should thank them for getting him high. The only thing was that it didn't seem so easy to eat dry pot, and he gagged a few times. But he took it slow, and eventually, after three mouthfuls - they had shoved a lot of pot into that vial - it was all gone.

'Now you faggots get the fuck outta here,' the cops ordered. 'And if we ever catch you again, you're going to jail. No more fuckin' around.'

They undid their handcuffs, gave them a final shove out of the triangle, and they were free.

'Holy shit,' Adam said as they walked back to his car. They were already seriously late for school, and had no intention of stopping by Stephanie's to tell her what had happened. Adam would call her later that evening. 'How are you feeling?'

If Stevie hadn't been as big as he was, he would have needed to go to the hospital, that's how fucked-up he got. He had eaten almost a quarter ounce of pot, and had to miss a day and a half of school.

Sitting in the back of Utah State Police car, they knew if they got caught with the pot they had on them, they wouldn't be getting off so easily.

'All right, just follow me,' the officer said, parked in front of the St. George police station. Stevie and Adam were dying on the inside. They looked at each other, and that look said it all, 'Whatever you do, be cool. Do not fuck up.'

The fact that they were put in the holding cell, the kind they had seen in almost every cop drama on TV – a small room within a room with bars on the front, and a few benches on the side – and the door remained unlocked was a very good sign.

'We're just keeping you in here overnight,' the officer who took charge of them from the highway patrol officer said. 'Any reason I need to lock you in?'

'Nope,' Adam said, choking down his heart-pounding anxiety. 'I don't think so. We really apologize for not knowing we weren't supposed to hitch. We should have known better.'

'Yeah, I love the police,' Stevie said. 'I play football back home.'

Adam was thinking, 'Again with loving the police and football... Please shut the fuck up.' Stevie was sounding as nervous as he was when they got busted the first time.

'You're friend there seems kind of nervous. You guys aren't doing anything stupid, are ya'?'

Adam's ears were burning with radiating fear. 'We've both lived kind of a sheltered life,' he said, 'so this is pretty... weird... being in a jail.' At that point it was all about trying to act as benign as possible. Luckily, Stevie picked up Adam's vibe and nodded benignly.

'All right,' the officer said. 'If you need to use the bathroom, just ask. It's down the hall on your right.'

'Thanks officer,' Adam said.

'Yeah, thanks. And have a... good night.' A smart move on Stevie's part; shut it down and fake sleep. There was no way either of them was getting any real sleep, or so Adam thought. Within minutes of him spreading his sleeping bag on the hard cement floor, Stevie was fast asleep.

'Maybe I should find a place to stash the weed,' Adam thought. 'Nah, no way. Fuck. This sucks. All right, just breathe.'

'Rise and shine,' a different officer said. Adam couldn't believe he had actually fallen asleep for a couple of hours.

Somehow, God had watched over them. They hadn't aroused suspicion, at least enough to warrant searching them. The next morning, after the police fed them coffee and donuts, they drove them over the boarder into Wyoming. Adam had never felt so relieved in his life. And he knew Stevie felt the exact same way.

'We catch you again,' the officer who drove them warned, 'You'll be spending some real time with us, understood?'

'Definitely.'

'Absolutely.'

CHAPTER 5

A little Providence

Adam needed a plan... figure out the next step forward.

'Maybe I should ask Scott if I could, at least, camp in his backyard for a day or two,' he thought. 'Nah. There's gotta be a place to camp around here. Okay, that's step one...'

That thought settled him a little – finding a campground within a reasonable distance. Maybe even meet up with other solo trekkers, one step leading to another, embracing the unknown. But hitching on his own - not exactly ideal. But it was either that or go home; spend the rest of his savings on a plane ticket, or save some and take a bus - accept his friend disregarded him and go home looking like a loser who couldn't do what he said he was gonna do, sometimes bragging about what he was going to do. Those were his options; get hacked up by some psycho-killer who picks up lone hitchhikers somewhere in the Colorado Rockies, or go home.

And then a little Providence. So unexpected. The sweeter for it.

Stevie had walked into town to get lunch alone. After he told Adam he was leaving, Adam wanted nothing to do with him. But he had to eat too. So, about an hour after Stevie left, Adam walked into town as well.

On the road, a road through the emerald-forest Colorado foot-hills that should have been a source of wonder because of the natural beauty all around, but wasn't because everything at that point sucked, was Stevie, talking to an incredibly beautiful girl; blond hair, short jean shorts, cowboy shirt tied at the waist and the rest of the buttons undone, a summer fantasy, the impossible dream. Adam was incredibly jealous. But projecting indifference or hostility would have only brought him down further, so he passed them with a slight nod and a non-committal 'How're ya doing', and continued his solo trek into town. Up to that point they hadn't had one single female encounter, and here was the guy who was ruining his summer flirting with a girl who probably didn't even register that he was walking by. Stevie's practiced, charming smile. And Adam was facing the unknown unprepared. He couldn't even enjoy the short-ribs and beer he had at the bar Scott told him was the coolest place around. To him, it could have been just another shit-hole diner they ate at on the road, that they probably would have been pitching their tent near if nobody picked them up before it got dark, which, throughout their hitch was more than likely.

When Adam got back to Scott's house his demeanor immediately changed. Because Scott had gone hunting right after he told Adam he couldn't stay at his house, and wasn't expected to return until much later that night, Stevie had extended an obvious invitation to make dinner for his new, extremely desirable friend. When she informed him she was traveling with her sister and another guy, he courteously invited her whole party, attempting to atone for his unilateral departure by providing Adam with possible female companionship.

'There he is,' Stevie said as Adam walked through the door, telepathically trying to convey the possibilities Adam had with the other girl in the room, whose presence Adam registered at once, and who he silently speed-prayed found him attractive.

'Hi Adam,' said the woman Stevie had been speaking to on the road. 'How was lunch?'

'Delicious.'

'I'm Lynn, by the way. That's my sister Chris.'

'Hey. Good to meet ya,' Adam said, still praying.

'Good to meet you too,' Chris said. Beautiful smile. Round mid-western face, German, maybe Irish. Not stunning, like her sister, but cute, same piercing blue eyes. Straight, light brown hair parted in the middle, beautifully formed smaller breasts needing no support. Being the second best looking ones in their respective pairs gave her and Adam an immediate common bond.

'And this is Tom Buck. We picked him up hitching in... Where was it Tom, Fort Wayne?'

'Yup.'

'We're driving him down to the Gunnison, where he's gonna cover the Blue Mesa Dam with riprap.'

Tom smiled and nodded. 'How's it goin' Adam?' Tom looked like Jesus in a denim shirt, jeans and construction boots. Another tall, handsome guy. Adam felt like a troll.

'What's riprap?' Adam asked.

'It's rock or sometimes concrete that's used to protect shorelines or bridge abutments or dams against erosion.'

'Don't want a dam eroding, I would imagine,' Adam said.

'You got that right. Good-bye Montrose,' Tom said.

'Come on and sit with us, Adam. Stevie's told us all about you.' Chris's mid-western accent was slower than the typical Long Island accent - more sultry, at least to him. At that point, any woman his age smiling at him and saying hello, especially if she looked like Chris, would have gotten him going.

'Did he tell you that he was leaving me high and dry?' He didn't say that. What he said was, "I hope it was good.'

'He told us you're a really good drummer,' at which point Adam's animosity toward Stevie subsided a little. Stevie had never done any matchmaking for him before. He was atoning. 'I'm a drummer, too,' she added.

Since Adam had started playing, he felt drummers were part of a brotherhood – finger and toe-tapping guys who marched to their own rhythm – less intellectual than other musicians – more primal. Although he had never met a female drummer, other than the girl who played snare-drum in the high school marching band, who tended not to hang out with guys, he felt a stronger connection to Chris because of their rhythmic bond. He thought she felt the same way, based on how comfortable they were talking to each other. The conversation flowed without inhibition. Her sister had been laid-off from the Richman Tire and Rubber plant in Akron Ohio, where they were from, and they decided to travel around the country for a while. Her tone suggested that life in Akron was less than complete. She had just graduated from high school as well, but didn't have any immediate plans to go to college, 'Maybe Ohio State in the spring. We'll see,' she said. 'They have a real good nursing program. Right now I'm hanging out with my sister. And Mr. Tom over there.'

She and her sister had been on the road only a few hours when they saw this guy, who looked like a cowboy Jesus, hitching a ride. Lynn, because she was feeling free and adventurous - this was a time when hitchhiking was still part of the American experience - decided to pick him up. She thought he looked like he knew his way around the open road and could suggest where they might find out-of-the-way natural beauty, as opposed to national parks, which Lynn felt she could see anytime, and planned to, a little later, when she married and had kids. Now, her wandering spirit was directing her to go with a less defined itinerary, more of a 'drive, and the destination will appear' adventure. As it turned out, Tom was exactly what Lynn thought he might be. He was a freelance construction worker on his way to the Blue Mesa dam project on the Gunnison River in the Black Canyons of southern Colorado, where he grew up. He had been hitching his way around America working on large-scale, well-paying building projects for about six years, and had a cool vibe and quiet confidence you appreciate in someone you just met. Lynn and Chris were going to drive him to the dam site, and he had promised he would show them places they'd remember for the rest of their lives on the way.

'What are you guys gonna do for the rest of the summer?' Lynn asked.

Stevie had neglected to tell Lynn he was flying home the next day, hoping for a quick 'here's your hat, what's your hurry'.

'I'm going home tomorrow,' he said, knowing instantly by her expression that Lynn knew he had been trying to play her. 'I need to sleep in a real bed.'

'I know what you mean,' Tom agreed. 'Hitching can definitely be intense. On my way down from this job in Toronto this guy picked me up and asked me if I wanted to get a hotel room with him. Damn. And after I said no he turned red as a sugar-beet, took a twenty-two from under his seat and started screaming that he was gonna blow my head off. But I'll be damned if he didn't just stop the car in the middle of the highway and tell me to get out.'

That story put the fear of God into Adam. What would he do if that happened to him? He couldn't believe, starting tomorrow, he was going to be hitching alone. Tom looked like he could handle himself. Adam had just been bar-mitzvah'd five years before, and had rarely been out of his hometown.

The thought of his brother pointing a gun at him popped into his mind. 'I can't believe he pointed it right at me,' he thought. 'I'm definitely not going home so fast.'

Chris must have seen or sensed his apprehension. 'So what are you gonna do?' she asked him, genuinely interested.

'I don't know. Hitch around myself for a while. I just found out he was leaving this morning.'

Chris looked at her sister for a brief second. 'You can travel around with us for a while... I mean, if you wanna.'

If he wanted to... He wanted to more than she could have known. He had just been delivered. From darkness to light in an instant – by a beautiful girl he felt an immediate connection to, like they were friends, even though they had just met. It was unbelievable, truly one of the most poignant moments he had ever known, right out of the book of miracles.

Lynn smiled. 'Yeah, Adam. We'd love to have you.' Lynn had been harboring a certain desire for Tom Buck since they had picked him up. Tom shared that mutual desire, but also let her know, through an unspoken understanding, that he knew she wasn't going to act on anything if it made her sister uncomfortable, which, being a third wheel would certainly have done. By extending that invitation to Adam, Chris was not only delivering him from the unknown, but freeing her sister and Tom to express their desire for each other. Stevie never had a shot. Lynn was just being cordial when she stopped to talk with him on the road. A New York woman would probably not have been as friendly; too random, one of the distinct differences between encounters in New York and the rest of the country. Ask a woman from the South or Midwest you've never met how she's doing and, chances are, she'd give you a smile, tell you she's doing all right, and ask you how you're doing. Women from New York tend to be a little more guarded. Stevie, being a quintessential New York guy, had mistaken Lynn's friendliness for an easy mark. Adam didn't know if it was going to happen with him and Chris either, but he wasn't going to jeopardize the invitation that was just extended to him by pushing his luck and coming onto her. He had learned his horniness, ninety-nine times out of a hundred, was not shared by the woman it was directed at. That's why God invented jerking off.

'Why don't I get the fire started,' he said. 'I'll cook us up some serious burgers.' Scott had told them they could help themselves to his chopmeat.

'I'd love to help,' Chris said.

'Well, come on.' 'Thank you, God,' Adam thought.

Chris joined him out back while he got the grill going, and further captivated him with her graceful spirit and flowing peasant dress.

'So which drummers do you like?' he asked. What an easy conversation for him to have. Once his brother went away to college, he started playing his drums, and took to it fairly quickly. It seemed to be a part of him, where he could forget about everything and just let go in the energy - a refuge.

'Well, I think my style is very much like Ginger Baker, although I don't play double-bass, but I'm thinking about it. And, you know, like, Buddy, of course. Oh yeah, I saw Billy Cobham, the drummer from the Mahavishnu Orchestra. Oh my God. It was incredible. It was like the best drumming I've ever seen. Double-bass also. I think that's the thing.'

Adam had seen Billy Cobham two months before Stevie and he left, and was so blown away by what he did that the next day he went out and bought another bass drum. He had just become a double-bass drummer, although when Charles came home he reset the kit the way Charles played it, not that he played it very often anymore. Adam stored the extra bass drum in the garage until Charles went back to school. But by buying that bass drum, Adam had made his first purchase on the way to owning his own drum-set. When he told Chris he had recently seen Billy Cobham, and that he inspired him to become a double-bass drummer, she smiled and shook her head. They were on the same wavelength.

'I know,' she said. 'That was some of the craziest energy I ever felt.'

'It definitely takes a while to get used to double-bass. I'm still working on it. But I never heard of a female double-bass drummer. You should go for it.'

'Yeah, we'll see.' It seemed there was a lot behind her 'we'll see'. Her tone became less buoyant, her eyes slightly downcast.

'When did you start playing?' Adam asked, trying to bring the focus back to something less involved.

'My dad was in the army drum and bugle corps. He was like amazing on the snare. He won a few national awards. But then my parents got divorced a few years ago, and he moved away. But he left all his drumming stuff, so I just started playing and got really into it. What about you?'

Adam went into his whole story about how he knew he wanted to be a drummer in the third grade, but his parents weren't into it, but then they brought his brother a drum-set, which he finally got to play when his brother went away to college. 'And I've been playing almost every day since, except when he comes home.'

'I bet because you had to wait, you're more into it. Like, you're finally getting to do it. That's the one thing I miss so far.'

'I know. You and me'll have to jam. We'll find a place.'

'I think your...' She redirected his attention to the grill.

'Oh yeah... Why don't you call everybody out.' The burgers were ready.

Adam almost felt like the lord of the manor, cooking for everyone – except for the fact that he knew he was trying, maybe a little too hard, to do everything he could so that Chris would find him attractive enough to have sex with. He couldn't help himself.

'Tom's been telling us some other pretty crazy hitching stories,' Lynn said, everyone sitting around on Scott's lawn chairs enjoying their well-cooked burgers and beer. Lynn had a way of keeping the conversation flowing without seeming to. You couldn't really help looking at her, and she had learned how to direct that kind of energy the way a talented moderator would, or a master politician, if that master politician looked like Miss July.

'A few years ago I was working on the Teton Dam,' Tom said. 'Man, that was a blow-out. Very poorly managed. So I left to go up to Toronto...'

'What were you doing on that one?' Stevie asked. Adam sensed a little healthy competition between Stevie and Tom for Lynn's attention. Even though Stevie's hand had been revealed, and not in the most chivalrous way, he was hormonally incapable of not flirting with a woman who attracted him like a prospector to a mountain of gold. Adam felt guilt that he was rooting for Tom, but Stevie had made his decision to leave and, out of spite and jealousy, Adam didn't want him leaving with such a magnificent conquest. He knew he was being less than a good friend, but at that point he didn't feel they were.

'I worked the RT, the rough terrain crane. A little too rough, I thought. Anyway...'

'I once worked at a construction site,' Stevie interrupted. 'They're building all these new condos in my hometown, right Adam?' meaning, 'Because of me, Chris is here, and I told them how great you were, now you build me up.'

'Yup,' Adam said, noncommittally. He wasn't going to support Stevie's cause, and Stevie knew it, although bringing Chris into his life had softened his animosity toward him.

'That's good,' Tom said. 'What did you do?'

'You know – sheetrock, spackle.' Stevie was way out of his league.

"So anyway, Tom,' Adam interrupted, 'what happened?'

'So this guy picks me up in Rapid City, and he seemed cool enough. He tells me he just has to make a stop in Fargo before heading over the boarder. I didn't think much of it. But when he pulls up near this bank and parks, and says to me, "Listen, why don't you take over the driving. And when I get out of the bank, you just take off as soon as I get in. Deal?" This guy was about to rob that bank and was gonna use me as his accomplice.'

'So what did you do?' Chris asked.

'I just told him thanks but no thanks, and got outta there as quick as I could. I'm telling you, as I was walking away, I thought he might shoot me in the back. It was one of the strangest feelings I ever had. I'll never forget it. Could o' just as easily been.'

'Did he end up robbing the bank?' Adam asked.

'I don't think so. I didn't hear anything. I was out of there pretty quick.'

'I once knew a guy who told me his father shot these guys who tried to rob his jewelry store,' Stevie said. Adam had to give him credit for trying, although all his efforts were in vain.

"Listen, I'm gonna clean up and get some sleep," Adam said, as soon as the energy in the room started to fade. He didn't want to get any more fucked up than he already was because that meant waking up with a hangover, and he was never his best in that condition. With the possibilities that had suddenly presented themselves with Chris, he didn't want to do anything to jeopardize them. He had already taken his sleeping-bag out of the room he shared with Stevie and pitched his tent by the stream that ran through the back of Scott's house.

'Yeah, I'm pretty beat myself. Where are you gonna sleep?' Lynn asked her sister, with an extra-sensory conveyance of understanding only sisters share.

'I…' and she looked right at Adam. 'I'm gonna sleep out back in Adam's tent. You want some company?'

This was really happening. Right there. Right then. Like he was living the movie where things like that happened. Adam didn't know what to say, although his shit-eating grin said it all. He managed a, 'Definitely', and was glad Chris stood up first, because he was dumbfounded. Then everyone stood up and started going to their various sleeping places, Lynn grabbing Tom by the hand and almost dragging him to the car where their tents were, although only hers would be pitched that night, in a secluded spot in the pine forest that bordered the property. Stevie was on his own.

What a timeless night. Adam had never kissed a girl with more hunger or passion. He didn't know what it was; the mountain air? the freedom of expression because he was on his own for the first time? Love? All of the above. They melted into each other, and didn't stop fucking until it had already started getting light out. There was almost no talking, except to say how beautiful what they had just done was, right before saying good night. Then sleep for a couple of hours. Lynn wanted to hit the road right after an early breakfast. The explorations into south-western Colorado's natural wonders Tom had suggested all sounded worthy of extended stays, and he needed to be at the job site in the next week or so or he risked losing the crane operator's job he had been contracted for.

After a couple of hours of 'shared sleeping-bag, shared body warmth in the cool mountain air' sleep, Chris and Adam got up, both of them a little nervous and shy. Even though they had made selfless, out-of-body love, the morning light illuminated the fact that they had only met several hours before. But knowing they had the opportunity, and were looking forward to getting to know each other a whole lot better mitigated most of the discomfort fairly quickly. After Adam cooked them omelets over a quick-built fire, any residual weirdness was long gone.

Chris, who was also eighteen, had been seeing an ex-marine, who, two years into their relationship, started drinking more heavily than he ever did and became gradually more abusive, although she said he never hit her.

'But did he, like, push you or anything?'

'Just once. Well, once bad. That was it. He knew it too. He needed help. He wasn't a bad guy. I just couldn't help him. I needed to get away from him'

'Good,' Adam said. 'You deserve better than that.' He really didn't know what else to say. Chris seemed too young to have had such darkness in her life. As self-serving as it was, Adam was going to do everything he could to redeem the male species in her eyes, simply by just not being a jerk-off, which he honestly didn't think he was – maybe a little naïve and inexperienced… and horny - but basically good.

'What about your love life?' she asked.

He told her about his relationship with Stephanie Millman, leaving out the 'Dear John' part. He didn't want Chris to think he was the kind of guy who got 'Dear John'd', blaming their breakup, instead, on Stephanie's parents, who found out they had smoked pot together, and half-heartedly, and unsuccessfully insisted they break up. 'I was bummed,' he added, 'but masturbated my way through it.'

'Seriously?' Chris asked, a shocked look on her face. She had no idea if he was kidding or not. And even though there was some truth to what he had just said, he had said it as a joke. After her telling him about being pushed around by an ex-marine, he felt it was important to bring the levity back.

'I'm just kidding,' he said, smiling.

After a delayed reaction, she smiled and shook her head. 'Sure you are,' she said. 'My old boyfriend used to get my mother pot. She was definitely a little sorry to see him go, but she'll probably call him when she needs some.'

Chris's mother's story, in the early years, was not dissimilar to Adam's mother's. Both were born in the depths of the depression to immigrant parents – Chris's German, Adam's Russian. Both had been bobbysoxers, and heavily into Frank Sinatra – Adam's mother even sleeping on line over-night at The Paramount Theater in 1944 to get tickets to his concert. Both had thought FDR would be President for the rest of time, and both had married honorably discharged military men several years older than them six or seven years after the war had ended. Chris's father supported his young family by playing drums in local and regional jazz bands - even some national acts like the Dizzy Gillespie Big Band, whose regular drummer got sick while they were passing through Ohio - while her mother took care of the family's domestic needs. When Chris was very young her father bought a small record store in Akron, which paid the bills for a couple of years, until the British Invasion, when it became a hub for the Akron music scene. With success came a bigger house and better cars and more parties and access to women, which Chris's father regularly took advantage of, eventually getting so wrapped up in his lifestyle that he neglected his business. Sales declined, money and inventory were stolen by unmonitored cashiers and stock-workers, bigger record chains had started to rear their corporate heads – all factors that lead to the decline of Chris's father's business, which he eventually sold in order to avoid bankruptcy. All of that pressure, and the fact that Chris's dad had been fucking around behind his wife's back, lead to an inevitable divorce. After the dust settled, Chris's dad moved to Cleveland, where he got a job with a wholesale record distributor, never missing an alimony or child support payment. Chris's mother got a job in the meat department of the local supermarket, where she was still working when Lynn and Chris decided to travel around. She had been seeing the head butcher for about a year, but both Lynn and Chris knew it was a relationship of convenience, as opposed to love, the butcher being a slightly older, balding, overweight, ex-slaughterhouse foreman who was always very nice to Lynn and Chris. He understood they were still deeply upset about their father moving away, and kept a low, supportive profile when they were together.

'He's a good guy and all,' Chris said. 'But I know my mom still misses my dad.'

'So, did you ever get stoned with your mother?' Adam asked.

'Just a couple o' times. She wasn't exactly fun to be around when she was stoned. Mostly Matt would sell her an ounce and then roll a joint out of her stash, and then she'd end up telling him all her troubles. It was weird. I could just see those two hooking up... Ugggh, I can't even think about it.'

Adam didn't know what to say. Her boyfriend hooking up with her mother. He went with levity, which he tended to do in uncomfortable situations. 'At least then I wouldn't have an ex-marine coming after me for sleeping with his girlfriend.'

'And he would'a, too. He could get pretty jealous.' She got the joke.

'Just, if you ever see him again, maybe you wanna neglect to mention that you and I… you know…'

'Oh, I'm writing him the first chance I get. I love it when guys fight over me.'

Adam actually, for a moment, didn't know if she was serious or not, one of the pitfalls of sleeping with a woman he knew nothing about.

'I'm just kidding, Adam. Jeez, not much for confrontation, are you?'

'I don't know. I've never really had many,' which was true. He had lived a pretty sheltered, middle-class life up to that point, except for his older brother, which may have been the reason he was so not into having anyone fuck with him anymore.

'Well, I'm trying to put all that behind me. That's why getting away has been such a godsend. And I think it just got a whole lot better.' She came over to him and kissed him with her warm, wet tongue, and drew him right back to that timeless, sensual place.

'It certainly did,' he thought.

CHAPTER 6

· ·

Like a-priori knowledge

After breakfast they packed up the car and, along with Lynn and Tom, who also seemed to be attached at the lips, were on the road before Stevie or Scott had even woken up.

If Adam didn't see Stevie in the future, he'd see him in the pasture. 'How appropriate,' Adam thought.

Their first stop on the way to the Black Canyon of the Gunnison was in Crested Butte, nestled in the Gunnison highlands, where Tom had some friends who owned a llama ranch. Not only did Adam not know that llamas were bred in the United States, believing them to be strictly indigenous to South and Central America, but he had no idea they spit. He walked over to a calm looking llama who was busy chomping on a bug-ridden pile of compost, and it spit on him - raised its head and hucked a slimy brown goober that smelled like cat piss onto his prized Led Zepplin tee shit, the one he had gotten a few months before when he had seen them at Madison Square Garden. He had planned to keep that tee shirt the rest of his life as a precious artifact, but had to throw it out two days after the llama spit on it because, even after a couple of washes in Tom's friends' washing machine it had this residual smell that was rubbing off on all the other clothes he had with him in his backpack, which wasn't a lot; a couple of tee shirts, another pair of jeans and a pair of cargo shorts. Walking into a diner somewhere smelling like cat piss was not how he wanted to present himself.

'Adam, you gotta wash yourself off in the river,' Chris said to him as he got into their tent the night they left the llama farm. He hadn't even been wearing the Zepplin tee shirt that day. 'And throw that shirt out, man. It stinks.'

Even though it was a bummer trashing a prized rock artifact, bathing in a lazy river running through the Colorado highlands, under one of the deepest, starriest skies he had ever seen, with Chris naked in the river next to him, jerking him off with the lavender scented body-wash she said would remove the cat piss odor made it all worthwhile.

Adam's cum disbursing in the water reminded him of footage he'd seen of fish ejaculating near the egg-colony their mate had laid, their milky-white semen, like fat-free milk dissolving in water, being carried by the current toward fertilization.

'Imagine if, by some perversion of zoology,' he said to Chris in their tent later that evening, 'I fertilized a fish egg. It would be like half man half trout.'

'Maybe that's how mermaids first evolved.'

'You think we could'a just created a mermaid?'

'No, Adam. I was just playing along.'

'I wonder if, in the history of evolution, one species was ever able to, you know, actually impregnate another completely different species and have like a mixed baby. I mean I've seen plenty of dogs humping almost anything, but I'm talking about actually fertilizing an egg and it growing into some kind of mutant.'

'Well, they cross-breed donkeys and horses.'

'Yeah, but that's kinda the same. I mean like an eagle with an antelope.'

'Oh, I know. Have you ever seen a duck-billed platypus?'

'Good one... That was the craziest looking thing I ever saw.'

'There's no way that thing evolved like that.'

'So you think a duck did it with an otter or something, and it went through?'

'A beaver. That thing had a duck's bill and a beaver's body and tail. It looked like its bill was just glued on. And they have a stinger that's poisonous.'

'You see. Maybe it's possible we really did make a mermaid.'

'Wait, you're not serious, are you?'

'And, now that I think of it... and I know we smoked a lot of weed tonight... but what's the possibility that, in the history since animals were on the planet, that some animal's semen fell on some plant, and that grew into some kind of hybrid living thing, like the trees from The Wizard of Oz that threw the apples at Dorothy. I mean, I gotta believe at some point in history some guy actually, you know, masturbated in the woods. Maybe... who knows? I don't know.'

'Why don't you try it?'

''cause I'm not gonna jerk-off in the woods. That's kinda creepy.'

'Okay, the next time we're in the woods I promise I'll play with your little friend, see if we can't make some tree people.'

'I think my little friend just heard you.'

'Lemme see. Oh my God. You're one horny guy, you know that?'
'How could I not be with you laying here next to me.'

The next attraction, once they were back on the road, was the annual Somerset Rodeo, which Tom had been to before and thought, having grown up in that part of the world, might be going on that time of year. Neither Chris nor Adam had ever been to a rodeo, and learned together that, at these traveling, roadside events, the testicles of normally docile stock animals are bound with a leather strap and then tightened in order to induce spasmodic hysteria. If the animals refused to comply, or are shocked into immobility, firecrackers were exploded directly underneath their bellies, at which point even the most obstinate or lazy cow will start bucking like a Brahma bull. Tom suggested that Adam might want to keep a lower profile because the cowboys might not take too kindly to a long-haired New Yorker, Adam's neo-hippie afro of the mid-seventies having gotten a little too overgrown. Even though Tom had longer hair, he was a good-ol'-boy from way back and could handle himself in any situation. Without condescending, he was suggesting Adam might be a little out of place and out of his league. Since Adam had no desire to upset a group of men who took pleasure in castrating livestock, Chris and he kept a safe distance from the congregation. And, in fact, a fight did break out between a cowboy and a hippie, the hippie knocking the cowboy out with a remarkable left hook that gained him the respect of even the knocked-out cowboy's friends. Ironically, the hippie turned out to be a two-time Little Britches Rodeo champ. He just happened to be deeply into The Allman Brothers. So were the cowboys, probably.

Feeling increasingly threatened as the massive consumption of beer continued, and a horse, who had broken its leg chasing after a frightened calf was shot right in front of the anxious crowd, Chris and Adam appealed to Tom and Lynn, who were genuinely enjoying themselves, to depart that circus of monogrammed belts and beehive hairdos and get back on the road. They had seen enough blatant animal abuse for one day.

'Not your cup of tea, huh Adam?' Tom said. 'To each, his own.'

One look at her sister and Lynn knew Chris had had enough as well.

How much more cosmic back at their campsite at the confluence of two clear-water streams running through a nature preserve Tom remembered hunting in when he was a young man, watching satellites slowly skating across the Milky Way with their pinpoint of light. It was incredible to trace their path, like a shooting star in extreme slow-motion. For the first time in his life Adam slept outside, under the stars. Stevie and he had never had a time camping when that seemed right. Not even in Canyon-lands. He hadn't even thought about it until Chris suggested it, that's how inexperienced a camper he was, him laying on his back on top of their sleeping bag, looking up at the western night sky, in the middle of a pristine wilderness, Chris riding him like a Little Britches Rodeo champ. The perfection of the moment was not lost on him. That night was the only time in his life he was able to stay hard through two orgasms. His erection didn't even think of coming down. He felt immortal.

'I feel well and truly fucked,' Chris said, right before dismounting. 'Let's get into the sleeping bag. It's getting a little cold.' They were asleep before ComSat 1 got from Cassiopeia to the Pleiades.

The next day they drove through rustic western Colorado small towns, stopping for lunch at a saloon not dissimilar to the one Adam ate at right before meeting Chris, the kind with the old-west motif, sometimes a façade, sometimes actually from a more authentic time, which the one they were eating at felt like. It was there Adam realized a burger was not just about the quality of the meat or the chef who cooking it. It was also about head-space and atmosphere. He must have been in a very good place, 'cause that was one delicious burger.

Then back in the back seat along a scenic mountain road that became less paved as they drove into the higher elevations, ultimately becoming a dirt road too un-navigable for their vehicle.

'This is it,' Tom said, getting out of the car and walking over to the tree-line at the base of the trail; trees so thick and plentiful that the last rays of sunlight dissolved over their tops, filtering down into a dark veil. Evening had begun to descend. 'Let's get our gear. I wanna get to the campsite before it gets too dark.'

After they stretched and unloaded the necessary gear, Tom lead them through the forest to a grassy clearing by the side of a crystal stream shadowed by tall fir pines, a hidden Eden, the snow-capped peaks, visible all around them, feeling much closer than at any point that summer.

Adam remembered the first time Stevie and he had seen snow-capped mountains, which was the first time Adam had ever seen them in person. They were blown away, more than anything just to know they had made it that far west. But at no point did they camp anywhere near them, other than the Tetons, and, at the time of year, they were snowless. All other ranges had remained a distant vision. Now it felt like they were in them, and it was a very different feeling from camping in lower elevations, much more isolated, clear, and rarified. The stars, too, were different. Adam finally understood what people meant when they said they could see the Milky Way. At higher mountain elevations on clear summer nights, there were no individual stars, but sheets of them, the night sky flowing with them. As Chris and he laid on their backs on top of their sleeping bags set up outside for another night of outdoor slumber, they saw shooting stars almost every second, so prodigious was the canopy.

After Tom and Lynn had retired for the evening to their tent, set up far enough away from Adam and Chris's that they couldn't see them, Adam asked Chris what was the best sex she had ever had. He was fishing for the answer that it was just the prior evening when his penis stayed hard through two orgasms. That was unquestionably the best sex he ever had, and he was trying to confirm his status as a sex god.

'Well, I always loved it when my ex, you know, went down on me.'

'Uh huh,' Adam managed to say, hoping his feigned grin didn't give away his disappointment and inexperience. He hadn't performed oral sex on her. He didn't even know to do that. The one time he had licked Stephanie Millman's vagina, he did it almost unintentionally. He had heard something somewhere about oral sex, although Stephanie had never performed it on him, nor him on her. The only reason he did it a tiny bit was because he had been kissing her body and found himself down there. And even though she coo'd like a wood-nymph when he did it, he didn't put it together that he should stay down there. At that point in his nascent sexual awakening, it was just about fucking; kissing, getting naked, embracing, and the shy act of sticking it in where it belonged, which was how he had approached sex with Chris. There he was, thinking he was the greatest lover since Valentino, and he hadn't even made honorable mention. He needed to redeem himself. What Chris had just said triggered what may have been his first 'ah ha' moment - 69, double-blow, eat a girl out, all of those mysterious sexual acts young boys hear about but never really quite understand, he suddenly understood, like a-priori knowledge.

'You mean like this,' he said, getting her pants off as quickly as he could.

'Ooh… Adam,' and he was getting more turned on knowing he was turning her on. Stephanie had never said anything about how their sex felt, especially during it, probably because he hadn't considered her feelings while they were doing it, and had clearly failed to inspire such vocal expressions of sexual arousal. That, plus being a sexual neophyte, it had never taken him very long to come - two minutes max - and he had never come more than once during any sexual encounter. Usually when he was done, they'd hug for a while, get dressed and go to a local diner for dessert before dropping her home. Eating Chris out, her, spread-eagle on their sleeping-bags, moaning, those moans getting louder until she ultimately climaxed was a revelation, the first time he understood what it meant for a woman to have an orgasm - the fact that by going down on a woman he could give her so much pleasure… That night changed his life.

'Can't you guys keep it to yourself,' Lynn yelled from somewhere just behind the tree-line. 'You better get some sleep. We're heading out early.'

They began their trek the following morning before the sun made its welcomed appearance. Walking at a healthy pace, Tom lead them through plush river valleys and over steep passes, stopping only for short meal breaks, mostly gorp and fresh beef jerky they had bought in one of the towns along the way - fresh molasses and hickory-smoke-cured beef, ice-cold pure mountain stream water – perfect hiking food.

'"Just keep your pace,' Tom encouraged.

Nobody spoke much during the eight-hour, up-hill hike. That type of mountain trekking was all about focus and destination. Because they were hiking mainly through the upper part of a pine forest, there wasn't much to see, other than the omnipresent, indescribably enormous snow-capped peaks which seemed to be getting closer every so often. Felling very small in the vastness, Adam followed Chris, who was right behind her sister, one foot in front of the next, ever upward. Maybe it was the thinner air, or the fact that he had never spent so much time in so concentrated a way as that hike required, but at one point Adam realized he hadn't thought of anything for longer than he ever had. He was just being – content within himself, focused but free, mellow. For a neurotic Jewish teenager, that was quite a moment of realization; him, mellow within himself. He wondered if that's what people meant when they spoke about meditation. And as he was thinking that, he ran chest-first into Chris's backpack, almost knocking her down. In his silent reverie he hadn't noticed she, Lynn and Tom had stopped for a moment to get their bearings.

'You all right there, Adam?' Tom asked, wondering if the thinning air was becoming an issue for him.

'Beautiful, man. I was just in my own little world.'

By early evening they had climbed out of the last of the trees and stood at the rim of a brilliant turquoise-blue lake surrounded on three sides by the towering snow-capped peaks of the Rockies. It's impossible to describe that kind of overwhelming natural beauty. It was Shangri-La, heaven, unbelievable yet real. They just stood there and took it in, the gravity of its enormous majesty rooting them.

'That's the most beautiful thing I have ever seen,' Lynn said. 'Cowboy, you did it.'

'You guys go find yourselves a place to pitch your tent,' Tom said to Chris and Adam. 'I'm gonna have me a little dip. Feel free to join me if you want.' And with that, he took off all his clothes and jumped right in the lake, Lynn right behind.

'Come on, Adam,' Chris said, unlacing her hiking boots.

Adam had never been naked in front of a group of people. Being naked in front of a group of people wasn't something he was especially comfortable doing, even with the sight of Chris's naked body walking toward the water.

'Fuck it,' he thought, and threw caution to the wind. But only for a second or two. That water was fuckin' cold, shocking. He had no idea how the three of them stayed in as long as they did, which was not that much longer than him, several minutes maybe, but certainly longer, and seemingly without the excruciating discomfort he felt. It was so cold, his balls shriveled up to the size of raisins, and he didn't get warm again until he had been sitting in front of the fire he had been charged to build for several minutes.

As he was building the fire, he happened to catch the three of them climbing out of the lake, naked and glistening. To a guy to whom a naked woman was the ultimate vision, two naked women, one with a body wars had been fought over, was double the pleasure. He was glad to see that Tom's balls, too, were in hypothermic shock – not that he was looking at his balls on purpose. He wasn't. But he was glad to know he wasn't as much of a pussy as he though he might have been. If Tom had come out of the lake hanging low and unfettered, it might have given him pause for concern.

As they all began to thaw, and the Milky Way once again overtook the night sky, and the serenity and majesty of where they were began to settle into his soul - Chris huddled next to him in front of the fire - Adam knew he was having one of the ultimate moments he would ever have in his life. He just knew it, and was thankful to be having it. He had no idea how his life would unfold in the future – going home after the trip, starting college. All he knew at that moment was that whatever had happened in his life had lead up to him being exactly where he was, almost as validation.

'Any of you ever climbed before?' Tom asked as they sat around the fire eating beef stew Lynn and Chris prepared. Eating well had been one of the primary conditions of taking their trip together, and their cooler was always well stocked – a little heavy, but well stocked.

Since none of them could answer Tom's question in the affirmative, he pointed to the smallest snowless peak directly in front of the turquoise lake and said, 'That's all right. Tomorrow, when we get to the top o' that little peak over there, we'll be able to look out over the whole range as good as we could from a twin engine. You up for it?' he asked, looking directly at Adam, without condescending, more out of empathy. Tom sensed Adam's apprehension about scaling the unknown.

'Definitely,' Adam said. If the girls could do it, he could do it too.

That feeling was seriously tested the next day as he clung to the side of the mountain, holding onto it for dear life, like he used to hold onto his father when they were in water too deep for him to stand in. He felt if he let go he was going to fall off the mountain. They had been climbing for about four hours with few interim breaks – reasonable climbing, like on a Jungle Jim. But as they got higher they reached a point where the rock path they were following got narrower and narrower until it was only about as wide as the souls of their shoes, requiring them to face the mountain and inch along, side-stepping, feeling for hand-holds to hold onto. Tom, who was directly in front of Adam, or directly to his left when they had to change position and stick their faces against the rock, was able to direct them to the best hand-holds. He had climbed that mountain before, and was familiar with its topography. It didn't matter. At one point Adam's fear became greater than his ability to overcome it. There was a small vertical chasm they had to cross over, about three feet wide. But in order to get across, they had to first reach across it, get a good hold of the little hand-hold Tom directed them to, then step across onto the ledge that was even less wide than the one they had been inching along on. Then it was a matter of pulling themselves over and feeling under their feet to make sure they had a good foothold. Tom said that was the only difficult part of the climb, and that they should be very careful when they pull themselves over. 'You want to keep your weight forward,' he instructed. 'Feel the mountain like it's a part of you.' But Adam must have gotten a little vertigo, and felt like the mountain was just a sheer wall without anything to hold onto. At that point he had to stop and go back to terra firma. The thought of going forward terrified him.

'I can't do it,' he said, knowing he was admitting defeat, and not caring. He'd rather be a living nebbish than a dead tough-guy.

'Yes you can, man,' Tom said. He was already across. 'As soon as you reach over I can get a hold of you. Just lean across and grab ahold of this rock right here, and step with your left foot. You'll feel it.'

'All right,' Adam said, taking a deep breath and trying to build up the courage to go for it.

'You can do it, Adam,' Chris said, by way of encouragement. It encouraged him to at least try.

As soon as Adam took his left hand off the rock-face to reach across, and was momentarily unsure what to do with his left foot, he knew it wasn't going to happen. He didn't feel it was worth it, possibly falling off a mountain. For what? To prove he could do it? At that point he could accept he couldn't. He had never been that type of afraid in his life, like in a nightmare where you can't hold on anymore and you find yourself falling, until you wake up and realize it was only a dream. This wasn't a dream.

'You guys go ahead. I'll meet you right back here.'

'All right,' Lynn said, 'I'm gonna come around behind you. Just move back down a little bit. Chrissy, move down a little,' which they all did. 'Get as tight as you can against the wall and don't move. I'm gonna show you how to do it.'

Hugging the wall like his and Lynn's life depended on it, Adam felt Lynn come around him, first her arm across his back, then her left foot to the left of his. He got the sense, from the way he felt her body move around him, that she didn't have much fear, and was going to be able to get across without any problem. Luckily, only Tom had worn a backpack. It was a few hours up, and much less back, and one backpack was all Tom thought they needed.

'Okay watch,' Lynn said, once she was standing to Adam's left. 'Just lean in and get your arm across, and hold here.' She stayed in that position an extra second so Adam could see what she was doing. 'Now just slide and step. And just... shimmy... across,' as she was doing it. 'And that's it. You can do it.' She had done it like she was Sir Edmond Hillary. Adam had whined like an infant.

He thought, 'If she can do it, so can I.' He wasn't being condescending or misogynistic, especially of Lynn, who had already shown herself to be mother-earth incarnate. If anyone, who had never climbed, who was roughly in the same decent shape he was in, could do it with such confidence, he should be able to. It was more of a challenge to himself. So he went for it. And did it. Following Lynn's lead, he took it step by step, and was amazed that, this time, his body seemed to end up where it was supposed to. He was still sweating it a little, but when he got across the chasm he realized how doable it had been, and that his fear might have been a little premature, a good lesson to learn; don't be so quick to give up. Challenge himself.

Then it was Chris's turn to get across. Because the ground underfoot was wide enough, Lynn told Adam to get on the other side of her so she could watch what her sister was doing, and make sure she was okay.

'That's it, Chrissy... exactly. Now just hold and bring your... good.' You could tell she was willing her sister across.

When they got to the summit Adam understood why people risked their lives climbing mountains. The infinite topography. In order to feel like you're standing on top of the world, you have to climb there. There's no other way to get there, to see and feel God's glory spread out before you in every direction – overlooking an entire mountain range, with their turquoise lake a little jewel below them. All Adam could do was stand there, holding onto whatever stationary boulder he could because he was still a little uptight about falling off the mountain, and take it all in. That's what you do on top of a mountain, you take it all in, because that's the place you can get it all – it's all around you.

'Pretty good,' Tom said.

Yup. Pretty fuckin' good.

But Adam could honestly say he didn't know which was better, the view from the top of a mountain, or the blow-job Chris gave him later that evening – his first. He hadn't been expecting it, but when Chris told him to just lie still, and she started kissing his body, getting lower and lower, and he's thinking, 'Is she? I hope... Oh my God, she's getting closer... yup, I think... ' and she started kissing his dick and then putting it into her mouth, every nerve-ending in his body started firing. It was like he was being made love to by a legion of angels. To say he came quickly would be an understatement. Luckily, by the time he finished reciprocating, he was ready to go for round two, riding out the waves of sensuality until exhaustion and sleep settled over them.

His first summit, and his first blow-job - easily one of the greatest days of his life.

In the morning, with the moon still hanging tough over the distant peaks, the sun yet to make it up and over, Tom, Lynn and Chris jumped in the turquoise lake for a pre-breakfast skinny-dip. Adam had volunteered to make breakfast because he was feeling happy and mellow, and didn't need the cold-water shock. It was a decision he was glad he made. Because the sun had yet to warm the water, it was much colder than it had been when they had jumped in the first time, and even Tom had to get out after his initial dive in.

'Yee haw,' he screamed the moment he surfaced, and he was out of there within seconds, as were Chris and Lynn, who immediately wrapped themselves in their towels, their lips almost as blue as the lake, both thankful that the fire had already begun to kindle. Then a quick breakfast of pancakes and eggs, pack up all the gear, and then a five, six hour hike back to the car.

How much less buoyant the hike back down to the car felt. Again, there wasn't much talking, but this time it felt less because they were contemplating the grandeur of space and time and more because something magical had just ended. Even though they still had weeks to go on their shared adventure, those two nights at the turquoise lake had been perfect, magic, and leaving left an emptiness that translated into monotony after three or four hours of downhill trekking. Adam felt it, and the head-slightly-down, silent, determined progress of Tom, Lynn and Chris lead him to believe they felt it too.

'How much longer, do you think?' Of course Adam was the one who asked, the impatient New Yorker.

''nother hour or so,' Tom said. 'You wanna stop?'

'Nah, let's just keep going.'

They did, their batteries slowly recharging. Back into the zen of trekking. The day was crystal clear.

'Listen,' Tom said, stopping them, motioning them to be quiet. Adam didn't hear anything. Then he saw it – an elk crossing their path not fifty feet in front of them. It stopped, turned slightly, and set them in its sights. It was magnificent, as big as the moose Adam had seen in the Tetons, the elk checking them out, them checking the elk out.

'I bet I can call him over,' Adam whispered. For some reason, when he saw large, non-threatening wildlife, he felt compelled to communicate with them, perhaps trying making up for the time in fifth grade when he went to the Bronx zoo on a class trip and he threw a rock at a buffalo, never expecting to hit it. But, not only did he hit it, the rock got lodged between the buffalo's horn and ear, causing it to start freaking out. A zoo employee had to clear the area. The reason he threw the rock was because some of the other tougher guys in his class were throwing rocks, and he wanted to show them how cool he was too. All he felt was guilt hurting that buffalo.

'Just let him be, Adam,' Chris said.

'Lemme give it a shot.' He got out a little handful of gorp from his backpack, and held it out as an offering. 'Here Mr. Elk. Come on. Come on. That's a good boy...'

'That's a cow,' Tom corrected.

'I'm pretty sure it's an elk. I mean, I know I'm from New York and all, but...' Adam knew female elk were called cows. Stags and cows. He went for the obvious humor.

The elk stood there stone still, staring at Adam like he was out of his mind – literally staring at him. He didn't know if she was going to charge, or what. After a moment or two, she nodded her head down, brought it back up, like she was bowing, turned and ran off. The humans were just a momentary diversion better left alone.

'I think she just nodded to us, right?' Adam said, feeling like they had just communed with one of nature's majestic creatures. There was no doubt in his mind that elk acknowledged them before departing.

'I think you're right, Adam,' Lynn said. 'That was awesome.'

After being such a pussy on the mountain, Adam was glad to redeem himself a little in Lynn's eyes. Maybe he wasn't the toughest guy in the world, but he made her and Chris laugh. He knew that counted for something.

By the time they got to the car, they were fully recovered from their lower-energy malaise and were looking forward to their next adventure.

'You ever shoot an elk, Tom?' Chris asked. They were driving along the open highway toward the night's campground.

'Many. Some of the best meat there is.'

'Aw,' she sighed. 'But she was so cute. She looked right at us.'

'Yes. Yes she did,' Tom said. Adam got the impression that if Tom had his rifle with him, they would have been grilling up elk steaks that night.

'I say we find a place that has elk burgers for lunch,' Lynn said. 'I'm getting hungry.'

'But we could be eating her children or something,' Chris said.

'So, you have whatever you want. I definitely wanna check out elk.'

'Me too,' Adam said.

Tom, of course, knew a place along the way that served elk, a food not uncommon in that part of the world. Even though Chris ordered a regular burger, when she took a bite of Adam's elk burger, 'just a little bite. I'm curious,' she liked it so much, they exchanged burgers.

Back on the road for an hour or two, country music on the radio, Tom directed Lynn to turn onto a road that was headed into a scene right out of a Fifties western – two, two and a half miles of flat, rugged terrain straight into the rock walls. The miles of uninterrupted, uninhabited flatland was deep enough that it created a vast perspective, like looking at a prairie night sky, which is unimaginably vast.

'Good call, Tom,' Chris said, hers and Adam's shoulders fitting together like sculpture.

That night they didn't bother to pitch their tents. Everything was so open, they wanted to be a part of it – to lie under it. Adam built a fire from scrub-wood Chris and he gathered, while Tom and Lynn looked for cool rocks and minerals.

'Just shine your flashlight on the ground,' Tom told her. 'If something flashes, go check it out.'

They came back with a beautifully formed, incredibly clear nine-inch, five-inch-around quartz crystal that had purple and blue, geometrically formed fluorite at its base. It looked like a large crystal dildo with geometric, smaller purple balls. It was a remarkably beautiful find, a museum-quality mineral which Lynn said she was going to keep forever.

'I bet you are,' Adam said. He couldn't resist. He had seen Lynn naked twice, although besides those two flashes, both she and Tom were naturally modest – no public affection, very little bad language. Still, he felt he had earned a little suggestive humor.

'Oh, cut it out. You're disgusting.' It was funny how she knew exactly what he meant.

Over pit-grilled chicken parts purchased from the butcher shop attached to the restaurant they ate elk at, the chickens freshly slaughtered, they talked about possible travel and living scenarios once Tom started working at the dam. It was kind of a given that they weren't ready to break up their little family unit just then. That was inevitable. Adam had to get back east. But, that was almost a month away. Right then, they were taking it week by week.

'I'm not sure what the set-up's gonna be,' Tom said. 'I'm guessing whoever's coming in can pretty much find a place to set up camp for a while. A lot of beautiful wilderness in the Gunnison. A lot o' guys'll stay in Montrose. But plenty'll stake a claim and live that way. Saves a lot of money. These crews are used to roughing it. And the Black Canyon is something else. You ever see The Unsinkable Molly Brown?'

'Of course. Debbie Reynolds,' Lynn said. 'I love that movie.'

'That was shot there.'

'Oh my God. Those scenes were...' And she started singing *Belly Up To The Bar Boys*. It was the first time she had spontaneously broken into song.

'There you go,' Tom said. Because he knew the area, he said he could keep them occupied with hikes and sightseeing and exploring until... 'I mean, I know you're not gonna wanna stay there too long, I mean...' He was looking at Lynn. Adam realized it was the first time he had seen Tom unsure of himself. He hadn't expected to fall in love on his hitch down to The Gunnison.

'Let's just see how it goes, Cowboy,' Lynn said. 'We'll figure it out.' Neither had she. But now that she had, she'd figure it out.

It didn't feel like Chris and Adam shared that kind of love - deep, soul-mate love, eternal and unbreakable. There were certainly many moments filled with it – love, joy, submission, depth. Adam loved being with her. And he thought, based on how they were with each other – tender, playful, protective – she loved being with him. But he was going back home at the end of the summer. Whatever happened after that would happen. But first there was going to be a big separation, one that was difficult to see across. Adam, abstractly and inconsequentially, thought about how great it would be to have Chris visit him at college. Of course. Keep the fantasy going. But he had no way to conceptualize, much less visualize what that meant. College was a completely foreign concept. And because of that, it might have weakened the bond of their love, or at least not have allowed it to reach its full strength. What was Chris going to do? Follow him to Cortland, New York? That didn't seem right, not even remotely. And not just from his perspective. Chris wanted to get out on her own. That's why she took this trip in the first place. She knew where she was in the world, for better or for worse, and knew if she wanted to achieve what she hoped to – a nurse, or hospital administration, definitely in the health-care field – she would have to start focusing on that, either applying to college next semester, or certainly the semester after that. Adam actually felt their feelings were mutual. It could happen with them. What they had was real. But there was a big inevitable unknown coming. Better to keep it at arm's length and make the most of the time they had.

CHAPTER 7

· · · · · · · · · · · · · · · · · · · ·

You can see it in the way
the world was made

The Black Canyon of the Gunnison – another mystical landscape, with its painted granite walls rising in some places to over a thousand feet, and not a quarter mile of straight track on it. Tom directed them to a secluded plot twenty feet away from the canyon's massive fissure and said, 'I'm glad this claim's still open.'

'Me too. Oh my God,' Chris said, taking in the sweep of canyon, forest, mountain range, valley. 'I could live here forever.'

'I'll come and visit ya,' Lynn said. 'If it's forever, I'm going with a house, and a pool...'

'And television,' Adam added.

'And a comfortable bed,' Tom said. 'I don't plan on sleeping on the ground forever either.'

'You guys know what I mean,' Chris said.

'I'm just playin' with you, Chrissy. Tom, let's go find a spot to set up. How about near that Juniper tree.'

'That'll work.'

The juniper tree, with its short curving trunk, growing just a few feet from the edge of the canyon, looked like it had been there since the beginning of time.

'You're gonna set up that close to the edge?' Adam asked.

'Yup,' Tom said.

Lounging around the fire that ethereal evening, getting hammered on Wild Turkey and weed, Tom educated the girls and Adam about the hallucinogenic properties of Morning Glory seeds.

'Morning Glories?' Lynn asked. 'Like I have growing all over my fence?'

'That's it,' Tom confirmed.

Morning Glories are common violet or white horn-shaped flowers that grow along fences, trellises, and gardens with vine-like adaptability. Seed packets are sold everywhere, in almost every hardware store and feed and grain depot in the country.

'Once you boil the strychnine off the seed-coat,' Tom said, 'you're left with a pretty potent hallucinogen. Not as powerful as peyote or amanita mescaria mushrooms, but psychedelic none the less. Maybe this weekend I can get a bunch of people together and we can go trippin' at the potholes. You won't believe how beautiful it is up there.'

'Don't get any of that shit for me, Cowboy,' Lynn said. She had mentioned many times that alcohol, and a little pot was where she drew the line when it came to partying. Chris had never done a hallucinogenic drug, but was willing to try. Adam had tripped twice, both times during the preceding year. The first time was on a quarter of a tab of windowpane acid at a Who concert in a thunderstorm outdoors at Forest Hills Stadium with Stevie. It was the most epic night he ever had. It was electric, drawing him into the music like he was living it. He didn't do enough acid to hallucinate flying pink elephants, but he was definitely in a surreal state of mind. Motion and color. And the music of eternity.

The other time he did a hallucinogenic drug was with Stephanie, at a party. They divided half a hit of mescaline and ended up making out for four hours straight. Mescaline was a much mellower high, still very psychedelic, but more internal, their kiss dream-like, waves of fluid oral sensuality, like being thirsty and drinking cold mountain stream water and you can keep drinking, never getting full or tired, every moment like the first... dawn tapping him on the shoulder when it was time to get Stephanie home.

The plan, the following day, was for Lynn to drive Tom to the dam worksite at around five-thirty, come back, have breakfast with Chris and Adam, and then the three of them would spend their first day as a trio at the Shavano Valley rock art site, one of the most spiritual and well preserved prehistoric art and habitation sites in the country. Some of the petroglyphs at that site were almost three thousand years old - Ute territory until the turn of the twentieth century. Once Tom was done with his shift, he was going to get a ride into Montrose, where he had left his old pick-up truck with some childhood friends. The truck wasn't in the kind of shape that could have withstood the trip to Toronto and back, but for local driving it was better than good.

'You guys ready?' Lynn asked, after all the breakfast accoutrements had been cleaned and put away. 'Do we have everything we need?' They did a final check – water-bottles, sandwiches, snacks, camera, snake-bite antidote...

'I doubt you'll need that,' Lynn said.

'Ya never know. I bought it. Might as well bring it.'

'Do you know how to use it?' Chris asked.

'Yeah… you…' Adam stalled, looking for the directions on the package. The directions were inside the package, which he didn't want to open, so he read what was on the package. 'Kit contains: detailed instructions, three pliable suction cups, an easy to use with one hand lymph constrictor – that's for people who only have one hand – a scalpel, and an antiseptic swab. So I'm thinking you…'

'All right, bring it,' Lynn said. 'If we need it we'll figure it out. Hopefully, we won't need it.'

Up the road they saw two pick-up trucks coming their way, one with Tom and another guy, and the other with a man and a woman.

'I knew I'd get you guys before you left,' Tom said, pulling up. 'How about you save Shavano for another day. Today we're going to the Potholes. Hop in. I picked up some fresh chicken salad and some cold beer for lunch.'

'We packed lunch,' Lynn said.

'Bring it. You never know.'

Tom's first day of work was only to fill out paperwork and get briefed on the overall scope of his job. His actual daily riprap grind didn't start until Monday, which gave him the rest of Friday, and the whole weekend to hang out with them.

'That there's Phil, and his wife Mary,' Tom introduced. 'And this here's Rat. Rat's our resident poet. Rat why don't you hop in the payload, let Lynn ride shot-gun.'

'No worries,' Rat said. 'Hello everyone. Damn, Tom,' meaning, 'You weren't kidding how beautiful Lynn was.' Rat was about Adam's height, maybe a little shorter, fit, with a solitary vibe and alert eyes. As for his name, he had a home-made Bic-ink tattoo of a rat's head traced into his forearm. He got into the payload of Phil's truck, and Chris and Adam got into the back of Tom's, the two trucks raising plumes of dust as they bounded over the quiet mountain roads and empty highways, looking for adventure. One thing Chris and Adam learned very quickly was that it's not a good idea to make-out in the payload of a pick-up truck traveling on a dirt road. One wrong bump and you can break your teeth.

'Adam, how many times do you think we've made love?' Chris asked. The cloudless sky was a perfect blue. Their butts were comfortably cushioned by two of Tom's blankets.

'Well,' Adam said, 'let's figure we've averaged... two times a day since we met, so... I think we've been doing pretty good.'

Chris leaned over and whispered in his ear, 'Maybe the next time you go down on me, you can play with my ass a little. I really like that.'

Adam sighed like he'd been punched in the stomach with a feather. He had never engaged in ass-play, and couldn't wait to add that to his growing list of sexual experiences.

Sitting shoulder to shoulder, hand in hand, leaning against the back of the truck's cab, they took in the moment. Although neither of them said it, in the short time they had been together, they had grown to love each other. Adam had never spent so much uninterrupted time with anyone, other than his immediate family, and Stevie, and all of it was beautiful. He looked at Chris and felt completely himself.

'I'm looking at you and it's like I've known you for way longer than we have,' he said.

'I know. I have this whole thing about... that feelings tend to be mutual because we project ourselves onto people. So, like, the way I feel about someone is generally the way they feel about me. That's what I go by, anyway.'

'Okay, so what else am I feeling?' Adam asked.

Again, she leaned over and whispered in his ear, '... that you can't wait to do what I just told you about...' at which point Lynn knocked on the window separating them, and shook her finger as if to scold them. She was smiling. She must have known they were talking about naughty things.

'What,' Adam yelled, playing innocent.

Adam read her lips, something like, 'Be good to buy sister.' He couldn't hear her above the din of the rushing air.

At one point Tom slowed down and turned off the highway in the middle of a tumbleweed prairie, driving over the rocky, roadless plain into the distant mountains – a direct route into a hidden domain. Forty minutes later they arrived at the foot of an antiquated wooden bridge spanning the Gunnison River. Built around the turn of the century, the wood and steel suspension bridge was originally intended for livestock and horse-drawn wagons and was now unable, mainly due to its advanced state of decay, to safely accommodate the weight of the trucks. Tom slowed to a stop, Phil pulling up next to him. Everybody got out and stretched their legs.

'Hi Adam, Chris,' Phil said, extending his hand, which both of them shook. 'A pleasure to meet ya.'

'Likewise,' Chris said. 'And you too, Mary.'

'Should be a pretty fun day,' Mary said. She was tall - almost as tall as Phil, who had an inch or two on Tom. Both were dressed in flannel shirts and jeans, although Mary was wearing jean shorts and had cut the sleeves off of her shirt. They both looked to be in their late twenties, and had that natural western ease Adam was hoping would rub off on him. Rat was wearing overalls, no shirt, old Converse sneakers, and was the only one of the seven of them who smoked cigarettes – Camel non-filters. Every drag he took he would stick the tip of his tongue between his lips and pick something off of it. He also looked to be about the same age as his friends. 'Tom wasn't kidding,' Mary continued, looking at Lynn and shaking her hand. 'How'd you get mixed up with a rascal like him?'

'I saw him on the side of the road, and he looked like he could use a friend,' Lynn said.

'He always said hitchin' was the best way to get around,' Mary said.

Mary, Phil, and Tom had known each other since high school. Phil, whose number had come up early in the draft, spent the last year of the Viet Nam war on a river patrol boat as part of the river patrol task force, stopping and searching river traffic on the Saigon River in an attempt to disrupt weapons shipments, and to bring Navy Seal teams in and out of the area. He had been part of the US Army's 458th Transportation Company, known as the 458th Seatigers. Phil and Rat met on their patrol boat and became comrades in arms. When the war ended, Phil asked Rat, who was originally from Pittsburg, if he wanted move out to Montrose, Colorado and work for the construction company Phil's father owned.

Luckily for Tom, he had drawn number 356 in the draft and was never close to being called up for active duty. On their six-mile hike through the unique granite and limestone mountainscape, which resembled a large-scale chessboard with half the pieces held captive on either end, Adam told Phil and Rat that his father had been in the navy, and his ship was assigned to bring marines on and off the island of Okinawa. He was trying to relate to them - bridge the decade separating them. That decade was the difference between revolution and corporate comfort.

'My old man was a marine on Okinawa,' Rat said. 'Small world, man.'

Adam immediately thought they could have...

'It's entirely possible,' Tom said, 'they could have shared a moment aboard ship... maybe acknowledged one another.'

'If I know my father,' Rat said, 'he wasn't in any kind of socializing mood right off-island. Probably took him a while to regain himself. That was hell on earth, man... hand to hand.'

'I could see that,' Tom continued. 'Still...'

'That is kind of amazing that your fathers could have actually passed each other like that during the war,' Chris said. 'And here you two guys are, in the middle of Colorado, forty years later.'

The connection wasn't lost on either Rat or Adam, like they were from the same neighborhood.

'By the way,' Tom said, 'getting back to the cars is gonna be a whole lot easier than hiking, especially 'cause it would've started getting dark.'

'You wanna do the river run?' Phil asked.

'Yup.'

'What's the river run?' Chris asked.

'Jump in, clothes and all, and have it run us on our backs all the way down,' Mary said. 'You all can swim?' They all could.

On the hike, Adam saw a flash of light on the ground about twenty feet to his left in a small scree pile, and went over to it to check it out. He remembered what Tom said about flashes of light when looking for rocks and minerals. Sure enough, he bent down and picked up a beautiful six-inch-long quartz crystal with a yellowish crystal at its base. It was like finding a beautiful gem.

'Good one, Adam,' Phil said, 'Those are gettin' harder and harder to find. People from all over the country are comin' here to collect those... sellin' them as healing crystals and such. Rat does a little collecting himself.'

'Quartz and citrine,' Rat said, looking at Adam's find. 'Nice. Real nice. Good energy, man. Use it well.'

Adam immediately gave the crystal to Chris, who loved it. 'I can't believe we both got these,' she said to her sister. 'That's gotta mean something.'

'I think it's nature's way of letting you know it knows you're sisters,' Tom said.

'I'm thinkin' it already knows that, Tom,' Mary said.

'I'm sure it does. But it just let them know it knows.'

'Do you think nature just kinda acknowledged your sisterhood?' Phil asked Lynn.

Lynn thought for a second. 'I think there's something pretty special about both of us getting these crystals,' she said. 'I don't know if it's nature, but it feels like something.'

'Maybe it's God,' Rat said.

'You mean like Spinoza's God,' Phil asked.

'Yeah,' Rat said.

'Well I'm glad Spinoza, or whoever's God made sure Adam found this,' Chris said. 'Can you hold it 'til we get back to our campsite?' She didn't have anywhere to store it, and the front of Adam's overalls had a pocket that was tailor-made.

'That's very sweet of you to give that to Chrissy,' Lynn said, putting her hand on Adam's cheek as a kind of benediction.

Twenty minutes later they were at The Potholes.

'Oh my God, that is so beautiful,' Chris said, taking in the unique terrestrial vision before them: a series of three crystal-clear, sun-heated pools about fifty to a hundred feet in diameter carved into the terraced mountain slopes, one pool careening in a silver-white waterfall into the pool ten-fifteen feet below, the bottom pool spilling off into a stream coursing to the river. Because of the topography, it was easy to climb up to the top pool and then jump down from pool to pool, which was what Rat did as soon as he got his sneakers off.

'Geronimo,' he yelled.

The whole area gave the impression of an enormous open-air, mystically conceived water park - the curved mountain walls embracing them as they jumped from pool to pool in whatever clothes they were wearing – all except Tom, who was hunched over a small pot of boiling water heated over a small fire he had built. Because they were going to be jumping in the river in a couple of hours to get back to the trucks, it didn't matter if they got their clothes wet. The air was so warm and dry, wet clothes felt good. Apparently, this was not a skinny-dipping crowd.

'The seeds are ready,' Tom harangued like a farm cook a few minutes later. 'Come and get 'em... Just make sure you chew 'em up real good.'

'I'm nervous,' Chris said. "Lemme just do a little bit.'

'You know what,' Lynn said, 'it's so beautiful here, I think I'm gonna partake. What the hell. Just don't gimme too much.'

Tom distributed what he felt was the right amount of Morning Glory seeds for each of them, erring on the very conservative side. The seeds had a consistency and taste not dissimilar to sunflower seeds, although with morning glory seeds you ate everything, shell and all.

Seventeen minutes later Adam began to experience a distinct neurological excitation. 'You all right, Chris?'

'Look at that mountain,' she said, a little slurry. 'I think it just waved. It looks like a mother bird and her two babies. Everything is so bright.'

'Your face has a violet halo around it,' Adam said. 'Like you're an angel.' Colorful light traced spiraling images across the universe, dissipating as if they were fragmentary thoughts. Chris and Adam were very high, but thanks to Tom's wise oversight, not too high – just enough to see colors and motion that weren't there, but not enough to hallucinate – not dissimilar to how Adam felt when he did mescaline, and ended up making out with Stephanie Millman.

'You guys get off yet?' Tom asked, approaching with vibrating, dilated eyes and a wide Cheshire cat smile.

'Definitely,' Adam said. Chris was looking in every direction at once, a big smile on her face as well.

'Okay,ifyouneedanythinglemmeknow.'

He walked back to Lynn, whose eyes and mouth were open in wonder. She leaned into him nose to nose and, with her right index finger, started tracing imaginary images on his face with Buddhist concentration. He just stared at her and let her do what she felt. Phil, Mary, and Rat had climbed into the top pool and were having a splash-fight.

'Let's go do that,' Adam said.

'Okay, but wait. Do you love me?'

'I completely love you.'

'Good. I'm having the best summer.'

The depth of their kiss could only be judged by the degree to which they lost themselves in it. It took Lynn a couple of attempts at calling them to come up to the top pool and join everybody before they realized they were standing on the ground on the planet Earth, and that there were other people around, one of whom was yelling to them.

'They look like living trees swaying,' Chris said, when they unlocked their lips. 'I love that color.'

Even stoned on morning glory seeds, the fact that Adam had just told Chris he loved her was duly noted. It felt good – a little confusing because he didn't know how to bridge the divide between where they were in the world, and the fact that in a couple of weeks he had to leave and start a different life. But right then, he was exactly where he wanted to be - watching Chris as she climbed up the terraced slope in front of him in her short jeans shorts on the way to the top pool in a magical landscape.

'Rat, do one of your poems,' Phil said after they had all finished a communal splash-fest and were sitting on the edge of the pool drying in the warm sun. The sky was a deep blue, which made the aura around everyone's body that much more electric. 'One of the free association ones.'

Rat stood up, closed his eyes, faced the sun, took a few deep breaths, turned back around to the group, put his hand up, palms outward, closed his eyes again, took another a very deep breath, exhaled, and started. 'I was standing against the background of a Hollywood movie with two pounds of relativity in my back pocket when it hit me… It's always been like that… like the time my sister saw the magic circle and she told me why nothing is faster than the speed of light except what's in front of it… and even then it's all a mystery… from wherever you're standing… You can see it in the way the world was made… You can see it on tv… the way the clouds tumble and roll as if I was dreaming someone else's dream that became louder and louder every time a new thought came into my mind… the phone ringing and there's no one there… It's just ringin'… those rings floating right over the horizon, the horizon floatin' right back… I mean, you could think about it, or you could do something about it... Do something about it... Don't wait for some Hindu deity to give you the answer... See it with your own eyes... That's why Jesus wasn't afraid... The eyes of the world were upon him... But glory's like a shot of tequila right after last call - when my spirit's running for cover like a fallen king knocking on heaven's door and no one's home... How can that be... I hear the music playing... It sounds like morning glory whispers at the Potholes in the beautiful key of tranquility... no more death... no more suffering... the spark of tomorrow's promise to light the way... To all God's creatures great and small, amen...'

'Wow,' Chris said.

'Good one, Rat,' Phil said. 'Very Albion Moonlight.'

'What's Albion Moonlight?' Lynn asked.

'A character in literature by Kenneth Patchen. The Journal of Albion Moonlight, one of the great allegories of all time. He was looking for Savior spelled backwards, right?'

'Roivas,' Rat said. 'Lemme go get my smokes. I am stoned, man.'

When Rat started climbing down to get his cigarettes, Adam looked over his shoulder and saw what appeared to be a natural trail further into the magic mountains – like a mini mountain pass just a few yards away.

'You wanna hike a little,' he asked Chris. 'That looks like amazing.'

'Be careful,' Lynn said. 'I know how fucked up you guys are. Okay?'

'It'll be all right,' Tom said. 'It doesn't let out too far. Make sure you look in the pool at the end. And come back pretty soon.'

Once they climbed up and over the graduated rock incline, the trail Adam had seen was wide enough for Chris and him to walk side by side, hand in hand. It was like walking through a pink stone movie set – like it was made out of papier-mâché and created to make you feel like you were in someone's private tripped-out stone labyrinth.

'How can this be real?' Chris wondered. 'It's so...'

'I know.' The blue sky made everything seem present, centered. 'Let's check out the pool.' Directly in front of them, about a hundred yards, in front of a thirty-foot rock wall with a trickle of a waterfall falling from above, was another pool, this one almost surrounded on three sides. Above it were more graduated mountain terraces.

'What are those?' Adam asked, looking down into the crystal water and seeing little black sperm-like things swimming around. He didn't think he was hallucinating them.

'They look like tadpoles. It's like they're skating underwater. Skriggly... Skriggly... Squiggly. Squiggly.'

'Tadpoles,' Adam said. What a strange word when you're stoned on morning glory seeds. 'Tadpoles. What are tadpoles doing in the mountains?'

'Maybe they came over the waterfall.'

'Over the waterfall. Somewhere over the... That's rainbow... I wonder where it starts.'

'What, the rainbow?'

'The waterfall.'

'At the beginning. I need to kiss you again.'

That's how Tom and Lynn found them, however many eons later – wrapped tightly together, making out next to the tadpole pool. They had come to get them because they were gone longer than Lynn was comfortable with them being gone for, in their condition.

'Lynn, look at this,' Chris said, showing her the tadpoles.

'They're so cute,' Lynn said. 'Tadpoles... Tadpoles.'

'Right?'

'Why don't you guys come on back and hang with us for a while. Then we gotta start getting back.'

The rest of the day they swam and played in God's water-park, an ever-changing array of drug-induced colors and images projected against the mountains and sky. For some reason, perhaps the tadpoles, Adam was hesitant to let his legs dangle too low or long in the pools for fear that something, some prehistoric animal, might rise up from the bottom and bite them off. So he kept them tucked up close to his body, and eventually got out of the water with the excuse that he just wanted to hang out in the sun. He seemed to be the only one afraid of the imaginary pool monsters.

When the sun crested sharply to the west they hiked to where the bottom pool's runoff met the river and jumped in, clothes, packs and all, body-rafting through the canyon walls, where the water was cooler than it was in the open air, but not too cold as to be uninviting.

'Always keep your legs down-river,' Phil explained. 'And use 'em to kinda spring off any rock you feel. It's slow season so not many rapids. Just mind what's in front of you and use your legs.'

At one point, Chris and Adam floated down-river holding hands, much more sober because of the passage of time and the fact that what they were doing required them to have their wits about them.

'I'm glad you didn't overdo it with the seeds Tom,' Chris said, all of them back-floating out of the last of the canyons into flatter, more open terrain, the water becoming warmer and calmer, the sun getting closer to the horizon. 'I was super-stoned there for a while.'

'Did you enjoy it?' Tom asked.

'Oh my God,' she said. 'That was amazing. All the light and colors... and the tadpoles. What about you Lynn?' Like Chris and Adam, Lynn and Tom were floating on their backs side by side hand in hand, as were Phil and Mary. Rat was behind them all taking it nice and easy.

'It was very intense,' Lynn said. 'I'm glad I did it, but I think once might have been enough.'

'Yeah, it's been a while since we've done it too,' Mary said. 'Nice to feel that again, but I think I'm getting too old to be doing hallucinogenics. Phil and I are thinkin' about startin' a family.'

''bout time, man,' Tom said. 'What 'a you been waitin' for?'

'To everything there is a season, my friend, and a time to every purpose under the heaven,' Rat said. Somehow he had managed to get a cigarette, which he had put in a plastic bag before jumping in the river, lit.

'You got that right,' Phil said.

As promised, the current delivered them, waterlogged and exhausted back to the crumbling bridge and the trucks. But departure had to be delayed because both front tires of Tom's pick-up had flattened during their absence, victims of the sharp tumblewood prairie sticks and stones that littered the ground. Since those tires were the spares of an original set, and no other spares were available, the only option was for Phil to drive into town, roughly fifty miles away, pick up two new tires and drive back to the disabled vehicle. Phil gladly volunteered.

'I got a couple right in the garage,' he said.

'Hey Phil, you mind if I tag along in the back?' Adam asked. They hadn't been to Montrose yet, and the thought of adding another experience to that remarkable day was very compelling; the vibration of motion, the zen of open-air travel.

'Sure,' Phil said. 'Glad to have ya'.'

'You wanna come?' Adam asked Chris.

'I don't think so. I'm pretty mellow right now,' she said. 'You go ahead. You should change into something dry. You'd be more comfortable'

Since Adam didn't have a change of clothes, he peeled off his wet overalls, handing Chris her crystal before draping the overalls, his underwear, and tee shirt over the side of Toms payload – which meant he was buck naked in front of everyone before he wrapped himself in one of the soft wool blankets Tom had brought along specifically for that purpose. Since he didn't foresee any reason to be away from the truck for a prolonged period, he felt it was safe to dispense with clothing and go with the snuggly insulation of the blanket. Mary had brought along sweatpants and sweatshirts for Lynn and Chris, anticipating their needs.

Once everyone had changed into dry clothes and good-byes were said, hands were shaken, and kisses given, Phil headed out to Montrose, with Rat and Adam in the payload.

'You a reader?' Rat asked, the night starting to descend.

'Not really,' Adam said.

'You should. That's how you can perceive genius. You gotta check out Gravity's Rainbow, man. Pynchon. It's the wildest thing I ever read.'

'What's it about?'

'Everything.'

'I know. I gotta start getting into books. I've been kinda bullshitting myself about it.'

'How'd you get though high school, man?'

'I just did. Reading wasn't one of the big requirements. You know, like 'Catcher in the Rye' and 'The Good Earth', but that's about it.

'I'm tellin' you man, read. It's the best way to pass tough time. It keeps your mind active.'

'Did you read a lot in Viet Nam?'

'Oh yeah.'

'Did you see a lot of crazy shit?

'I was a Seatiger on the Saigon River. Enough said.' He reached into the chest pocket of his overalls, took out a cigarette and lit it, cupping both hands around the flame of the match with a fluid, practiced motion.

'Got it,' Adam said. It didn't seem his war experiences were something Rat wanted to discuss, at least not with Adam right then. 'That was a pretty wild poem, by the way.'

'Yeah, psychedelics seem to open up my stream of consciousness. Usually I'm a little more focused.'

'Maybe you'll be a famous poet someday, and I can say I knew you when.'

Rat smiled and nodded. Both of them had almost completely come down from their trippy afternoon, and a quiet, slightly tired calm had replaced the electricity. Less than an hour later they pulled up in front of a small wood-framed house on a quiet street just within the Montrose City limits. Rat hopped out.

'Good hangin' with you, man.'

'Take care you yourself, man,' Adam said.

To Phil and Mary he said a quick, 'Monday, boss. Good night, Mary.'

'Good night, Rat,' Mary said.

They drove about ten minutes to another part of Montrose – newer, bigger homes with sweeping views of the surrounding mountains – and pulled into the driveway of Phil and Mary's home.

'Wow, man. This place is beautiful,' Adam said. Their home looked like it belonged in that part of the world, with its natural wood exterior and fifty-foot picture window facing the mountains out back.

'We just moved in,' Phil said. 'It's one of the models we're building out here. Montrose is really starting to come into its own. Do me a favor, Adam, gimme a hand in the garage. I gotta move some stuff to get the tires.'

'I'm… kinda naked under here.' That he was naked, in a strange city, with people he had only met that day felt strangely familiar, like déjà vu, like he had dreamed something like it a long time ago. There was a purity about it, combined with a little vulnerability and embarrassment about being so helpless.

'No worries. Honey, you wanna get him something to wear while I start movin' stuff.'

'Sure. Come on in, Adam,' Mary said.

Because both Phil and Mary were quite a bit taller than Adam, the legs of the slightly worn pair of overalls Mary brought out had to be rolled up at the cuffs. It felt like Adam was wearing his father's clothes. At least the area around the crotch was comfortable because he declined the pair of underwear Mary offered.

'Those look cute on you,' Mary said. 'You look like you're wearing your dad's clothes.'

'I had an amazing day with you guys,' Adam said. 'I hope to see you again before I have to go.'

'Likewise. You can get to the garage down those stairs and to the right.'

When Adam got to the garage, Phil had moved most of the stored items out of the way – skis, a generator, a portable tool rack. He lifted out the first of the two tires and set it down in front of Adam.

'Why don't you roll this out to the truck,' he said. 'I'll be right there.'

Once both of the tires were secured in the payload, Phil and Adam got into the cab. As he had done thousands of times before, Phil turned the ignition key and, for the first time, the truck wouldn't start. Completely dead.

'What the hell,' he said. He tried it again. Nothing.

'Must be the starter,' he said, looking under the hood, trying to see if he was overlooking something obvious.

'So, what are we gonna do?' Adam asked.

He thought for a moment. 'I don't think there's anything we can do tonight.'

'But what are they gonna do?' Mary asked. She had joined them when she saw, out her kitchen window, that they were just sitting there. As circumstance would have it, Mary's car was also in the shop due to mechanical problems.

'Well, lemme see,' Phil said, evaluating the situation. 'They got dry clothes, blankets...'

'I saw Lynn brought all that extra food,' Mary said.

'Yup. And it's supposed to be a beautiful night. I think they'll be just fine. I'll call Bill first thing in the morning. He'll come right out and get us fixed up before church traffic. Looks like you're our first house-guest, Adam.'

How weird it was to be standing there, separated from his adopted family, in a strange city, in front of a strange house, barefoot, in someone else's clothes that were way too big on him, without underwear on, with no money, nothin'. He felt like a stranger in a strange land. But he knew Phil was right about Chris, Lynn, and Tom having everything they needed for a safe, pleasant evening. Tom could handle himself in much more challenging situations. They'd probably let Chris sleep in the cab of the truck, and they would sleep in the payload wrapped in those wool blankets, under the stars, the sound of the running river filling the night, no one around but the ghosts of the cowboys who had been driving their cattle over that weather-worn bridge for almost a hundred years.

'I just hope they don't think we got into an accident or something,' Adam said. 'That would suck.'

'What time is it now,' Phil asked.

'Almost ten,' Mary said.

'Bill opens at seven on Sundays. Figure he can be done here by nine. And we can be out there by ten. Twelve hours. That's the worst it's gonna be.'

'All right,' Mary said. 'Why don't you come inside. I'll make some dinner. When's the last time you slept in a bed, Adam?'

Over lamb chops and applesauce, Adam told Phil and Mary about the summer he was having and how he had come to meet Tom, Lynn and Chris.

'Sounds like your friend left you kinda high and dry,' Phil said.

'Yeah, but look how it turned out,' Adam said.

'Someone was looking out for you,' Mary said.

That night they watched Mary Tyler Moore and Bob Newhart, the first television Adam had watched since leaving Baldwin. They also watched a PBS news segment on Mother Theresa – images of her in Calcutta taking care of the most destitute people on the planet – loving those children who didn't have anyone else to love them, and her love sustaining them. To Adam, she looked out of place in formal settings, like news conferences – like a penitent in a boardroom among corporate functionaries. But once she got going, you knew you were listening to the gospel. When a reporter asked her what could be done with all the orphans and forgotten children around the world, she said, 'Give them to me.' You knew she meant it.

'Who else is like Mother Theresa,' Adam thought, under the covers and drifting off in Phil and Mary's guest room. It was too dark to see the mountains, but he knew they were out there, silhouettes against a starry sky on a quiet summer night. 'Lincoln... Gandhi... Moses... Jesus, I guess.' Being Jewish and uninformed about other religions, he didn't know enough about Jesus to have a definite opinion about his mythology. Moses he got. Jesus as the son of God, he had no idea what that meant. At his bar-mitzvah, there was just God, and a lot of him. But he was a firm believer in 'to each, their own', so he wasn't worried about his religious shortcomings. Seeing Mother Theresa carrying on Jesus's blessing, he got the message.

'Okay Adam, we're ready to go,' Phil said, sunlight streaming through the open window. 'I got a muffin and coffee for you in the truck.' Adam had slept through everything Phil had said he was going to do in the morning.

'Wow. Whoah. All right. Let's go.' He gave Mary a hug and a kiss, and they were on the road just before nine.

'What kinda music ya'into back home?' Phil asked, after he saw Adam fumble with the coffee lid and asked him, very nicely, to try not to spill any.

'Mostly this year it was a lot of Jimi Hendrix, Zepplin, Bowie.'

'Rock.'

'Heavily. I know you're a country guy.' It was all he had heard Phil play, and the radio was always on in the car.

'I like the outlaws: Jonny Cash, Waylon Jennings, Willie, Merle. But I guess I also like the good ole' boys like George Jones. Check this out,' and he cranked up the volume on the radio. 'That's him,' he said, almost yelling. 'It's called *The Door*.' And he starts singing along, '... with tear-stained eyes I watched her walk away...' And a couple of seconds later, '... and the only sound, the closing of the door.'

That car-ride was where Adam learned to appreciate country music. He had never heard a voice like George Jones - velvet and real, and deep. Some of the popular songs failed to draw him in, like *Devil in a Bottle* by T. G. Sheppard, and *Linda On My Mind* by Conway Twitty. But that zen-like, country music-filled hour was well worth the time. He wondered if the fact that he had done a hallucinogenic drug and burned out a few brain-cells the day before contributed to his enhanced mellowness. It was one of the rare times in his life he hadn't felt the need to fill in the silent spaces in a conversation with talking. They just drove and listened to the radio.

'I told you they were all right,' Tom said, as they pulled up to the bridge.

'The starter,' Phil said to Tom. 'You wanna gimme a hand getting the tires out the back?'

Through an initial glance Adam tried to communicate to Chris that everything was all right, that he was glad to be back to her, that he knew how silly he looked in the overalls, that he hoped she had a good night, and what an unbelievable, magical day the day before had been.

'Everything good?' he asked her after he asked Tom and Phil if they needed a hand changing the tires and they told him they were good. She knew he meant about coming down from the morning glory seeds.

'We were just worried about you guys was all,' she said. 'Tom said it was probably that his truck broke down, but I could tell he was a little concerned. We all were.'

'I figured. And all we were doing was watching Bob Newhart.'

'Oh, I love that show.'

'And I slept in a bed.'

'I'm jealous. How was it?'

'Lonely.'

'We'll have to make up for that tonight.'

Perhaps it was because he had declared his love, or because they had missed a night of love-making the night before – whatever the reason, their sex that night was hotter than it had ever been, Chris reaching down and grabbing Adam's right hand while he was going down on her, and directing his forefinger near her ass. They were of one mind, her whole body relaxing and heating up the second he got his fingertip inside her. She grabbed his wrist, and, for a moment, he thought she was going to pull his hand away, that he had misread her intention. Instead she pulled it toward her. She was wetter than a juicy plum, and his finger slid in and out naturally, like he was conducting the sexual rhythm. He was so turned on that he didn't realize he was humping the ground until it was too late to stop himself from coming, and when she started to orgasm, he humped the tent floor like it was Chris beneath him. They came together.

'Ooohhh… com'ere,' she said, wanting him to climb aboard and make love to her.

'I… uh… kinda came…'

'No problem,' and she sucked him hard again in less than a minute. And then again after the second time he came, another first from that night, coming three times in a row.

When they were done he rested his head on her stomach, the smell of their sex all over them, natural and beautiful, with the Black Canyon of the Gunnison right outside their door, one of the great atmospheres to fall asleep in.

The next morning, Tom's first official day at work, Lynn, Chris, and Adam headed out to the Shavano Valley Petroglyph Park.

'Let me just call home. It's not gonna be long,' Adam said. They were at the Shavano Valley Petroglyph Park visitor's center, using the facilities, checking out the displays, reading some of the park literature, not looking in the gift shop until after, so they'd know if something captured the essence of the place, even if it was only a shot-glass or a key-chain. The two available phone-booths, near the soda machine caught Adam's attention. It had been over a week since he had called home.

'Let's call mom too,' Lynn said.

'Yes, I accept the charges… Hi!,' Doris said. No one would ever be as glad to hear from him. 'How's your trip? We miss you.'

'I miss you too. It's amazing. We're at this place today that's one of the oldest habitations in the country. It's like in the middle of nowhere. It's beautiful.'

'Oh, I'm so glad. And how are the girls?'

'They're doing good. They're in the phone-booth right next to me talking to their mother.'

'Listen, I'm glad you called. I don't want you to get upset, but your car was stolen.'

'From where?' Not exactly the news Adam was expecting to hear. It brought him back down to a reality he hadn't had to deal with since meeting Chris. Life wasn't all a timeless adventure.

'Well, Charles was at the Belmont Racetrack, which I didn't even know he went to, and it was stolen from the parking lot. We got the police report, so if there's any insurance claim, we can put in for it.'

'Ma, that car wasn't worth anything.'

Kenny Sackler had told Adam, not long after alerting him that Charles had threatened to shoot him, that he heard that Charles and some of the guys he went to the gym with had been going to Belmont Racetrack and shaking down people in the parking lot. They would hang around the cashier windows after each race, see who had won, then follow them into the parking lot. Knowing Charles was into guns, it wasn't a far stretch. Adam did see the irony of his brother holding someone up, and then getting ripped off himself. Although he didn't get ripped off. Adam did.

'What a fuckin' dick that guy is,' Adam thought.

'I know. But you worked very hard for it,' Doris said. 'Even though you weren't planning on bringing it with you right away, if you feel you need a car at college, Daddy and I will get you one, okay?'

'All right. Any other good news?'

'Nothing, other than Barry jammed his toe on the diving board. It's probably broken but there isn't much we can do about it. The doctor at the hospital taped it up, and Barry was right back outside. The kid doesn't miss a beat.

'All right, well tell him I said hi, and daddy too, and I'll call you soon.'

'All right sweetheart. Take care of yourself. And give the girls my love.'

'I will.'

'Don't worry about your car.'

'I'm not.' He wasn't going to bring up the reason Charles was at Belmont. At one point, Charles's decisions would find their way back to him, one way or another. Adam wanted as little to do with that psycho-drama as possible.

'I can't believe that fuckin' guy,' Adam thought, as soon as he hung up. 'He really did that shit... Rolled people in the parking lot of Belmont Racetrack.' Charles wasn't there watching the races, that was for sure. Even though his mother said she had thrown his gun into the creek, he wouldn't have put it past Charles to get another one. 'Or maybe someone else had one...'

'What's the matter?' Chris asked as soon as they were done with their call. Adam must have been wearing his emotions on his sleeve.

'My car was stolen.'

'How'd it...'

'Forget it. I'll tell you later. I don't want it to ruin our day.'

'I had my car stolen once,' Lynn said, as they were walking out of the visitors center into a very ancient environment. 'I had like three thousand dollars worth of coke in the glove compartment. God, was my ex freaked out.'

'I really liked Mark,' Chris said.

'Ancient history, Chrissy. Speaking of which...'

None of them had any idea there were such ancient markings in the United States.

'They look like mini NISCA lines,' Lynn said. 'I had no idea. Do you guys know what the NISCA lines are?'

Neither of them did.

'They're those figures in South America – southern Peru I think, that you can only see from the air, they're so spread out. People think they were made by aliens as kind of landing zones or points of demarcation. That's the only way to explain 'em. I'm telling you, these markings look just like 'em.'

Carved into the rocks around 42-acres of rugged terrain were images of dancing bears, cosmic trees, footprints, squiggly insects, and a vast array of religious iconography whose original meanings have been lost over the millennium. Standing in front of the petroglyph panels they felt transported back in time thousands of years.

'I wonder who carved these?' Chris asked.

An older gentleman, clearly native American, by both dress and visage, who was standing with, what turned out to be his eight year old grandson, overheard Chris' question and came over to answer it.

'I didn't mean to eavesdrop,' he said, 'but these were carved by our ancestors. We're Ute. This is my grandson Orrin.'

'Nice to meet you, Orrin,' Chris said, extending her hand.

'Go ahead,' his grandfather prodded. Orrin hesitantly grabbed Chris's hand without saying anything, and let it go just as quickly.

'Our people have been living around this area since... well,' and he acknowledged the petroglyphs. 'These markings represent our heritage. We're glad you're here today to share that. Heritage is people. I'm Severo.'

After everyone introduced themselves, Severo bent down to whisper something in his grandson's ear.

'My grandfather wants to know,' Orrin said, shy, but also a little confident, 'if you'd like to join us at our drum circle. We're gonna start in about twenty minutes. If you want, you can walk with us.'

'I'd say that was tailor made for the two of you,' Lynn said.

'We'd love to join you,' Chris said.

'We would,' Adam said, 'but we don't have any drums.'

'We have drums,' Severo said.

Drumming with native Americans, drumming with Chris, on a beautiful, warm, western summer day, at a mystical ancient art site, another day unfolding with wonder...

But, as they were walking to where Severo was leading them – through a landscape that had acres of open spaces, but was very mountainous – not towering peaks, but big enough, rocky - and Adam didn't see anyone else around, and, more importantly, didn't hear anyone else around, he started to think there was a possibility... He wasn't freaking out or anything. He just had a suspicion that they could be walking into something not good... that all of a sudden they would find themselves in a bad situation, and Severo and Orrin had been shills, luring them in.

'It's right up around here,' Servero said. He was referring to one of the smaller rock formations much closer to solid ground a half-mile away from the area where the petroglyphs were concentrated. It rose from the earth about eleven feet and was about twenty feet long, forming a natural amphitheater. Adam actually considered not going any further, but he didn't want to let on that he was suspecting a grandfather and grandson of anything other than hospitality. Then he heard the sound of a drum, then another drum, and his paranoia began to abate. The amphitheater had muted the voices, but not the drums, of the people sitting behind it - ten in all, three boys, three girls, two men and two women, all native Americans, ranging in age from eight to octogenarian, sitting or kneeling on the ground in a circle toward the center of the monolith. The older couple sat on lawn chairs.

'This is the Ouray Rock,' Severo said, 'A very good place. Wait until you hear the acoustics. Why don't each of you pick out a drum, and we'll widen the circle to accommodate you.' There were four or five extra drums in the center of the circle.

Boy, did Adam feel like an asshole for suspecting Severo and Orrin of being anything other than the sweet, good people they were. How far was he from transcending the baggage he had accumulated up to that point in his life. Pretty far. What a rude awakening. As he was walking to get the drum, Chris next to him, full of excitement, he realized he was someone who could get it wrong, who could suspect falsely, a kind, older man who had asked them to join a true, genuine, native American drum circle... And Adam was becoming a drummer. Man, did he need to learn... something. A healthy skepticism was one thing. Paranoia was something entirely different.

'You look serious. Long live your Dodge Coronet 440. Which drum are you going for?' Chris asked, snapping him out of his quandary.

Both Chris and Adam chose hand-drums carved out of a single tree-trunk, that were about two-feet deep, about a foot in diameter, and covered both on top and bottom with a natural animal hide, all the hair scraped off so that all that was left was a smooth tough hardened skin. Lynn chose a gut-covered frame-drum you held in one hand and hit with a leather-topped stick held in the other hand.

Once the drum circle was enlarged to accommodate them, Severo stood and address the circle.

'First, I want to welcome our new friends.' He paused, and the rest of the circle nodded to Lynn, Chris and Adam. 'We drum,' he continued, 'to communicate with our ancestors, whose legacy we represent. May their spirits be forever free, their spirit voices receding in time, like buffalo clouds in the distance. Once we moved around like the wind. Upon the wind ancient whispers, secrets of the remembered earth, when the Great Spirit danced in the moonlight. We will always remember the earth. We will always remember our past. We will always follow the eagle. We will dance the eternal dance.' And with that he sat down and started playing the drum in front of him, a drum similar to Chris's and Adam's, that he played with a leather-topped stick. His rhythm started out as the classic Native American single-stroke beat, which everyone joined in on. Several measures later, one of the guys - around Adam's age, maybe a little older, long black ponytail, jean-shirt and pants, turquoise and silver bolo tie – started weaving a rhythm around the core of the single-stroke rhythm, different accents, off the one, on the one, everybody, because the core rhythm was so simple, in complete unison. Adam understood what Severo meant about the acoustics. The drum sound radiated back to them, off the rock walls, in waves, their rhythm in time within the dynamic interplay. Adam felt the rhythmic echoes. Everyone did… looking at a cute eight-year-old girl in flip-flops, her face as native as her ancestors who carved the petroglyphs, eyes closed, head and long straight, jet-black hair bobbing on the one.

The guy with the bolo tie played his solo for a few measures, then settled back into the original single-stroke beat, the eight or nine year old boy next to him immediately assuming the solo mantle, also weaving a simple rhythm around the core rhythm, using accents to differentiate himself from the group. When the older woman next to him did the same thing, both Chris and Adam realized that that was how that drum circle worked. It wasn't a free-for-all or a jam session. It was a simple rhythm everyone got into and everyone had a chance to individually express themselves in. When it was Adam's turn to solo, he was a little nervous, like when a teacher picked on him to read aloud in class, but he kept his improvisation simple - doubling the single-stroke beat, keeping the accent on the one – and he felt the integrity of the rhythm and the circle had been maintained. Chris swung her solo, keeping it perfectly in line with the Native American rhythm, and looked at Adam with a happy smile after she had passed the solo onto Lynn, who, because she had never played drums, kept to the core beat, just playing it with a little more energy before passing it on. That rhythm went around a couple of times, and then Severo subtly changed it, speeding the new rhythm up a little and placing the accents on the two and four instead of on the one. And round and round that rhythm went, until the next one, all of it played without tension, in harmony with the sun, the deep blue sky, the ancient whispers. Lynn, Chris and Adam felt like they were communing with these members of the Ute nation, and when it was time to bring the drum circle to a close, after about forty minutes of almost constant playing, they shook everyone's hand and told them how much they enjoyed sharing that experience with them. Saying good-bye, Severo and the two older people took their faces in their hands and touched their foreheads to theirs. Adam felt like he had been blessed.

'Oh my God was that fun,' Lynn said, driving back to their campsite.

'You were doing some jazz riffs,' Adam said to Chris, who was riding shotgun.

'Was I all right?' she asked.

'It was perfect. I think the guy with the ponytail wanted to jam.'

'I have to tell you something,' Lynn said. 'When Severo grabbed my face and touched his forehead to mine, it felt like I was a young kid and my father was giving me a big hug. Did you feel that way Chrissy?'

'Not exactly that daddy was hugging me. It was more like I was receiving a blessing or something.'

'Yes,' Adam said. 'I think we did.' And he had suspected Severo of being a shill.

'So, how'd your car get stolen?' Chris asked.

'So this is really not good.'

'Really?'

'And… I don't think I'm betraying anything by saying something about it, especially if it's true. But I could see it. My car was stolen at a race track where my brother, I think… listen, this is crazy…'

'What, was he ripping people off?' Lynn asked.

'Yes.' It was amazing how quickly Lynn surmised that. A sixth sense.

'How was he ripping people off?' Chris asked.

'I think he watched the cashier's window, saw who won, and followed them into the parking lot.'

'Mark knew guys who did that. Not good guys. Whoah. I'm sorry Adam. It's okay to detach from him. Probably a good idea you did. That's a whole 'nother world.'

'Does he use a gun?' Chris asked. 'I thought your mother through it in a creek.'

'I don't know. These are really big guys, so they must have figured out a way, but...'

'Oh my God that's terrible.'

'So he was ripping people off while someone was ripping him off,' Lynn said. 'How perfect it that? Instant karma. The pressure in that realization could have turned a lump of coal into a diamond. It's almost worth it, Adam. There is little question, no matter how 'out there' your brother is, he knows he... got served. The second he knew the car was stolen, he knew how bad what he was doing was. It probably hit him like a ton of bricks. I'm sure it won't change him. Sometimes. Sometimes that's the only justice you get.'

'Yeah,' Adam said, wanting to change the subject. The last thing he wanted to think about, after that incredible day was Charles. 'Did you guys ever see the episode where Superman crushed the lump of coal in his hand... until it became a diamond?' Adam asked.

'That was an old one,' Lynn said. 'He had to put the diamond back... into like an idol or something. Someone stole the original one.'

'I loved Superman,' Chris said, 'I watch the reruns. You know what I think about sometimes, since we're talking about it, the episode with those little, like, beings with the rounded cone-shaped heads who... I think they came from inside the earth, but were from another planet? It really must have captured my imagination.'

'I think that was the only two-parter,' Adam said. 'That was definitely a darker episode, like Superman noir. I remember the one with the robot McTavish.'

'Bock McTavish,' Lynn, who had never before spoken in a Scottish accent said. That was how the actor, who played the inventor and controller of McTavish spoke when giving orders to McTavish to either go forward toward Superman, with the chunk of Kryptonite in his metallic grip, weakening and possibly killing Superman, or calling him back, away from Superman, giving Superman the space to get his strength back.

'Wait, didn't Superman also crush the diamond to give to Lois Lane?' Chris asked.

'I don't think Superman and Lois Lane ever got to that point,' Lynn said.

'I wonder if Superman ever thought about sex,' Adam asked. 'He seemed pretty oblivious to Lois, and she was throwing all of her best stuff at him.'

'I'm gonna say that in the best of all possible worlds, Superman didn't think about sex,' Chris said. 'He was beyond that kinda stuff.'

'Or that he just hadn't met his soul-mate yet, and he is forever faithful.'

'Or that he was in the closet. I don't know if he'd be… No, he'd have to be. He's Superman, with all his powers. He should be happy no matter who he wants to love. He's fighting evil… which, in a way would be the people who would ridicule him for his sexual orientation if, in fact he was gay. I don't remember, do they show him like a Ken doll… or a, you know, defined crotch area? His costume was tight.'

'Wow. I don't know,' Chris said.

'It was a little like a ballet dancer's,' Lynn said.

'Look at you,' Adam said.

'Sounds like you guys had yourselves a day,' Tom said, back at the campsite. 'I was thinkin' we could go out to dinner in town tonight to celebrate my first day on the job. There's this cool place that has live music. Y'up for it?'

Adam played drums that night too – twice in one day, both times with other people, something he had never done before. Whenever he had played his brother's drums it was either just soloing, working out rhythms, or playing along to records. That night, at The Saloon in Montrose, a classic western bar and grill, there was a country rock and blues band playing, and Tom, after a couple of beers, went up to the rhythm guitarist, someone he knew from the area, and asked if they minded if his friend from New York sat in. Tom was just spreading the love.

'I never played with anybody,' Adam said, really nervous, after Tom told him he could sit in for a song or two.

'You just spent the day playing with other people,' Tom said.

'Yeah, but that was just a simple beat on a hand drum. This is…'

'You can do it,' Chris said. 'It's all pretty much straight rock and blues they're playing. You'll feel it.'

'Ladies and gentlemen, we're gonna have a guest drummer for this next song,' the rhythm guitarist, who was also the lead singer, announced to the rest of the restaurant. All the way from New York. Come on up, man.'

While not The Allman Brothers or Little Feat, the band was a serious unit who had been playing together for years. All Adam could do was pray that instinct took over and he would know what to do. He had been playing along to the greatest bands on record for almost two years, so he understood the nature of drumming in relation to playing songs. It was the idea of fucking up in front of a room full of people that had his stomach in knots. All he could do was go for it. Jump and the net will appear.

'Thanks for doing this, man,' the drummer said, as Adam walked over. 'I could use a break,' and he handed Adam his sticks.

When Adam sat down and got himself acquainted with the setup - the classic Ringo setup - the lead singer turned to him and said, 'How about *Key To The Highway*?' Straight blues. Not too complicated.

'Go for it,' Adam said… A slow, four bar guitar intro right into the type of blues Adam loved to listen to, and had played along to many times: *Red House, Sitting On Top Of The World, It Hurts Me Too*. Adam was able to settle into the groove, everyone doing their thing but being part of something bigger. He felt the music. It felt natural, even the concentrating on everything around him. He was conscious of keeping himself together, but not overly worried that he wouldn't. He got so into it, his eyes closed, just grooving, that he almost missed the signal from the singer to end the song. He just happened to look up the moment the singer turned to him. A smooth landing.

'You up for one more?' the singer asked.

'Definitely,' Adam said, and the singer nodded to the bass player, who started playing the unmistakable opening riff from *Whipping Post*, a song Adam had worn the grooves out of listening and playing to.

He couldn't say the experience of playing *Whipping Post* with a band who knew how to rock was better than sex, but it was right up there. He had let himself go, playing along to that record many times, but that was nothing compared to playing it live with other musicians. To be in that heavy groove, riding the rhythm with all the intensity he had in him was exciting. All the pieces of the living puzzle fitting. Pure energy. There were moments he had to bring the energy down – the dynamics of the song demanded that. In those moments he was conscious that he was the beat and had better not fuck the beat up. Thank God he didn't.

'Thanks, we're gonna take a short break,' the singer announced to the restaurant and bar. 'I hope you'll stick around for the next set.' Then, turning to Adam he said, 'That was great man. Really sounded good. Thanks.'

'Thanks. That was awesome,' Adam said.

'Look at how happy he is,' Lynn said as he walked over to the table.

'That was great, man.' Tom said, standing, his hand extended. 'You know you make some pretty funny faces when you play,' and he made one; like he was bearing down to give birth. Lynn and Chris laughed. Adam was still a little in shock to feel self-conscious, or even to comment on what Tom or Lynn had said. He sat down, had a sip of beer, turned to Chris, who was looking at him with such tenderness that he felt he'd known her all his life, and asked, 'Was it okay?'

'Are you kidding,' she said, loud and enthusiastically, 'That was wild.'

'Really?'

'Really.'

'Thank God… Why don't you get up there? I…'

'No way.'

The lead singer, whose name was Rich, and who looked a little like Bob Weir from The Grateful Dead, came over, shook Tom's hand, was introduced to Lynn and Chris, and said to Adam, 'You playin' with a band back in New York?'

'Actually, that was the first time I ever played with a band.'

'Come on, man. Seriously.'

'Seriously.'

'Well, I hope it was as good for you as it was for us.' They all got his virgin reference. 'Anyway, I gotta go mingle. You guys gonna hang out for the next set?'

'Not too long,' Tom said. 'I gotta get up early.'

'I heard you were working up at the dam.'

'Yup.'

'Good. So, we'll be seein' you around. Nice meetin' you guys. And you keep playin' them drums.'

'I'm gonna,' Adam said.

After Rich left, Tom told Chris that, if she wanted, they could stay and he would try to arrange for her to sit in. Over the course of their many conversations about drums, drummers, and drumming, Tom knew Chris was into drums as well.

'Not tonight, Tom,' Chris said. 'I already did my drumming for today.'

'What about you, Lynn. You wanna give it a shot?' he asked.

'Very funny, honey,' the first term of endearment Adam had heard either of them use toward each other. 'I've never been very musically inclined. Our dad tried, but gave up after about the fourth grade. He knew my time was better spent elsewhere.' Lynn had shown an aptitude for math and science, and finally mechanical engineering, which was what she went to college for – Kent State – Class of '71. She was a junior when the National Guard shot the four students. She was at the protest - had been involved in the coordination of it. She hadn't seen anyone shot, but heard about it within moments, and sought cover. There was electricity in the air. As she was being herded off campus by the authorities, a Playboy Magazine representative, who had seen her at an anti-war rally in Washington, DC, and was currently covering Kent State, asked her if she would consider posing for the next issue, as part of the 'Girls of the Movement' series.

'You're out of your mind,' she told him.

After college she got a job helping to automate the Richman Tire and Rubber Plant, a large employer of people in and around Akron, transitioning from labor to management fairly quickly to help oversee the technical operations. She was one of seven Automation Controls Engineers involved with maintaining the new robotic machinery Richman had installed – the only woman. She also helped design a new QC process that was supposed to go on-line about a year before the factory closed. Funding for that project kept getting delayed, and when the Company's relocation to Macau, China by the summer was announced at the beginning of the year, Lynn understood why. The Senior VP of Technical Operations – the COO of Richman – asked her if she would consider relocating to Macau.

'Lemme think about it,' she told him. She knew it wouldn't be such a bad idea to get away. After college, she had moved in with the guy she had been seeing, a successful restaurant owner eight years her senior, who owned a beautiful house on Portage Lake. They were living the disco high-life. And Ohioans knew how to shake their groove thing. Unfortunately, the steady supply of cocaine her boyfriend always had was also being dealt to his restaurant patrons, and he was busted about four months before the Richman Tire and Rubber Plant announced it was closing its doors and moving to China. Although she was allowed to stay at her boyfriend's house while he was incarcerated – three to five in FCI Elkton – she had decided to get away, with her sister, for a few months. Break the ties that bound. Cold turkey – not that she was a cocaine abuser, just a recreational user. But she wasn't naïve. She knew she had been doing it too much, and was looking forward to being away from that whole lifestyle. She hadn't even thought about meeting someone like Tom Buck. In fact, she thought she was going to be taking a break from men for a while.

'You did make some pretty funny faces, Adam,' she said.

By that point, after the day they had, Adam was pretty mellow. He thought, 'I must have made some pretty funny faces,' if both Tom and Lynn mentioned them. He knew it was part of the rhythmic flow, as was the beer, which went down very smooth. He was right where he wanted to be; in a western Colorado bar and grill having the summer of his life. 'That was amazing,' he thought - rocking out on *Whipping Post*. 'I love when Chris is like this.' A little drunk. Alotta vibe. 'I can't wait to get her in the tent.'

'You guys about ready to hit the road?' Tom asked.

'Love to, Cowboy,' Lynn said. A woman after Adam's own heart.

Chris could have hung out, drank a few more beers and listened to the next set, probably the third one as well. But once they were in their tent, Adam was down on her like a bear on honey.

'Hold on a second,' she said, taking off her western shirt and trying to wiggle out of her jeans, which Adam cordially helped her out of. 'I wanna get comfortable. Ah, that's better. ' She turned over onto her stomach and pushed up onto all fours. 'Not in my ass,' she said. She wanted him to fuck her from behind, a new position for them. He slid in like greased lightening, her sigh as he entered her soul-deep. They fit together, moved together, Chris looking out the mesh window at the stars. He couldn't hold on for very long, pulling out at the last second, buzzed, euphoric, his cum landing in her hair and on her back, well before the cum on his face had a chance to dry.

'Here, use this,' she said, handing him the shirt she had worn that evening. When he had cleaned them both off, they crawled into their sleeping bag and fell asleep in each other's arms.

That was the beginning of the end of their summer together.

CHAPTER 8

· · · · · · · · · · · · · · · · · · · ·

Why change a good thing

River-rafting down the Gunnison River Gorge, a perfect fourteen mile run through the towering black granite cliffs and pristine backcountry of the Black Canyon. Lynn, Chris, and Adam were up with Tom at six in the morning, day two at the dam, and were at the river as the sun was rising above the canyon walls. Although it was mid-august, and run-off was at its lowest ebb, there were still some dam-regulated class-III rapids to be run, which their appointed guide, Jonathan, a bearded, grizzly-looking middle-aged man - huge calves, looked like they belonged on a much bigger guy - guided them through with skill and confidence, although at no point were the rapids anything close to threatening or un-navigable. They screamed anyway, as if they were tempting fate at every wave.

Dropping out of the first set of rapids into a glassy river pool, with cottonwood trees along the riverbanks, their excitement having given way to a quiet, introspective appreciation for the grand, mountainous, blue-sky wilderness they were smoothly floating through, they happened upon a male bighorn sheep mounted behind a female bighorn sheep, going at it with everything he had. They couldn't have been more than fifty feet away, up a little farther on the left bank of the river. Adam was about to yell, 'Atta boy,' remembering himself in the same position less than twelve hours before.

'Hold on,' Chris whispered. She knew Adam was going to do something obnoxious. 'Don't scare 'em. I gotta get a picture of this.' She quietly took her camera out of her waterproof carry-all, focused, and got a shot off before the click of the shutter brought the two sheep out of their reverie. Both sheep turned and looked at them as if to say, sarcastically, smugly, 'Thanks.' They immediately decoupled, the male sheep's penis about ten inches long, bright pink and glistening in the midday sun, prompting both Chris and Lynn to say, 'Oh my God,' at the same time. Then the sheep quickly traversed the side of the canyon walls until they felt they were a safe distance away from their gawkers.

'I can't believe we interrupted those two sheep,' Lynn said, over lunch a few minutes later. They were on the beach where the sheep had been fornicating, enjoying the tuna-fish and bologna sandwiches the rafting company provided – a welcome break from paddling. The beach was about twenty feet deep and fifty feet long, and was composed of sand and river rocks, a perfect place for an early afternoon interlude in the sun - the quietness of the slow-moving river, the canyon walls muffling all sound into a whisper, except the song-birds, whose songs seemed to get louder as soon as they started eating. It was quintessential wilderness river-rafting, a thousand miles away from civilization, the only things real, those which they could apprehend with their five senses - the universe boiled down into the eternal vision in front of them.

'So, Adam, what are your plans?' Lynn asked, bringing Adam out of his sunshine daydream. 'Don't you have to get back pretty soon?'

There it was - the interjection of the inevitability Chris and Adam had been very good at keeping in abeyance. Lynn asked because she was trying to formulate her own plans with Chris, and Adam's timing was part of the equation. Even though her time with Tom had been every bit as beautiful as Adam's and Chris's, she wasn't planning on living in a tent in the Gunnison forever either. Life had to be reckoned with. The four of them had been very good about living in the moment. There had not been one discussion about long-term plans. Whether Tom and Lynn discussed their future in private, Adam didn't know. They were both honest about who they were. And their love seemed to be growing. The limitation on Adam's relationship with Chris was established at the beginning. At some point he had to get back home. Their few weeks together had been so concentrated, so fantasy-filled, it felt much longer, which was what the rest of the summer had started to feel like - the end, a concept a long way off. But it was getting close to mid-August, and Adam needed to get back to Baldwin sometime at the beginning of the last week of August to get everything together so his parents could drive him up to Cortland on the Friday before school started, Monday, September 1st. That left about two weeks between then and now.

'Two weeks,' Chris said, looking straight ahead, not focusing on anything in particular, her easy smile turned pensive. 'Wow... This summer's flying...'

'Just so you know,' Adam told both of them. 'I'm having the greatest time of my life.'

'You ain't kiddin'' Lynn said. It was hard to see her and Tom going their separate ways at that point. It was more about being where they were while they were there, and moving on when the time was right. No one knew where the future would lead. They were busy creating it. 'Listen Chrissy, we gotta figure out what we're doing too,' Lynn continued. 'Tom's working, and I wanna get back kinda by the end of September... figure out what I'm doing. You gotta, too.'

'I know,' Chris said. 'We were planning on hitting New York at some point. We could come and visit you.'

'How about you guys drive me all the way back to Baldwin. My parents would love you. My mother asks about you every time I speak to her. Then we could all drive up to Cortland.'

'I'm serious,' Chris said.

'Me too. I would love for you to visit me.'

'You guys about ready to put back in?' Jonathan asked. He had spent their lunch break exploring that section of the canyon, and had come back with an Indian-head penny from 1899, soiled but legible, which he gave to Lynn as a memento from their time on the river. It was a great find – a great gift.

'You guys are my two-hundredth tour,' Jonathan informed them, pushing off. 'Still love it... AAAAHOOOO!'

The rest of the afternoon was as beautiful as the morning, floating through the ever-unfolding Black Canyon landscape – the sheer scope of the canyon, massive in parts, Grand Canyon massive. To be at the bottom of that, at one with nature, having serious fun... Everything felt in balance – even the two five-foot egrets watching them float by from their perch upon another rocky river beach.

'Imagine if they were goin' at it too,' Chris said.

'This is the magic land of, as Marvin Gaye would say, getting it on,' Lynn announced. 'Around every corner, a new species engaged in procreation.'

'Sounds like an erotic Disney ride,' Adam said.

'Okay, we're coming up to Rocky Point,' Jonathan said, pointing to the whitewater ahead. 'Today, we'll be able to see pretty good. But when it's running, this place can be immense. Call 'em if you see 'em. And don't be afraid to use your oars.'

Again, it was on the lower end of the class III spectrum, but they screamed anyway as they paddled through it, as if it was more treacherous than it was. When they dropped into a calmer section of river, they felt like they had conquered the elements. Their discussion about how the future was going to take shape – not necessarily specifically, but simply that over the next two weeks they had to think about it – had once again given way to living in the moment. They weren't avoiding dealing with change as much as waiting for the appropriate time before they had to reckon with it, which was probably a day or two before Adam actually had to leave. Two weeks still felt like a solid chunk of time. It was still summer. Lynn and Chris had almost two months before they planned on heading back, so they were still heavily in vacation mode. Perhaps it was as Chris had said, that feelings tended to be mutual. Adam wasn't freaking out that their summer was coming to an end sooner rather than later. And he didn't get the impression Chris was either. If she felt the same way he did then she loved him, but not to the point of dropping everything for that love. Their love was about being together on a teenage adventure that had an expiration date. Whether that love could endure outside their adventure, they would have to wait and see. Certainly, knowing Chris planned on visiting Adam at college helped softened the idea of separating. But a lot would happen before their love would have a chance to prove itself eternal. The fact that neither of them ruled that out kept their spirits buoyed.

'There's no way we're not coming to visit you, by the way,' Chris said later that evening in their tent.

'I can't wait.'

'Watch. You'll meet someone right off, and I'll be just another summer romance.'

'What do you mean another. This is the only one I've ever had.'

'Am I really only the third girl you've ever had sex with?'

In addition to Stephanie Millman, Adam had told Chris about Beth Fishbein, a moderately attractive girl two years his senior who he met at her brother's post-season soccer party a few weeks after Stephanie and he broke up, who fucked him in the back of her Plymouth Valiant after she asked him if he needed a ride home. She drove to the back of the Baldwin Park parking lot, well beyond the light-posts, down by the bay. 'I knew we were gonna do this as soon as I saw you,' she said. 'Why don't we climb in the back.'

That random, unexpected, deeply appreciated offer lead Adam to understand that his sex life was probably going to be an unforeseen continuum. Hang in. It'll happen, whenever it happens. Try not to get too freaked out about it.

The fact that Chris was rubbing his balls when she asked made his past irrelevant.

Tom and Lynn's future came a'calling that Saturday morning. Chris and Adam had taken Lynn's car into Montrose to do some shopping – food, toiletries, other essentials. Montrose was a quintessential Colorado town, built in a huge, sprawling valley with the Rocky Mountains all around. It even had its own historic district, which was starting to become a high-end tourist destination because Montrose was perfectly situated for four seasons worth of vacation activities – skiing, hiking, river-rafting, hot-air ballooning. Main Street literally looked like Main Street in Disneyland, except in Montrose it was real, the mountains in the background giving it a grounded vibe.

'Hold on one second,' Chris said, window-shopping at the historic district's shoe and boot store. 'I really wanna get a pair of cowboy boots.' The hiking boots Chris wore almost every day were starting to show signs of wear.

'Let's go in,' Adam said.

Chris was very serious about which boots spoke to her. She picked out three pairs to try on, walking in them, looking at them on her feet in the mirror, not asking Adam's opinion until she tried one of the pairs on for a second time - a pair of black, lizard-skinned Justin's with a pinkish floral stitch.

'What do you think?' she asked, modeling them for Adam. There was something about seeing Chris in a pair of short jeans shorts and cowboy boots that really turned him on, his eyes following the line from the top of her boots, up her inner thigh, past the bottom of her shorts, into the promised land.

'They look amazing. I'm getting them for you.'

'No way. These are way too expensive.'

The truth was, Adam had spent much less money than he had anticipated up to that point. With a little over a week to go before he had to start heading home, the almost four hundred dollars he still had in reserve was more than enough. Even accounting for unforeseen events, he could afford to buy Chris her boots.

'Please. I really wanna,' he said.

'You sure?'

'Totally.'

Their next stop was a combination hiking gear, jewelry store, rock and mineral shop.

'Would your sister wear this?' Adam asked, holding up a sterling silver bracelet about three-quarters of an inch wide, with turquoise inlaid in a pattern reminiscent of the petroglyphs at Shavano.

'I think she'd love it. No kidding.'

'What about you,' Chris asked, after Adam paid for the bracelet.

'I'm not really...'

'I know, how about we get you an earring. Look at these.'

There were some very cool silver earrings Adam wouldn't have minded wearing. The problem was his parents had always been against him wearing an earring. They were old-school Eisenhower-era parents. And even though the '60's revolution had broadened their social conscience, they still insisted on a conservative mentality, at least until Adam was on his own, which, at that point he was.

'Let's do it,' he said.

Chris picked out and paid for a silver hoop the saleswoman said was from Tibet – a mystical land, infusing the earring with even greater coolness. The saleswoman also told them the store didn't do piercings.

'Me and Lynn can do that when we get back. We just gotta remember to bring back a cup of ice.'

When they got back to the campsite, Lynn and Tom were cooking ham and cheese melts over the fire – the perfect lunch.

'Just in time,' Lynn said. 'Whadja get?'

Chris modeled her boots for everyone, and Adam gave Lynn her bracelet, which he could tell she loved. She put it right on.

'This is so sweet of you Adam,' she said. 'It's beautiful. I love it.' She couldn't stop staring at it on her wrist.

'We have some pretty interesting news,' Tom said.

Over their melts, Tom and Lynn told Chris and Adam that Phil had stopped by earlier that morning. He told Tom his father's and his company had just been given the commission by one of the biggest real estate developers in Colorado to build twenty to thirty new homes in and around the Montrose area in anticipation of the overall growth the area was already beginning to experience. They expected that overall commission to take about three years, after which their company would be one of the premier home-building contractors in south-west Colorado. Most of the homes would have mountain views and would be anywhere from three to six thousand square feet. As a way to vertically integrate that type of expansion, Phil's father put a bid on the small, local lumberyard with the expectation of expanding. That bid had been accepted.

'I used to work for Phil's father.' Tom said. 'That's where I learned my trade. Phil asked me to come aboard again.'

'He wants you to be his partner,' Lynn said.

'Well, we have to work out those details,' Tom said. 'But he did talk about a buy-in.' Tom would run a crew and Phil would run a crew. Rat, Phil had told Tom, didn't want the responsibility. He'd rather just work and write his poetry.

As an incentive for coming aboard sooner rather than later - Tom would have to give notice at the dam a few months before the end of his proposed, although completely non-binding term of employment – Phil had offered Tom the first model home they had built in the development Phil and Mary currently lived in at cost less depreciation already recorded; about one-fifth the asking price, definitely affordable with the salary Phil had proposed, some of which would be invested back into the business as Tom's equity in the company, eventually acquiring a maximum of fifteen percent of the company stock, which, if they continued to grow, would be worth a considerable amount of money in years to come. The company would guarantee Tom's mortgage, if that was the financing route he wanted to go. The home was a thirty-two-hundred square-foot chalet with a forty-foot picture window looking out at the spectacular mountain views. Phil gave up a little more of the business than his father had wanted, but since they both wanted to insure success, which, with Tom, was a good bet, they went with the offer Tom couldn't refuse.

'And that's a lotta house for...'

'So Tom and I were talking about me coming out here and living together,' Lynn said. 'See how that goes.'

'Chris, just so you know how I feel about your sister... And I don't want you thinkin' I'm some kinda dishonorable guy,' Tom said, 'I went a little farther than 'see how it goes'.'

'He wants to make an honest woman out of me,' Lynn said.

'Oh my God!' Chris yelled, and grabbed her sister in her arms. That was a beautiful moment to witness – two sisters sharing the joy of love. Chris went up to Tom and gave him a hug, and whispered in his ear, 'I'm so happy for you guys.' In that instant, she felt much closer to Tom, like she was hugging a member of her family.

'Anyway,' Lynn said, not wanting the moment to be completely about her. She knew Chris was genuinely happy for both her and Tom. She also knew her sister was the only one without a foothold into the future, and that her relationship was coming to an abrupt end in about a week. Lynn loved her sister too much to dwell on her good fortune when her sister's was so uncertain. 'We're not rushing into anything. We still have a lot to figure out.'

'We could always live in this tent here,' Tom said, beaming. He had met the woman of his dreams, asked her to marry him, and had gotten a definite maybe in response – kind of like a rental agreement with an option to buy. At least he was in. Considering the way things were going, he wasn't worried about the future. He knew Lynn was his and he was hers. If she wanted to wait before she accepted his marriage proposal, he understood. They had known each other less than a summer. 'Why change a good thing...'

''cause I saw those houses,' Adam said. 'It feels like you're living in a permanent vacation. We need to celebrate tonight.'

'Did you call mom and dad?' Chris asked.

'I will,' Lynn said.

'Do you think your parents'll like me,' Tom asked.

'I think they'll love you, Cowboy,' Lynn said, looking into his eyes and caressing his face with such tenderness, you couldn't help but believe those two were meant to be together.

'I don't have a house,' Adam said to Chris. 'But I may have a dorm-room you can crash in for a while.'

'I may just take you up on that.' Chris was going with the flow. 'Oh yeah, Adam's getting his ear pierced. You ready?'

'Absolutely.'

'Why don't you go get the cup o' ice and start numbing out your earlobe. I'll get the needles and the alcohol.'

'Adam's gettin' hippie on us,' Lynn said.

'Finally,' Adam said.

Getting his ear pierced with ice cubes and a sewing needle hurt more than he was lead to believe. Especially when Chris had to aggressively push through the mid-line cartilage. He heard and felt it pop.

'What was that?' he asked, a little concerned.

'Oh yeah, I forgot about that. That's just the cartilage,' Chris said. 'I'm almost done.'

When he looked in the mirror, it was worth it. Even though his ear was very tender, and it felt weird to have something pull at it from a central point, he felt it looked much cooler than he had imagined – pirate, hippie, musician, him more mature.

'Just make sure you clean it with alcohol twice a day,' Chris said, 'You don't want it to get infected.'

'And keep moving it around,' Lynn added, 'so the hole has a chance to form.'

'Lemme see the mirror again.'

They celebrated that night at The Saloon. Tom didn't know anyone in the band, although he did offer to go up to the lead singer and ask if Chris or Adam could sit in for a song or two.

'Not tonight, man,' Adam said. Both Chris and he were more into hanging out together than losing themselves in the rhythm individually, although when the band started playing *Jack Straw*, Adam did feel the pull.

'Here's to Tom and Lynn,' Chris toasted, all of them lifting their shot of tequila and throwing it back. Then Tom lifted his beer, all of them following suit. 'I'd like to propose a toast,' he said. 'To the four of us... How we all came together and everything we've shared. This is just the beginning.' They all drank to that.

'This is for Adam getting home safely,' Lynn toasted. 'And us visiting him at college.' They were all starting to feel the warm embrace of the tequila and beer. Plus, they had smoked Adam's last joint on the way to the restaurant – the last time he would ever see Panama Red. 'So here's what Tom and I were talking about in terms timing and everything,' Lynn continued. 'What do you think about the three of us heading out next Saturday – give you enough time to get home without stressing about it. We'll drive you to Cheyenne, Wyoming where Route 80 is – get you right to the main road east… And, if nothing happens, you can get on a bus there, which, the more I thought about it, the more I think it might not be such a bad idea.'

'Imagine if Tom had done that,' Adam said, trying to be cute.

'Yeah. There is that,' Lynn said. 'But this is a little different.'

It was different. Adam had a limited amount of time, her sister's heart was involved, and Adam wasn't Tom Buck. He got that. He appreciated her candor. It helped him focus. Lynn was the kind of woman who made men want to be better men.

'Anyway,' Lynn continued, 'then you and I could head up to Yellowstone, and from there, the Pacific Northwest, or down to Yosemite. Either way I wanna see Yosemite. Then Route 40 through the south for a few weeks, head up the east coat and hit New York around the end of September. Niagara Falls after we visit Adam, and then home. But I do wanna spend a night or two in New York City, like we said. I'm seeing *A Chorus Line* this summer. That's how long we were planning to be out anyway. Sound good?'

'Sounds… okay.' Chris was thinking that everyone but her was starting a new life. That was the moment she decided that when she got home she would apply to nursing school for the winter/spring semester. The pieces had fallen into place. She immediately felt a little lighter. 'Yeah… I like it.'

During that time Tom would finish up working at the dam, and start getting ownership of the house in order before Lynn made her official move sometime mid-October. Although he was supposed to be working at the dam until the end of the year, he felt a month notice was fair. Riprap required much less building skills and much more grunt-work than he had hoped. Although he appreciated the weekly compensation, and being back on native soil, the work wasn't challenging or fun. Management would find someone to replace him. He even knew a few people he could recommend. He planned on recommending Lynn to the engineering department. Along with riprap, the dam was also getting new turbines, which were in the process of being built for installation the following spring. The whole area was planning for expansion. It had already started. Tom knew that, once he introduced Lynn to the crew chief, she had a good shot at getting a new gig, if one was available, which Tom thought one or two were. A wise, beautiful, competent woman was always a welcome addition to a technically challenging, all male work environment.

'Wow,' Adam said, when Chris and he were in their tent.

'Wow what?'

'... Everything.'

'I know. I can't believe Tom asked Lynn to marry him.'

'I'm really happy for them. It's like they were meant to be... And I gotta tell ya, I can't believe I'm getting on the road alone.'

'Should we drive you further?'

'No... Actually, it's really good you're driving me all the way to Route 80. That's the road I need to get to, and getting there might have been a problem.'

Because everything had turned out the way it did after Stevie told him he was leaving, Adam was actually looking forward to seeing how he could do on the roads alone. He felt that would be an adventure unto itself. If things didn't work out the way he needed them to, he had enough money to hop on a bus and be home in two days. But the unknown didn't feel threatening at that point. It was part of the summer, the last leg of the adventure.

'It's so bittersweet,' Chris said. 'I never expected to meet you... You were trying so hard to be cool. By the way, I'm definitely applying to nursing school as soon as I get home. That's one thing I gotta do. And maybe you'll be able to come visit me around the holidays. Whadda you think?

'I think... I'm glad I tried to be cool. Look what happened. Here we are. It's crazy... Oh my God. I'm really into you right now.'

'Good.'

They fucked with abandon, Adam on top, pushing up a little, palms down, leaning over her, kissing her passionately – kissing and fucking at the same time, the ultimate full-body experience, the kind of love-making that feels like what sex should be, what love feels like. Coming together while they made out, still buzzed, fully engaged.

'I'm gonna miss this,' she said after, drifting.

'You still have seven nights of it.'

'... Six.'

'Oh yeah, six.' It still felt a long way off.

CHAPTER 9

The separation of law and gospel

Sometimes we awake before our most promising dreams have reached their climax, and try as we might to fall back asleep and recapture the sequence, a different series of images has moved onto the viewfinder. That's how Chris and Adam felt the following Saturday morning as they broke down camp and packed up the car.

'Don't go falling in love too fast, okay?' Chris said. The little plot of canyon they had called their own for a few weeks looked like they had never been there. How quickly nature reclaimed itself.

'Yeah, I wouldn't worry about that,' Adam said. 'Right now it's just you. I feel like I felt when the wind changed and Mary Poppins left.'

'I know.'

Sadness mixed with loss and change, and the reality that they were growing up and becoming responsible for themselves. Their summer-long dream was ending and could never be reclaimed. The possibility existed that their separation was part of a grander scheme, that eventually the wheel would bring them together again. But the wheel always turns and never slows down. It never stops and never stands still. The entire universe would have to be traversed before they could arrive back at their point of departure.

'You be careful on the road,' Tom said to Adam. He and Lynn had finished packing up everything she and Chris would need on their continuing adventure. 'I'm sure I'll be hearing all about how you're doing. You have Mary's number just in case. You keep going, man. You were a pleasure. And keep playing your drums. That seems to be in ya.'

'I will... Okay, man. You take care of yourself. This was pretty wild,' meaning everything – how they met, their time together, his future with Lynn. Adam hadn't expected that saying good-bye to Tom was going to feel like he was losing something: like an older brother. 'Anyway, I'm sure I'll see ya.'

'You will.'

''bye Cowboy,' Chris said, emotional, holding onto the hug, and Tom feeling the warm embrace. The sudden realization of departure. In those moments Chris sensed a subtle shift in her self-awareness - not that she was on her own, but that was coming, sooner rather than later. Time's winged ships were at full mast. She didn't feel intimidated. She believed in herself. 'I'm gonna see you at the holidays, right?'

Tom loved it when Chris called him Cowboy, which she did very infrequently. He felt like he had two strong, good women looking out for him. And, because they were sisters, their power was multiplied. 'Before,' he said.

'He's helping me get all my stuff out here,' Lynn said. 'I'll call Mary tonight, let her know when I'll call you. I love you, Cowboy. I miss you already.'

'I love you. Call me soon.'

'I will.'

Although they weren't officially engaged, their farewell hug and kiss was convincing. It was the only time Adam had seen Tom so passionately express his affection for Lynn. He caressed her like she was the most precious thing he had ever held. For Lynn it was abandon. She found the man she was going to marry. She was going on a month vacation with her sister to the most beautiful places in America, and coming back to start a life with Tom, in an unbelievably beautiful home with a view of the Rocky Mountains. Even the name, Lynn Buck, like she'd heard it all her life. She had said it a thousand times since Tom asked her to marry him. It had started to feel like who she was. Lynn Buck.

Chris held Adams hand. They looked at each other. Chance had brought them together. They both jumped and the net appeared. It was timeless, until it was time to go their separate ways. That very day. Their bond was breaking. Chris could feel it, just like Adam did, at the edge of their love, just a tiny bit. It felt like, 'nothing lasts forever', and 'I can't predict the future. Maybe....' Right then, they were not enough in love to change everything to be together – the unconditional love of eternity. They had allowed themselves to be swept up in the fantasy summer, and now that September was knocking on the door, that fantasy was walking out, just like George Jones sang. Their love was like the falling of an autumn leaf. The deepest love is evergreen.

And, as much as Adam wanted to diminish the psychological impact of knowing he was going to be hitching on his own for the first time, two thousand miles from home, it definitely weighed heavily. He had a hundred-forty-seven dollars left, and a maximum of four days to get home. If he saw it was going to take longer than that, he was going to buy a bus ticket, no matter where he was. That meant he had to keep at least seventy dollars in reserve, which left the remainder for food and anything else he might need. He was well aware of his apprehension, and did his best to hide it.

'You ready for this?' Chris asked. The fact that he had to pee for the third time that morning gave Chris the hint he might have had other things on his mind.

'I have no idea,' he said.

'All right Cowboy. We're gonna hit the road. We have everything? Oh, wait.' Lynn searched in the new hand-tooled, natural-leather backpack Tom had bought her – southwest themes, with a silver and turquoise florette as the main clasp - and took out the quartz and fluorite crystal she had found, what seemed like a lifetime ago. 'Do me a favor,' she said to Tom, 'when you get into the house, find a special place for this. No comment from the peanut gallery… It's good luck.'

Adam held his hands up, innocent of even the suggestion that he might make a dildo-related comment.

Tom took the crystal, smiled and nodded. Adam was glad something they shared together meant so much to Lynn. Chris kept hers in her backpack, wrapped up in a tee shirt and a hand towel to protect it.

'We ready?' Lynn asked.

'Yup,' Adam said. 'Bye Tom.'

'See ya, Tom,' Chris said.

'I love you, sweetheart,' Lynn said. And they drove away.

It felt like Adam was being swept away by the tide of time. In about six and a half hours he was going to be on his own facing the unknown.

'I can't believe we're on the road again,' Lynn said, keeping everything light and positive. 'It feels so weird.'

'I know,' Chris said. 'Maybe you should just get on a bus.'

'Nah. First, I wanna see if I can hitch. I'm not gonna be stupid about it. I'll know if I shouldn't do it. I hope, anyway.'

'That would give you a few more days with us,' Lynn said.

'I know. But I really wanna see if I can do it.'

He was genuinely into to testing his mettle as a man, a direct influence of Tom Buck. Prolonging the inevitable was a pretty enticing offer, but for some reason he felt it was time to start heading back. He hoped Chris didn't take it personally. He would have loved to spend the rest of eternity living the way they had been living – an endless summer. But at that point, knowing the summer was rapidly coming to an end, his focus had started to shift. He wanted to get home, safely. After that, he'd be able to think about his future. Right then, he was feeling kind of antsy, although he was trying his best to hide it. He got the impression Chris, too, had an eye on her future, without him in the picture. She still had a month of touring around the country, and then applying to, and then attending nursing school. She would have loved to continue their endless summer as well, but life was beckoning. Would they find their way back to each other? That was a question neither of them had the answer to. Yet neither of them, as they drove along Route 133, felt the overwhelming loss of love. Loss of a friend, certainly; apprehension about change, definitely; the fact that they would soon be on their own, yes. It felt kind of like breaking up, without any hard feelings or regrets, which lent itself more to introspection than outward expression. Because of what they meant to each other, they were doing the best they could with the few hours they still had together.

'Okay, look for the signs for 70,' Chris instructed Lynn, 'and we're gonna take that all the way into Denver. Then 25 to Cheyenne. I'm calling you in five days at your parents' house. If you're not there, you're in trouble.'

Adam thought, 'If I'm not there I *am* in trouble.'

'I'll be there,' he said.

The few moments of silence that followed was indicative of their individual states of mind – watching the trees and open spaces roll by – always the mountains in the distance – Lynn thinking about things she wanted to bring with her to Montrose, and what she was going to leave. Tom told her she didn't need to bring any furniture, only things she really wanted. Chris was floating in and out of memories of tadpoles, and the drum circle and feeling the beautiful sentiment of Severo's words; heritage is people. She was wondering who her people were; her parents and sister, Adam – maybe. Tom. For Chris, it felt like Tom had become an enduring part of her life. She thought about her ex-boyfriend. She was glad she closed that chapter.

'I wish you were going to Yellowstone with us,' she said.

Adam was in the back seat not thinking of too much. It felt good to be on the road. He had just had the most amazing summer of his life – the most amazing time of his life. He had spent it with a guardian angel. He didn't know how it happened, but it happened. He felt a much more mature sense of himself than he did when Stevie and he first put out their thumbs. That felt like the distant past. The unsettling fact that he was going from sex every day back to the unknown was overshadowed, in his mind, by the abstract idea of Chris visiting him at college and them continuing where they left off, until *The Door* by George Jones came on the radio, a song they had heard many times over the past few weeks, and the three of them sang along as the world rolled by. Then a commercial for Pup N Taco, the jingler singing, 'At Puppy's Pup N Taco we hope that we please you, Pup N Taco, Pup or Taco 29 cent drive-through.'

'Oh my God, Pup N Taco,' Lynn said. 'I haven't had that in years. We have to find that for lunch.'

Once they got within the general Denver area, Lynn pulled into a gas station to fill up her tank, and ask the attendant if he knew where the Pup N Taco was, which he did, giving her directions to East Colfax Avenue.

'This is our last meal together,' Chris said. They were sitting at an outdoor table on a beautiful summer day at Pup N Taco trying to enjoy their tacos, the first Adam had ever eaten. They probably would have been even more delicious if it weren't for the fact that it was, perhaps, their last meal together. Not even the '50's nostalgia vibe could lighten the mood. In around two hours they were going their separate ways. Both Chris and Adam were starting to feel what that meant much more acutely than either of them expected.

'I can't believe the summer's over,' Adam said. 'It flew.'

'You just make sure you get home safe,' Lynn said. 'Chrissy has your address, right?'

'Yeah.'

'And your parents'll know to forward her letters?'

'Yeah.'

'I know this part's kind of a drag. You bring out the best in each other. Just keep an open heart and an open mind. It'll work out.'

'I hope so,' Adam said.

'It will.'

Chris took one bite of her taco and put it back down in the paper wrapper it came in. 'I'm not really hungry,' she said. She just sipped her diet coke, and took a few deep breaths every once in a while.

'You sure you're not gonna eat that?' Adam asked.

'You have it.'

Even though the somber mood of their lunch had made food less relevant than it had been, when Adam finished his taco, he was definitely into having another.

Two hours later, as Chris and he stood in front of a Safeway store in Cheyenne saying good-bye, they both felt the full weight of the end of what they had shared. It was much sadder than breaking up with Stephanie. This felt like he was losing his best friend, for no other reason than that was the way it was supposed to play out - like the script had already been written and they were living it. For Chris, who had lived through her parents' divorce and her father moving out, it was even sadder. Behind her tears, Adam sensed a loss he would have given anything to fill. But there was nothing they could do except say good-bye.

'This is crazy,' he said, standing there, holding her hands, looking at her, knowing how strong she was and how quickly she'd get back into the groove of exploration. Lynn and he had hugged outside of her car and said good-bye as if they were two old friends who knew that life had many twists and turns. Then he put his backpack on, and Chris walked him over to where he planned on starting his hitch eastward.

'I wish we could have done this forever,' she said through tears. 'Please take care of yourself. If it starts getting dark, just get on a bus. You don't have to prove anything. You already did that. I love you.'

'I love you too.' The weight in Adam's chest was suddenly very heavy. He took a deep breath to try to lighten it a little. 'Wow. Please write. And I can't wait for you to come to New York.'

'I will... All right... I guess this is it... 'bye Adam.' A final hug. A lingering kiss on the lips. A last look. Her walking back to the car. And they drove away. Waved, sadly, and drove west, toward the mountains. From Chris to without her, just like that. Adam had never felt so alone in his life. Not lonely. It was more like, he was truly on his own - there was everything in the universe, and then there was him, right in the middle of it, pulled down by gravity, and the knowledge that a once in a lifetime experience had come and gone. For the first few seconds it was surreal – kind of like, 'What the fuck just happened?' Then, just as quickly, reality returned, and with it a sense of resolve. His insecurities were there, but he knew he had no choice. He had to seize the moment. How quickly his focus returned to the task at hand - two thousand indifferent miles of open highway to hitch alone, and a hundred forty dollars in his pocket. It wasn't that he could so easily disregard Chris minutes after she was gone. It was more like self-preservation. The reality of the situation only became apparent when he was standing in the middle of it. He wished Chris was standing there with him. But she wasn't. No one was.

'Okay, let's do this,' he said to himself.

Not twenty minutes later, in front of the Safeway store he was hitching across from, two seriously inebriated middle-aged Native American men started yelling at each other. They had just stumbled out of the Safeway store, slurring and yelling, both of them missing front teeth, both of them wearing jeans and denim shirts as haggard looking as their wearers. Then one took out a knife out from his belt, a serious hunting blade. Then the other took his knife out from his belt – all this in broad daylight, on a main thoroughfare, although traffic was light. Because they were so fucked up, their slower-motion lunges and parries looked like a slovenly rum-go. It was almost like insane theater, until the cops showed up. Then it got brutal. The police arrested those guys with professional prejudice. Not because they were Native American, but because they were violent, wasted, and unpredictable. And their knives could kill. Adam couldn't believe that so soon into his new adventure, the harsh realities of the world had reasserted themselves. Not that he had forgotten they existed. It was just that he had been living the utopian dream for weeks, and within twenty minutes – a few people had stopped, but no one was getting onto Route 80, just up the road – that dream turned to ugliness.

'Oh, please let me get home safe,' he prayed. He decided right then that if he didn't get picked up by someone going a fairly good distance on Route 80 before the sun went down, in about two hours, he was walking over to the Greyhound terminal a few blocks away and buying a bus ticket home. Chris telling him he had nothing to prove resonated within him. He even considered forgetting about hitching altogether, but decided to give it a shot before throwing in the towel.

Less than an hour later an older nun in a Dodge Dart pulled up beside him.

'How far are you going, young man,' she asked, sizing Adam up at a glance.

'All the way to New York.'

'I'm on my way to Chicago. So, if you want, you got yourself a ride. I could use the company.'

Chicago was more than half the distance home, almost a thousand miles, and Cheyenne to Chicago was the most difficult part of the excursion.

'That would be amazing,' Adam said.

'Why don't you go ahead and put your backpack in the back seat.'

'Someone's looking out for me,' Adam thought, opening up the back door and taking his backpack off. He wished Chris and Lynn knew this was happening. They'd be glad.

'There's just so may times I can listen to the same songs over and over. You ready? Please put on your seatbelt.'

'Oh, sure. I can't believe this. Is this really happening? Thank you so much.'

'You're welcome so much. I'm Sister Evangeline,' she said, not taking her hand off the wheel.

'I'm Adam.'

'A name of great import. And quite a distinct New York accent.'

'It's that obvious?'

'Oh, absolutely. But I love New York accents. They sound so... Edward G. Robinson. What are you doing hitchhiking in Cheyenne Wyoming?'

Adam proceeded to tell Sister Evangeline he was on his way home after having spent the summer hitching around the country. When he got to the part about Stevie leaving and Chris coming into his life that very day, and that her and her sister had begun their journey from Akron, Ohio, Sister Evangeline ears perked up.

'The man I'm going to meet is from Akron,' she said. She proceeded to tell Adam she was a professor at the Arizona Christian University since its founding in 1960. She taught classes in systems of cosmic redemption, which Adam had no idea what that meant, although her picking him up when she did and driving him all the way to Chicago felt like cosmic redemption. She also taught the separation of law and gospel, and Apostolic succession, which he also had no idea what it meant.

'Is that like apostles leaving the church?' he asked, flaunting his ignorance.

'I think that would be Apostolic secession. Apostolic succession is the continuity in doctrinal teaching from the time of the apostles 'til the present – the continuity of Christian experience and the continued proclamation of the message. But there are other interpretations, more personal, such as the apostles appointing bishops as their successors, and the bishops in turn appointing their own successors, but that's getting into more detail than I think we need to right now.'

Sister Evangeline was on her way to The University of Chicago, whose press was publishing a massive five-volume work entitled 'The Christian Tradition: A History of the Development of Doctrine', by Jaroslav Pelikan, the guy from Akron. Sister Evangeline was going to deliver, in person – because she loved road trips, hated flying, and couldn't wait to meet the esteemed Mr. Pelikan – her work on the criteria of apostolic continuity, and systems of cosmic redemption to be included in Mr. Pelican's definitive history.

'All the contributors will be presenting,' Sister Evangeline said. 'Well, not all. Those who are part of this volume. It should be very enlightening. Have you had any religious education?'

'Hebrew school. Until my bar mitzvah.'

'Was it helpful? Did it teach you anything?'

'Sister, to be honest, at that point in my life, I really didn't take it seriously. More than anything, I was bummed out that I had to miss The Beatles cartoon every Saturday morning. I don't think I got much out of it, although I still remember a little of my hof-torah.'

'I'd love to hear it.'

'Okay. Ready? Call amoo-day hechatzair tzaviv, mechooshakeem kesev, vavyayhem cosef, vadnayhem nechoshet.'

'Very good,' she said, smiling. Sister Evangeline looked a little like an older version of Adam's seventh grade English teacher, Mrs. Hunter, who was austere, in a western European way – straight nose, thin lips, a slight wave in her short salt-and-pepper-hair brushed straight back. She looked the way you would expect a late-fifties, early sixties teaching nun to look – unadorned, very real, alert. She seemed genuinely pleased with what she heard. 'I don't know what it means, but it must have meant a lot to you if you still remember it like that.'

Adam told Sister Evangeline about the piece he had seen on Mother Theresa, trying to exploit his limited understanding of, and exposure to her way of life. With hours of open road ahead of them, and the comfort of knowing he had successfully bridged the gap between the fantasy summer that had just come to an end a few hours before, and getting home on his own, he gave voice to whatever he was thinking and feeling, so happy was he to be living in the moment.

'And what did you think of Mother Theresa and the work she's doing?'

'Well, to be honest, it felt like Mother Theresa is the only other person I could call mother, for, like, you know, real – like she really is that. I don't know how anyone could do what she does. But there it is. I wish I could get a hug from her.'

'Maybe someday you will. If you feel that way, you may want to think about volunteering at some point. It does the spirit good knowing you're helping make the world a better place - giving back. That's why we're here. Are you hungry?' It was dinnertime.

On the floor in the back of Sister Evangeline's Dart was a cooler filled with food and beverages – six cans of Tab - she had packed for her road trip. Rather than stopping to eat along the way, Sister Evangeline wanted to drive to Lexington, Nebraska, about four and a half hours from Cheyenne, where she planned on spending the night, before heading straight through to Chicago the following morning. 'There's a few movies out I'd like to see. Would you like to see a movie?' she asked.

'I would love to.' Adam hadn't been to the movies all summer. 'I grew up on Lexington Ave. in my hometown.'

'Oh… Lexington and Lexington… And Akron. I think the Lord's watching over us.'

'Sister, there is just one thing. I don't really have enough money for a hotel or motel room. Can I maybe like crash in your car... or if it's possible to find a local campground?'

'My car will be fine,' she said, without qualification.

'Wow,' Adam thought. 'Perfect.'

'But if you don't have enough money, how are you going to get home? How are you going to eat?'

'No, I have enough to get home. I just wanna make sure that I have enough to get a bus ticket in case I need one.'

'Oh, I see. All right. Why don't you grab two sandwiches from the cooler. I hope you like meatloaf? And if you wouldn't mind handing me a Tab. Take one for yourself.' Adam's mother drank Tab.

The meatloaf was delicious, on white bread with ketchup, a perfect road dinner, as evening turned to night on Interstate 80. 'It's as good as my mother's,' Adam said.

'How does she feel about you hitchhiking?'

'She was definitely nervous. But I called her at least once a week to let her know I was okay.'

Sister Evangeline nodded, her eyes on the road. The only time she took one of her two hands off the wheel was to pick up the meatloaf sandwich she had resting on her lap, on top of the wax paper she had wrapped the sandwich in. She was a study in efficient movement. Even reaching for her can of soda in the cup-holder was done with the least amount of distraction.

After checking into the Minuteman Motel, a clean, respectable 1950's-model roadside motel, Sister Evangeline came back out to the car and told Adam the motel's proprietor told her that *Jaws* was playing at the local movie theater. He highly recommended it.

'He said that's what it was like in the Catholic school he went to.' She smiled, chuckled once. 'Very good.'

Sister Evangeline was visibly upset after the first shark attack, and shielded her eyes from the rest of the frightening parts. Overall, she loved the movie – not as much as *Young Frankenstein*, which, for Sister Evangeline, whose fifth favorite movie of all time was *The Bride of Frankenstein* – was the funniest thing she'd ever seen. Her favorite was *Wuthering Heights*. And a close second was *Gone With The Wind*. But she knew she had just had an amazing cinematic experience. The other movie patrons, a dozen or so, also loved it, based on their animated discussions afterward.

'What'd you think, Sister?' a contemporary of Sister Evangeline's in jeans and a flannel shirt asked. He had just lit a non-filter cigarette and coughed a few times into his hand after each exhale.

'That shark looked real to me. I'm glad I live in Phoenix and not Los Angeles.'

'What about Long Island,' Adam thought. 'That guy should give his lungs a break. I bet he's gonna...'

As soon as Adam thought it, as soon as the guy was turned away from Sister Evangeline, Adam heard him huck up a loogie and spit, exactly like his father, who was a heavy smoker, would have done.

'That's disgusting John,' the guy's wife said, as Adam's mother would have. The guy didn't respond. Nor would Adam's father have.

That night, as Adam laid comfortably on his back across the blue naugahide backseat of Sister Evangeline's Dart, the widows rolled down, a perfect nighttime summer breeze circulating, Nebraskan fresh air, the only sounds those of night insects and the occasional car traveling on Plum Creek Parkway, Adam thought about Tom and Lynn - how real their love was, their preternatural bond. Like they were meant to be. And would be. He didn't feel he was belittling what Chris and he had by recognizing the differences in the relationships. He wasn't sure he was even mature enough for that kind of relationship. Not only were Tom and Lynn older, with a lot more real-life experience, but they seemed to have older souls – Chris, too. Adam's soul was still in its adolescence. He hoped what Chris and he had would empower them. He hoped it was balanced – that she wasn't into him more than he was into her – that she had the same perspective on the future he did, that it was open and full of possibilities.

'Maybe I'll get on a bus in Chicago... I don't know,' he thought. 'I'll see. At least I'm here... It's so peaceful... Wow, Chris. How did that happen... I hope it happens again.' He pictured them driving away, and felt that longing again. But, steadily, he began to feel satisfied with the way things were going. He had just gotten laid every day for '...Oh my God. That was amazing. Chris's pink nipples and how sweet her cum tasted... feeling her start to sweat before... Wait a second... What am I doing...' He realized he was thinking about masturbating in the backseat of a nun's car, a nun who was sleeping in a room not twenty feet away, who was also a guardian angel. Then he thought about something he had seen Mother Theresa say, something about being married to Jesus. It was the only thing about her he didn't quite understand. It was too abstract, being married to a concept. But she had said it with such certainty, he just accepted it. 'I wonder where that falls on the bell-curve of love? That's a whole different bell. I wonder if Sister Evangeline feels that way, too. Maybe I'll ask her tomorrow... Oh my God, I can't believe I made it out of Cheyenne. I wish Chris was here... feel her tongue... Oh my God, again?'

The golden wheat-fields extended in endless waves through America's heartland. Absorbing the sun, each radiant stalk seemed to acknowledge their passing as they drove through towns with names like Avoca and Walnut, each town and city broadcasting their own brand of country music, Sister Evangeline's favorite.

'Sister, can I ask you something?' They still had roughly eight hours on the road before they reached Chicago.

'You can ask me anything.'

'The only thing I didn't understand about the piece I saw on Mother Theresa was when she said she was married to Jesus. She said it like she really was.'

'She is. I know it's hard for you to understand, but in our vows we pledge our souls to Christ. We think of it as a mystical marriage, and in that marriage our soul receives a sudden augmentation of charity and a deeper connection with God. I think what Mother Theresa was trying to convey was that, as a wife shares in the life of her husband, she had entered into a more intimate participation in Jesus' sufferings. A mystical union with God is the most exalted condition a soul can attain in this life. That's what Kabbalah seeks to achieve in Judaism. And Sufism in Islam. And, you've heard the term nirvana, I'm sure. To me they're all ways of becoming one with God.'

'Are you married to Jesus?'

'Very much so. It's my highest calling. If there's one thing I'd like for you to remember from our time together, it's that you should aspire to be the best you can be; realize your God-given potential. Everyone has that, and there are no shortcuts getting there. I tell my students to use Jesus as the mirror. I know that's a little out of your purview, but I think you understand. Abraham Lincoln wasn't a very religious man, but I loved what he said about it. 'When I do good works, I feel good. When I do bad I feel bad.' That about sums it up. You have a long road ahead of you, Adam. Make the most of it.'

By six o'clock that evening they had entered the Chicago city limits.

'Sister, I don't know how to thank you for your kindness,' Adam said, standing outside of her car, putting his backpack on. She had pulled up in front of the Chicago Port Authority building. After the summer he had, and then getting the ride from Sister Evangeline, it was the perfect time to close the show – end his hitchhiking experience on a high note. He didn't feel like he was short-changing his adventure. He had nothing else to prove, and he wanted to get home. It was a great weight off his shoulders when he made the decision to take a bus from Chicago. Sister Evangeline seconded that decision. Knowing his time constraint and human nature, she thought that the wisest path as well.

'You can thank me by taking care of yourself and those around you,' she said. 'It was fun traveling with you, I must say. Good luck in college. It's where you'll set the groundwork for the rest of your life. Let me know how you're doing. I look forward to hearing about it. You have everything you need?'

'I think so.'

'Why don't you take the last meatloaf sandwich from the back - save your money in case you need it.'

'Really?'

'Of course.'

'You're too much, Sister, you know that?' Adam put the sandwich in his backpack. Since it was getting toward dinnertime, he planned on eating it as soon as he got on the bus.

'Are there any more cans of Tab?' she asked.

'One more.'

'Oh, good. I'll take it.' He handed it to her. Nothing left to do but say good-bye.

'Thanks again for everything. It's like you're my guardian angel.'

'It was my pleasure, Adam. Just remember to work hard. I want to hear that you aced all of your classes. Freshman year sets the tone.'

'I will.'

'I know you will. God bless you.'

CHAPTER 10

· · · · · · · · · · · · · · · · ·

Charles, are you there?

For the second time in two days Adam felt like a stranger in a strange land; cars driving away, people passing through his life. The idea that no one was creating his destiny but him was becoming an important sense - how random it all felt, how much seizing the moment in time meant. It was easy for those moments to slip away, like he did most of his senior year of high school, getting high in the morning, not caring about what he was learning.

All those thoughts were going through Adam's mind as he stood in line to buy a ticket for the first Greyhound to New York, a meatloaf sandwich in his backpack, a little of his summer adventure starting to sink in. The abstract, the dreamy, and the tasks at hand. That was how time was unfolding – thinking about Chris and Lynn coming out of the Turquoise Lake naked and glistening... And in reality, the overly-made-up, way too much rouge Greyhound ticket-lady telling Adam the next bus to New York Port Authority leaves at five AM.

'Really?' he asked.

'I ain't lyin', Shorty,' or, that was what he thought he heard.

'I wonder if she said surely,' he thought.

Greyhound ran three New York buses a day; five, noon, and five.

'All right, eleven hours,' he thought. He was a little bummed, but not enough to forget about the bus and start hitching. He was surprised at how over the idea of hitching alone he was. The sure thing completely trumped the unknown.

Waiting is rarely pleasant, but waiting all night in a neon-lit public-transportation hub among mutants and thieves was a test of endurance. Adam couldn't allow himself to fall asleep for fear of being ripped-off or worse. So, he spent more money than he wanted to on coffee, chocolate bars, and newspapers, and established his own little fiefdom on an empty bench centrally located in the Port Authority's main concourse. Because the media and the mountains had been relatively exclusive domains, Adam had very little awareness of what had been going on in the outside world. It wasn't until he started reading one of the newspapers that he realized how out of touch with the modern world he had become, and how little it had mattered, although he was interested to learn that a second assassination attempt had been made on President Ford's life, that Pele was coming to the New York Cosmos, that Elizabeth Taylor and

Richard Burton were going to remarry after getting divorced the year before, that Mother Seton had become the first American saint – when he read that, he thought of Sister Evangeline, and how happy she probably was to be so represented, although she hadn't mentioned anything about it during their time together – that scientists had synthesized the first artificial gene, and that Larry Fine of The Three Stooges had died, all important bits of information that hadn't made it into The Gunnison.

Sometime after midnight, with the steady buzz of the overhead florescent lights the only constant sound, Adam was unavoidably beckoned to the Port Authority's public restrooms. He had hoped, in vain, to wait until an hour when the regular daily traffic began to converge, very wary of the nocturnal element who were possibly living in the lavatories, as they did in New York's Port Authority and Penn Station. But the combination of coffee, chocolate, and meatloaf proved too strong. So he gathered his belongings, found his bearings, and climbed the linoleum stairs to the even more desolate second floor, where the bathrooms were located. Breathing through his mouth to avoid the strong piss and shit-tinged odor, he walked into the men's room, like a horse with blinders, and went directly to the first available stall – standard, light grey, steel, moderately unclean – he'd seen worse, he'd seen cleaner - not too much graffiti – some. When he went to close the door, he realized the stall had no door. He went to the next stall, which was also doorless, and occupied by a seemingly unconscious, ragged alcoholic whose filthy American flag dungarees were around his ankles. He was sprawled on the toilet, leaning into the corner of the stall, like gravity had continued to pull him down after his initial squat. And there he stayed, as still as the night.

'Fuck,' Adam said under his breath, bummed-out he wasn't alone.

The last two stalls didn't have doors either. All the doors had been removed. But the pressure in Adam's stomach left him no choice but to sit down in the second-to-last stall – the last stall felt way too threatening - and pray that the comatose alcoholic remained comatose and that no one else wandered in seeking refuge or trouble.

As soon as Adam was sitting on the toilet, his pants around his ankles, he noticed the toilet paper dispenser, which he thought started in a horizontal position, had become vertical, and that there was an enlarged hole where a smaller screw-hole should have been. Someone had inscribed, in the chicken-scratch penmanship of a first-grader, 'insert penis' next to the enlarged hole. He lifted the dispenser back into the proper horizontal position, hoping it had slipped of its own accord. But a second later it slowly spun back down in an arching motion too slow and deliberate for gravity, as if a magnet were directing it from behind the divider. Then, personifying his dread, the alcoholic appeared in front of him, his flag pants still around his ankles, his gaunt white chicken-legs and dead cock just about eye level, his arms outstretched, palms skyward, pleading, wasted, 'Lemme have a li'l touch,' he drooled. 'Jus a li'l one...'

'Please get the fuck away from me.' Adam was scared, and preparing himself for whatever he had to do to get the fuck out of there safely. Luckily, the pressure in his stomach had subsided. Adrenaline had taken over.

'Come on, jus a li'l one... please... jus lemme touch it.' The guy slurred so heavily he sounded like a chanting Tibetan monk. His runny eyes were swollen and red.

'Listen, leave me alone and get the fuck outta here, all right?'

At which point the guy stepped forward, leaving Adam no other choice but to stand up, with his pants around his ankles, and cold-cock the guy in the mouth. He threw that punch with everything he had, and felt the pain of it connect. It was the first real punch he had ever thrown – the only other, a wild rabbit punch at a neighbor when he was seven. When he fought with his brother, it never involved fists; pushing, wrestling, slapping, screaming, but never pugilism. He had always felt like a pussy because he had never been battle-tested. He was afraid to fight. His method for dealing with aggression was generally to turn it around into humor, if he could, and if he couldn't, he extricated himself from the situation. After the fight with his neighbor, he knew how much he hated fighting. But this old codger left him no quarter.

The guy fell back against the wall behind him and slid down into a lifeless slump. He never saw it coming.

When everything became quiet again, which Adam prayed it would – he even gave it a few extra seconds to see if anyone would come in – he knew he was going to have to do what he had to do.

'All right. Fuck it,' he said to the bathroom spirits.

It was very weird taking a shit with an unconscious homeless alcoholic sociopath he had just punched in the face and knocked out a few feet from him.

'Is he dead?' Adam wondered. The guy hadn't moved, no discernible chest-rise, nothing.

After Adam finished doing his business, he cautiously walked over to him. For a moment he thought the guy could be playing possum, and was going to reach up and grab him, like the hand that comes out of the rubble at the end of the movie *Carrie*. No. He was out cold, but not dead. Adam could see he was breathing, by the thin saliva arches that clung to his ever-greying lifeless lips, that sucked in when he breathed in, and arched out when he breathed out. Adam was considerably relieved. Knowing he had killed someone would have altered the course of his life irrevocably, even if it was self-defense. Looking down at the guy he felt a tiny bit of empathy. Mostly he felt nothing, maybe a little relief that things hadn't gotten medieval. Also, that this guy was a sick fuck. Adam had no hesitation about looking in the guy's wallet, which had fallen out of his pocket and was lying next to his boney knee. The impact must have dislodged it. Adam wouldn't have thought to rifle through his pockets to rip him off, but his wallet was right there. He didn't know what he expected to find, money, treasure, some magic talisman. Money, mostly – after buying the bus ticket, he had twenty-two dollars left, which had to get him to New York, and then home on the Long Island Railroad – and the guy was a child molester. Fuck him.

Crumpled up in the corner of the guy's billfold were two of the oldest, dirtiest most faded greasy dollar bills Adam had ever seen. The type of bills the Treasury takes out of circulation and burns. He carefully extracted them and threw the wallet on his benefactor's chest, causing him to look up and catch an unintended glimpse of the guy's scrotum, which looked like a very old goat's scrotum.

'Ugghhh,' Adam said to himself, getting those bills out of his hand as fast as he could, like a hot potato. 'I don't want this guy's money.'

Without looking back, he quickly washed his hands and vacated the premises, finally breathing through his nose once he had cleared the bathroom's periphery. It felt good to take a deep breath, unlock the tension a little bit.

'That was insane,' he thought, sitting back down on the bench he had vacated earlier, knowing there was an unconscious sociopath in stall three upstairs. His right hand hurt a little, but his punch had felt solid. He knew he'd be all right. That punch had come out of his sub-conscious like a bullet. No hesitation. The guy's face just crumpled. Adam knew he'd gotten off lucky.

He didn't even think about getting any sleep after that. Just a few stretches resting his eyes.

As morning light thought about beginning to creep over the darkness, a voice over the concourse PA announced that the boarding of the Greyhound express to New York City Port Authority would begin in fifteen minutes.

'Finally,' Adam said under his breath. That was the longest night he had ever spent, longer than the few nights at the beginning of the summer when the police kicked Stevie and him out of where they had set up camp, leaving them no alternative but to wait on or near the highway until morning traffic started. He couldn't wait to get on the bus and into those upholstered seats, and close his eyes. Just a few semi-comfortable hours of sleep the night before in the backseat of Sister Evangeline's car, and none that night. He was running on empty.

Handing his backpack to the bus driver for storage underneath the bus, Adam had completely put the events of a few hours before, in stall three of the Chicago Port Authority second-floor men's lavatory, out of his mind. How happy he was to be boarding, finding his seat, a window seat mid-bus, the seat next to him empty, at least for the time being. Things were finally progressing as he hoped they would. He sat, looked around, at nothing in particular, took a deep breath, closed his eyes for an extended blink, opened them, looked out the window, and there... 'Oh my God...' he said out loud, causing the older man walking down the isle past him to do a nervous double-take, was Mr. Flag-pants stumbling head-first out of the building into the maze of surrounding side streets. Initially, Adam felt disgust mixed with a little aggression, but a moment later lightened up. What a pathetic, painful life the guy lead. He was a lost soul stuck in a revolving door. And Adam was on his way home to begin his college career. 'I can't believe I saw that guy's gross dick,' he thought. 'Ugghh. Living in a public toilet, I can't even imagine... I can't believe Larry from The Three Stooges died... I wonder if Moe or Curley are still alive... or Shemp... I hope so.'

The person who sat next to Adam – it ended up being a crowded bus - was a late sixties, early seventies African American man who was traveling with his daughter and granddaughter, who ended up sitting a few rows behind. Even though it was summer, the guy was wearing long, nicely pressed slacks, and a plaid windbreaker, out of the pocket of which he surreptitiously took a pint bottle of wine. Adam got a cool vibe from him. He wasn't some crazy wino, or a derelict like Mr. Flag-pants.

'Can't let my daughter see me wi' da hooch,' he said, leaning at an inside angle into the backs of the seats in front of him, and taking a low-slung swig. 'You want?'

'Sure,' Adam said. It was a little after five in the morning, but because of the transient nature of his life at that moment - for the last couple of hours and the next couple of hours - he felt he could suspend reason for a unique experience, sharing a partying moment with an older black guy, something he had never done, and which he thought was cool. Something about it seemed rebellious, but not too, like petting a pit bull whose owner tells you he wouldn't hurt a fly. Adam wasn't planning to bogart the bottle.

'Jus maybe be a little on the down-low,' the guy said.

Even that part of it, having to sneak it, was fun. The wine was a little syrupy, but not bad, not moonshine-bitter. After two smaller swigs Adam was ready to close his eyes and let his mind drift away. After the Port Authority bench, the bus seat felt like he was resting on a cloud.

A lot of highway miles later, the last part through rush hour on the New Jersey Turnpike, and then the Long Island Railroad home, Adam came full circle, filled with mixed emotions. He didn't take for granted, not for a moment, how mind-blowingly unbelievable the summer was, how blessed he felt to have had it. But as he got off the train at the Baldwin station with the tail-end of the rush-hour crowd, a little melancholy set in. The lament of the loss of the endless summer. He had never had one where it meant that much for it to end so soon.

Before he walked home he felt compelled to stop at the creek at the very end of his block, where, eight or nine years before, he had taken his first and last drag of a cigarette with Kenny Sackler, the neighbor who called him at Stevie's to let him know Charles had threatened to shoot him. It was the same creek his mother had told him she had thrown Charles's hand-gun in. Standing on the shore amid rusty beer cans and other discarded memorabilia, he took out his earring, and came to terms with the summer's end. Taking the earring out was symbolic – the adventure was over. He was back under the influence of his parents, who had always forbidden him from getting an earring, although he knew he could have kept it in without too much opposition. His parents would have recognized it was appropriate, and even that it looked cool. It was entropy, maybe even a little self-inflicted humility that lead him to take it out, that he shouldn't forget who he was and where he came from.

'I guess this is it,' he thought, staring into the dark, dirty water. 'I hope Chris comes to Cortland. I can't believe I met her... I can't believe I punched a guy in the face. What a pisser... I wonder if Stevie's still around... All right...'

He heard the earring hit the water's surface, and then he made his way home. Halfway there, a quarter of a mile, he regretted throwing the earring away.

'Oh well,' he thought. 'Nothing I can do about it now.'

His parents didn't know the exact day he was getting home. Because it had been a while since they'd seen each other, he wanted to surprise them.

As he approached his house, a three-bedroom, two bath, split-level in a typical Long Island suburb, the first thing he felt was how weird it was that he was there and his car wasn't, nor was his parents', which could have meant a few things. First, since it was dinnertime, his parents and younger brother were probably at the diner having dinner. The problem was Charles. Was he at home or was he back at school? It was unlikely he had gone to the diner with their parents, although that was a possibility as well. Since Adam had left his house keys home for the summer – no sense risking losing them – he knocked on the front door, and then rang the doorbell to see if Charles was home. No answer. He was locked out. But he had been locked out before, and had a relatively easy way in; climb onto the roof of the storage shed at the back of their house and slip the screen out of the window of Charles's bedroom, which was right above the back of the shed roof. Easy. The front lip of the shingled storage shed was only about seven and a half feet off the ground, and pitched upward in slant against the back of the house. Adam hadn't employed that method of breaking into his house often because his older brother never responded well to being awakened in the middle of the night. But Adam knew it was the best way into his locked house. He also decided that, in the off chance his brother was home, even though he hadn't answer the front door, waking him up like that, at a little after seven in the evening, for the first time in three or four years – that was the last time Adam had to employ the 'climbing on the shed' method – was an acceptable average. Plus, he didn't think Charles was home. For the last two years, he had gone up to Brockport a full week before school started.

So, he walked around to the back of the house, jumped up and grabbed the bottom lip of the shed roof, pulling himself up until he was able to get his right foot onto the shed's door-knob, at which point, using his hands and feet, he was easily able to climb onto the roof. Because the roof was pitched, he kept a lower center of gravity, the course salt and pepper shingles giving his hiking boots sure-footed traction. When he got to the window he decided to knock one more time to make sure his brother wasn't home. He couldn't imagine how startled Charles would be if he woke up and saw someone breaking and entering into his room. What Adam didn't know was that the prior evening Charles had seen *The Exorcist*, which had just come out, and had given him nightmares, something he had, not frequently, but enough to be noted. And there something was, knocking on his window, chanting, beckoning, 'Charles, are you there? Charles. Let me in…' in kind of a whisper. He had no idea it was Adam. He thought Adam was still out west. Out of sight, out of mind.

The next thing Adam knew, the shade ripped off the window from the inside, and there was his brother in his underwear with a terrified look on his face, his shotgun held at a threatening angle. It was a moment frozen in time. Charles about to shoot him. Charles standing in front of him with a loaded shotgun pointed at him, a crazy look on his face, like he was defending against an alien invasion. Thank God, a split second before he pulled the trigger he realized it was Adam. Adam thought he was gonna die, his body position and chemistry instantly adapting to the possibility that it was about to get hit with a full cartridge of buckshot.

Then, literally in real time, he felt his brother's transition from fear to recognition, and knew he had just gotten in under the wire.

'What the fuck are you doing!' Charles screamed through his mask of fear and loathing. 'I thought someone was... I almost killed you!'

Adam thought about pointing out that he had knocked on the front door, and rang the doorbell, and that he had already threatened to kill him earlier that year, and that it was nice too see him too, and that he had let him use his car all summer and he had gotten it stolen, and that it was dinnertime not bedtime, but decided a heated dialogue was useless. Also, because of how fucked up what had just happened was, he had almost lost his footing and fallen off the roof, which certainly would have broken a few bones or worse. He was shaking, and doing everything he could to keep his feet planted under him.

'Do me a favor,' he said, 'just unlock the front door,' which he did, without any further conversation. Charles went back into his room, and Adam put his backpack down and walked over to the Rainbow Diner, less than a half mile away, where his parents and younger brother were surprised, and very happy to see him.

'Look at this,' his father said loudly, lovingly, seeing him walk over to their table. He gave Adam a big hug and kiss and so did his mother. It was nice to feel their embrace, like he was a little boy. He gave his younger brother a kiss on the cheek, the first time they had shown that type of affection for one another. Before that they were just brothers being brothers, too young to appreciate each other. It seemed as if Barry had grown several inches since the beginning of the summer. He was leaving boyhood behind. With a smile that brought Adam joy.

After he gave them a brief rundown of how he got home, his mother asked me if he had seen his older brother when he stopped home.

'For a second,' Adam said. He didn't go into what had transpired. That wasn't the type of homecoming he wanted. They knew it wasn't a warm reception, and didn't pursue it, other than to tell him his bus up to Brockport was leaving at eight the following morning from New York Port Authority. The day after that, they were going to drive Adam up to Cortland for the start of his college career. He thought about telling his mother she should probably confiscate Charles's shotgun as well, but that would have taken the conversation in a direction Adam had no desire for it to go. So he kept his mouth shut and enjoyed being back with his family. At some point, sooner rather than later, he would let his mother know what happened, for everyone's benefit. He didn't think that was a betrayal of trust. Trust wasn't something they shared. That was just getting a gun out of the hands of someone who shouldn't have guns.

CHAPTER 11

. . . .

Let's see what you've learned

'You will look back on your years at college,' faculty members and school administrators predicted during freshman orientation on the lawn in front of the State College of New York at Cortland library, 'as the best years of your life.'

'That's a pretty bold prediction. We haven't even been here ten minutes,' Adam said as a matter of introduction to the eighteen year old co-ed he sat next to. He hadn't planned on playing the field, less than an hour after saying good-bye to his parents. He was looking for a place to sit, saw this girl; straight black hair, denim shirt and jeans, Frye boots, sitting alone... He felt the pull, a new environment. Be who he wanted to be. Not that he was reinventing himself. It was just that this girl reminded him of his summer, and new possibilities, so he went for it.

'At least we have four years before we go into decline,' she said.

She got it. Adam immediately felt more at ease.

'My size,' he thought. 'She could be Native American... maybe Italian. Really cute.'

'Only four?' he said. 'Does that mean by the time I'm thirty, I'll be living in a trailer in like Bayonne, New Jersey?'

'Hey, I'm from Bayonne.' She was more surprised than offended.

'I think I feel my decline starting already,' Adam said, back-peddling. 'I didn't mean...'

'Don't worry. Everybody makes fun of New Jersey. Actually, there are parts of Bayonne that are beautiful. Where are you from?'

Adam's face flushed and his mouth became a little dry. Within one minute he had insulted that woman's hometown.

'Baldwin, Long Island,' he said, hoping no damage had been done.

'Baldwin. I went to camp with a girl from Baldwin. Do you know Franny Berringer?'

Finding common ground was the quickest way of getting past the awkward first moments of a random encounter, even if the one person from Baldwin that woman knew happened to be the one girl, Adam's backyard neighbor, he inappropriately touched thirteen years before. Franny had been one of his earliest friends. Her mother was one of Adam's mother's best friends. One day, when he was six years old and Franny was five, he asked her if she wanted to play husband and wife. They were in her bedroom, where they had played many times before.

She agreed to the premise, reluctantly honoring his suggestion that she lift up her dress. Adam knew what he was doing was wrong, but he did it anyway. He couldn't help himself.

Unfortunately, Franny's mother interrupted their game with his fingers in the proverbial cookie-jar, the plate of yodels and devil-dogs she had brought crashing to the carpet. Adam instantly realized the full extent of his transgression.

'What are you doing?!' Mrs. Berringer screamed. 'Get out of here! Now! I'm calling your mother!'

Adam knew he had better flee and think about it later. Scrambling like a cockroach avoiding a loaded shoe, he headed down the stairs, out the back door and straight over the fence. Then he heard the phone ring, followed shortly thereafter by his mother slamming the phone back down.

After she finished beating the shit out of him for molesting her best friend's daughter, Adam's mother banished him to the corner of his bedroom to think about what he had done. What he came up with was that he had better stay away from Franny's holiday package.

'She's lives around the corner from me,' he said, a second dose of guilt more deprecating than the first. He started to feel like a gambler who found out seconds after placing his bet that the jockey of the horse he had wagered his life savings on had been paid to come in last.

'You're kidding!' she said. He was waiting for 'So you're the guy who fucked up her whole life.' 'I went to camp with her for like seven years. If you see her tell her Molly Jupiter says hello.'

'I definitely will. I'm Adam, by the way.' He tried to regroup after so close a call with karma.

'So far, you're the only person I've met.'

'Unfortunately, my roommate was unpacking when my parents dropped me off. The guy put up a poster of Neil Diamond over his bed. At least he's probably mellow. I really don't want to have to deal with a psycho everyday. What dorm are you in?'

'Alger Hall.'

'I'm right up the hill from you in Bishop... I don't know if you know this or not, but there's a dance tonight at the Student Union. Do you wanna... Or... Are you, are you going with anybody?'

That was the first time Adam asked a strange woman on a date. All prior dates were with women he had known from school. And Chris, that was more like divine intervention, or perfect timing. He definitely felt guilty hitting on Molly. Chris and he had said good-bye only a week before, and there he was betraying her love already.

'No, I'd love to,' Molly said.

'Really? Just so you know, I usually don't go up to strangers and ask them to hang out. But if all we have is four years before it all goes downhill, I might was well go for it. Right?'

'You're weird, you know that? But that's cool.'

At the party, Molly and Adam danced to David Bowie and drank cup after red plastic 16 oz. cup of Budweiser, their intimate conversation about their dreams as continuous as the flow of time. Soon they were discussing the virtues of life with alcohol-enhanced Socratic fervor.

'In a perfect world we'd all benefit from everyone else,' Adam emphasized, agreeing with Molly's beliefs about pure ideological communism.

'Exactly,' Molly continued. 'No one would need to be self-sufficient. The farmers would provide the food, the builders would provide shelter. There would be tailors and artists...'

'Yeah but I'm wondering if that ever works. There always seems to be like some politician making a deal with someone.'

'What about Gandhi?'   "Yeah, I know. But while he was liberating India, India was being ripped apart by civil war.'

How glad he was to have been forced to learn certain aspects about world history in his senior year of high school. Until then, he thought they were irrelevant to his life.

'You're such a skeptic,' Molly said, looking him in the eye, her smile momentarily faded.

'I'm not being skeptical. I'm just being a realist,' he said, holding his ground as long as he didn't tip the balance toward dissent. 'If it sounds so good, why aren't people living like that?'

"cause we just haven't evolved to that point yet.'

'Did you see the last *Planet of the Apes* movie?'

'Oh my God!, where they could read each other's minds? I can't believe you just thought of that. I always think about that.'

'That's how I wanna evolve.'

'Me too!'

'All right, let's see if you can do it. I'm gonna try to send you my thoughts telepathically... OK, what did I just think?'

The first nanosecond had a topless Molly offering herself to him. He quickly wiped that image clean because desire and disrespect could decide to become vindictive.

'I don't know - that you can't believe you're at college? No. I know. That you become best friends with those guys over there.'

Near the DJ's table, a group of young, drunk jocks wearing Smithtown Varsity Wrestling tee shirts were playing 'flinch', a game whose object is to smack your opponent's hands before he has a chance to pull them out of range.

'I could never be that cool,' Adam said. 'Actually, I was wondering if you wanna go outside and check out the campus.'

'Yeah. Definitely. Let me tell my roommate. I'll be right back.'

He watched Molly cross the dance floor, gently swaying to the rhythm of the music, a living brushstroke in tight jeans.

In every corner of the room, men were trying to impress the women they were talking to, mostly with tales about themselves. The five drunk jocks from Smithtown had overthrown the DJ and were screaming *Don't Let Me Down* by The Beatles in disjointed harmony while shotgunning whole cans of Genesee Cream Ale. The dance floor pulsated with the abandon inspired by knowing you're free to create your own future. In that tentative balance of sight, sound, spirit, and beer, Adam felt the pull of a desire more than sexual from a girl he had met that afternoon.

The night air was cool and crisp and foretold the end of summer. Crops had been harvested, oceans had grown darker, and schools all around the country had come alive with the controlled insanity of anticipation and promise.

'That's my room up there,' Adam said, pointing to the top floor of his dorm. 'There's a ledge on the back window you can sit on that looks out into the woods. You can even see the mountains.'

'All I see out of my window is a parking lot, and a little bit of the quad,' Molly sighed. 'Wow, there's the Big Dipper. I used to be able to see that from my bedroom. And, you know what's amazing? I used to be able to see Venus...'

'What was that?'

From close by they heard an ominous, high-pitched squeal.

'I don't know,' Molly said, pointing to the slow flying creature darting in and out of the light illuminating the top of the Humanities Building. 'It looks like a weird bird.'

'I think it's a bat.'

'A bat!? Oh my God!' She looked like she was ready to bolt.

'Don't worry,' he said. 'Most bats are harmless. Mother bats even tenderly care for their young.' Another high school fact he was glad he had been force-fed.

'Are you sure?'

'I think so. He just looks like he's trying to find a way into the building. Maybe he goes here. Bat studies or something.'

'Did you ever see the movie Dracula? Maybe that's where his coffin is.'

'You think that's him?'

'It could be. Couldn't Dracula turn into a bat?'

'So, we gotta find him a drive a stake through his heart. You up for it?'

'Maybe another time. I don't wanna risk a confrontation with a vampire on our first day.'

'All right. I might as well tell you. I'm not really from Baldwin...' shifting into a thick eastern-European accent. 'I'm from the Carpathian Mountains, and I've come to suck your blood.' As soon as he said it, he regretted it. He shouldn't have been talking about sucking Molly's anything. He was getting ahead of himself. It was time to walk her to her dorm. In another couple of seconds he would be saying things better suited for a more established relationship. 'Anyway,' he continued, in his normal Long Island accent, 'I'm glad I gave that bat ten bucks. If I only gave him five, he might've just done a fly-by.'

'What a day. Our first day,' he said outside Molly's dorm. He had contemplated going in for a good-night kiss, but decided to play it a little cooler. He was attracted to her and planned on pursuing her, and didn't want to blow it by seeming over-anxious or aggressive.

'I had a great time,' Molly said. 'Thanks for inviting me. I am so tired. I can't believe tomorrow's registration. Will I see you there?'

'I hope so.'

'Okay, good night.'

She hadn't turned to go inside yet. Adam wondered if she was waiting for him to lean in for the kiss. But if read it wrong, he was doomed.

'Good night.' They were still both standing there. 'How 'bout a hug.' Adam knew that was a safe bet - the perfect way to bring that milestone day to a close. A warm, upstate New York night. Plenty of stars. The freedom of knowing they were on their own, their bodies pressing close together. It was a moment filled with new beginnings.

'Sorry Chris,' Adam thought, trying to keep how unfaithful he felt at bay.

'That guy was cute,' Molly's roommate, Sharon Rubenstein, said after Molly was back in her room. Sharon was short and heavy, with a blond perm. She reminded Adam of some of the girls he had gone to Hebrew school with. She was also studying to be a teacher.

'He's a little young,' Molly said. 'He's really funny though. Don't you think he looks like the drummer from the Monkeys.'

'I was thinking more like Frankie Avalon. So, are you gonna see him again?' Sharon asked.

'Maybe. I don't know. Today's our first day. I got a good vibe from him though, you know?'

Molly had only had one serious relationship in her life, which lasted from her junior year of high school right up until a few days before leaving for college, when she told her soon-to-be ex, who planned on attending a community college in a town close to Bayonne, that she didn't think a long distance relationship would work. When asked how she could know that, she told him she just did. Besides, she added, she needed her freedom. How could she know if what they had was real if she didn't have anything to compare it to? He told her he was pretty sure their love was real. She again asked how they could know for sure.

Seeing Molly at registration the following morning, in a crowd, talking to others, being herself, being beautiful, Adam realized how little he knew her and how many other guys were going to try to get to know her as well. Even though they had spent the prior evening together, it wasn't officially a date. It was more like two people who didn't know anybody finding each other so they wouldn't be alone on an important day. And even though it was fun hanging out, Molly's point about breaking up with her boyfriend because she wanted her freedom was not lost on Adam. Still, he was looking at her and couldn't help wanting her.

'Adam!' she yelled when she saw him, excitedly motioning him over. 'I've been saving the last spot in Introduction to Human Sexuality for you. Here, sign here.' They had spoken the prior evening of some of the course electives they were considering. Molly thought she might want pre-med or psychology. Adam felt redeemed.

Walking out of registration, he asked Molly if she wanted to have dinner with him that evening. He knew he might be pressing his luck, but with all the competition he saw that afternoon, he felt he had better give it a shot. She told him she had already made plans with a few people from her corridor, but invited him to come along.

'If you think it's all right,' he said. He felt like the younger sibling the older siblings are forced, by their parents, to drag along.

He was glad he went. Although Molly's dorm was co-ed, the corridors were not. He entertained the group of freshman women with stories about his high school drug experiences, embellishing the absurdity of those experiences for comic effect. He felt a little guilty telling them that the police officer made him eat the pot, instead of Stevie, but if that little white lie helped his cause with Molly, he wasn't going to sweat it.

'Play it cool,' he thought, walking the girls back to their dorm. Getting too familiar with Molly in front of her friends would have been inappropriate and probably the end of his chances with her. So he bid the entire group good night, resting his gaze on Molly, who smiled and blew him a quick, heart-felt kiss. She appreciated his restraint. He walked away as happy as if he had just gotten laid.

Thoughts of Molly dominated his mind the following day. Because of their schedules, they hadn't run into each other.

'Maybe I'll stop by there tonight,' he thought. 'Nah, she'll think I'm stalking her.'

'How come you didn't come to dinner with us last night?' Molly asked in Introduction to Human Sexuality class the following day.

'Because my therapist said I have to stop being one of the girls,' he said, imitating a drag-queen. He was relieved to know Molly had thought about him. 'By the way, there's a band...'

'Please refrain from speaking unless you'd like to share it with the rest of the class,' the teacher admonished.

'Well...'

He was going to do it; throw caution to the wind. They were learning about human sexuality. Might as well apply it practically.

'I was just mentioning to this young woman,' Adam continued, calling the teacher's bluff, intending to impress Molly with his bold individualism, 'that there's this band from my hometown playing at the gym tonight...'

'The Good Rats. Yeah,' someone yelled. Half the school was from Long Island, and half of them had probably heard of The Good Rats, and would be at the concert.

'And I was gonna ask her if she wanted to go with me.'

'Well, now that you've put this poor, unsuspecting girl on the spot,' the teacher said, 'I'm sure we'd all love to know her answer.'

'I'd love to,' Molly said, smiling. The class erupted in hoots and applause.

'A little decorum, people,' the teacher insisted. 'Please open your textbooks to page three; under the heading 'Survival of the Species'.'

The Good Rats must have turned Molly on because her good-night kiss with Adam outside her dorm-room door was filled with passion. He was a little self-conscious of the erection he had no control over. But Molly didn't seem to mind. She was pushing up against it, almost like a vertical dry-hump.

'I hope she asks me in,' he thought.

Not that night.

'Please be patient,' she said a few evenings later, after he slipped his hand down to her belt intending to unbuckle it. They were alone in her room after dinner, making out on her bed. 'I want you to be able to make love to my mind, not just my body.'

If their relationship was to be real, she said, they needed to become friends first. She wanted to be able to look into his eyes while they made love and feel wild and free. He said nothing, nor was he disappointed. He would wait until the return of the Messiah for the possibility of wild and free sex with her. She had the largest, most perfect breasts of any woman he had known. It was very hard to not want to dive into them. More importantly, she had a beautiful mind and a good sense of humor.

Feeling that way, how could he have answered Chris's letters honestly? How could he tell her he met a girl he wanted more than any girl he had ever met? Molly represented a next step, a better reflection of himself.

Chris had written a four-page letter from the Grand Canyon describing how moved she was by the canyon's beauty, and how she wished he was there. She told him Lynn took an incredible photograph of a lone buffalo walking through the mist of the plume of Old Faithful.

'We (I) can't wait to visit you,' she wrote. 'You can show us autumn in New York, just like the song.'

They had arranged a system for him to correspond with her – send his letters to her mother in Akron, and she would figure out how to get them to her. He didn't answer her letter. He didn't know what to say, so he didn't say anything. He took the immature way out. A better man would have let her know what a good friend she had been, and that he hoped she found happiness. A more evolved, mature man would have been honest, and written that he hoped they could, somehow, remain a part of each other's lives. He knew it and still he didn't do it. He just wrote her off like she was someone he needed to avoid.

Her next letter, a few weeks later, from Carlsbad Caverns in New Mexico, was a postcard. Instead of describing the spectacular wonder of the caverns, and their life on the road, she wrote that she missed him, and asked if the reason he hadn't answered her last letter was because he had met someone.

'It's gotta be,' she wrote. 'I'm sad. But if you love someone, set them free.' She also asked if they should change their itinerary.

'Yes,' he thought, intending to let that letter go unanswered also. As his love and desire for Molly grew, thoughts of Chris became more nostalgic, like a first apartment when you move into a house. It wasn't a reflection on Chris. She had her place in his heart. Molly pervaded the essence of his being.

There were no more letters or postcards from Chris.

Autumn leaves began to change color. The entire Cortland landscape looked like it was consumed in flames, so vivid were the yellows, oranges, reds, and violets. Sometimes that impressionistic scene filled your whole field of vision, like Ansel Adams captured in a few of his masterpieces. Night fell earlier, and you needed a sweater. On weekends Molly and Adam hiked through the painted woods and picked apples by the bushel at nearby orchards. They saw Billy Joel and Bruce Springsteen in concert at the school gymnasium. One weekend they went climbing in the Shawangunks, world-class vertical cliffs two and a half hour's drive from Cortland. Another of Molly's camp friends, Joy, who was also a freshman at Cortland, and who also knew Frannie Berringer, and her boyfriend, Doug, were going climbing and asked Molly and Adam if they wanted to go. They had hung out as couples a number of times. Joy lived right down the corridor from Molly. Doug and Joy were cool. They got high, and were up for an adventure. The thought of getting back out into nature struck a deep chord with Adam; hiking, climbing, that part of himself and the planet he had explored so extensively just a few months before; this time with Molly... a beautiful transition from season to season.

'Any of you ever rock-climbed before?' asked the guide the four of them hired in town. Because Doug had climbed the Shawangunks before - he wasn't an avid climber but loved the rush - he knew it wasn't simply hiking up steep inclines. Rock climbing at that level required the proper equipment; harness, helmet, rope, shoes, pitons, crampons, a lead guide, and a set of balls Adam wondered if he had, once he followed the guide about ten feet off the ground and found himself, again, hugging the side of a mountain, this time without anything underfoot. He felt like a fly on a wall. Even though he was roped in, and would fall only as far as the length of the rope above their anchor below, about five feet, and end up dangling until he got his hold back, the feeling of being in that nightmare scenario of falling off a mountain into the unknown was almost overwhelming. It went from his stomach, all the way around to his bowels.

'I'm shaking,' Adam admitted, to the guide. He was having a hard time stopping it, and that stopped everything else. 'Is there anything you can...'

'I gotch'a buddy,' Tim, their guide said. 'This is easy. Here's what I want you to do. Can you free up your right hand? Stay steady and lean in. Good. That's it. Now slowly start pushing your palm against the rock. Nice and slow. That's it.'

Adam immediately felt the shaking start to lighten. That settled him, knowing there was help on the way.

'Okay. Now do that with your left hand. Nice and steady.'

His upper body was more or less under control.

'Okay. Now right toe. You got it.'

He did. He was ready to go on. During that interval Molly was almost level with him.

'How're you doing?' he called over to her. She was following the other guide who had joined their little expedition, and who had established a line up the cliff-face about twenty feet to their left. The guides were a husband and wife team who charged the same as a single guide. They were clearly soul-mates. It made you feel safe in their care.

'I'm not sure,' Molly said. 'So far, so good.'

'Just follow my line,' her guide said. 'Look for my chalk marks. You're doing great.'

'I'm definitely not,' Joy, who was only two hand-holds off the ground, said. 'Why'd I let you talk me into this?'

'You said you wanted to do cool stuff,' Doug answered. He was following directly behind Tim, about ten feet above Adam, and was clearly the best climber of the four of them.

'You think this is cool? I feel like a monkey.'

'Okay, who's gonna say it?' Adam said.

'Say what?' Molly asked.

'And you look like one too,' Doug yelled. He was beginning to get some real elevation; two, three stories above terra firma.

'Very funny. How do I get down?'

'Come on. You're doing great,' her guide said. 'Just follow my...'

'Cathy, the only place I'm following you is to the bar after we're done. Seriously, is all I have to do just climb down and unhook myself?'

'Are you sure?' Doug yelled.

'Totally.'

'Okay, then just hang out at the bottom and catch us if any of us falls.' At which point Adam happened to look over his shoulder, and, for a split-second, saw one of the best reasons people climb the Shawangunks, the endless view of the Catskill Mountain region and Hudson Vall...

'Oh fuck...'

Adam felt himself falling, an instantaneous paradigm shift into confusion and horror... during which he heard Molly scream, and then Joy scream right after her. 'Oh no,' he thought, as he tumbled. But then he stopped. The crampon held. He had fallen about five feet, and was dangling at the end of his rope... from which position he happened to catch the sight of Molly dangling at the end of her rope. They had both fallen at the same time.

'Are you all right?' he called over.

'I think so.'

'Holy shit.'

'Holy shit is right.'

'Okay, try to steady yourselves against the wall,' Tim instructed. 'Try to get vertical. That's it.'

'Molly, I see a hand-hold about a foot to your right. Do you see it?' Cathy directed.

'Hold on,' Molly said.

They were both in the process of righting themselves, and happened to look over to each other. They started laughing hysterically. The shared experience of the nightmare fall, and knowing they lived to tell the tale allowed them to see the humor in that kind of fear. It was laughter because they were happy to be alive. Adam was laughing so hard that he couldn't hold onto his hand-hold, and ended up letting go again, just dangling at the end of his rope, laughing, as was Molly.

Finally regaining their composure, they righted themselves once again, determined to conquer the wall. Now that they knew what falling meant, they weren't as afraid to risk going higher. The potential was always there that something wouldn't hold, but there was no question Tim and Cathy knew how to mitigate trouble.

When they got to the top - over an hour to climb a distance less than half a football field - they were able to look out over the Hudson Valley as far as the eye could see. It was a vision out of any high-end travelogue; endless sweeping views, enormous, majestic, Fall foliage colors still radiating their impressionistic beauty, a perfect blue sky that went from almost white at the horizon, to a deep, velvety blue closer to heaven.

'Congratulations,' Cathy said to Molly.

'That was by far the hardest thing I've ever done,' Molly said.

'I gotta tell ya. You looked like a natural. You should keep at it.'

'Yeah, I don't know. I think I may have fulfilled my quota for rock climbing.'

'Me too,' Adam said. As beautiful as the view was, what he had to do to see it was so strenuous and scary, he didn't think it was something he would want to do again. Hiking was one thing. Scaling walls was a whole 'nother activity.

'You'll see,' Doug said. 'You'll never look at a wall the same way again.'

'You got that right. No reason to limit yourself,' Tim said. Tim had a 'semper fi' tattoo on his right calf.

'No. I know. That was just insane,' Adam said.

'Hey, what do you mean 'limit myself'? I did it, didn't I?' Molly insisted.

'Yeah, honey,' Cathy said. 'Give the girl some credit.'

'You're absolutely right,' Tim said. Then he turned to the vast expanse of New York and the blue sky and announced, in a very loud voice, 'Let it be known that, on this day, in the year of our lord nineteen seventy-five, Molly... What's your last name?'

'Jupiter.'

'Molly Jupiter conquered the Shawangunks.'

From below them they heard Joy whoop.

That night still no full-on sex. But Molly, feeling her oats, did a strip-tease to her panties, while Adam sat on her desk-chair. When she was almost naked, she sashayed over to him, sat on his lap facing him and shoved her perfect beautiful tits in his mouth, him ecstatic, her dry-humping in fluid waves. In the dark stoned light of making love, she looked to Adam a little like Cher, but with her own unique beauty; smaller features, yet voluptuous, soft, smooth, fuckin' hot... her leaning forward, eyes closed, riding it, pumping herself and him into a beautiful orgasm. Adam knew how good it was because of how deeply they kissed after. They were definitely progressing. He knew it was only a matter of time. Plus, he came while he was sucking his girlfriend's tits. It was hard to argue with a day like they had.

The rhythm of college life pulsed through their veins. Adam made Molly bracelets and rings in his jewelry and metal-smithing class; beautiful interwoven bands of silver, and a silver ring with a small lion's head he molded in waxed sand. They had dinner together almost every night, usually in her dorm, where he and, often, Doug, would entertain the rest of the girls on their corridor. It became the routine, part of their freshman college experience. Afterward Joy and Molly and Adam and Doug walked to the library where they studied together, Molly and Adam often taking breaks to make out in a secluded corner behind the Humanities section.

Classes were, for the most part, interesting. Molly was taking Intro to Biology I, American Lit, Sociology 101, Psychology 101, and Human Sexuality. And Adam was taking Introduction to Eastern Philosophy, Jewelry and Metal-smithing, Child Psychology, Yoga 101, and Human Sexuality. The first couple of weeks of school, Adam had a little bit of trouble adjusting to the amount of responsibility he had; to do well, the abundance of school-work, tests a few times a week. College was the real world where, if he fucked up, it would affect the rest of his life. He knew it was simply a matter of buckling down, not letting the work get ahead of him. So, as he had seen so many other students do, he went to the library every night and studied two, sometimes more hours learning what he needed to know. It made him feel like he was using his time wisely, especially with Molly often studying next to him.

One particular night – a cool, late-October upstate New York, 'smell the trees and the Appalachian breeze' kind of night, studying for their Human Sexuality pre-mid-term, they got so turned on reading about 'Propagation; instinct and desire', they went to their spot and started making out, and, without a conscious thought, almost on its own, Adam's right hand floated over to Molly's crotch, slowly at first, apply a little pressure… Could go one of two ways; she takes his hand away, or she pushes in. She pushed in, against his increasing pressure. It got very hot very fast.

'Let's go to my room,' she said.

It was like awakening from a dream for Adam, so absorbed was he in the moment, the anticipation, going to Molly's room, lighting candles, getting her naked, giving her a beautiful massage – a little baby oil, her lying face down on her bed, head at the edge, starting at the shoulders, using the leverage, down her back, to the top of her ass, a little over. Feel every inch of her. Massage it. The top of her thighs, like satin, down to her toes, in between her toes, get in there, her fingers, the muscle at the base of her thumbs, back to her shoulders and neck.

'Okay, why don't you turn over,' he instructed.

At that point everything was about getting her so turned on that she'd be yearning for him to crawl between her legs and go down on her… massaging her shoulders, her chest, lightly rubbing her hardened nipples… going around to the other side of the bed, rubbing her feet, her thighs, getting closer, crawling up, getting down in cat position, leaning in, licking her jet-black muff, feel her immediately respond, like a shiver that ran through her entire body, her pussy opening up, getting wetter, his tongue seeking out the right spots, the right pressure, the only sound that of her breathing, which was getting a little quicker, a moan or a sigh every now and again.

Adam lifted up his head and asked, 'Is this okay?' He didn't want to overstep his boundaries.

'Yes.'

Adam was back down on her quicker than gravity.

After Molly climaxed, Adam entered her, riding her slowly at first, then building up speed until he was ready to come, pulling out at the last second, a little quicker than he would have chosen had he been given the choice, but not so soon as to be concerned about his performance. The massage into the sex felt pretty complete. And it still had a little bit more to go.

'Where'd you learn to do that,' Molly asked, when they were cuddling side by side.

'Some things you just know,' he lied. He had learned about a woman's desire for oral sex from Chris, something he was eternally grateful to her for. 'We're still not done with your massage,' he continued. 'Do me a favor, lay on your back and put the top of your head right at the edge of the bed.'

'You don't have to.'

'I want to. You're gonna love this.'

'Wait. Lemme get my robe on. I don't know when my roommate's coming back. You should get dressed too.'

Adam appreciated the quick transition. They made love and were moving onto the next thing, which was still a part of the other thing.

Dressed, Adam massaged the pressure points on Molly's face, starting with her cheeks, under her cheek bones, press in with his fingertips, then around her nose, press in against her nostrils all the way around, her chin, moving up to around her ears, around the halo of her scalp.

'That feels amazing,' Molly said. 'And talk about perfect timing.' Just as Adam was applying pressure above Molly's brow, one of the last spots to be massaged, they heard the door-knob turn.

'Hey,' Stacy said. 'You're back early. Oh...' Molly in her robe had given it away. 'Naughty, naughty.'

'All right, I'm gonna head back,' Adam said. 'Good night.'

He walked over to Molly and gave her a kiss on the lips. She held his head there for a deep breath through the nose in and a deep breath through the nose out. Adam floated back to his dorm, *I Am The Walrus* playing in his head.

Adam went down on Molly every night, timing his penetration for maximum pleasure, trying new positions, quietly if Sharon was sleeping or pretending to be asleep, wild and free if she was out. Established very quickly was the understanding that Molly and Adam would be having sex in her room as often as they could, and that Sharon was welcome to try to sleep through it, or whatever she needed to do, which she did. When she was there the nights were quieter, but no less sexual. When she was out, things usually started with an erotic massage, which not only didn't get old, but got hotter as they became more familiar. All he had to do was offer her a massage, and it was go time. After, he'd walk back to his dorm whistling a heavy tune; *Close to the Edge*, by Yes. *Fracture*, by King

Crimson, *Quadrophenia*. Not since making love to Chris at the turquoise lake had he felt so confident and alive. The copy of the Kama Sutra Molly bought him showed she thought of him when they weren't together.

'So, my friend and his girlfriend are coming to visit me this weekend, from Oneonta,' Doug said at the library two weeks before finals, 'and he told me he's bringing 'shrooms. Ya interested?'

Other than beer, there wasn't much partying going on within Adam's small circle of friends. A shared joint on an occasional Friday or Saturday night, the one or two times Doug had a little cocaine. Generally, drugs hadn't taken hold of the student population at Cortland, as it had at some other party schools in the SUNY system.

'Are they like a mellow head, or is it really heavy?' Adam asked.

'My friend said they were pretty mellow, although he said some people were really wasted. I haven't done 'em in like a year.'

'Whadda you think?' Adam asked Molly. She had told him she had tripped once in high school, on windowpane acid, so called because it was a clear, quarter of an inch square. She laughed hysterically for a little while, loved the halos and colorful diffusion around everything. Then she became withdrawn, not sure about the loss of her center of focus, the ability to think linearly. She said music was definitely important in helping her regain her equilibrium.

'Are you gonna do it?' Molly asked Joy.

'I think I wanna try it. Just a little. I don't wanna be tripping my, you know what off.'

'Your what?' Doug said.

'Her balls,' Adam said.

'But she doesn't have balls,' Molly declared.

'I think when it comes to tripping something off, even girls can trip their balls off. Right? You're tripping.'

Molly saw the logic. When you were tripping, anything was possible. 'Her balls it is,' she said.

Doug's friend couldn't connect with his 'shrooms guy. He brought LSD instead. Blotter acid, each little half-inch square tab stamped with a picture of Mr. Natural. Two bucks a tab.

'Do you think I should do the whole thing?' Molly asked.

'Why don't we split one,' Adam said. 'We have all day tomorrow to chill out. We can start studying after dinner. You should do what you're comfortable with.'

'I'm gonna do like a half, too,' Joy said.

'Me too,' Doug's friend Alan's girlfriend Janie said. Janie was classic neo-hippie; big, thick, long light-brown hair, headband, embroidered, middle-eastern shearling jacket, bell-bottoms, from Huntington, Long Island, about half an hour east of Baldwin on the LIE.

Doug's friend Alan was from Bay Ridge Brooklyn, where Doug was from. He reminded Adam of his friend Stevie – tall and congenial, which allowed Adam to feel closer to him than if there was no kind of connection, other than Doug.

Twenty minutes later, everyone was starting to get off, to feel the energy radiating off of everyone and everything around them. The lysergic acid was starting to have its way with their synapses.

'Wow, that looks like another world... like we can go into it,' Adam said. They were in Doug's room looking through the frosted glass window at the lights along the walkways around his dorm.

'It's like geometry... with light,' Molly said. 'I feel like I'm floating.'

'I'm starting to get really lit,' Doug said.

'Let's go to the Black Oak,' Joy said. The Black Oak Tavern was their bar of choice; everything a college-town bar should be. Young, packed, and fun. 'I think I wanna be outside.'

'Outside in the distance, a wild cat did prowl,' Adam sang. 'Two riders were approaching...'

'And the wind began to howl...' Alan sang.

'I'm so comfortable,' Janie said. I juss wanna lay herrrrrrrrrrrrrre.' She and Alan were laying on their backs on the other bed in the room hallucinating images onto the white stucco ceiling.

'Look at my hand.' Molly was standing at the window staring at her hand. 'I can see the blood circulating. What's that called?'

'What?' Joy asked. She was walking back and forth from the desk to the door.

'That tattoo...'

'Oh I know... from India?' Joy asked.

'Yeah.'

'Henna,' Joy remembered.

'Henna Youngman,' Adam said. 'Didn't he... Doctor, it hurts when I... So don't...'

There was a delay, and then Alan exploded in laughter. He got the joke. 'That's the funniest thing I ever heard,' he stammered, the grin on his face taking wing at the corners, the kind of sustained grin that hurts the next morning.

'What about pizza,' Joy declared.

'The perfect food,' Doug said. 'A piece o' pizza, a pizza pizza.' He started to giggle.

'Two pizza pizza.'

The instant Adam said that, he knew he was gone. His laughter caught hold, started to roll, in his breath and chest, and quickly overtook him, into a world where it was impossible not to feel electric mirth. Lost inside the laughter. It was like a full-body orgasm.

'I'll have two pizza pizza,' Adam slurred.

'A pizza pizza,' Alan was just barely able to say, he was laughing so hard.

'Who wants to go outside with me?' Joy asked.

'I'll go,' Adam said. 'You wanna go outside?'

'I'm really comfortable,' Molly said. 'You should go outside. I'm really... really....' She waved her hand by her face. 'Do you see 'em?'

Adam waved his hand in front of his face. 'Definitely.' Trails; the phase-shifting of reality. 'Your face is coming to me in like waves.' He could feel them landing.

'You look like Cher,' Doug said to Molly. 'I mean, you know... Wait... You look like my friend Sal's sister. She's like amazing... Molly. We never hung out like this. This is my best friend Alan. I've known him since we were five.'

'You have beautiful eyes,' Janie said. She had a Mother Earth vibe. Very grounded. Clan leader in another incarnation.

'All right, you guys. We'll be back,' Joy said. 'If I don't see you in the future, I'll see you in the pasture.'

'Hey, I...' Adam said, then thought, 'Wow, that was like...' His summer seemed many seasons gone. 'Molly, you sure you don't wanna go?'

'I don't wanna be left alone with these two,' Janie said. Alan and Doug were standing nose to nose, saying what sounded like 'raaaw', slowly, full mouth extension, repeatedly, one after the other.

'Come back,' Molly said.

'We will,' Adam said.

The initial shock of cold was invigorating, walking outside, down the path to the parking lot to catch the campus bus downtown. But both Adam and Joy knew that type of cold, upstate cold, in the teens, only lasted until the cold took hold, which didn't take long. Luckily, the bus was just pulling up when they arrived at the bus stop, like it had read their minds.

'Yay,' Joy said, inside the warm, familiar, way too bright campus bus. 'I want something cold and sweet. I wish they could turn the lights down.'

'It's so warm,' Adam said. He was feeling comfortable with Joy. And not in any possessive, objectifying way. She'd always been cool with him; treated him with respect. She was a friend, a good person to be tripping with, more than anything because she had her shit together.

'This is like an adventure,' Adam said.

Joy was staring out the window. 'Wow, look at that.'

Adam had no idea what she was looking at. It was pretty black outside, except for house lights, which radiated geometric patterns as they passed them.

Standing up and walking off the bus, Adam felt propelled by a round, fluid energy. 'One foot in front of the next,' he told himself.

'Whadda you want?' Adam asked Joy, shimmying up to the Black Oak bar.

'Something frozen, like a pina colada.'

'Two frozen pina coladas,' Adam told the bartender. He had never had one, but he was into experimenting, at which point the bustle of the crowded bar grabbed his attention. The auditory distortions were greater than the visuals; sounds becoming indecipherable from one another, blending into a totality, nothing lasting long enough to be distinguished above the echoes. A total soundscape in which there were messages Adam was way too fractured to decipher. He instinctively told himself to just let it bathe over him. 'Just concentrate on Joy' he told himself. Everything had halos. He was about as high as he'd ever want to be. His inner voice was still his own, even if he had a hard time holding onto thoughts. Somewhere within his racing mind was the settling thought that he had only done half a hit, sharing the other half with Molly. He wondered how fucked up Doug and Alan were. They had each done a whole tab.

'You cool?' he asked Joy, handing her her drink.

'Oh yeah,' she said. 'And my favorite seats are open...' a love-seat in the corner along the same wall as the bar. 'Let's go snag 'em.' It was perfect, snuggled up in the corner, everything happening in front of them.

'I wish everybody came with us,' Joy said. 'I'd rather be out than inside.'

'I'm sure their just as fucked up as we are.'

'Alan's girlfriend's really hot. I'd love to be with her.'

'You mean like...'

'Oh yeah. I love girls, man. I love guys too. But girls are so much sof...' At which point she closed her eyes, and seemed to be having an erotic daydream, leaving Adam to contemplate Joy and Janie having sex. Ordinarily, that would have started his engines racing. But the speedy nature of his stoned condition kept his sexual impulses less engaged, more like an awareness wrapped in a hum, which was an unexpectedly mellow place to be; a beautiful vision without the selfish desire, although the more he thought about it, the more the hum started revving up.

He was watching Joy's physical characteristics morph with the vibrations emanating from the room, her eyes closed, a serene smile, the veins in her face prominent against her pale skin. When she took a deep breath and moved her head back, trails followed her movement. All motion was followed by trails, the edges of reality sequenced into still images fading into the distance.

'Oh yeah,' Joy said, opening her eyes. She was staring at Adam with huge black pupils. He stared right back, watching her face radiate energy.

'What?' Adam asked.

'I was... Do you wanna another pina colada?'

'Definitely. It's like the most delicious thing I ever had. I'll get...'

'No, it's right here.'

They were close enough to the bar that Adam could keep an eye on Joy, make sure nothing went wrong.

'I can't believe she's into girls,' Adam thought, watching her back expand and contract as she ordered drinks. 'I'd love to watch her and Molly...' That thought, again, remained a cerebral concept, although Adam could feel time and alcohol diminishing the fluttery, speedy feeling that had pervaded his nervous system. He was feeling a bit more relaxed. Still super-high. But everything felt interwoven. The good vibe of the bar. Not many sad faces on a Saturday night in a college-town bar.

'I can't believe how delicious this is,' Adam said, taking a huge swig of his drink. He could taste that drink was stronger.

'He put more rum in. I wanna get fucked up.'

'I'm pretty fucked up.'

'Yeah. Wow.' She stared into the crowd, her mouth open, drink in her left hand, completely still. Just staring.

After about a minute she said, 'First time I got high was with my brother. When he got back from Nam, he was heavily into partying. I love him so much. He's such a good guy. I wish he was hear right now. I'm gonna channel 'im.'

She closed her eyes, and Adam could tell she was seriously trying to make extra-sensory contact through the ether. He was watching her, and almost, internally, seeing the connection Joy was trying to make. Then, for a moment, he lost focus, requiring him immediately to remember where he was, and what he was doing...

'Okay... All right...' he thought, getting his bearings. He was tripping... waves, like the flutter of film images... all sound blending into one sound, yet each sound distinct. Joy was... her brother... That thought transforming into Adam thinking of Charles, which was weird when he was tripping, like the two worlds were so incongruous that they would cancel each other out.

'I hope he's okay,' he thought. Then that too was gone, as he watched Joy's face turn feline, in a very psychedelic and curious way... still Joy... morphing... was definitely feline in another incarnation... morphing back...

'Wow, I'm fuckin'...' Then, even the thought to say, 'stoned' was gone. Adam wasn't able to hold onto anything. The LSD was making everything different; an altered reality, one Adam had little control over. It was a little scary. He was definitely way higher than he realized he'd be. Nothing to do but let it roll. Give in to the surreality... Into the next thing... how incredibly delicious the frozen pina colada was, the cold sending a shiver over Adam's entire body, almost like a mini-orgasm, without any sexual origins.

Joy looked at him with pupils dilated to their fullest capacity, letting in maximum light.

'That's why the halos...' Adam realized. 'Like when you go to the eye doctor,' he thought.

'What halos?' Joy asked.

'Everything,' Adam managed to say.

'I think we should go back. I swear I think I could feel Doug wanting us to come back.'

'Really? Let's go.' He wanted to get back. Hang with Molly. Let his mind wonder with hers. There was usually a good connection there. He flashed back to standing at top of the Shawangunks with her. Looking out onto forever. He wanted to be outside with her, right then, like he was with Joy as they waited for the campus bus. He felt alive. The slap of cold, now around twelve degrees, the quietness and peacefulness of upstate New York, alcohol, time, all combined to progressively lessen the effects of Mr. Natural. Not that Adam was straight. Not by a long shot. The halos and altered perceptions were still distorting reality. But his mind was back under his control. He could keep a thought. And right then it was about standing outside with Molly, at the place near the stream behind Adam's dorm they hung out at a few times. It felt like the middle of a forest. Look up at the clear, radiant points of light against the pitch-black night sky. Smell the crystal north wind, at one with nature.

Doug met them coming out of his dorm. He had his coat on.

'I was just coming to get you,' he said, highly concerned. 'Molly's bumming out. She's been asking for you.'

'Fuck,' Adam said. From stoned bliss to buzz-kill. Molly was having a bad trip. It was written all over Doug's face. That straightened him out even more. He took a deep breath in, checking internally that he had his wits about him – no racing, lost thoughts, familiar inner voice.

'I'm so glad you're here,' Janie said, as Adam walked over to Molly, who was crawled up in fetal position on Doug's bed. Janie had been administering to Molly, trying to talk her down. Adam could sense her relief that help had arrived.

'Molly, you okay?' Adam asked.

'I don't… can't stop thinking… Adam can… Talk to me…'

'Of course. Listen, I just went through the same thing,' Adam said, bending over her, kissing her lips, her cheeks, her forehead. She was burning up. 'Everything's racing. It's just the drugs. They'll make their way through your body. You'll be all right.'

'No but, I can't… think… shit… shit…'

'I'm gonna get you outside, and get you back to your room.'

'I'm afraid to move.'

'I'm tellin' you. Everything'll be okay.' At that point, Adam wasn't so sure. He'd never seen Molly lost within herself. He'd never seen anybody like that. He knew it was only a matter of time before the drugs made their way through her. But he was a little afraid of the damage they could do on their way out. 'Come on. I'm gonna help you sit up. That's it, grab around my neck.' When she was sitting up, Adam reached around his neck, pried apart Molly's hands, which were clutch him tightly, and held them in front of him. Looking her in the eyes - huge dilated eyes that were full of other-worldly fear - his heart broke a tiny bit knowing she was going through what she was going through. He said, 'I have a good idea. Try to fill your mind with light. Give your brain a rest. I'm gonna get your stuff, and then we're gonna try to head back.'

'Molly, I love you,' Joy said. 'You're gonna be okay. I like the light thing.'

Molly tried to concentrate. 'I can't. I'm really scared. I can't stop…'

'Okay, sweetie. It's gonna be okay,' Janie said. 'Let's get your coat on. That's it.'

'Do me a favor,' Joy said, 'Drink some of this. You gotta hydrate.'

Molly took a long swig of water, and handed it back to Joy. She needed to cleanse. She needed to burn away the impurity. Her difficult

LSD trip was a refiner's fire. She was still going through the process. But things were progressing. Not as magically as Adam would have hoped, but she was up, her coat was on, and he was certain the fresh air would do her good.

'We love you Molly,' Doug said. Adam and Molly were walking arm in arm out the door. 'We'll see you tomorrow.'

'Keep yourself together, Molly. You got this,' Janie said.

'I'll see you tomorrow,' Joy said.

Adam sensed they were relieved to be relieved of the responsibility of watching over Molly. Not that they would have ever have forsaken her. They knew Adam was up to the task, and was the right person for Molly to be with. They could finally enjoy their elevated consciousnesses. 'I wonder if Joy and Janie…' Adam thought, but immediately shifted to Molly. It was the quickest sexual thought he had ever had. 'I just gotta get her back to her room, keep her as mellow as possible…' Let the drug run its course. She was holding onto Adam as if her life depended on it.

'Lemme get your hat on,' Adam said, right before they stepped outside. Molly's face was pastier that he had ever seen it. A real life Keane painting, with the flu, in a red-into-yellow ombre ski hat, a big, red, wool scarf her mother knit, and shearling LL Bean mittens.

'Ahhhh,' Molly said, stepping outside into the bitter cold. 'That feels good.'

As good as it felt, Adam knew he had to get Molly inside as quickly as he could. Upstate New York cold is unforgiving. Things could go from bad to worse in a single wind gust.

'You okay?' Adam asked. They were walking briskly along the path leading to Molly's dorm.

'Adam… When'd we get outside?'

'You warm enough?' He knew not to engage the discord. Keep going forward.

'I'm starting to get cold.' As she said that, he could feel her starting to shake. He put his right arm around her back and held onto her right bicep, his left hand around her left bicep, guiding her a little more quickly along. Luckily, they didn't have far to go.

'How 'bout taking in a deep breath with me through your nose, and letting it out through your mouth, and saying ahhh when you do.' That was a relaxation technique Adam learned in Yoga 101. His mother had said she thought that was a silly class to take. Maybe. Maybe not. He did it first. Breathe in, which was less than relaxing because they were walking briskly. But the 'Ahhhhhhhhh,' the vibration in the head and chest, that's what Adam was going for.

Molly did it. Breathing in, feeling the tingling cold on her nostrils… 'Ahhhhhhhhhhhhhhhh…' Another deep breath in, and they were inside her dorm.

'Sharon, um, could you…'

'Are you all right?' One look at Molly and she could see she wasn't. 'Let's get her into bed.'

'What…'

'We'll tell you tomorrow.'

'All right.' Sharon knew it was drugs, and was both disappointed and concerned. She didn't approve of drugs. She was studying to be a teacher. 'Let's get you in your robe.'

She brought the robe over to Molly. 'I'm here if you need me,' she said. 'I'll be right down the hall.' Sharon was gracious enough to sleep in Joy's bed when the situation warranted and allowed.

When she was gone, Adam helped Molly get undressed, which at no point was lost on him. She could be puking up last week's tuna casserole, but if she was naked, Adam would be turned on.

'Okay,' he said, wrapping her robe around her, 'under the covers.' Which she did, two seconds after which, he was right there with her, naked. He knew his intentions were less than honorable – he was thinking of fucking her, and she was trying to reclaim her sanity. He was hoping they could do both. It was warm, calm, and comfortable under the covers. Adam knew it was just a matter of time.

'Am I gonna be able to do math?' Molly asked. She was lucid enough to begin assessing her mental condition, as opposed to being overwhelmed by it.

'The bad part of the drug is already working its way through your body. It's just time now.' They were both cuddled up in fetal position, forehead to forehead, knees to knees, the blankets over their heads, like they were in a mini pup-tent.

'But how do I know.'

'How much is one plus one.'

'Two, but that's not what I mean. I don't know if I'll even remember where I live.'

'You will. Breathe in, and then breathe out, and then I'm gonna breathe that in... take all that bad shit outta ya.'

She did.

'Oh, I can feel that bad shit coming outta ya. Can you do that again?'

She did. 'I'm starting to get really warm,' she said.

'I'll lift the blankets up a little. Why don't you take your robe off.'

As she did that, Adam shifted his position to his back.

'Why don't you lay on top of me... let our hearts beat together.' He thought that might be a good way to keep her calm. He was playing it by ear... and a little by penis. He was naked in bed with Molly on a Saturday night, and he was beautifully stoned. He knew he was being a little disingenuous, but he hoped the good he was trying to do would cancel that out.

Her body was burning hot. She had the flu, or pneumonia.

'You okay?' Adam asked. Molly was resting her head on his chest.

'This is so fucked up. I don't know why I can't...'

'You know what we should do? I'm gonna do it too. I'm gonna try to empty my mind, just concentrate on my breathing.'

'Am I gonna be able to read?'

'Yup. I'd go get you a book right now, but I'm so comfortable.'

'But how do you know. I think I might have fucked up my whole brain.'

'It's just the drugs. In another couple of hours you'll be as good as new.'

'A couple of hours?'

'Listen, we're not going anywhere. Just try to stop all the activity in your head, and just feel the breath coming in through your nostrils... and out... in... out... Now, try to think of light. Don't think of anything else. Just try to fill your mind with light.'

Adam could feel Molly really trying to concentrate, felt her deep breathing, her heartbeat begin to slow down a little.

'My poor brother,' she said.

'Yeah, but he made it.'

Molly's older brother had a motorcycle accident while stoned on Quaaludes, doing permanent damage to his right leg.

"Thank God... Why did your brother pull a gun on you?'

'Well he didn't actually... although...' The image of Charles standing in his underwear with his shotgun pointing directly at Adam flashed into his mind. He quickly shifted his thoughts to how good it felt to feel Molly resting naked on top of him. No sense letting his mind go where he didn't want it to, now that it was back under his control. 'It's a rough world. You know what the four noble truths are?'

'No.'

'It's like one of the things in Buddhism. I just learned it. Anyway, the first one is that all life is suffering, and the other three are about transcending the suffering, by things like getting away from desire, and living a good life. What I'm trying to say is, just tough it out. Work through what you're going through. I think I know what that is right now 'cause my mind was really racing before. Just tell yourself you're gonna be all right, cause you are. I promise. I *am* wondering why you're so hot though. If you're still like this when you come down, I think we should call your parents.'

'You don't think it's gonna fry my brain do you?'

'No. I do wanna get you some water though. Joy was right. You should stay hydrated... get this shit through your system. I'm gonna...'

'No, don't move. This is good like this.'

'Okay, I ain't movin'.... Did you know Joy was into girls?'

'Yeah. She told me anytime... whoooo, I just had a... oy yoy yoy...

'You okay?'

'Hold on... oy... oy... okay... awright... whoah...'

'Take a deep breath...'

She did.

'Settle your heart...'

She took another deep breath.

'What were we saying?' she asked.

'We were talking about Joy.'

Besides the selfish motives, he was groping at straws. If he could make the connection, any connection, from before the swoon to after, he'd know they were through the worst of it.

'Oh yeah.'

'Thank God,' Adam thought.

'Would… are you?'

'You would like that, wouldn't you…'

Now that Adam's mind and penis were almost back to normal, his natural reactions once again manifested themselves. The thought of a ménage a trois with Molly and Joy got him as hard as steel.

'Adam, I don't…'

'No. I know… Let's just breathe together, okay?'

'What a bummer,' he thought.

That was the way they stayed until about four in the morning, when Molly felt together enough for Adam to get up and get her a glass of cold water. She was still burning up.

'We need to call your parents,' Adam said.

'Not yet….'

'Okay, but I think you're really sick. I think that's why you had such a bad reaction.'

'Oh my God was that scary. I'm never doing that again.'

'You and me both.' Seeing the dark side of tripping was enough for Adam to swear off that kind of partying forever. Pot, okay. Anything else, no way. It wasn't worth it.

By five in the morning, her fever hadn't abated one bit.

'Do you have a thermometer anywhere?' Adam asked.

'I think there's one in the top draw of Sharon's desk.'

The thought of telling Molly he wanted to take her temperature anally, to get a more accurate reading, crossed his mind, but never made it into words or action.

'All right, I'm calling your parents.'

'How much?'

'A little over a hundred and four.'

'Oy.'

'What's their number? They need to come and get you.'

'All right. But don't freak 'em out.'

'I won't.'

As Adam was getting dressed, he wrote down Molly's number.

'I'll be right back, okay?' There was a payphone at the end of the corridor.

'Okay.'

'Hello?' Mr. Jupiter said, immediately concerned. Calls that early in the morning are rarely good.

'Hi Mr. Jupiter, it's Adam Strulovitz...'

'Is Molly all right?'

'Who is it,' Adam heard Mrs. Jupiter ask in the background.

'It's Adam,' Mr. Jupiter said.

'Molly just has a pretty high fever...' Adam threw in before their concern escalated.

'Molly's got a high fever,' Mr. Jupiter told Mrs. Jupiter.

'How high?' Mrs. Jupiter asked.

'How high?' Mr. Jupiter asked.

'A little over a hundred and four.'

'Tell her we'll be up as soon as we can. Thanks for calling, Adam.'

'What'd they say?'

'They're on their way.'

'Okay. All right. I gotta rest before they get here. I still don't feel together. They're gonna know I'm fucked up. Definitely.'

'Just let 'em just take care o' ya.'

Adam looked down at Molly. She had been through the ringer. And she wasn't out of it yet. She had questioned the very essence of her mind, if she had lost it? And it wasn't hyperbole. The drug was so overwhelming, it took over. Too much heroin and it takes over your body and you die. At points, Adam was afraid Molly really hurt herself, which freaked him out. 'Poor Molly,' he thought. 'Holy fuck. Thank God. Thank God.'

'Is that okay?' she said a few seconds later, meaning she didn't want him there when her parents got there, and needed some time to herself before they did. He understood. He wouldn't have wanted to hang out with his parent in the condition he was in either.

'You sure you're okay?'

'I feel like such shit, I can't believe it. What happened?' More than asking Adam, she was asking God.

'I think you transcended the first noble truth.'

'What? Oh.'

'Are you sure you're okay?'

'I gotta close my eyes. Oy...'

'All right. Try to get some sleep. Your parents'll be here in a couple of hours.'

'I'm so glad you came back. I didn't know if you were gonna come back.'

'Me too. I'll call you tonight.' He bent over her and kissed her face, her cheek, her forehead; held his lips there. He was relieved help was on the way. She was burning up.

'Hi Mrs. Jupiter,' Adam said over the phone later that evening. He waited until after dinner to call. He wanted to give Molly the day, to feel the embrace of her family. 'How's Molly doing? Is she around?'

'She's resting right now. My husband would like to talk to you.'

Adam's first inclination was that Molly's father wanted the truth about why Molly was in the condition she was in; know what he was dealing with, maybe recognizing Adam's care of his daughter...

'I want the truth,' Molly's father angrily demanded. 'Did you do drugs with my daughter?'

Blindsided. Adam never thought he was going to be chastised, scolded for what happened. He quickly thought, 'Did something really happen?' Give the guy the truth, and find out what the fuck was going on.

'Mr. Jupiter, we did. If I could take it back I would. Is she all right?'

'She'll be all right. But I can't have this happen again.'

'We both said...'

'I'm not talking about you. I just went through this with my son. I have to do what I have to do. It's the only way I know how. I'm protecting my daughter.'

'Of course, I...'

'You don't get it. I want Molly to keep away from you.'

It went all the way. Adam was paying a steep price for a rough night. Somewhere in the matrix of his mind he understood how a father would want to exorcise any potential demon from his daughter's life. But he felt he was being miscast. He was stunned. What could he possibly say to change a protective parent's mind? He was exposed as a drug-taking teen, not the greatest endorsement. What father would want their daughter going out with a guy who does drugs, especially a father who had already been burned by them. He had met Mr. and Mrs. Jupiter twice. They were both teachers; Mrs. Jupiter, a Middle School health teacher, and Mr. Jupiter, a High School science teacher. Mr. Jupiter served under General Patton during World War II, and was very direct with Adam when he first met him, asking about his parents, and letting him know he wouldn't tolerate anyone or anything that could hurt his daughter. At the time, Adam felt he had nothing to worry about. Adam, in his own way, shared his concern, minus the fact that he was banging his daughter.

'I think that's...' Adam said, thinking, 'crazy, unfair'. He remembered when Stephanie Millman's parents forbid their daughter from seeing him because they found out they had smoked pot together. The fact that Stephanie had gotten the joint from her older brother had a lot to do with her parents' weakened resolve.

'I'm sure you do,' Mr. Jupiter interrupted. 'I'm usually a fair guy, but I gotta circle the wagons. My family's too important. You blew it, son. Whether you think you did or not. I hope you straighten your life out. It's worth it. Good bye Adam.'

'Did I just lose Molly? I'm gonna call her. This is bullshit,' in the same instant realizing how bad of an idea that was, to defy her father right after betraying his trust. That would guarantee he remained a pariah, if there was even a chance that status could be lifted. He was stuck. He'd have to wait until she got back to school. At the latest he'd see her in their Human Sexuality class the following day.

She wasn't there. Nor was she in class on Wednesday.

'Fuck this,' Adam decided. 'I'm calling her.' He had to find out if she was okay. It felt irresponsible not to.

'She was quite ill, both mentally and physically,' Mrs. Jupiter told him. 'But she's on the mend. We're just being a little overly cautious. I appreciate you calling, Adam. But we've been pretty clear with Molly about how we feel. We'd appreciate it if you didn't call here again. I hope you understand.'

'Mrs. Jupiter, I'm so sorry Molly had to go through that. I want you to know I did everything I could. I can't take it back.'

'No you can't. Please respect our wishes.'

The mark of Cain. They were pushing him out of her life. He was heartbroken. The punishment didn't fit the crime, yet he knew he was destined to endure it. He went back to his room filled with anguish.

The first thing his eyes settled upon was the biography of Lord Byron he bought to impress Molly. Many were the nights he read Byron's poetry to her, from there branching off to other poets; Whitman, Keats, Patchen, Lowell. Of all of them, *When Lilacs Last In The Dooryard Bloomed* by Walt Whitman blew Adam's mind the most. But Lord Byron, who felt his life singled out for affliction by a vengeful God, marked with a crippled gait and a heart of darkness – that was the story Adam would never forget. A tortured soul trying to exorcise his demons by the most selfish and destructive means he could find, while also translating them into poetry.

'That's what I gotta do,' Adam thought; shut his mind off, turn the anguish into poetry. Until he heard from Molly, there was a possibility of redemption. Although she cherished her parents' love, support and wise council, maybe this time she would go it alone, reject her parents' wishes. 'But what happens if she doesn't. But why wouldn't she? She knows what happened. Fuck, I gotta talk to her. But they won't... Maybe I can... Nah... Fuck... All right, shut it down.'

Adam took the Byron biography down from the shelf and thumbed through it, looking at the passages he had highlighted, words that had struck him while he was reading. Two days later he had written his first poem, one he was burning to read to Molly.

The Mark of Cain

Born with the mark of Cain, a peer of the realm and an empty purse
Elevate the ambiguous thrill of identity to the grandeur of a curse
The sins of the father through forces much darker, shading into blasphemy
Willing anti-hero as rude as the rocks that sheltered his infancy
Beauty before the fall... No fear of destiny's call

Into the river, a child of sorrow to swim out beyond the Aberdeen wall
Run through the maze of sin with a conscience that was deaf and blind
Passion's delirium haunting his tortured and strangely glowing mind
The pleasures of Sodom with an innocent child rescued from the rain
To never again deny the sins worthy of the mark of Cain
A monotony… of endless variety
Tried every kind of pleasure and it was all vanity
Death is eternal sleep… lust sharper than the sword
Conquest the only consideration of the hopeless lord
Without shame… a dangerous game
The love that dare not speak its name
So do the dark in the soul expire
Or live like vengeance wrought by fire
Narcissus born to opposition and fame
The roar of the bull was the point of the game
But the bull was struck down in a riot of lust and was dragged from the
ring by the guardians of trust who feed the crows on Avalon's plain and
fertilize the fields that each would gain
The love where Faust had set his seal
Not age can forgive nor judgment steal
Thus the august moon did perverse passions awake
To curse the withered heart too selfish to break
For the first step of error none could recall
The son and the moon once fallen must forever fall
No salvation could be found in his blasphemy
A child of scorn, to misery born, sacrificed to save the guilty
And his the guilt, and his the hell… his soul's desolation dooming
And he has earned those tortures well… tortures still consuming
Seek out, less often sought than found, a soldier's grave, for you the best
Then look around and choose your ground, and forever take your rest
You, who left something dear to this world

'I gotta read this to her,' Adam thought, putting on his coat, intending
again to show up at her room unannounced. 'I hope she doesn't throw
me out.'

'She's still not back,' Sharon said. Molly had missed the whole week. 'Have you spoken to her?'

'Her parents won't let me.'

Sharon didn't know what to say, in a cynical way. Adam knew she also held him partially responsible for what happened to Molly. As he had disregarded her feelings about having sex with Molly almost every night whether she was in the room pretending to be asleep or not, so did Sharon not feel inclined to comfort Adam. You do the crime, you do the time.

'I'm sure she'll be all right,' she finally said. 'She's gotta come back. Finals start Monday.'

Adam knew, as soon as Molly walked into the Lecture Hall Seven for their Human Sexuality final, there was a wall he wasn't gonna be able to knock down - something in the way she scanned the room, uncharacteristically nervous, like she was carrying a weight, even though she smiled her recognition when she saw him, and sat down in the seat he had saved for her.

'Hi.'

'Hi.'

'Please tell me you're okay.'

'I'm okay. I know you're upset. That thing really manifested…'

'Please. There's no talking,' the proctor insisted. 'Everyone please take your seats, and I'll begin handing out the packets.'

'Can we talk afterwards?'

'Sure.'

Not 'I can't wait,' or even 'Of course.' 'Sure', empathetic, deference for the condemned.

'All right. I gotta concentrate on this test,' Adam thought. 'Fuck. This isn't good.'

'When'd you get back?' Adam asked, the second he met Molly outside Lecture Hall Seven. Luckily, he had studied for the test so, at least, he felt good about that. The one thing he knew he blew was, he couldn't remember the period men go through right after orgasm… 'Refractory, uh,' he remembered as soon as he started talking to Molly.

And then he realized that's where Molly and he were - all of a sudden, withdrawn, energy spent. Things were forever changed because of a bad decision. From that point on, try to keep the bad decisions to a minimum. They have bad consequences. Adam knew he had better take better care of himself. He just got his ass kicked. A whole new future had to be conceived. Not that he didn't see it coming over the past week. But until he got there, there's still some connection.

'Last night.' She was still a little pale. A little vulnerable. Molly. How much he loved her, wanted her. How much he wanted her to want him. He couldn't believe he was losing her. Everything in her interaction spoke of distance, separation; no touching, restrictive body language, forced smile. Another powerful and real relationship, a friendship, over. Two in a row. Different endings. Same ending.

'I thought I was losing my mind. And the flu didn't help,' she said.

'I think that's what caused it.'

'That's not what caused it.'

'Yeah. I know... But I have no idea why I'm taking the fall.' He went for it. Why fuck around.

'It's not that. I gotta take care of me. I can't ever let that happen again. You have no idea.'

'Maybe a little idea,' meaning, he was there.

'Yeah, but then... Thank God I was home. I spoke to my brother every night. It was like two wounded soldiers talking about their war experiences. I know you think my family's blaming you for what happened.'

'Um...' He was starting to grasp the extent of what Molly had gone through. It was no joke. It wasn't just the drugs. The drugs triggered something deeper and then distorted it. He wished he had been there to help her through it. Apparently, he was part of the problem. 'It definitely feels a little like that,' he said. 'But I know there's a lot more to it. Oh yeah, I wrote this poem. I'd love for you to read it.' He had fantasized about reading it to her. Her on the bed. Him at the foot, standing up facing her.

'All I wanna do right now is get through this week, and then take a break.' She didn't acknowledge his declaration.

'From us?'

'From everything.'

'There it is,' Adam thought. He felt like the rug had been pulled out from under him, a momentary dangle. He had to respect her wishes. She was trying to heal. He didn't want to be an impediment. Fate would determine the rest.

'Are you sure that's what you want?' he said, finding his way back to the center, but also feeling himself slipping into defensive mode. 'I...' but he stopped himself. Anything he said to try to prolong the inevitable would have only brought him down further. He had actually played out the noble break-up scenario in his mind, in anticipation of the possibility that what just happened might happen, except in that fantasy she'd find her way back to him. This didn't feel like that.

'You're really a great guy and...'

'Obviously not that great if you're breaking up with me,' he thought. After that, he didn't really hear much of what she said, something about she was only eighteen, and that she was thinking of transferring because she needed a new environment, all things that let Adam know her need to move on. But as Chris's last note had taught him, real love includes freedom and acceptance, even if it meant breaking up.

'I'm sorry, Adam.'

'Me too. Can I ask you something? No. Forget it...' He probably didn't want to know the answer.

'No. What?'

'If that night never happened, would we be... doing this?'

'No idea. If you really wanna know, and at this point, I just wanna be honest, I was starting to think we're too young to get so involved. I met you like the first day. We both have to experience life.'

All Adam could think was, 'This is life. Our life.' What Molly said sounded like a conversation she had with her parents many times over the preceding week, an attempt to move her forward, to see the possibilities the future held. At no point during their relationship had she given him any indication that she was thinking of breaking up - some frustrations, maybe. Mostly harmony. 'Was I that blind or naïve?' he wondered. Perhaps it was the belated effect of his prepubescent transgression with Molly's old camp friend Frannie Berringer. 'Probably a little of that, too.'

'Wow, this sucks,' he said. But knowing the hell Molly had just gone through, he didn't want to be another brick in her wall. Nor could he rewrite reality.

'I'm sorry Adam… I guess… Okay…. I'm gonna...'

She walked back to her dorm. He stood there feeling somewhere between numbness and the wrath of a spiteful God. He knew this was the one that got away.

Even though it was sub-zero outside, he went back to his dorm room, got the drum-pad and sticks he bought the first week of school – wanting to impress Molly with his spontaneity, he went inside the music store in town they were walking by and bought the set - and sat outside on his window ledge, playing to every song on *Layla*, by Derrick and The Dominoes, until he had blisters on his fingers. He sat there not trying to think about too much. He, basically, understood what happened, and why. His relationship with Molly wasn't meant to be anything more than what it was; a transition between one paradigm, life before college, and another. Still, like his perfect summer, why not have it go on forever. He had few regrets, but the ones he had were big, the biggest being he didn't know how to hold onto a woman he loved. One very bad night and it was over, possibly not long after that if that night never happened. He didn't know what to do about any of it, which only proved how much he had to learn. He was also sorry for the way he had disregarded Chris. He hadn't answered her letters because of his transferrable commitment, and her letters stopped coming. He felt guilty about betraying Chris, sick about losing Molly, and insecure about the future. His social life had imploded, his proverbial little black book as empty as a drunk's dreamscape.

In the days, weeks and months that followed, if Adam wasn't in class, he was on his ledge playing his drum pad, trying not to obsess about his problems. Because of the way the dorm was built - recessed windows, with a deep seat, and boarder - he was able to sit outside, far enough back toward the window that he wasn't afraid of falling off. Every time his problems bubbled up to the surface, he concentrated on the moment, feeling the wooden sticks in his hands bounce off the rubber. Sometimes his anxiety disappeared, sometimes it joined him in his paradiddles. But his emotion was energy and he was learning to channel that energy into creativity. He had been good about sticking to a regular practice schedule of five or six hours a week. After Molly broke up with him, he was playing that daily. Drumming freed his mind and inspired him with thoughts of self-improvement. When in doubt, he took his drum-pad out. With the approach of spring, his drum-pad was never put away, and the loss of Molly didn't loom as large. Time heals, and positive reinforcement helps the process, and drumming was positive - a way to understand a deeper aesthetic and establish a wider range of personal expression. Luckily, nobody cared that he was playing his pad outside, even though he was, generally, the only one making a racket out there. Because college life was about doing things, as opposed to thinking about doing things, no one wasted too much time thinking about what other people were doing. They were too busy doing their thing. So Adam did his thing, always stopping by ten o'clock.

One day he was on the ledge, four stories up, playing his pad to *Black Magic Woman* by Santana, feeling the groove, looking out at the hilltops that lead into the Appalachian Mountains. Warm, spring, early evening. He had finished studying for his Child Psychology 202 final, memorizing the major attributes of the five major stages of development:

1. Infancy: birth to 18 months – trust vs. mistrust... basic strength: drive and hope
2. Early Childhood: 18 Months to 3 Years - Autonomy vs. Shame... Basic Strengths: Self-control, Courage, and Will
3. Play Age: 3 to 5 Years - Initiative vs. Guilt... Basic Strength: Purpose
4. School Age: 6 to 12 Years - Industry vs. Inferiority... Basic Strengths: Method and Competence
5. Adolescence: 12 to 18 Years - Identity vs. Role Confusion... Basic Strengths: Devotion and Fidelity

Adam sensed a career in child psychology was not in his future. Not because it was an unworthy subject, but because he didn't feel he was the type of person who would be engaging other people in so intimate a way. He didn't think he needed psychological intervention, nor did he think he would be the one intervening. That was an academic path he didn't relate to, although he did relate to the stages of development, and appreciated having had them defined so succinctly. At least he was studying about something. He recognized how easy it was to fuck off, to not think about a career, and allow himself to believe that one thing would lead to another, and eventually everything would lead to the full realization of his potential. That's how he got through high school, a B+ average and three varsity letters; soccer, wrestling and lacrosse, although he didn't play lacrosse in his senior year of high school because the coach was a sadist, and Adam hated getting hit on his forearms and hands by the opponents' sticks, even though he wore gloves and arm-guards. It still hurt like shit.

Adam recognized he had to start taking college more seriously than he had taken his education up to that point. His classes his second semester of freshman year were: Anti-lit and Pop Culture, Introduction to Western Philosophy, Intermediate Child Psychology, Accounting 101, and Acting 101. After Molly, the idea that he had better get his shit together started coalescing.

Jamming on his ledge to *Oye Como Va*, the idea of transferring to a better school with an accounting curriculum started forming in his mind.

'That's it,' he realized.

He knew immediately he was going to make that change - if not the following semester, then certainly the one after that. He remembered Chris told him that as soon as she made the decision to move forward on nursing school, she felt empowered. That's how Adam's decision felt – keep going, keep working toward the future. No one was telling him what to do. He was figuring it out himself.

'This is the real Bar Mitzvah,' he thought.

From there it was easy to slip back inside Santana's heavy groove, riding it, looking out at the distant Appalachian ridge, thinking of some of the things Chris and he did at higher elevations... 'Maybe I should write to her,' he thought. 'Nah, I was a jerk-off. I blew that... Wait, is that the door? Shit.' If someone was knocking, that could only mean they were coming to ask him to turn the music and his drumming down. So much for his theory that he wasn't bothering anybody because they were too busy doing their own thing.

'Yeah,' said a guy Adam had seen around the dorm. 'How's it goin', man.'

'Good. Listen, I know I'm playing too loud. I'll…'

'Too loud for who? Me and some guys from my band were just watching you from my room. Your shit is out there. We were wondering if you're free Saturday night. We have a gig at The Rat and our drummer can't make it.'

'Wow. I'd love to… Come in.'

'Okay, but I gotta get back and study for a Trig test tomorrow.'

'Okay…. I just gotta tell ya though. I've only played with a band once, and that was just for two songs.'

'How'd it go?'

'It was really good.'

'Excellent. I see you out there all the time. I'm surprised you don't fly off the way you freak out,'

'Oh man, are you kidding? It's so great sitting up there going wild, with the mountains right there.'

'I know, man. I'm the trumpet player from the second floor. But I don't play outside. I think that'd be a little much, like Gabriel calling his children home.'

'I've heard you practice. It sounds great. Am I ever too loud?'

'No. Not really. At least I don't think so. I heard you jamming on some Coltrane the other day.'

'Yeah. I just got into it. *Afro-Blue Impressions*. It's like Hendrix.'

'That's one of the greatest albums of all time. That's what we're into. We like to take it out. Start off on a groove and see where it goes. I'm Gary, by the way.'

'Adam. Wow. All right. This is wild. Oh yeah. There is one really big problem though. I don't have a kit, so…'

'No, no problem. You can use The Rat's house kit. It's all you need. It's a really good kit, a Slingerland four-piece I think. Cool ride. It's really good. So you in?'

'I'm in.'

'Cool. Why don't you get there a little before seven-thirty, give you time to adjust the kit. And we'll be on for like an hour. Then we can hang out and have a beer.'

How fortunate Adam had gotten into jazz a few months before, and had been listening to and, more importantly playing along to *Kind Of*

Blue, Afro-Blue Impressions, Mingus Ah Um, Straight No Chaser almost every day since then. He couldn't wait to apply what he had learned on his pad.

He didn't have to wait long. Saturday was only three days away... and before he knew it, it was showtime.

With major butterflies in his stomach, he took his seat behind the vintage white-pearl Slingerland drumset set up in the corner of the bandstand and waited for his cue. The Rat, short for Rathskeller, was the on-campus bar and grill Adam had spent many nights at. With its low ceilings and dark, subterranean vibe, he felt like he was in someone's basement waiting to jam. Since the band, which consisted of a pianist, a bass player, a trumpet player and a sax player, were all in front of him, and he was in the corner, he felt insulated, away from the scrutiny of the bar patrons, like he was in his own little world, like he felt on his ledge. Gary caught his eye, nodded, turned back around to face the audience and began blowing the opening refrain from Miles Davis's *All Blue*, a song Adam had worn the grooves off of playing along to. Although this was a different arrangement from the record, Adam got the sense the next instrument in was the drums, his right hand dancing over to the ride cymbal grooving in a steady six-eight.

'All right,' he thought to himself. 'Feels good. Just keep it together.'

When the rest of the band joined in he started swinging like a smooth flowing river. He felt the rhythm from within, and was able to translate his thoughts and feelings onto the drums. It was like singing, dancing, and meditating, all at the same time. The bass player, a tall, heavier-set guy who was in Adam's Western Philosophy class, although they had never acknowledged each other, opened his eyes, looked at Adam and nodded his smiling approval.

They continued their set with *A Love Supreme* by John Coltrane, Charlie Parker's *Billie's Bounce*, and *Freddy the Freeloader* by Miles Davis. The only time Adam got into trouble was during the drum solo on *Take Five* by Dave Brubeck. He lost the five-four count somewhere along the way and found himself playing a straight four-four. In order to compensate for his mistake, he went as wild as he could, and when he brought it back to a mellow five-count, he heard the audience applauding over the repeated first verse he had come back in on. His first drum solo.

'I hope I didn't fuck that up too bad,' he thought, right after *Take Five* ended. 'Nothing I can do about it now.'

When the set was over, Gary came back to the drums and extended his hand in gratitude and appreciation.

'Adam, man, you swung it. A little up-tempo in places, but we all dug it.'

'It felt really good. I know I lost the five there...'

'I wouldn't worry about that. It almost sounded like it was part of the solo. Why don't you hang out with us at the bar, have a few beers. Oh yeah, this is for you.' He slipped Adam forty unexpected dollars. Getting paid to swing...

Adam was hanging out on cloud nine, tipping back a frosty Heineken, listening to the harmonic blend of conversation, jukebox music, glassware, cash register, laughing, thinking about how natural drumming felt, but how the more difficult rhythms required greater concentration. Riding a jazz groove felt like flying. Rock was more of a full-body immersion, heavier, more primal. Jazz, you can leave a little more space, lay out a little bit...

CHAPTER 12

. . . .

It took a special type of person to be so distant

A few months after Charles graduated from college, with a degree in Recreational Administration, he moved to Los Angels to pursue a career in sports hypnotherapy. He believed in his ability to transform people's lives, to help them achieve their potential. Motivation through hypnosis, regimentation, words and will – the hammer forging people's better selves

Because Adam had never seen his brother motivate anyone, he couldn't make the connection. But that didn't mean there wasn't one. Maybe he just couldn't see it. Not that it mattered, or that he cared. He didn't wish Charles ill or luck. They were distant, estranged. It was easier when Charles wasn't around.

Adam wondered, the few times he saw Charles looking at his body-building magazines, adoring the male physique, if he was gay and afraid of coming out, which would explain a lot about why he was so difficult within his family, and more centered in a community he felt he belonged. Certainly, body-building was his community. Somewhere in Adam's sense-memory, he felt how impossible it would have been for Charles to come out to their father, not that their father would have reacted differently than most other first generation, depression-era Jewish fathers. He would have weathered it, accepted it, in his way. Their relationship was so fucked-up anyway, it might have even brought them closer.

Charles never came out to anyone they knew, although, one of the times Adam saw him looking at one of his magazines, he turned to Adam, showed him the center-fold guy he was staring at, made the universal jerking-off gesture, looking Adam right in the eye with a 'how fuckin' great is this' look on his face.

'Wow,' Adam said. He was shocked at how enormous, defined, and indescribably muscular the guy was, like a computer-generated caricature of what the most super-human guy would look like.

'He just did that,' Adam thought. 'He just made the jerk-off gesture to a guy... In a g-string... Okay...'

Charles had only one girlfriend, for a few weeks, back in tenth grade. Other than that, it was pretty much a man's world. It didn't seem that women were all that relevant to his life-style.

The one masturbatory gesture he made was the only clue. Yet, Adam could have completely misread it. Charles could have loved women. That was how little Adam knew him; how little his parents knew him. When Charles spoke about women, he was generally degrading, but that was more a projection than a clue to his sexual orientation.

Again, it didn't matter. Adam knowing if his brother was gay or not did nothing to change their relationship. Charles wanted nothing to do with his family.

Adam saw him only twice after he moved to California. He came back to Baldwin for a few days the following Thanksgiving, and was civil. No drama. Very little interaction. He was at the gym, or wherever, most of the time. He seemed uncomfortable being home, but accepted it, and smiled when Adam told him he practiced drums every day. Because Adam was studying accounting at school, Charles asked him to look at a financial projection for an idea he had about selling hypnotherapy cassettes; by word of mouth, from the backs of fitness magazines, at local gyms: stop smoking, lose weight, get in peak physical condition. It seemed like a pie-in-the-sky projection - all profit, which, Adam supposed, if you sell something for a lot more money than it costs to produce, and you sell a lot of them, was possible. Adam told him he thought if he met his sales goals, he'd be in good shape. At no point during the few hours they spent together did he ask Adam or Barry anything about their lives. When he engaged Adam, it was about his financial projection, which he asked him about several times. His lack of regard was notable. It took a special type of person to be so distant to his brothers, to care so little about them, to be so uninterested. They weren't kids anymore. He was letting them know, in no uncertain terms, that he wanted nothing to do with them. Same message as always, only now, the idea of forever was creeping into the equation.

Yet his trip home was enough for their mother to hope she could salvage some kind of future for them, suggesting, months later, that Adam fly out to California for a few days, maybe take a Friday off and come back Sunday night. She would bank-roll the whole thing - enough money to try to make the trip fun, or to use in case Adam needed to.

"What, I'm gonna just show up there?' Adam asked.

'I just wanna know if you're interested or not.'

Spending time with his brother held very little allure for him. Once bitten, twice shy - the hundredth time, only because where was Adam gonna go? Run away? Live on the street? But he knew how much his brother's lack of contact, once he moved out to California – months without speaking, longer than it had ever gone before, was hurting his mother. Her suggesting he visit Charles was more a recon mission for her than a fun weekend for him.

'Ma, if he's into it, I'll go. I'll take one for the team. But just what you said; Friday, and I come home Sunday.'

'All right. Let me call him. Hopefully, I'll be able to get in touch with him.' Hope, as it related to Charles, was a precious commodity. Their mother had mentioned that he never answers the phone and rarely calls back.

At the time, a few months after graduating from college, Adam was working as an accountant at Bimstein, Stein and Abramowitz, a mid-sized New York City accounting firm with a concentration of small to mid-sized Garment Center companies as clients. Adam's father worked for one of those companies, Frohman and Frohman. They imported, and he sold piece-goods, the cloth you make clothes from. He heard that Bimstein, Stein and Abramowitz, liked to hire graduates from SUNY Albany, and gave Adam Mr. Stein's phone number the next time he saw him.

Adam had transferred from Cortland to SUNY Albany at the beginning of his sophomore year. Cortland was fun, but Adam had no career focus. SUNY Albany was known for its business school. Since he hadn't shown an aptitude for any specific profession or trade up to that point, he followed his father's advice and pursued a degree in accounting.

'People always need a good accountant,' his father recommended.

Accounting was not Adam's strongest subject. He spent three years at Albany putting numbers in boxes and graduated somewhere in the middle of his class. There was a disconnect at the higher levels of financial theory and practice - the mathematical, real-world problems Adam didn't give enough of a shit about to want to take the time it took to learn how to solve – net present values, M&A, investment strategies. He studied every day from five to seven at the library. Then he'd walk over to the Arts and Humanities Building and practice drums until exhaustion. The problem was, he should have studied 'til exhaustion, like many students did. Instead, he followed his insecure awakening-artist's instinct. Drum. Don't think about it. Do it. Do it enough hours to keep the deeper questions, like 'Why haven't I gotten laid in almost a year?' from hanging around. There were no meaningful answers. It was what it was. If he had the answer, he would have employed it. What he was learning was about distraction; put something in the way of wondering why his life wasn't where he wanted it to be. It was about time; spend it being neurotic, or replace some of that with the sheer joy of playing the drums.

He had bought the rest of his kit – two tom-toms, a snare drum, a hi-hat, a ride and a crash cymbal, and a double-bass pedal – toward the end of his sophomore year with the money he made driving the campus ambulette. He had seen an ad posted in the Student Union, and immediately knew it was a good thing to do. The training was two three-hour classes that taught very basic medic skills and interventions. After passing a just-as-basic emergency medical care exam, he started working; three on-call overnights at the infirmary a week, almost always uneventful. They fed him, paid him, and it was warm against Albany's fierce winters, a good atmosphere to study in - come in after a shorter night of drumming, settle into the infirmary vibe, like a chilled-out mini ER, and hit the books.

The calls he went on were ninety-percent transporting sick students to and from the infirmary. There were broken limbs, which he wrapped ice-packs around, and calls transporting students to essential medical appointments and procedures. Real emergencies were called into 911 and attended to by EMS. But he knew what he was doing had merit. He did feel a small sense of purpose after a few of the calls.

'You're the guy that drives the ambulance,' students who saw him on campus or in a bar on the weekend would say. In that capacity, twice weekly, he took the stool and urine samples to Bender Lab.

Accounting and drumming, and introspection. Albany was a time for learning that success was not easily attained, and that personal growth was slow and subtle - that life could be difficult and lonely, and that we are each responsible for our own happiness. At Albany, Adam was constantly preoccupied with passing one of the accounting curriculum's rigorous weekly exams, and even more concerned with why he seemed to be invisible to women. Was he *that* on the periphery? 'What the fuck?' he constantly thought. 'All right, shut up and practice.'

Rhythm was starting to become a very fluid energy running through him. He allowed it to overtake him, regularly. Build up a sweat and keep going – walk outside, after practicing for hours, into an Albany winter night, where temperatures regularly got to twenty below, the condensation on his exposed skin immediately vaporizing, enveloping him in his very own cloud.

'You know you're smoking, right?' was the most common comment. 'The Human Cloud,' his stock response.

Forget about falling in love. Love was a level of fulfillment he accepted might have been beyond his grasp. How about a few nights of female companionship, a little yang to his yin. His standards were not that high. He just wanted to have a few beers and make-out with someone, flirt. But for whatever reason - immaturity, timing, a grand scheme - he didn't. And because he didn't he questioned the nature of his existence, and was practicing twenty, sometimes thirty hours a week in order to justify that questionable existence. Drumming became a compulsion. There were times when he'd look down at his hands and realize he was still clutching the same pair of drumsticks he thought he had retired for the night, so second nature was the sensation of having them in his grasp. All he had were his drums, and want to or not he practiced.

And, after all was said and done, Albany lead to his first job at Bimstein, Stein and Abromowitz, which allowed him to make enough money to move into an apartment soon after he graduated.

CHAPTER 13

· ·

The general cacophony

'Fish, do you know anyone looking for a roommate?' Adam asked, over fondue. Fish and he were having lunch at a crowded mid-town French bistro on a work-day Wednesday afternoon.

'Interesting,' Fish said. 'We are just living it out, aren't we? Like, if we think it, we help bring it about. My roommate just told me he was moving back to South Carolina, and I was actually thinking of you.'

''Cause I'm the only one you know who's still living with his parents, and if I don't get out soon I'm gonna freak out?'

'Exactly. You need to get out on your own... There is something you should know if we're gonna talk about you moving in with me.'

'That you wear diapers, and you're into bondage.'

'No, I'm serious. I'm... bisexual.'

'What, every time a woman tells you she wants to have sex with you, you say, "bye? Fish, I've known you were into men ever since I saw you leave The Black Oak with a guy wearing a 'Damn Straight I'm Gay' tee shirt. I admired your openness.'

'I don't remember that.'

Fish's dimpled black cheeks turned crimson. He had the longest, most naturally curled eye-lashes Adam had ever seen, with a Far Rockaway, Beach Street vibe that radiated out of his big jet eyes. When Fish looked at you, you knew you were being looked at. He was magnetically handsome, half African American, half Native American. Every girl Adam had ever met who knew him or met him was instantly smitten, including Adam's mother. She met Fish Adam's first day at college when his parents dropped him off. Standing at the entrance of his dorm with his Sly Stone afro, Elvis muttonchops, dashiki, and water-buffalo sandals, Fisher Huff extended his hand in a gesture of true friendliness and support.

'I'm one of the Resident Advisors,' he informed Adam. Resident Advisors volunteered to help incoming freshman get settled into dorm-life. 'If there's anything you need, just let me know.'

'Do you know where I can cop some herb?' Adam whispered. He was trying to impress this impressive looking black guy with his limited street cool.

'Why don't you come by my room after orientation. A few friends are gonna be hanging out.'

They had been friends ever since; not seeing each other often, twice a year, go out to dinner or a movie, or just hang out at Fish's apartment getting high and talking. There was definitely kinship, like they had been friendly in a past life or something. They ended up working a few blocks from each other, Fish in the garment center, where he sold suits for a high-end French designer, and Adam near Rockefeller Center, so it was easier to get together.

From the beginning Fish hypnotically transmitted his inclination not to talk about his sexuality. Respecting his privacy, Adam slid by the subject of his befriending a gay man surprisingly less affected than he thought he would have been. To pass judgment on someone's sexuality was as ignorant as racism or religious persecution. And as self-serving as patronization can be, he thought it was pretty cool that Fish was gay. A gay friend added to his reservoir of experience. It showed an increased sensitivity which, he hoped, made him more attractive to women. But that was just a potential fringe benefit. The core of their friendship was mutual respect. Fish could only be who he was; son of a preacher, old, grounded soul, a Whitmanesque, Melvillian love of men. Adam got the feeling Fish knew the ways of the world, and laughed at how absurd it all was sometimes. To be a gay black man anywhere couldn't have been easy.

When Fish graduated from Cortland, he moved into a spacious two-bedroom apartment in Forest Hills, Queens. A few days after his 'coming-out to Adam' lunch, Adam moved in with him, for less than three-hundred dollars a month. At twenty-two Adam was getting out on his own. Maybe that was the real bar mitzvah.

For obvious reasons, drumming doesn't belong in apartment buildings, unless it's an apartment building full of deaf tenants. Even Adam's practice of 'playing the air' – sitting on a stool, stomping the ground, and flailing in rhythm with sticks in his hand – wasn't suited, because his floor was his downstairs neighbor's ceiling, and his stomping shook them both.

The Yellow Pages directed him to The Music Building, an old converted textile factory squatting on the corner of Thirty-Eighth Street and Eighth Avenue in Manhattan. Hell's Kitchen, a crossroads for humanity's outcasts. At any given point on any given day one could find a heroine addict drag-queen prostitute in a matted wig hoping to work for bus-fare home – false eyelash hanging loose, smeared lipstick, a mess. Some of them reminded Adam of the guy in stall three in the Chicago Port Authority. The Music Building was twelve floors of both recording studios and rehearsal space, where, legend had it, Madonna, Iggy Pop, The Plasmatics, and many others had spent more than a little time. It was a two minute walk from the E train, which was a two minute walk from work. Within ten minutes of contacting the building's managing agent, Adam worked out a viable weekly schedule at a reasonable monthly rent. In a cool building. Even though the noise from his nightly practice was incorporated into the building's general cacophony, he was self-consciously driven to fully let go within the rhythm, drive it wherever it wanted to go… play his best in case someone heard him and asked him to join their band. It wasn't out of the realm of possibility. He rode the elevator with Lenny Kaye, Patti Smith's guitarist, and Lenny asked him if he knew a great bass player, which he didn't.

'You play drums,' Lenny said.

'I do.' Adam's backpack was a leather snare-drum case.

'Maybe one day we'll jam.'

'Love it.'

Life for Adam became a little less stressful, a little more complete. He got a seat on the subway every morning. He started reading, something he had never done. The first day he took the subway he sat there like a bored yuppy just staring at his fellow commuters for almost an hour. He hadn't thought commuting through. Seeing another urban professional across from him, in her own world, reading, he knew that was how he should spend that time, as Rat had recommended. The next day he went to Coliseum Books and bought a copy of *How To Talk Dirty and Influence People*, Lenny Bruce's autobiography, which he had heard was really good, which it was. When work was done, the ledgers shut, more numbers in boxes the next day, he walked to the subway, and then his studio and practiced for his scheduled time, five to nine. Then the subway home, and dinner with Fish in front of the television, usually Chinese or Italian take-out. Or the Mediterranean place on Queens Blvd near Sam Ash. On weekends he practiced at the studio all morning and all night sometimes.

The one distinct difference between his and Fish's lifestyles was that, as the midnight hour approached and Adam thought about going to bed,

Fish, who by that time had drank a few beers, done a few bongs, and smoked a few Newport 100's, announced he was going to go to his bar for a drink, which, loosely translated, meant he was going to pick up a guy and have penis for desert before going to bed. Sex in the gay world, Adam had come to learn, was often as frequent and natural as his fantasy of it in the straight world. Almost every night Fish would scrape himself off the couch, go to the local gay bar - and that was a densely populated part of the world – and have sex with guys from differing nationalities. The International House of Blow-Jobs. Adam admired Fish's fortitude. He rarely brought his dates back to the apartment, and when he had no choice, he did his best not to disturb Adam. The one time Adam realized the sounds that had awakened him were of two men fucking in the room next door, he did get upset, an initial discomfort, angry at himself and Fish. What was this saying about him? He was tense. He was living in a gay world.

'All right. Relax,' he said to himself.

First thing to do was stop-up his ears. Because of how loud Forest Hills at night was, Adam sometimes slept with earplugs. Queens is a big part of the city that never sleeps. But Adam needed to. Earplugs took the sting off.

'All right. Lemme get the pillow around my ears,' he directed himself. 'Anything? No. Good… Wait. Is that? No, that's a truck downshifting. All right, lemme try to get to sleep.' Successfully muffling the grunting, he calmed down enough to try to see it from Fish's perspective. Fish was just doing his thing. If Adam could, he would, too. It had been seven months since he had any sexual contact with anyone other than myself, and five before that. Another prolonged dry spell, humbling.

Only once during the entire three years Fish and Adam lived together did Adam come home while Fish was entertaining a friend. They were having a candlelight dinner together.

'Sit,' Fish's new friend Dean told Adam, patting the empty chair's seat cushion, his 's' sounding like steam escaping from a radiator valve. Out of courtesy, Fish had set a place anticipating his return.

'Fish tells me you play the drums.' Dean was like a black Joan Crawford.

'Dean, forget it. I told you he's straight.'

If Adam had been having dinner with a woman and she started openly flirting with his roommate, he would be very pissed off. But Fish calmly reiterated Adam's sexual orientation and offered him another helping of his homemade mashed potatoes. So many men. So little time.

'Oh Fish, come on. There's no harm in flirting. You remind me a little of my brother,' Dean said, turning to Adam. 'He's a bass player. Plays with that whole underground rock scene. Do you know the Bad Brains?'

Adam had. Bad Brains rocked.

'Really heavy,' Dean continued. 'A little too heavy for me.'

Ordinarily, this would have been the perfect set-up for Adam to describe how he like his rock, an expression he used numerous times. But he just couldn't tell Dean, 'For me, the harder the better.'

'I should tell my brother to give you a call.'

'I would love that.'

Adam thought, 'Maybe that's how it happens. Why not from a Fish boy-toy...'

'He needs to start getting out there,' Fish said. 'You should see him play.'

'Do you mind if I ask you a question. And I'm not coming onto you, per se. Have you ever considered being with a man?'

Fish hung back. He wanted to hear what Adam had to say.

'Not really,' Adam said. 'But at the rate I'm going...'

'Just let me know when you're ready,' Dean said.

Adam did recount the time he slept at a friend's house when they were eight years old, and, at his friend's suggestion, ended up tickling each other's wieners over their pajama bottoms.

'But other than that, nothing. Not even a gay dream.'

'More's the pity,' Dean said. 'I grew up on a farm, so all bets were off with us.'

After dinner, Adam went into his room to read, earplugs in. He knew what was going to transpire, and he needed to be as removed from it as he could. Right on cue, he felt the door to Fish's bedroom close, Fish and Dean quietly doing their business, which was done before the ice in Dean's half-filled water glass had a chance to melt.

'Was he suggesting that he had sex with farm animals?' Adam asked Fish later that night while were watching *The Tonight Show*. He realized there was virtually no shot that Dean was going to remember to tell his brother about the straight roommate of one of his one-night stands who was looking for a band. That was just party talk.

'Who knows? Probably.'

'Oy.'

'Oy is right. Speaking of oy, when are you going to out California to see your brother?'

'A week from Friday.'

'Oh, you're taking off a day. I hope it's good. Don't be surprised if his lifestyle is a lot different than you expect.'

From everything Adam had told him, Fish thought Charles was probably gay; the obsession with male bodybuilders, spending hours looking at their pictures in magazines, his low opinion of women, the fact that Charles had said to Adam, during one of their hypnotherapy cassette sales projection reviews, 'Sometimes you have to suck a man's dick to get ahead in this world. Literally.' When he said that, Adam up-thought, 'Oh...kay.' Then he thought, 'maybe you do, but...'

'To be honest,' Adam said, 'I'm not expecting much. Anything goes wrong and I'm outta there.'

'Well, I know your mother would love for it to work out. What else can she do but keep trying.' Adam's mother loved Fish. With her, he was himself. She felt protective of him. A tall, beautiful, young, hip, gay black-man making her feel like she still had it goin' on. Adam's father, Fish was more reserved around. He suspected Fish was gay, working in the garment industry, knowing about the business of men's fashion, Fish's subtle deflections of questions about his social life. But he was always warm and cordial toward Fish, and genuinely liked him. He knew Fish had Adam's best interests at heart. Adam's father never thought Adam was gay. His oldest son, maybe, maybe not. He didn't have a clue.

'Who knows? Maybe he'll surprise both of you,' Fish said.

'Yeah... Nah...'

It was hard to describe to someone how little chance there was that Charles would have a change of heart. Nothing had happened that would have precipitated one. He'd never been wired for compassion or courtesy.

All Adam wanted from the trip was for them to be civil, and for life to go on. Chances were, Charles wasn't someone Adam was going to be friends with. A lot of water had flowed under that bridge, all hope tinged with threat and self-preservation. Charles didn't deviate. All Adam was hoping for was a little less animosity, get rid of some of the baggage. Lighten the load a little.

It was also a good time to get away. Adam had interviewed with the media company Telecom for a Senior Accounting position for their newly acquired broadcasting division. If he got the job, which he felt he would, it would be a while before he would be eligible for a vacation. Almost from the beginning, he had been reaching the end of his appreciation for the straight accounting world of Bimstein, Stein and Abramowitz. Accounting, by nature, accounts for business that had already taken place, like the guy who sweeps up after the parade. Adam wanted something a little more progressive, a little more creative. So, after two months, he contacted a few headhunters, one of whom had learned that Telecom had just bought the maximum number of owned and operated radio and television stations allowed by law, and was looking to hire a new financial team to integrate the new division into the company fold.

'Oh my God do I want this job,' Adam thought, after the interview. TV and radio. Media and entertainment. He felt that was a much more appropriate industry for him than being a digit-brain for a CPA firm, although, because he was such a digit-brain during the day, he tried to redeem his self-esteem at night by letting go on drums, pushing himself beyond the pain barrier. Sometimes, in the middle of going off, he looked up and saw his right hand riding the cymbal as if disconnected from his mind, like muscle-memory from another incarnation. He felt the balance, the energy, free, in the humming blue twilight of the neon night, Eighth Avenue, where right outside his window was inner-city chaos.

But getting away from the drums for a few days would be a welcome break as well, allow Adam's shoulders to heal a little, like big-league pitchers, one day on, four days off. Adam didn't want to be done before his time. He was just getting near the end of the beginning of his musical education. There was still a long way to go.

CHAPTER 14

. . . .

That looks exactly like...

As the day of departure drew nearer, Adam became excited. He hadn't been to California since he hitched there a few years before; crawdads at Big Sur with the Mormons, Disneyland as anti-climax, the threat of the desert. And he had never been on an airplane. It was about time. He also figured not much could go too wrong in two days. If it did, he could get a cheap hotel to stay at, and then he was outta there.

'How cheap?' his mother asked, the Sunday before the trip. Adam had driven the Honda 450 Nighthawk he bought a few months before out to visit his parents, let them wish him a bon voyage. Having a car in Queens was impossible. There were no available parking spaces, at least not without going through a Kafkaesque nightmare. A motorcycle was the answer, quickly becoming an integral part of Adam's life, right down to how it affected his wardrobe – a drumming, MC jacket-wearing accountant.

'Why don't you give me, like, an extra... four-hundred, and if I don't spend it I'll give it back to you.' She knew she'd never see that money.

'Here's and extra three-hundred. It's more than enough. Try to have a good time. Maybe he just needed to be away.' She was getting choked up. 'If you're not feeling that it's right, it's okay to leave. You know it's not you. You're doing everything you can. You always did. Be safe. I love you.'

Charles wasn't at the airport to meet Adam. No olive branch. Same as it ever was.

'Just take a taxi,' his mother said. He called her from an LAX payphone, after leaving a few messages on his brother's answering machine. 'You have his address. Don't make a big deal out of it.'

'I really didn't expect anything else. But... Anyway, I wish I had that extra hundred.'

'What for?'

'I don't know. Buy some good California weed.'

'Very funny. Don't be an idiot, all right? Just watch yourself. Call me when you get to his house. Please take care of yourself.'

'I will.'

When Adam got to his brother's house, the doors were locked, and there was no one home. Charles lived in a middle-income suburb about forty minutes from the airport in a small bungalow that appeared to be in the backyard of a larger split-level house facing the street named in his brother's address. That explained why his address was 1428 ½ Second Street. His house looked like it could have been a converted, free-standing two-car garage. Adam noticed that a lot of the houses in the neighborhood had bungalows in their backyards.

'Definitely a California thing,' Adam thought. 'Okay, what the fuck am I gonna do now?'

He walked around the neighborhood for a while, see what he could see. He was on vacation. Time to take a deep breath and let the tension go, under a beautiful blue California sky.

'He's gotta come back eventually,' Adam thought.

The neighborhood was mellow. The houses were a little smaller than a typical Long Island suburb, a lot more flowers and color, a little less front lawn.

After about twenty minutes Adam realized he was walking for the sake of walking. It was a suburb. He wasn't going to suddenly find himself gazing upon some natural wonder. He headed back to Charles's house.

'I'll give him another two hours,' Adam thought. 'What time is it? Wow, it's already three.' The plane landed around noon. 'Okay, five. Then I gotta find a place.'

Plan B: Find a place, spend the night, maybe see a movie, definitely have a good dinner, stop stressing about Charles. He would call again in the morning. If they got together, and it was good, great. Adam didn't want to freak out over it. It wasn't as if he had come to California with unrealistic expectations. In fact he was expecting exactly what he was getting. He was participating in it. He was a part of the equation, like Einstein's theory of the observer and the observed, their interrelatedness.

Sitting in front of his brother's house, leaning back against his backpack, the one he used the last time he was in California, he read *War And Peace*, getting lost in its profound beauty and depth. The early evening air was warm and pleasant, and quiet, like the neighborhood was deserted. Adam was mellow. His first plane-ride. He got a little nauseous during take-off, and a few other times during the flight, mostly if the plane was banking. But other than that it was good. It got him across the country in around six hours.

'I wonder if there's a motel around here,' he thought. 'There's gotta be something near the airport.'

At around 4:30 Adam heard a car pull up in front of the house on the street.

'There you are,' his brother said, coming around the side of the house. 'Where were you?'

His feigned aggression was his way of letting Adam know he knew he should have been at the airport to welcome him, or at least been back sooner, although he offered no excuse. The fact that, after not speaking for so long, he hadn't evolved beyond the subtle bullying was disappointing, and at the same time indicative. Adam knew he should watch what he said and did.

'Maybe I should get the fuck outta here right now,' he thought. 'Nah, let's see what happens.'

At least Charles wasn't being a psycho. He had started losing his hair – at the time he was twenty-five – and was pale, with a darkened, somewhat sunken look around his eyes. He had also gained weight, not in a muscular way. It was sad to see him looking like he was headed in the wrong direction. It was also very apparent how estranged they had become. Adam felt very little connection to the man standing in front of him. But that seemed like a good thing. He thought they both were glad they didn't have much to do with each other. Neither of them needed the drama.

'Anyway, it's good that you're here,' Charles continued. 'Why don't you bring your backpack in. I know this place is a shit-hole, but as soon as I get a few more clients, I'm gonna fix it up. You should see what some people do with these. Sorry I don't have a full couch, but you're welcome to that,' a threadbare, worn-smelling loveseat that would have required Adam to sleep in extreme fetal position. 'Or I have a sleeping-bag, and you can sleep on the carpet over there,' between the wall and the side of the loveseat.

'I'll go with the sleeping-bag.' Adam would rather stretch out than sleep all bunched up.

Those were more civil words strung together than Charles had spoken to Adam in longer than Adam could remember.

'All right. Let's see how this goes,' he thought.

It took Adam a few moments to take in who his brother was and how he was living. His house looked like nothing had been done to it since it was built in the late '50's; the paint on the walls discolored, the linoleum floors uneven, and in some places chipped. The kitchen had the standard cheap white wooden cabinets, with the black ace-shaped wrought-iron pulls. A few of the cabinet doors were hanging a little off-center. And the old, white, round-edged Kelvinator had a noticeable hum. On the walls, throughout the four rooms, including the bathroom, were hand-written notes written on ripped pieces of scrap paper, and scotch-taped randomly to the walls, with lines like, 'You are the master of your destiny' and 'You are the best you can be.' All of them were positive messages, daily affirmations. It just felt a little weird to Adam the way they were displayed, like reminders in an otherwise troubled world, lifelines. The need to keep being reminded. Better to assimilate those sentiments enough to not need to be reminded every day, randomly taped to the wall, in Charles's habitually poor penmanship.

'Those are my affirmations,' Charles said, noticing Adam notice.

The notes were all over the place. One said 'Win' and another 'Mind is power'.

'Like this one, "Work sweat conquer". It's all in your mind,' Charles said. 'You should write down what you want, get your mind used to believing you can achieve it.'

'Actually, I have been writing, just a little… just starting. It's good. I can see it being something. But more than anything I've been practicing drums every day for like hours a day. I'm really into it.'

Adam thought because Charles had been a drummer, he could relate. Adam saw, by the way Charles said, 'That's great,' that he could give a shit.

'And I started riding a motorcycle.'

That brought Charles out of his affirmation reverie. He was genuinely surprised, a little taken back. He realized he had no idea who his brother really was. Adam driving a motorcycle? He actually seemed a little timid for a few moments. Adam felt good redefining Charles's image of him, let him know he was his own man, or at least on his way.

'You'd fit right in out here. Everybody's got a motorcycle. Yuppie bikers. ' He was so used to thinking it, he didn't think to not say it.

'Still a dick,' Adam thought. 'Unbelievable. All right, let that one go.'

'You've been out here before, haven't you?'

'I was out here when I hitched across country.'

'Oh yeah. What's his name left. Great friend.'

Actually, Stevie and Adam stayed in contact through college. Stevie was working in computer sales, living in Manhattan, and still fucking very beautiful women. He still had an irresistible smile, which he wore way more often than not. His and Adam's roots ran deep. And Adam met Chris through his intervention. If he hadn't gone home, that never would have happened.

Even though Charles knew Stevie was Adam's good friend, had seen him at their house many times, he ignored him when he saw him; at school, at a sporting event, wherever. Refused to acknowledge him. That was Charles.

'So whadda ya got planned?' Adam asked, steering the focus away from negative energy toward anything else.

'I thought we would go to this Thai place, and then we're gonna meet a friend of mine at the movies. Mommy's paying, right?'

'Yes.'

'But first I wanna rest. Gimme like an hour. Please let me rest.'

What was Adam gonna do, sing a-cappella? He sat on Charles played-out loveseat, and was swept away by *War And Peace*.

An hour and twenty minutes later they were driving through Charles's neighborhood in his old beat-up jeep. Adam realized it might have been the first time he had been in the passenger seat with his brother behind the wheel. Try, as he did, he couldn't remember one time his brother had driven him anywhere.

'He must've,' he thought, although he was still drawing a blank. Usually, the three boys had been in the back. And when they got older they weren't in a car together much.

'I think we're seeing *Fast Times At Ridgemont High*', Charles said, reaching into his pocket and pulling out a joint. Adam had never gotten stoned with his brother. He didn't know Charles smoked so casually. Adam had never even smelled pot around him, although he had stolen pot from him a few times.

'Okay,' Adam thought. 'Give it a shot.' Kind of like when Native Americans share tobacco. By some law of magic it forms a bond.

Charles lit the joint with the car lighter, took a hit, took the joint out of his mouth and held it. After he exhaled, he took a deep breath, exhaled again, and on the beginning of the intake of the next breath, he took another hit.

'Okay,' Adam thought, 'a double hit.'

When Charles didn't pass the joint after the second hit, but just held it, keeping his eyes on the road, in his own world, and then took another hit, Adam began to wonder if he was actually not going to pass it, a level of disconnect Adam had to wait around to see to believe, just to see if it was possible that Charles could be so, either completely in his own space and time, or that much of a scum-bag.

After Charles actually didn't pass it, Adam decided not to say anything. He wanted to keep the chasm between them as wide as it was, maybe even let it grow, in silence. Forever distant. Charles wasn't withholding the natural, friendly act of passing a joint to the person next to him out of deference to or concern for Adam's well-being. It was something else, something Adam was trying to define as it was happening because of how extraordinary it was. He couldn't. The disconnect was too great.

'This guy is wigged out, man,' Adam thought. Not that he hated Charles. It was yet another indefinable act in a long line of indefinable acts. If it didn't escalate, let it alone. Path of least resistance. Everything else led to stress.

'At least I'm not gonna run into a buzz-kill', he thought. He wasn't buzzed. He was a little relieved that he didn't have deal with his brother with anything other than his full wits about him.

Dinner started almost pleasantly. Charles was really stoned, and that seemed to smooth out the rough edges of his personality. It seemed pot was good for him, under certain conditions. Adam was seeing it happen. To account for Charles not including him in the ritual of getting stoned together, he couldn't. At least his brother and he were having a normal conversation about fitness and self-improvement.

'It's all in your mind,' Charles was saying. 'You should wake up every day and say 'I am. I will.' Say it. Be who you wanna be.'

'You mean say it now?'

'Yeah. Every time you say it, you feel stronger.'

'Okay… I am. I will.'

'What will you?' he asked, with elevated intensity.

'Well… right now I will use my chopsticks to pick up this piece of shrimp. I'm just kidding. It's been about drumming, and starting to think about things to write about. I mean, I just got this new job that I start on Tuesday…'

'You have to manifest the power of your mind. Embrace it… beyond the pain; all the shit we've had to live through. Transform the pain into energy, and focus that energy. With that focus, you can achieve anything you want.'

'Yeah, doing it,' Adam concurred. 'I'm learning there's no shortcuts. Progress is slow. You better than anyone know what Arnold said, 'No pain, no gain.'

'Fuck Arnold.'

Adam sensed trouble in the bodybuilding world. But, of course. It's extreme competition. Your opponent is your enemy, especially the alpha male.

'Let me ask you something,' Charles continued. 'Have you made a dime from your drums?' A challenge. Unnecessary.

'Actually, I have. Not a lot. That's so not what it's about for me right now.'

'That's bullshit, and you know it.'

Adam thought because his answers to Charles's questions were reasonable, Charles was getting a little put off. He had never really thought of Adam as someone with a heart and soul, especially one who could implement some of his motivational ideas in a practical way, independent of his guidance. Neither had he thought that he would be preaching to the choir from a pulpit the choir had long before stopped attending.

'Listen, let me tell you something,' out of nowhere, 'the shit I had to deal with in that house…'

'What shit?' Adam was surprised Charles went there so abruptly, so definitively, but was right there with him, glad to have him lay some cards on the table. Adam lived in the house with Charles their entire childhoods. There wasn't that much shit, other than what Charles generally instigated. True, their mother could get scary, and follow through with a slap in the face, a few slaps, when all was said and done. But Adam believed, or remembered, or had blocked out reality and replaced it with a symbolic counter-narrative that Charles caught much less of the physical punishment than Barry or him. Hitting Charles was like baiting a wolverine. It wasn't worth it; sometimes necessary, and seen through, but mostly redirected out of helplessness and frustration.

'Yeah, what about the time mommy broke her arm, she hit me so hard?' he said.

'That's not how it happened,' Adam insisted. 'I was there. You said you wished I was dead, and she was so pissed off at you, that she went to grab you, and she fell forward. That's all it was. She didn't hit you.'

It was sad to see Charles shrink back into himself like a lost child. He had smoked the whole joint, and, Adam was guessing, had never been that stoned in so surreal a moment; busted... by his brother? Adam saw the confusion, and palpably felt Charles's panic, like the bottom had gone out, like Molly must have felt in her drug-induced swoon. Charles had come to believe the lie about how their mother had broken her arm. He had built a whole mythology around being an abused child, a mythology so serious that it was calling him to leave his family; like the rules of a cult bound by fear. That was one of the main reasons it felt so weird for Adam to make that trip in the first place. Neither of them really wanted it. Adam certainly didn't want to be the mirror reflecting the hard truth, at least not on a long weekend that was supposed to be a vacation, not some gestalt therapy session exposing a lifetime of his brother's bullshit.

Regaining his composure – Adam could see the process of Charles trying to reclaim himself, mentally reciting his affirmations – Charles continued to try and justify his actions.

'Well, there's plenty of other shit. I'm glad to be out of there. There's a lot of things I wanna do. TV appearances, articles. I'm supposed to start writing for Joel Weinreb, an article every month. I'm telling you, I'm gonna make this thing huge. I'm sittin' on top of the world, pal.'

'I'm just going on record that I think you may have talked yourself into something that didn't actually happen.'

'We'll see,' Charles said, smug.

'We'll see what?' Adam thought. Either it happened or it didn't happen. And it didn't. It was such a fundamental disconnect that it, once again, confirmed how uncool Charles was. Individually, a mis-remembered memory was nothing. Everyone tended to remember some things the way they want, or need to. But knowing his brother was using a false pretense to justify his life choices was ridiculous, but also, Adam realized, typical. Charles's wall was so thick, there was no sense trying to get inside. There was nothing there Adam wanted. Better to stay on the outside, which, as he looked at the strange man, his brother, was where he intended to stay, unless Charles underwent a transformation, which wasn't likely.

'You know what I wanted to see,' Adam said, completely changing the focus, 'the Le Brea Tar-pits.'

'What the hell is that?' It seemed Charles was glad the subject was changed.

'It's like this pre-historic place where they found saber-tooth tigers and dinosaur bones. It's gotta be a designated tourist kinda place. I see La Brea all over the place.' Adam was surprised Charles hadn't heard of it. Adam had been hearing about it since he was young.

'When you get back to my place you can look it up. By the way, I have to see clients tomorrow, so you'll have to figure out something to do. I should be back around five. And tomorrow night there's a live Grateful Dead concert that their showing on TV and playing on radio, like a simulcast. I thought for your last night, we could hang out and watch that together. Whadda you think?'

'Wow... Wow.'

It was the first time in longer than Adam could remember that Charles had made such a gesture of inclusion. It was almost like a door was opening, and out of it, the negative energy... To let that shit go... Was that what just happened?

After a few frames Adam thought, 'Nah, I don't think so.' Too many winters spent keeping out of Charles's way. But Adam knew this gesture, watching a live Grateful Dead concert together, was genuine, a beautiful proposition. The thought of it silenced some of the clatter of the past, recent and distant; Charles not meeting him at the airport, not passing the joint, twenty-odd years of reproach, threatening to shoot him, pointing a gun in his face. His gesture was so unusual Adam thought it could be a trick. But that was not how his brother expressed himself. He was more direct, almost always out front. In one gesture, Charles made Adam feel the whole trip might have been worth taking. A mother's distant dream.

The rest of the night continued the trend of possible transformation. They met Charles's friend in front of the movie-theater – the biggest guy Adam had ever seen. He was one of those guys in the magazine. Wild looking in person. Beaming. Skin-tight tee shirt, arms as big as Adam's thighs, and a neck as wide as his head. It was intense just to be around him. Heavy athletic energy. A magnified smile. Steroid intensity. When the guy got excited, which he did about most of the things he liked to talk about, he got as red as a stop sign, and his veins really started popping. Adam was not naïve about steroids. A majority of professional body-builders overdid it. But if achieving that level of physical human potential required chemical enhancement, Adam believed you go for it. Go for the limit. If you over-juiced, you were gonna pay somewhere down the line. But there was a way in and a way out, when your body can metabolize it all, the window of peak performance, part of the regimen, without causing any damage. People drink, smoke, do drugs, stop, no problem. No vice in moderation is going to be that bad for you. In fact, it may enhance your life. Just because someone tells you something is bad for you doesn't mean that it is. You have to follow your own instincts. As long as it stays within 'metabolizable without doing permanent damage', you go for it, if you hear the calling. And a lot of guys, and some women heard it.

'Adam, this is my friend Paul. He's gonna kick Arnold's ass,' at which point Paul howled like a howler monkey, so loud that everyone within a twenty-yard radius stopped what they were doing and looked over, giving Paul all the attention he needed to take off his shirt and go through an abridged but unbelievably surreal, but at the same time professional pose-down. The movie didn't start for fifteen minutes, Paul had an audience, and he knew how to work it. The people loved it. Cheered. Whistled. He was massive. Literally muscles on top of muscles.

'You're outta your mind,' Charles said smiling, and shaking his head.

'You love it,' Paul said.

Even in the movie-theater Paul was compelled to entertain, yelling one or two comments at the screen, which the audience generally laughed at. He even did a quick pose sequence, standing up into the classic flexed-bicep pose at an appropriate point in the movie, the scene with bodybuilders on the beach checking each other out. And there was Paul, on screen, a real-life extra doing one-hundred-eighty-pound free-weight tricep reverse-curls.

'Go Paul,' someone in the audience yelled. People knew who he was. It was very fun energy to be around. It took nothing away from the movie, which was also fun. And zero negative vibe from Charles, who was at times engaging and considerate. Adam couldn't help thinking, 'So, this is what it's like.'

'You wanna come out with us for something to eat,' Charles asked, outside the theater after the movie. Charles had ordered and eaten two full dinners at the Thai place, and drank a gallon of water. Since he had started lifting weights, Charles's food consumption was at least double the normal adult. The problem was, he didn't metabolize it into ultimate muscle growth. That wasn't his physical make-up; he didn't cut like an Adonis. He got huge, powerful, but without the hyper-definition, without being able to see the sinews between the six-pack. As hard as he worked out, and he generally worked out as hard as the most dedicated body-builder, he never became as physically defined as the men in his magazines. But that didn't stop him from trying. Or believing he was that.

Adam saw his brother compete in one body-building competition. Charles had just graduated from college, a few months before moving to California, and, more than wanting Adam to come to see him compete, he needed Adam to drive him to the competition. He said he needed to mentally prepare, and not be distracted by traffic. It was Adam's pleasure to see his brother compete in something he believed in, something Adam thought was pretty cool, too. Charles had been working out like a madman for a few years. In fact, the group of people he used to work out with, one of whom was a world famous karate sensei known for the intensity of his commitment, used to call Charles 'Madman' because he, apparently, was more intense than all of them. Adam wasn't sure how much steroids played a part in that, but it didn't take anything away from the fact that his brother poured everything he had into the thing he believed he was meant to be and do. Unfortunately, as big and strong as he was, he wasn't nearly as defined as some of the other guys he posed-off with. Yet when the MC announced third place, then second place, and Charles's name hadn't been called yet, he actually thought he had won. And when he realized he hadn't even placed, he was shocked, not so much because he had lost, but because he believed he had been ripped off.

After the competition they went to a burger joint where Charles scarfed down three burgers in complete silence.

'You looked huge out there,' Adam said, trying to boost his brother's morale.

'Nothin' I can do about it now. I'll show 'em...'

It was about eleven o'clock LA time, which meant two New York time. If Adam went out to eat with his brother and Paul, he wouldn't get to sleep for at least an hour. Considering he was still full from dinner, and he had been up since six-thirty, and it was an emotionally draining day, he declined Charles's invitation. He told him it was probably a better idea if he dropped him off at his house.

'I'm really beat,' Adam said.

'Listen,' Charles said, leaning into Adam so no one else could hear, 'I know mommy gave you some money for me, so let me have it, all right?'

Adam wasn't sure what their mother had told Charles; something, Adam got the feeling, to the effect of, 'I'll send him with enough money for you guys to have a good time.' She had never mentioned to Adam that the money she gave him was specifically for his brother. She had given him five-hundred dollars altogether; two-hundred for food and fun, and three-hundred just in case. But since nothing seemed to be going wrong, he didn't think twice about giving his brother some money.

'Yeah, okay.' He gave him a hundred dollars.

'Is that it?' Charles asked. It felt like Adam was getting shaken down. He gave his brother another hundred just to bring back the harmony that had momentarily, and so easily, vanished.

Charles genuinely appreciated the extra money, like he had a weight lifted from his muscle-bound shoulders. Adam still had more than he would need. The next night they were staying in to watch the Grateful Dead on television.

'Okay brother, nice to meet ya,' Paul said, pulling Adam into his all-encompassing hug. Charles had pulled up in front of the house his house was behind. It was nice that Paul got out. It all felt heightened - being in southern California, the unique calm and quiet, this guy, who had nothing but good crazy energy... That, plus a weakening of the defense mechanism Adam had been twenty-some-odd years building. Everything seemed to be in balance. No negative energy.

'The door's open,' Charles said, staying in the car.

'That was really fun,' Adam told Paul.

'You know your brother's a wildman, right?'

'So they say.' They didn't have to grow up with him.

When Adam was alone on top of the sleeping bag, he let the quietness settle him. It was a warm night, too warm to sleep inside the sleeping-bag, especially one that smelled like it had never been cleaned. But it wasn't too warm that he would be uncomfortable.

'That was good,' he thought, his brother as a nice guy. 'Why couldn't he have been like that before? Whadda ya gonna do? What am I gonna do tomorrow? Definitely try to hit the Le Brea Tar-pits. Maybe just do the touristy thing in Hollywood... I still can't believe Nancy ended up making out with that guy right in fronna me.'

There was an accountant at Bimstein, Stein, and Abramowitz Adam had become friendly with. Nancy Kalper; very cute, almost always smiling, Long Island born and bred, Ashkenazi. Although they had never been out on a date, they had been out together a few times as part of an office group, and always ended up hanging out with each other. Adam had been building up to asking her out, until the appropriate time presented itself. She beat him to it, or so he thought. She asked him if he wanted to go out to the Hamptons with her. She was a little nervous when she asked, but also resolute. She rented a house with many others, some friends, some fellow random renters. One of the people she shared the house with couldn't make it out that weekend and she asked him if she could ask a friend if he was interested. Her body language and presentation lead Adam to understand her offer was more platonic than romantic. He knew she wasn't coming onto him. She was being cordial, friendly. But he couldn't shake the vibe that he had a real shot with her.

Everything was about groups in the Hamptons. Groups out to dinner, groups going to parties, groups having fun. It was like Club Med - all the ingredients for a really good time, do with it what you will. Nancy and Adam hung out with a group of her housemates, who were all young urban professionals, who knew how to party. After dinner at a local bar and grill - delicious burger and fries, a little pricey; with a few beers about forty bucks - Adam thought things were going well with Nancy. The whole group got into their respective rides and ended up at a party at a house on Dune Road, right on the ocean, with an 'all the beer and wine you can drink' cover-charge of twenty dollars a person.

'Lemme get that,' Adam said, as Nancy was taking out her wallet.

'No. No. That's very sweet.'

'Okay,' he thought. 'This may be a little farther away than I thought, but not insurmountable.' It was going to need some something, some quality time, when talking together felt really good and they both knew it. If she gave him that, he would find a way in. Much of her attention hovered around them. He appreciated her trying to include him in her group. Even at the party, they were mostly hanging out together, sometimes going their separate ways, always coming back together for a beer and a laugh.

'I'll be right back,' Adam said to her, on one of their longer rendezvous by the pool. Still nothing suggesting intimacy, but he thought he would try to steer it in that direction, hopefully subtly, after he took a much needed piss.

The piss took a while, which sucked. It took so long that Adam considered going back to Nancy to explain what was taking so long, insuring that he would lose his place on line for the one bathroom on that floor, still not having pissed, after five beers.

Coming back from the bathroom, reenergized, thinking, 'This could be good,' and seeing Nancy making out, a full-on mug-down, with a guy she had introduced Adam to a little earlier, was a buzz-kill unlike any he had ever experienced. Stopped him right in his tracks. He felt defeated. He hadn't even realize he was competing. Maybe that was her plan all along. So close, yet so far. He had badly misread Nancy's invitation. Yes, some hints along the way that it was a 'we work together, you're a really nice guy but...' friendship. Still, he thought he had a shot. Apparently, he had never been in the running. She actually looked a little annoyed when she saw him looking at her with dismay, like she was thinking, 'I can't believe you thought that.'

He watched her compose herself before she came over to him hand in hand with the guy she had been making out with, a cute guy in an Izod shirt, a little taller than Adam, beautiful, happy, suntanned smile. In a different scenario, Adam would have liked the guy.

'Adam, this is John.' They shook hands. 'You having a good time?'

'Yuh.'

'I'm gonna tell my friend to let you know when he's going back to the house so you have a ride.'

'Thanks.'

Adam didn't know what to say. He needed a minute or two to get his bearings. All of a sudden he was out in the Hamptons alone having already drank five beers. He felt like the odd man out.

He did end up talking to a girl who hated the Hamptons scene but knew you got out of it what you put into it. Not really feeling a rapport with his new junior account manager at a big advertising agency friend but hoping for the long-shot, he was buzzed enough to go where the evening took him, which, ultimately, was back to Nancy's house alone, and then on the first Hampton Jitney home.

Nancy and he didn't speak much after that.

'Cunt,' he thought, laying on top of his brother's sleeping-bag, wondering when sleep would overtake him. 'No, not really,' he internally corrected himself. 'That's just me projecting. She was just being friendly. She invited me out there, didn't charge me, introduced me to a lot of people. It was more than most people do. I wonder if that's how she was thinking of it. Probably, since that's what she did.' He felt like the dog along the water carrying a white dove in his mouth, who sees reflected over the waves the shadow of a bird overhead, and drops the white bird in the sand and chases after the reflection, losing at the same time both the image and what's real. 'Nice goin'…' he admonished himself.

When Adam finally got comfortable – he hadn't slept on the floor or the ground in years - he realized how tired he was. But for some reason he couldn't get to sleep, like some kind of annoying effect of jet-lag. He was tired, his body was still, he could shut off his mind to everything but his breathing... And still he was conscious that he wasn't asleep yet. Minutes. Hours. His 'don't think of anything and just feel the breath through his nostrils' not transitioning. All he was doing was thinking that he was trying to fall asleep by trying to feel the breath through his nostrils.

When he heard his brother come in, he knew immediately he was going to feign sleep. There wasn't a chance he was going to engage Charles in any way unless Charles initiated it, which he didn't. He went into the kitchen, turned on the light, opened the faucet, drank two glasses of water, turned off the light, went into his bedroom, got undressed, went to the bathroom in his underwear – Adam peeked – and took the longest piss Adam had ever heard. Nobody pisses that long. He pissed longer than the fire alarm that went off after he had started to piss. When the sound of the siren started to die away, a minute or two later, Adam could hear his brother still pissing. Massive steroids, gallons of water to flush it out, he stood in front of the toilet exhausted and just let it go. Then he went back into his room, closed his door, and went to sleep.

The last thing Adam remembered at 7:42 when he awoke, was that it was 6:16 the last time he had looked. One hour and twenty-six minutes of sleep. And, try as he might he couldn't get back to sleep, until, at 8:31 he gave up, and decided to get up. He was on vacation.

Charles was still sleeping when he was out the door looking for a fun LA breakfast place. His plan was to have breakfast, then go to The Le Brea tar-pits. After that, since he had to be back by five, he had to see how the day went. It wasn't a lot of time. In most cities, you have to allow for time to get around. Cities where the cars are concentrated. Traffic was inevitable.

He found a coffee shop in a little strip-mall on Santa Monica Blvd. that had an easy Southern California vibe. Organic products. Delicious blueberry/banana pancakes. Reasonably priced. A perfect vacation breakfast place.

'It would'a been more perfect if I was hangin' with someone,' he thought on the taxi-ride over to the tar-pits. 'Don't worry about it. Enjoy the day.'

Oil had been bubbling up to the surface of the area around Hancock Park for tens of thousands of years, forming deposits that got thick and adhesive enough to trap animals. Easy prey. But the predators became trapped prey themselves. And their predators after them. Millennia later, the city of Los Angeles erected an enclosed observation area and museum to commemorate that prehistoric wonder. The pits themselves looked like the ponds of hell; huge black bone-filled holes in the ground – right on Wilshire Blvd. The museum had some incredible exhibits; ground sloths, saber-toothed tigers, dire wolves.

'I didn't know they actually existed,' Adam thought, looking at the ancient skeleton of The Dead song's namesake. 'That thing musta been huge.' But it was dwarfed, as most other animals were, by the perfectly preserved skeleton of a Columbian Mammoth, whose tusks were bigger than the spears and men who hunted them.

With the song *Dire Wolf* looping through his head, he thought about the evening to come, hanging out alone with his brother.

'I hope he's cool. If he's not, I'm outta there in a second. This whole thing could change in like...'

He realized what he was doing. He was at a beautiful, interesting place stressing about his brother; not seeing the wonders of nature around him, but going inside and dwelling on negative energy. A sense memory followed. 'The same thing happened... where was it... the petroglyphs. I started buggin' 'cause o' my car, in the middle of a sanctified reserve... I can't believe I thought that guy was a shill. What a great guy. Severo...'

Since it was still early, a little after eleven, he had plenty of time to check out Venice Beach - the quintessential LA experience. Fish had recently been there on business and told Adam he had a really good time. Adam told him he probably wasn't gonna be hanging out in the same circles he hung out in.

'I'm not talking about a gay thing,' Fish had said, one of the few times he had referred to his sexuality. 'You should check it out. You'd love it.'

Even though he had grown up less than five miles from the Atlantic Ocean, and spent every summer on the beach, Adam definitely felt the eclectic party vibe more at Venice Beach. It was a microcosm of all that was free-spirited and eccentric; musicians, surfer dudes, girls in very-skimpy bikinis, bodybuilders, street performers, hacky-sack players, and the Pacific Ocean. The state-street area in Long Beach, Long Island had that kind of vibe; a beach community with small, cool houses close together, and bars and shops, then the dunes and the majestic ocean. But Venice Beach was a carnival of life.

As Adam walked along the sidewalk right off the sand – a promenade along one of the most colorful beach scenes on the planet – something caught his eye. He was looking for a spot where he could lay his towel down and hang out for a while, maybe go for a swim, body-surf.

'I could show these guys a thing or two,' he thought. He had been body-surfing his whole life. 'Wow, that looks exactly like...' Chris. As soon as he thought it, she looked up and saw him looking. Instant recognition. She was pleasantly shocked, a huge smile of reunion he was drawn to. She looked exactly the same, in the best way.

'Adam... Oh my God, what...'

She hugged him with conviction. He breathed it in.

'You're not real, right?' he said, a convergence of time and place. 'This is an amazing dream.'

As he said that, he felt he was being disingenuous. He had been a dick to her. She, a remarkable friend, and he treated her like a pariah, because he was too immature to know how to be friends with her, with a girl; the very definition of a dick-head.

But he wasn't getting any sense of inhibition from her.

'I know. I'm having it too,' she said. 'What are you doing here? I swear to God I was just thinking about you the other day.'

The three some-odd years after his relationship with Molly were the leanest Adam had since losing his virginity. Less than a hand-full of less than meaningful sexual encounters. Zero female companionship... And there was Chris in a string bikini top and short jean-shorts. He had never seen her so tan. It made her blue eyes radiant.

'And I appeared. *That* must be why I'm here,' he said. 'Or am I dreaming this, and that's why *you're* here?'

'Maybe we're both having the same dream.'

'Wow. Chris. I can't believe it.' Out of his periphery Adam perceived a juggling unicyclist, and the mime. It was all surreal, Chris there, him confronting his weaker self, trying to soft-pedal around it, keep them in the present... a mime. He hesitated. He knew he shouldn't be so care-free with someone he had been so dismissive to. 'I...' He couldn't find the words to let Chris know he knew what a dick he was, or even to try to make some lame apology... one of the rare times he couldn't even begin to bullshit his way out of something, kind of like Charles must have felt when Adam corrected him about how their mother had broken her arm.

Chris picked up on the vibe. She always did.

'Oh. Got it,' she said, 'Listen, I would have loved to have kept what we had. God. But, if I could be honest, though. I did think, more than a few times, a letter would've served you better in the long run. I'm just saying.'

'Yeah.'

'Yeah... You do what you have to do, I guess.' She was smiling.

'Not so sure how great that is either. Can I get a do-over?'

'Nope. Isn't that an expression, 'There are no do-overs.'? Anyway, you're here, so... It's crazy. I'm glad. I hope you can hang out with me. What are you... do you live out here?'

'No, I'm actually visiting my brother.'

'He's going to school out here? Barry right?'

'No, my brother Charles.'

'Oh... Good. You guys worked it out.'

'No. No,' Adam said. It was funny how far away somebody saying those words 'you guys worked it out', and reality were. Charles wasn't the kind of guy who cared to work things out with Adam. One civil night did not a chasm bridge. 'It's more kinda like a last ditch effort. Although last night, for the first time, we hung out.'

'Okay. That's good. One step at a time. So, are you here for a while, or...'

'I got here yesterday afternoon, and I'm leaving tomorrow morning.' Again, the mime, out of Adam's periphery, closer this time. 'Is he coming over to us?' Adam thought. He did. As Chris and Adam were standing on the warm sand next to Chris's blanket-sized, rainbow-colored towel, the mime got down on one knee in front of Chris and started pantomiming a love scene, which Chris, based on her expression, thoroughly enjoyed. But because Adam's time was limited, and he didn't want anyone, mime included – he recognized he was being uncharacteristically rigid - stealing Chris's attention, he fished a five dollar bill out of his wallet, and with a smile and a head-bob suggesting 'thank you' and 'scram' handed it to the mime who, with a truly mute thespian flourish, thanked them profusely, miming his way to his next audience.'

'I think that mime just proposed to you,' Adam said.

'I see him here all the time. This place is like that. I love it though.'

'So, are you living out here?'

'For almost two years. But I'm moving back home in three weeks, two weeks, oh my God. Soon. First I'm gonna spend a week with Lynn and Tom. I can't wait to tell 'em I saw you. They'll flip.'

'Oh my God... They need to have a happy ending. That's the shit that keeps the world in balance. If they're good, the world's good.'

'Well, they're doing good so far. They have a two year old daughter who kills me, in her little cowgirl boots... and number two's due in a couple of weeks.'

Adam laughed. 'Good. Please give them my love.'

Knowing that his summer adventure with Stevie and then Chris had important elements that continued and flourished and might be eternal grounded Adam for a moment – sensing the rhythm of life, the interconnectedness, Chris, a lost friend found, deeper than that.

'Do you accept my apology for being a dick?' he suddenly confessed. 'I know I should've been a better man. I'm sorry. I really am. You deserved way better than that."

'Yes I did. And I do... Wow, I'm actually getting to say that to you. It feels good... You have to ask me for my apology again.'

'Do you accept my apology for being such a dick?'

She took two beats before saying, 'Yes. Was it worth it?'

'No way.'

Adam knew that was the only thing to say. He didn't know if he meant it or not. The question of possibly losing Molly earlier, or making love to her less because he had engaged Chris through the mail needed more thought – but right off the top, no way.

'Plus,' he added, 'if anything had changed, I might not be standing here talking to you right now. So wait, how come you're moving home?'

'I moved out here 'cause the girl I was in a band with, who I met in nursing school, came out, and she put this whole thing together, so I took a leave of absence... And it was really good for a while. We played all over the place. There's this whole hard rock scene out here… You still play drums, right?'

'Oh my God yes.'

'Good. Wait, are you free this afternoon? We have our last rehearsal. You should come. You could sit in. Please tell me you still play double-bass.'

'That's all I play.'

The thought of hanging out with Charles later that evening suddenly became very unimportant. The moments were creating themselves; from an empty slate, to playing music with Chris. His trip to Los Angeles was turning out to be much more than he had ever thought.

'Good. Wow. I can't wait to tell Lynn… Are you playing with anybody?'

'Not really. I'm trying though. I go on all these auditions from The Village Voice and from the signs posted in the place where I have my studio, but nothing's really worked out yet.'

'Wait 'til you meet my band. You're gonna love 'em.'

'So how come you guys are…'

'It's a long story. The bass player, who I came out here with, is going back to school, and our lead guitarist thinks we're getting too heavy metal, which is kinda what we've been getting into… you know, Motorhead, Metallica. Not that she can't play it. She's got some other issues she's got to work on. It's a pretty heavy party scene out here, which is one of the reasons I'm looking forward to taking a break. Do you still get stoned?'

'Only when I play drums, which is pretty much every day… every night. I've never been stoned at work. That would just be too weird.'

'Yeah, it's a little bit heavier out here. A lotta drugs. I mean, it was cool for a while but… Anyway, I never got into it that heavy. No heroine or anything. But I felt like I was starting to become a rock-scene cliché… It was just weirding out…'

'So you wanna hear something really cool? I just read the greatest book that's ever been written, *Gravity's Rainbow* by Thomas Pynchon, and it was the guy from our trip, Rat, who had recommended it to me, and all through-out reading it I thought of him, and us… this is just like a month and a half ago… and the reason I'm telling you this is because the main character weirds out, or everything around him does, and the whole point is that, that's the way it happens. Everything weirds out.'

'Well, I'm gonna try to make it a little less so. No blaze of glory for me. You seem to be doing well. So tell me more. What are you doing besides playing drums?'

'Well, I graduated last May, and I'm working as an accountant, although hopefully when I get back I'll be starting a new job. And I ride a motorcycle. And I'm living in Queens in a two bedroom apartment with a gay black man.'

Chris got a little nervous, thinking Adam might have come out during their intervening years.

Picking up on it, he played along. 'Yeah, after our summer together, I swore off women.' In the gayest accent he could muster, he said, 'And it's been wonderful.'

'Are you serious?'

He was surprised there was any question.

'Not even a little.'

She laughed a little. Then a brief moment of realization. Then she laughed harder.

'Are you really living with a gay black man?'

'That part's true. I met him my first year of college, and kinda kept in touch after he graduated. It's definitely weird living with a gay man, but he's a really great guy, and he tries to keep his… stuff away from me, so it's okay. I love living there. And I have a really cool studio in the City, in a building where supposedly Madonna had a studio. That's what I've been doing. Working and practicing.'

'The girls are gonna freak when I bring a guy to sit in. I don't think they ever…'

'Are you sure it's cool?'

'Definitely. At this point it's just about having fun. We don't have any more gigs after next Saturday.'

'All right. I'll rock 'em.'

'Good. I remember you sitting in on *Whipping Post*. Wasn't that the first time you ever played with anybody?'

'It was.'

'That's crazy. I can't wait to see how you're playing now.'

'You know what's sad? I haven't played with many people since then. I'm trying, but… At least I practice. That keeps me from thinking how far I am from where I want to be.'

'That's exactly why I'm going back to school. And I'm sure you'll fit right in. Have you ever heard of Bad Brains?'

'Definitely.'

Adam thought of going into the story that he met the gay brother of a guy who plays bass in that whole underground NYC rock scene, who blew his roommate and was gone faster than a two-dollar hustle, but decided that was a whole different world that wouldn't have translated well. So he left it at knowing about Bad Brains.

'That's kinda like what we like to do,' Chris said. 'Rock it out. We're not near that, but there's a pretty heavy engine inside what we're doing. You'll see. Although lately it's been… Our keyboard player went into rehab a few weeks ago, so we're kinda missing a whole… Wait, what are you doing tonight?'

'My brother and I are supposed to watch this Grateful Dead concert on TV…'

'Oh my God! I'm going to it! It's right at The Grand. Do you wanna go? Can you go? I was supposed to go with my keyboard player but she just called me this morning and told me they're not letting her out. How crazy is this. I'd love to go with you.'

Adam couldn't believe he had to decline one of the great offers he knew he would ever, in his life, get. It was an arresting feeling, like missing your flight because you got caught in a traffic snarl and you weren't gonna get to where you needed to be and you knew you were fucked. But how could he have canceled on his brother, brush aside the only olive branch Charles ever extended? He couldn't. It was a relatively easy decision to make, which in no way diminished how crushed he felt having to make it. It felt like he was being physically restrained by Charles, in the abstract. He knew it was a coincidence. There was no guilt or blame. But the irony. The one time Charles was cool, and it had to cost Adam dearly… seeing The Dead live with Chris… making love to her after they got back to her apartment, or wherever she lived, after the show. Instead, he had to shut the fantasy down. Out of guilt? Yes. For the greater good? He wasn't sure. He had started to understand that his weekend with his brother, regardless of how it went, was not going to lead to the enduring legacy their mother had hoped. That wasn't who his brother was. Charles was into sports hypnotherapy and promoting his own interests. If you were with the program, there might be mutual benefit. If you weren't, that only lead to conflict or estrangement.

'So should I just fuck it?' Adam thought. 'He would do it to me in a heartbeat...This is fuckin' ridiculous.'

He just stared at Chris… literally at a loss for words.

'I don't even know what to say,' he said. 'I can't. Can you believe it? How fucked is this?'

"No, I completely understand. I do. You should try. Family is most important. If I can't find someone to go with, I might sell the tickets and watch it on TV too.'

The thought of sitting on a couch with Chris on one side of Adam and Charles on the other was so incongruous to him that it was dismissed before it had a chance to be considered, much less offered.

It took him a few moments to collect himself. 'This only means we're gonna have to do something like it another time,' he said, wishfully thinking.

The way Chris said, 'Okay,' almost like it was a question, gave Adam the distinct feeling there wasn't going to be another time. Their encounter was too brief, too random. If they had spent the day and night together they could have built some momentum. The balance had already started to shift toward the renewal. But a few hours wasn't gonna do it. Adam had to let it go – accept losing. Hopefully, it wouldn't cost more than an emotional bring-down every once in a while - when he remembered what he had to choose between.

The only consolation for the only decision he felt he could make was in the act of submission itself, like a martyr, only no one would be benefitting from his sacrifice. At that point it was a fine line between morality and stupidity.

'So where are we going to lunch?' he asked.

'The shit she let me do to her,' he thought.

'Any good romances?' asked Adam at an outdoor café near the beach. He thought that would be a good way to relate to Chris on a deeper level, especially after turning her magnificent offer down.

'I've, uh, seen a few guys. Nobody right now. I can't even really think about it. Especially going back home and going back to nursing school. I have to get my head back into that.'

'That's right, Sally,' Adam improvised, in an old mid-western high school girl's soccer coach voice, 'If you can see it, you can be it. Go out there and give it everything you've got.'

'Good advise, although you have to learn to adapt also. I can always set my kit up in my mom's garage. I love it in there… What about you?'

'I love it in there too.'

'Very funny.'

'What about me….?'

Adam assumed she meant if he had had any good romances.

'Look at you getting all defensive on me… What, you can ask me and I can't ask you?'

'First, you can ask me anything. Can't guarantee I'm gonna answer it. But you can ask it. My social life…' Adam felt spontaneous laughter bubble to the surface. He felt it catch in his chest, and he realized the laughter was coming even before the full formulation of the reason. At the center was the fact that he was just asked to reveal how pathetic his love life was, almost as karma for the way he had treated Chris. An accountant by day, and a solo drummer at night, unable to connect with either a woman or a band. Apparently, he wasn't exactly the pick of the litter. He didn't know why he found that funny but he did. And Chris found his laughter funny, and she started giggling, and then laughing. Within one intake of breath, they were stricken with a severe case of the giggles, which, if left to their own devices, will go until they wind down of their own accord.

'What's so funny?' she managed to stammer out.

'I've only… had…'

He knew he wasn't going to be able to get the fact that he only had three dates in over three years, out. It felt great to laugh at the absurdity of his life. It beat the alternative. People stared. Some even started laughing themselves.

Eventually the endorphins were satiated and calm once again settled over and around them.

'At least you can see the humor in it,' Chris said. 'That's not exactly how I've been processing it. I usually get...' a giggle escaped, 'so pissed,' and that set her off a little, which set Adam off – that's how close the giggles were to the surface, right into round two of their laughing fit. They actually had to consider leaving the café because they knew they were creating a disturbance, which made them laugh even harder. Even as Adam thought how fucked up it was that he couldn't spend that potentially magic night with Chris, he couldn't stop laughing.

'Oh my God. That was crazy,' Chris said once round two settled back down into normalcy. 'I haven't laughed like that in I don't know how long.'

'I think I'm just really jet-lagged. I haven't slept in like two days. I have no idea how I'm gonna stay up tonight watching TV.'

'Why don't you go back and take a nap?'

'Because,' he thought, 'I have no idea if my brother's home. And even if he isn't, I'd rather hang out with you.' Since they still had many hours before Adam had to get back, he was hoping upon hope that after her rehearsal, there would still be enough time for her to take him back to her home and make love to him for old-time sake.

"Cause I'd rather rock. What's the name of your band?'

'Eden.'

'Look at Chrissy totin' a new beau,' said the six-foot blonde with a bass guitar strapped to her shoulder, and a very thin black ring through her left nostril, which on her looked very sensual. Chris had driven to an industrial area closer to downtown LA where their rehearsal studio was. The rehearsal space itself was set up in a non-descript warehouse's second-floor loft, with an open view of the entire inside of the building, which was filled with cars, boats, tractors, motorcycles, jet-skis, engine parts, statuary, lighting fixtures. It was immense.

'Old,' Chris corrected. 'And he's a drummer. I can't wait to see where he's at. We'll indulge each other. Adam, that's Susan.' The bass player.

'Indulge we shall,' Susan said. 'Can you play?' She didn't want some drumming wanna-be sharing any part of their energy.

'Pretty much,' Adam said. His hours of obsessive practicing had started to infuse a cautious confidence in him. It was the first time he felt that. Generally, he was insecure about exposing himself musically. He hoped he didn't end up embarrassing himself, especially in front of Chris. 'This place is amazing. What is it?'

'It's my dad's,' said the girl who was walking over to a multi-cabinet guitar rig. She also had a nose ring, and was in semi-Goth attire; long black coat, straight black hair shaved on one side, black lip-stick.

'That's Shelly,' Chris introduced. 'You wanna hear something crazy? And we didn't even figure this out until we were playing together for like a year. Shelly's dad and mine played together in the Stan Kenton Big Band. In the late Fifties.'

'Just a few shows,' Shelly said. 'But yeah...'

'Wow. Swinging and rocking together. That pretty much covers it. They both know you guys are playing together?' Adam asked.

'Oh yeah. They're totally into it,' Shelly said.

'So, does your father own all this?' Adam asked, prying, just a little. That was a lot of stuff. From a different angle of the loft was a small jet, and other assorted aircraft.

'For a while. Then he sells it and gets new stuff.'

'It's called a really good exporting business,' Susan said. 'And we love him. He lets us do whatever we want here. And we've done it,' suggesting heavy playing and partying. 'What do you think about getting your friend right into it?'

'I don't mind,' Chris said. 'You wanna go for it, Adam?'

'I think we have to get stoned with him first,' Shelly said. 'See if he gets goofy on us.'

'Light 'er up,' Susan said. Shelly did, a joint of very good pot.

Adam guessed he passed the stoner part of the audition, because as soon as they were primed, they were ready to play. He was a little nervous, mostly because he hadn't been stoned with Chris in years, and he had no idea what kind of music he had gotten himself into, other than Bad Brains.

'Hard and fast,' Susan instructed. 'Try to listen for the changes.'

'Do you know Motorhead? *Ace of Spades*?' Chris asked, a last-minute tutorial.

'Definitely,' Adam said.

'Same kinda beat. If it's easier, just run your feet, and do a two-four off the snare.'

'You ready girls?' the bass player continued. 'One, two, onetwothreefour...'

Progressive punk. Original, but heavily influenced by The Ramones and Sex Pistols, with some Metallica, a new breed of heavy metal, thrown in. It was the kind of music Adam could rock as hard as anyone. He didn't even need visual cues. The straight four-four bass-line would tell him everything he needed to know.

Susan stopped suddenly, the rest of the band right behind. Adam thought he had fucked up. He looked at Chris, almost as an apology for denigrating her trust and her band. She looked at him with eager anticipation.

'Okay,' Susan said, 'when we get to the next section, just try to hit it and go as fast as you can. We'll hook in. Can you work those pedals?'

Adam was a double-bass drummer. That's how he rolled. 'Yup,' he said.

'Okay, lets take it from the top. Remember, just freak out when we get to the end of the second chorus. Okay, you ready girls? One, two, onetwothreefour...'

Right back into the music. This time, because Adam knew what to expect, he was relaxed enough to listen to some of the lyrics:

Seeing Without Illusion

Finally figured out the rules of the game
Accepting what was always there
Wind is gonna blow through the trees
Hanging on the leaves like a shattered prayer
Rhythm of the angels banging on the moon
Climbing up the tree of life to see the view
No more confusion
Seeing without illusion
All those years I felt behind
Seemed so real... I was blind
As the symbols of a higher way flashed across my soul

Then he had to go back inside the zone quickly. The thrash section was coming up and he needed to feel it.

Boom, right into it, as fast as he could go, his feet running like an Olympic sprinter. No thinking, just doing, full-body freaking in a straight four/four. He had no idea if the rest of the band was with him. When he let go like that on drums, the sonic overtones in the middle of the cymbals and skins were generally louder than everything around them, especially when he went from zero to eighty, or in this case, punk to speed metal, in a heartbeat. But the fact that he didn't hear any dissonance drew him back into the collective consciousness of the other players. They were in rhythm, playing harder and faster than Adam had ever played, so hard and fast that he couldn't think of opening his eyes. This was all internal; maximum explosive energy.

Somewhere in the electric metal flow, he sensed how the song might be structured. They were gonna bring it back to the verse at some point, almost as if the thrash section was the bridge. He opened his eyes to see if he could get any visual cues and saw Chris at the mike stand with Shelly. Everyone was into it.

'… three, four, Now,' Adam said to himself, trying to time the exact end of the bridge. He stopped playing, on a dime - hit it almost exactly, a milli-second before the rest of the band did. 'Yes,' he thought. He was about to go right back into the verse, but happened to look up and caught the bass player's eye, who signaled for him to wait for it, wait for it… 'One, two, onetwothreefour…'

Now I know how to feel the rain
To see beyond deception
Going back doesn't mean the end
Knowing when to move ahead again
No more confusion
Seeing without illusion
This doesn't mean I won't fall from grace
A few steps back to the other place
It all comes together eventually
I'm following my destiny

Adam couldn't believe how all-encompassing playing hard rock and heavy metal was - a full-on release. He understood what Chris meant about 'being inside a heavy engine'. He had never had a more complete musical experience, all parts of the machine working at peak performance. And the lyrics; real poetry. It gave him a deeper insight into how beyond his imagination playing music could be. One song. Like being transported. Plugged in. Bigger than the sum of its parts. With Chris right there, singing lead. His trip to California became that moment. Far more than one normal evening, or perhaps two, with his brother. This was an awakening. The better the players, the greater the synchronicity between them, the deeper the magic, the higher the energy.

'Wow,' Shelly said. 'That was insane... I loved sharing the mike with you. We never did that.'

'It felt great,' Chris said.   'I wanna do it more.'

'I can't believe how fast that was,' said the other guitarist, Allison, precision rhythm, who played the whole song with her eyes closed, and hadn't said a word up to that point. She seemed to be all about the music, which she wrote, lyrics and all. She was also into tattoos, which covered her right arm all the way to her wrist. She wore tight Levi 501's, a tight white v-neck tee shirt, was around five-nine, and had an 'approachable only if she wanted you to approach' kind of vibe. Adam respected that, and was honored to play with her.

'Seeing without illusion. Like stripping away veil of maya?' Adam asked, trying to impress Allison.

'Exactly,' Allison said.

'And did I hear a little I Ching in there?'

'You did.'

'Adam, I think you just sealed the deal. We've heard it all already. How about he keeps playing and I sing,' Chris said. 'I cannot believe how great that felt. You wanna keep playing?'

Adam felt like he was right where he belonged, behind a drumset. But it was Chris's, and he didn't want to steal her thunder, especially with how gracious she had been about letting him sit in in the first place. And, at one point he wanted to check her drumming out. He had looked up during the song, completely in tune with the rhythmic harmony of the universe, and saw her singing with abandon.

'If she could play like she can sing...' he thought. Then he thought, 'Maybe.... I might have a shot,' the way she was looking at him with discovery and wonder.

'You sure?' he asked.

'Totally,' Chris said. 'This may be the last time I get to do this. And I never did it before.'

'Don't say that,' Susan said.

'You know what I mean.'

'You'll see. Another few semesters of changing bed-pans and taking blood and we'll be right back out here.'

'Eww,' Shelly said.

'It's not as bad as you think,' Chris defended. 'It's all a part of it.'

'Better you than me,' Shelly said.

'I'm just fuckin' with you honey,' Susan said. 'Okay,' turning to Adam, 'this one starts straight ahead speed-metal. Then you cut it into a kind of *Sweet Leaf* crush, then back into the speed-metal, and then into the crush, like this...' She did a quick demo. 'We may jam on one or a few of the sections. Let's just see how it goes. *Antique Heroes*, you ready? You start this one off.'

Adam was lost. 'Can you just play it one more time?' he asked. 'Play it full on so I can...'

'I'll show him,' Chris said, walking over to the kit. 'This,' and she laid down a running rhythm – steady and strong double-bass work, riding the cymbal at the farthest edge of the beat, two and four on the snare.

'I can't wait to see you play,' Adam said.

'I will. I promise. You got it?'

'Got it,' he said. 'Just give me a few seconds to get into the groove, then come in when you want.'

How happy was he that he had learned how to play double-bass.

Antique Heroes

Like the Great Blondin across the falls
You better feel your center
You wave to the crowd
'cause you know why they came

Blondin bending rules like a yogi
Everything according to the laws of reason
Subdivide the world one footstep at a time
Feel the balance carefully

Don't end up like Steven Peer
Thought he was immortal
It's all performance, isn't it
Up until the long way down

Balancing... Knowing... when the time was right
Carried Harry on his back and he kept on going
Then he said goodnight

How're they gonna write your history
He bet against himself and won

The Great Blondin inside crystal walls
Feel the balance like the moon and tide
The Price of Wales was on his feet, delighted
Each footstep falling like suicide

Then there's John the American icon
Five, six packs a day
And the last few drags of every cigarette
Taking all he can get before he throws it away
Blondin played it straight
Wasn't tempting fate
Maybe pushed the boundaries a little
Showed the world a new frontier

To see the world through Duke's eyes
Before and after the turn
The whole point of view... you learn
Though real our love, you who are what men are made of
A little bit of trouble and a little bit of innocence

A little bit of rising… a little bit of falling
You can go pretty far before you've gone too far

And on, through the afternoon, all original songs, all with a 'heavy flow', as Susan liked to describe them. Chris's playing was as good as her singing, and she sang like a gypsy caller. Certainly one of the best female drummers Adam had ever seen. She was the real thing. Adam couldn't believe he had been so into her and he didn't even know she did that. That required a serious evaluation of who Chris was. She was a serious woman, an artist. It made Adam want to try to be a better man. Don't be so shallow. Everyone's got their own story. Most are trying write it as they go along… get to the happy ending… to figure it out. Some get it. Some never do. The bell-curve of life. Adam was an accountant and a drummer. Chris was a nurse and a drummer. He silently vowed to be ultimately respectful and caring of her. Be a positive part of her journey. He sensed he should be that for everyone, and a millisecond later sensed how impossible that was… locking into Chris's steady drum-beat. 'Good song,' he thought. Something about, 'Revolution Running/where the fires burn the sky/ all the false prophets lose control…

When Adam let go when he was playing drums he tended to be more like Keith Moon; high-speed fills, syncopated rhythms, crash accents. Animal from The Muppets. Chris's playing was straight-ahead, more out of the punk world. Chris was a punk-rock drummer, Allison taking them a little farther, a little deeper, the evolution of rock.

During one of the several party breaks they took - very trippy weed, and Kona coffee with organic sugar - Adam said, 'This must sound insane with keyboards.'

'Oh man, Patty…,' Shelly said. Shelly was a good player who covered her fret-board limitations with sustain, which, because Allison kept the rhythm tight and moving, and Susan drove the bottom hard, made the music more spacy. Keys would add color and texture. 'You wouldn't believe it. She's… Well, that's a whole 'nother story. What are you doing with her ticket tonight?' she asked Chris. 'She told me they're not letting her out, which, we all know, is probably a good thing. The last thing she… Well anyway….'

'I don't know. You wanna go?' Chris asked.

'Fuck yeah.'

'Hey, what about me?' Susan said.

'You wanna see The Grateful Dead?' Shelly asked.

'Are you kidding. Phil Lesh is a genius.'

'Then you go,' Shelly said.

'Really? No, you go.'

'No, I'm telling you, you go.'

'Oh my God, I couldn't have written this any better,' Allison said. Not only did she write the music and lyrics, but she was an assistant writer for a popular police drama. 'I was gonna surprise you guys when we finished, but since you've given me the perfect lead-in, my dad got us three VIP passes.' Her dad was a senior executive at Warner Brothers and was connected enough to be able to get tickets to almost anything anywhere. 'We can all go together, and then I'll figure out a way to get you backstage with us. Why don't I pick everyone up at like around seven-thirty.' She drove the Econoline van the band used for their gigs. 'Adam, do you wanna go? Chris, you want him tagging along?'

At that point, seeing The Dead on TV with his brother, in Charles's sour-smelling low-rent mini-house seemed much smaller than it did when he initially turned Chris's offer down. Then, he felt almost like a sadhu, renouncing earthly pleasure for a higher spiritual purpose. Now it just seemed like penance for sins he hadn't committed. VIP tickets to a Dead show at an old LA theater with Chris and the all-girl, very real hard-rock band he just spent the afternoon rocking out with. VIP tickets. How many times had he said he would give anything to see The Dead up close, to be inside the energy. The evening itself had become Adam's aspiration, even without making love to Chris. That would have been fantasy on top of fantasy.

'I do,' he said. 'More than you know, but...'

He explained his situation, and let them know how much he would have preferred hanging out with them.

'Hey, no worries, man,' Allison said.

'Yeah, no worries,' added Shelly, the Goth guitarist. 'It's cool what you're doing. How about we finish up with some jamming in honor of tonight.'

'What do you wanna jam on?' Susan asked.

'How about we let our honorary drummer drive this one,' Allison offered. 'Go for it.'

Adam went right into a rock fusion Eleventh House groove off the hi-hat that subtly morphed into more of a straighter rock rhythm as each of the players joined in. In the middle of the jam he felt his energy starting to wane – they had been playing for almost three hours, and he hadn't slept the night before.

'Just keep it steady,' he said to himself, so the other players could have a solid foundation to do their thing over, including Chris, who was improvising lyrics Adam was only able to make out intermittently; something about seeing the world through far-away eye/what she just saw/what she wanted to see/to lose herself/ in the rhythmic depths/a history/ yet to be written...

He had to stop trying to make out what she was singing and concentrate on the rhythm. Since this was their last song, he wanted to give it everything he had left... to be inside the cosmic flow only double-bass drummers know...

It was an unbelievable afternoon, one Adam never could have imagined. It just unfolded, like a movie, and he was in it, costarring with four really good, really impressive women who rocked as hard as he did.

'So how are you not going for this?' he asked Chris during the twenty-minute drive to his brother's house. 'You guys totally have it; the songs, the vibe...'

'Yeah, today was amazing,' Chris agreed. 'I can't believe it. Everything was faster and louder. Mr. Keith Moon over here. I can tell you they never played with a drummer like you. You made 'em work. That was sick.'

'Yes it was... You are, by far, my favorite female drummer. I can't believe how you fuckin' rock. I can't believe I didn't know that.'

'I wasn't doing that at eighteen. It's really been the last few years. Playing with them.'

'And you sang your ass off.'

'Wow, that was... Yeah... We'll see. Right now I think we need a little... If I don't go for my degree like soon, I never will. I know there were some labels that were interested, but they were much more interested in Allison, and she can be pretty intense.'

'She's certainly a woman of few words. But her songs definitely have unbelievable energy. Oh my God, *Antique Heroes*... I gotta be honest with ya. I rocked as hard as I ever did.'

'You still make really intense faces. You're fully immersed. This is what you are. It doesn't matter how you do it...'

'It's definitely a part of it. Seems to be the thread. Just keep going. I've left bars on Friday and Saturday nights and gone over to my studio and played naked for hours. Lights off. No one can see me. Just get naked and let it go, with New York City all around me.'

'I have to try that. That sounds really good.'

Adam stared a moment, his mouth open, his heartbeat racing at the thought of jamming naked with Chris, in the humming blue neon twilight of Eighth Avenue. He saw it in his mind's eye. He realized how he felt about her, how he wished he could jump in, see where a relationship with her went. He felt the potential, the depth of possibility. The only problem was that at no point did Chris suggest anything resembling intimacy. Their afternoon was strictly old-friend nostalgia and rock and roll. 'Burn me once...' Adam quickly thought. But a millisecond later he thought about Chris's theory of mutuality, that feelings in interpersonal relationships tended to be mutual. Then he realized there were a lot of other factors to consider, like time and place, which directly influence someone's emotional state. Adam knew imbalanced relationships, which is what he sensed his and Chris's was at that moment, tended to weird out, bringing him right back to where he was before his flight of fantasy. It was a non-starter. They were approaching his brother's neighborhood. They both realized their chance encounter was coming to an end, the transition from nostalgia and a shared rock and roll afternoon back to where they were before they ran into each other.

'Yeah,' Adam said. 'I'm lookin' right at you. I'm...'

'I've seen that look. You have no idea... We did this tour through Portland and Seattle... You can't believe the bands in that area. Oh my God. We played almost every night. Everybody did. It was amazing. Really shitty weather, and an unbelievable music scene... A lotta drugs. A lotta everything. You kind of get caught up in it.'

'Sex drugs and rock and roll.'

'It got me loopy,' Chris said.

'I think it might be good to get a little loopy every once in a while. And that's coming from someone who puts numbers in boxes every day.'

'Yeah, you think so. I guess it all depends on who you are. Some people can handle it a lot better than others. Look at Hendrix, and Janice Joplin, and Jim Morrison. I'm telling you, I saw stuff that was not cool at all. That's why I'm swearing off the sex and drugs part of it for a while, except pot...'

'Sounds like my life, only I didn't do no swearin'.' Adam was smiling as he said this. He wanted to suggest how opposite the rock and roll fantasy his life was.

'Grass is always greener... Whadda they say? 'Be careful what you wish for'. Anyway, it was an amazing afternoon. I'm nicely stoned... Oh yeah, how are you getting to the airport tomorrow?'

It sounded like Chris had lived many lifetimes since their summer together. Not that she was a stranger. It was just that Adam realized she had moved well beyond the time they had shared. The last thing she needed was a hard-up ex-boyfriend who had treated her like shit trying to get over on her. He recalled the vow he had silently made.

'A cab's coming to pick me up.'

'I'll drive you.'

'No, it's really early. You don't have to do that. I'm getting picked up at like eight.'

'You don't want me to take you?' She knew he did.

'Of course I do. I wanna spend every second I have out here with you. Are you kidding? I just...'

'Okay, I'll be here at eight.'

'Are you sure?'

'Come on, man. When's the next time we're gonna have a chance to see each other?'

Adam sensed the only way he was ever going to see Chris again after his trip was if they had another random encounter somewhere down the line. Or if she became a famous drummer, and he saw her on TV or in concert. Not that any of that was impossible. There were some people he went to various schools with that he had seen more than once over the years. No way to predict any of that.

It was bittersweet, a few fleeting hours of bliss. From the subdued nature of what he thought his California trip was going to, at best, be, to being transported to a world of rock and roll fantasy. Even if it was a one-off, cut short of its climax.

'Better a partial one-off than a whole never-been,' he thought, trying to celebrate what he had, rather than lament what he didn't. He was spent and happy. There was no denying it. Just like there was no denying how much he wished Chris would pull over, look at him with that, 'I want to fuck you right now,' look, lean into him and start lapping up his tongue.

'Yeah, keep dreaming,' he thought.

'That's it over there,' he said, pointing to the house his brother's house was behind.

'Crazy, right? What goes around...' she said, putting her car in park. 'Just so you know, I'm disappointed we didn't... get to spend the night together, all things considered.'

'Tell me about it.'

The fact that Chris felt that way about Adam settled his spirit. At the end of the road not taken was the world as he had hoped it would be. It helped balance out the world that was.

'How about a hug.'

She leaned in with a pouty face for a quick kiss on the lips, and a heart-felt, front-seat, torso-twisted hug. It was a moment Adam breathed in for all it was worth. It felt like he was letting go of something he wished he could hold onto.

'Okay Chris. I had an amazing day,' he said, opening the car door.

'Me too. I'll see you in the morning.'

'Good timing,' Charles said. He was in the bathroom taking one of his steroid and dietary supplement-induced extended pisses. It was already in progress when Adam came through the front door, continued as he went into the living-room and did some stretching, continued through sitting on the worn loveseat with his eyes closed, trying to let his stoned and happy, yet at the same time a little bummed-out head settle, which it couldn't because all he could concentrate on was the sound of his brother pissing like a racehorse. Fish, who drank a six-pack of Heinekens almost every night, had sometimes pissed Adam off with the distracting sound of his extended bladder-emptyings. Charles put those to shame. It was all Adam heard - the sound-track to those few minutes of his vacation where what might have been stood in stark contrast to what was.

'Let's go to dinner,' Charles said, when he was dressed and ready, twenty minutes after he finished pissing, enough chill-time for the tiredness that had started settling into Adam's body and soul to manifest. He had actually fallen asleep for a few seconds sitting on the loveseat. 'And when we get back, The Grateful Dead... Hey, come on. Don't fall asleep on me.'

'What? No, I'm just resting my eyes. I need a cup of coffee or something.' What he needed was a nap. He had a restless night Thursday night because he was anxious about spending the weekend with his brother. And the prior evening he had gotten almost no sleep at all. That, plus jet-lag and getting stoned and playing hard rock for hours – he was exhausted. At least his brother's wistful excitement about seeing the Dead concert with him dispelled a good amount of the second-thoughts he had about hanging out with him instead of Chris and the band. Two days in a row of civility and recognition.

'How about just giving me like a half an hour to take a nap,' he said. That would have been all he needed to recharge his batteries.

'You can sleep when you're dead,' Charles said, the irony and hypocrisy not lost on Adam. 'Come on. Throw some cold water on your face, and let's get outta here. We'll eat at this Italian place.'

'All right,' Adam thought, trying to will the tiredness away. 'It's just a couple of hours.'

He almost made it, finally succumbing to sleep a few songs before the first encore. By that time both Charles and he realized that the idea of a televised Dead concert simulcast on radio was much more compelling than actually watching it on a discount-brand nineteen-inch TV and listening to it on the stereo his brother got for his fifteenth birthday. Not that it wasn't without moments of sublime beauty. The magic flowed through the screen. And Charles actually passed the joint, which Adam took two hits of, just to know that he had gotten stoned with his brother. The fact that he wasn't getting any more stoned than he already was was why he let Charles finish the joint by himself, which he didn't need to be told a second time to do.

240

They didn't engage each other on an intimate level, or even a personal level. It was more about the music and the fact that they were hanging out together. The music had a unifying effect. It made them feel good, *China Cat* into *I Know You Rider*, singing along with his brother, and the band, and almost everyone else who was plugged in. Adam knew, while it was happening, that he would always remember that experience.

The spell weakened during the space jam, which, more than any other part of the concert didn't translate very well over the less-than high fidelity speakers. The dissonance of that particular jam was an uncomfortable backdrop to the awkward silence they had no idea how to navigate through. So rather than try, Adam closed his eyes to see if he could hook into the cosmic nature of what the music was supposed to represent.

'Wait, what's that sound?' he groggily wondered. 'Oh...'

He had fallen asleep, and was awakened by the unmistakable sound of his brother pissing, equally as loud and atonal as the space jam. It was a strange reality to wake up into. 'All right. Try to stay awake,' he thought. But he couldn't. He was fighting a losing battle. Even his brother's insistence that he was missing the best part couldn't stem the tide, and he finally let nature run its course. The next thing he knew, it was six-twenty in the morning, he was curled up in fetal position on the loveseat with a little bit of a stiff neck, the television was off, and his brother's bedroom door was closed. Chris was going to pick him up at eight o'clock, plenty of time for his nine-forty flight.

'Shit,' he said out loud. He forgot to call the taxi company to cancel the car. As quietly as he could, he called the dispatcher, who kept saying 'What?' as Adam tried to tell him what he wanted, requiring Adam to speak louder than he wanted to. The fear of waking Charles up was so tangible that Adam told the dispatcher, in a voice only slightly quieter than his normal speaking voice, 'I'm gonna say it one more time, and if you don't hear me, I'm hanging up. Please cancel the car coming to Second Street at eight o'clock.'

'You want car...'

Click.

'What an idiot,' Adam thought, listening to see if he had woken Charles up. Silence. 'Thank God... I can't believe I won't get home until like eight... I should wake him up and say good-bye. Lemme see if he left me a note or something.'

He did. It read, 'Take care. Please don't wake me up. Charles'. That was it. Adam actually thought of taking the note as a kind of historical document, but decided just to walk away clean, with the few hours he had spent in harmony with his brother the only take-away necessary.

'I should really wake him up and say good-bye,' he second-thought, about to head out the door to the coffee shop a few blocks away. By the time he got back Chris would be there. He stood in front of Charles's bedroom door fist forward, ready to knock, but something told him, 'Don't do it. Let it alone,' which is what he did.

Walking out Charles's front door was like walking out of an ulterior reality back into his normal life. He had no illusions that anything had fundamentally changed between his brother and him. Charles was as much of an enigma as he had always been.

'Take care of yourself,' Adam thought, as a kind of prayer for his brother's well-being, looking back at his mini-house, knowing he was in there, sleeping, battling his way through the world, trying to prove he had something important to give to humanity, if they would just listen. The saddest part was knowing how little Charles had, how much the two-hundred dollars Adam had given him had meant, how impoverished his lifestyle was; a little, poorly kept apartment in the back of the beyond, ocean dreams against reality's jagged edge. Adam thought about going back and leaving him the extra hundred dollars he had, but decided against it, for a number of reasons. Mostly, because he didn't want to risk waking Charles up. But also because he didn't mind having some extra money in his pocket. His starting salary as a junior accountant was eleven-thousand dollars a year.

'All right, man,' he thought, offering his good-bye and heading out. 'What a beautiful day,' another warm sunny morning in Southern California. He felt the future was filled with possibilities – that he was his possibilities.

'How was your night?' Chris asked as Adam was buckling his seatbelt. She was there at eight, and offered her lips instead of her cheek for a good-morning kiss. A small gesture, but one that Adam appreciated. Her friendship ran deep.

'It was good. No trauma. And the band was...'

'I know. Can you believe they ended with *Saint Steven* into *The Eleven*? I always wanted to hear that.'

So did Adam, who realized he had fallen asleep before he got to. But he didn't tell Chris that. There was no reason to go into the specific details of his evening with Charles. That was a whole different self-contained world, with little relevance to anything other than itself.

'I would have loved to have been there,' Adam said.

'I did bring you a present. And just so you know, these are real.' She reached down to the space between her seat and the door and brought up two pairs of drumsticks, which she presented to Adam. 'The ones with the sixes are Mickey's, and the ones with the eights are Billy's.'

'Holy shit! Are you kidding!? This is unbelievable!' A pair of Mickey and Billy's drumsticks. Holy relics of rock and roll.

Adam had started collecting drummer's drumsticks in college when, after a Bruce Springsteen concert, he went up to the stage and asked the drum roadie if he could have a pair of Max's sticks, one for Molly and one for him, impress her with his spontaneity and ability to procure fun things. Realizing all you had to do was ask, and the worst that could happen was that you were ignored, Adam went up to every concert stage since and told someone, a roadie usually, he was a drummer and a collector, and asked if he could possibly have a drumstick to add to his collection, a broken one was fine. Nine times out of ten he was presented with one. To date he had about thirty drummer's drumsticks. Mickey and Billy were magic acquisitions.

'How did...?'

'It just happened. Allison got everybody backstage, and there was a big meet and greet, and someone told Mickey I was the drummer for Eden, and he heard of us. He's completely into drumming. He wanted to know who my influences were, and how I got into drumming. Oh my God, his father was in the Drum and Bugle Corp, just like my dad. It was crazy. And then I just told him I had a friend who collected drumsticks, and asked him maybe could I get one... And you're not gonna believe this... He takes me by the hand, walks me out to the stage, goes to his and Billy's kit, and gives me a pair of drumsticks from each of 'em. He even said to tell you to keep collecting...'

All Adam could do was live vicariously through Chris, without any regret at not having been there. She brought him a piece of it, a piece of the history. It was another defining moment of his trip, the perfect ending, an affirmation that his decision to collect drumsticks was more than just an immature whim. He was putting together something he knew, if he kept collecting, would have historical significance. From jazz to rock, get 'em all. Every drummer he possibly could. A whole greater than the sum of its parts. The history of drumming from the early part of the twentieth century, even before, revolutionary war drumsticks, civil war drumsticks, through speed metal and beyond. Adam felt the direct connection to Mickey, and The Grateful Dead, through Chris.

'Unbelievable,' he said. 'Do you want one of each? You can start collecting yourself.' Secretly, Adam was hoping she'd say no.

'No. No. They're for you.'

'Wow. Thank you. I'm usually the guy at the end of the concert who's hassling the drum roadie. You made this one easy.'

'What are you doing with them?'

'I have them in a leather drumstick case. Actually, I just had to buy a new one 'cause I couldn't fit any more in the first one. And their hanging in my room.'

'I love it. Good energy. You gotta keep filling those cases. You might be the only one collecting drumsticks.'

'I'm trying. I just saw the Rolling Stones a few months ago, which, by the way, was the greatest rock and roll show I've ever seen, and I had to ask like five people before somebody finally just went over to Charlie's kit, took out a stick and gave it to me. I'm telling you, I wasn't leaving there without a Charlie Watts drumstick. I was even trying to figure out how I could climb over the barricade if I had to.'

Chris smiled and shook her head. 'I'm sure you would'a too.'

'Oh definitely.'

'So who's next on the list?'

'Well, the most important is Ringo, and then Keith and John Bonham.'

'I can't believe they're both gone. It's doesn't even make sense. I have no idea how you're gonna get their sticks. But if there's a way, I'm sure you'll figure it out. What about Buddy?'

'Got 'im.'

'Nice. That's like an anchor in any drumstick collection. Build it from there. How'd you get that?'

'I saw him about a year ago, maybe a little more, in this club in Albany. I was actually sitting next to this like ten year old kid who had just lost his father, and his mother told me this whole story of how much her husband had wanted to take their son to see Buddy because he had just started playing drums. So after the show I went up to the bass player and asked him if I could get a pair of Buddy's sticks, and I told him that I was going to give one to this kid who just lost his dad. So, the bass player went backstage and must have told Buddy the story, 'cause out comes Buddy, and he finds the kid, and not only hangs out with him, but he gave the kid his whole kit. It was amazing. You should have seen how happy that kid and his mother were. And Buddy was wearing a NORML tee shirt... Here's what you have to do. First, do you have a pair of drumsticks with you?'

She thought for a moment, 'No.'

'Please send me a pair. I saw the way you play. You're going in the collection. You belong there. Especially being the only female. You gotta represent your entire sex. If you don't send it to me, I'm gonna figure out a way to get it. Even if I have to do what I had to to get Art Blakey's stick.'

'What'd you hold him up?'

'Nope. I spied around after the first set at this little jazz club in The Village until there was no one around the bandstand, and it was actually empty enough for me to slip under the backstage curtain, and slip one of his sticks out of his bag. It was amazing that I was able to do it, which only means it was meant to be done. Not that I'm justifying stealing someone's personal property. But after all is said and done, the collection will be something, and Art Blakey, who blew my mind, had to be represented, along with Elvin Jones, and Ginger Baker... I'm telling you, this collection keeps getting more serious. This is no small thing,' referring to Mickey and Billy's sticks, which were still in Adam's right hand.

'Well, I promise if I come across any good drumsticks I'll send 'em your way.'

'You already did. All I need is yours… This is like one of the most flipped-out weekends I've ever had.'

'And what's crazy, it was for me too. I met The Grateful Dead, and jammed with you. And I'm on my way to see my sister soon, who I love that you know the way you do. They're still that, by the way. Country music and all.'

'All right,' Adam said, taking it all in, feeling their last few shared moments together winding down. Signs for the airport started to become more prominent. 'Nothing wrong with that… I'm just being honest and telling you that if we could, I'd jump all the way in with you right now. And I'm only saying that because I completely would. I don't want to make you uncomfortable. And I know that could probably be pretty creepy coming from someone you don't want it coming from. But there you go.'

Chris smiled. She felt safe. "There you go. I don't think it's creepy at all. You'll find what you're looking for. I hope we all do. Who knows? If things were a little different…'

'Yeah I know. If. That always reminds me of…' and he started singing *If I Were A Rich Man*, from Fiddler On The Roof. Chris joined him at 'biddy biddy bum.' She had done theater in her last two years of high school and actually played Tzeitel in her junior year.

'You I'm gonna keep in a special place,' she said, pulling up to the terminal after singing the full version of *Matchmaker*. 'Try not to take you out too often.'

'It's like the movie *The Way We Were*.'

'We had a chance to straighten things out. That's a big one. I remember hearing somewhere that one of our greatest emotional desires was wanting to get back to the happiness we knew as children. We were at the tail-end of that. Then it kinda got a little weird there for a while. But now I think we're good.'

'We definitely are. You can't tell me this isn't good. This is good. The only thing bad is having to say good-bye to you… again. Please take care of yourself.'

He leaned in for a good-bye kiss, hoping for a small kiss on the lips. She met his lips with hers and held his there, pushing just a tiny bit more than a standard good-night peck. He pushed back, just enough so that she didn't think he was being disrespectful, but enough to test the waters. Within a heartbeat, they both opened their mouths and kissed as though they were the sole inhabitants in the universe. It was instant transcendent pleasure, filled with love and innocence, friendship and longing. It was a kiss by which other kisses would be judged, without time or space, until a cop had to knock on the driver-side window to tell them they had to move.

'Sorry, you're in a no parking zone,' the cop said, a little embarrassed. It probably wasn't his first emotional separation.

'Sorry,' Chris said. 'Wow, I didn't expect that,' turning to Adam.

'I think I could live on that. Please remember to send me your drumsticks. And call me whenever you want. I promise I won't be a dick this time.'

'Deal. As soon as I have a place I'll send you the address... You gotta go. You're gonna miss your flight. I can't believe you're still carrying around that backpack.'

'I'm keeping this forever. I agree with what you said about the happiness we knew as children. It definitely feels right. Anyway, I gotta get going. I love you.' It just came out, like a prayer, unfiltered.

'Oh wow...' She seemed surprised, reflective. 'I love you too,' she said, feeling no tinge of regret. It felt good to say it. 'Take care of yourself, all right? And I promise I'll send you my sticks.'

CHAPTER 15

. . . .

His own self-fulfilling prophecy

That trip turned out to be the last time Adam ever saw his brother Charles. No more olive branches. No more attempts at reconciliation. The estrangement that had begun in college, and deepened when Charles moved to California, and was temporarily put on hiatus during Adam's trip, was enacted anew after Adam left. Charles didn't even bother to return the call Adam made several months later, after he had seen The Grateful Dead at Madison Square Garden and thought it was a reasonable conversation initiator. Adam had debated whether he should call him, whether he should be the one to initiate contact, and decided what the fuck. So he left a message on Charles's answering machine. Charles never called him back. At that point Adam knew he wouldn't be making another attempt to be his brother's keeper. If Charles wanted nothing to do with him, it was his pleasure to oblige.

He did, however, speak to Charles one more time, several years later. Yelled, actually. Adam had been visiting his parents for a standard Sunday afternoon visit, and couldn't help noticing how upset his mother was, even though she tried to hide it.

'What's going on?' he asked.

'Nothing,' she said

'Bullshit.'

After more prodding she said, 'It's not important.'

'What's not important?'

'Your brother's up to his old tricks,' his father finally said.

He told Adam Charles had returned the two-hundred-fifty dollar birthday check their mother had sent him. She sent him a check every year on his birthday. Some he returned, some he cashed. The latest was returned with a hateful note full of condemnation and accusations and demands that they leave him alone. And, Adam learned, it wasn't the first time Charles sent their mother hurtful notes. Adam grew up in his parents' house. He was there every day. He saw everything that went on. At no point did his mother or father abuse, hurt, defile, or in any way try to diminish his older brother. In fact, they did what they could to make him feel good about himself. He was handsome, a good athlete, intelligent, and they loved him. They certainly could have done a lot more – counseling and medication, for instance. But there was no basis for the accusations and vitriol Charles leveled at them. Sure, their mother was a strict disciplinarian, a smack or two in the face her preferred method of engagement. Barry and Adam took what she dished out in due course, even when they didn't deserve it. Many was the time they caught a smack or two for fighting with Charles, and they had done nothing to instigate it. Even though it generally takes two to tango, Adam and Barry's experience with their brother was completely one-sided. Charles needed no reason to be a scum-bag. Even though he would sometimes accuse his brothers of somehow baiting him before he acted like a scum-bag, Adam and Barry knew it was nonsense, the way a rapist uses the excuse that his victim was wearing provocative clothes. It was nonsense with their parents too. Charles had proven that when he erroneously recounted to Adam how their mother had broken her arm. That one attempted historical revision had revealed more about Charles's character than almost anything else. He was creating his own myth as a defense against his inner turmoil, blaming his parents mostly as justification for possible future failure, in essence creating his own self-fulfilling prophecy, something that felt very similar to how their father dealt with reality. Their father had very few good things to say about his family, and had nothing to do with them either. The difference was Charles had something to apply this abundant neurotic energy to, something that could absorb it; athletics, bodybuilding. Forget that he wasn't the best body-builder. That type of extreme athletics was about the act of becoming the best you could be. But Charles could never see it that way. He was looking for something he could never find, a validation few ever achieve. And because he was so driven by that impulse, he overlooked what was already there; in his energy, in his family, almost as if his inner-child was in free-fall, and he was going to take his parents down with him. Not if Adam could help it. He was so pissed-off Charles was still hurting their mother, after all those years, that he decided to call him and insist he never hurt her again. Charles was well over his quota for inflicting pain. It was time to shut his bullshit down. Luckily, his number was listed.

Adam felt momentarily transposed, detached, hearing Charles's voice on the answering machine message. It suddenly became real. Re-engagement, with probable malice. That seemed to be the way history was going to be written.

Charles's voice on the message no longer had any type of Long Island accent, and was spoken in a cadence unlike any Adam had heard him speak in before, like an erudite mid-westerner. But it was him. As soon as Adam heard the beep, he went off. A lifetime, less a day and a half, of being treated like shit by him flew out of him. He had no idea he was going to get so hyped-up. It was just there.

'You gotta stop hurting mommy,' he demanded. 'Do you understand? If you can't be normal, then leave her the fuck alone. Enough of your bullshit...' At which point Charles picked up the phone.

'Who the fuck are you!' he yelled. 'Don't you ever call me ag...'

'Stop hurting her! Do you understand! You're just lying to yourself!'

'Who the fuck are you to tell me what...'

'I hear you do anything like that again, I'm gonna come out there and fuckin' kill you!'

'You piece of shit! Don't ever call me again! Don't you ever fuckin' call me again! Do you hear me! You're nothing!' And he slammed the phone down. That was the last time Adam ever spoke to him.

CHAPTER 16

Yes she does

Over time, funny things happen. Everything happens. Love, war, oceans, deserts, The Beatles. Past experiences, which we assumed would remain in the past; memories - some pleasant, some not - sometimes find their way back into our present. Such is the random nature of the great world continuing to spin. That's why there are expressions like, 'you can't escape your past', and 'don't burn bridges', and 'karma'. You never know when the past will find its way back to the present.

'What's this?' Adam wondered, trying to figure out what was in the eighteen-inch long, two-inch in diameter cylindrical package that was jammed into the mail-slot of the apartment in Manhattan he had moved into roughly four months before. Fish had moved to Hawaii to pursue a career in home-goods exporting; soaps, candles, exotic wood picture-frames, and Adam had taken that opportunity to finally move into The City, where he worked, practiced, and partied, and around which, to most young urban New York professionals, the rest of the world revolved. Moving into Manhattan was the next step in Adam's personal and, he hoped, social development, even if he did end up christening his new apartment, the second night he was there, with the fight he had with his older brother over the phone, the last contact they would ever have, and which was still reverberating around the apartment, but getting dimmer as time went by.

The cylindrical package had originally been addressed to his apartment in Queens, and was forwarded, by the post office, to his new address. There was no return address on it.

Back inside his tiny one-bedroom apartment - a converted studio apartment someone had thrown a wall up in in order to have a separate sleeping space, creating two tiny living spaces that cost almost half of Adam's monthly take-home pay as a production accountant for public television, a job he had gotten about a few months prior - he anxiously opened the cylindrical package. He sensed it was something good, something fun. He never got fun things in the mail; presents, award-winning notifications, love letters. Just bills. And junk. Inside the cylinder was a pair of drumsticks, and a note that read:

'Hi Adam, Better late than never. How are you? I hope everything in your world is the way you want it to be. I'm sure this is a surprise, but I always wanted to send you a pair of my sticks. And here they are.

I wanted to wait until they legitimately belonged in your collection (you're still playing and collecting right?). I don't know if you've seen our video, but they started to play it on MTV, mostly at night, but we're really excited. And we're opening up for Joan Jett on the west-coast part of her tour (I moved back out here after I graduated nursing school... long story). Anyway, I don't know if you're still living where you were, but hopefully this will find its way to you. I'm all over the place, so it's not going to be too easy to get in touch with me. But please check us out on MTV, and if we're ever in New York, I hope that you have a chance to come to the show. You'll love it. If you do, I'm sure you'll find a way to find me (crawl under the curtain like you did for Art Blakey. I always loved that). Anyway, I hope all is well, and I hope my sticks make it in. Much love, Chris.'

She never mentioned the name of her band. That night, after getting home from practicing, Adam turned on MTV, starting at like nine-forty, something he rarely did. Mostly he rented movies from the local video store, which was around the corner from his apartment. It had become a part of his routine; work, practice, stop at the video store (that evening he had rented *Night of the Hunter*), home, shower, dinner, a movie, bed. MTV generally gave him a headache after a few videos; too many jump-cuts per second. But he persevered through every type of video image he could ever want to see, and after about an hour he heard the intro to a harder new wavy song that was playing behind the image of a young guy at a party showing off a pistol to his friends. According to the MTV identifying lower-third graphic, the name of the song was *Johnny, Put The Gun Away* by a band called No Nurses.

'This has got to be it,' Adam thought. It was. After way too many quick cuts of the different expressions and actions of the teenagers at the party, a montage that lasted through the entire first chorus of the song - Jonny put the gun away/no one gives a (...)/what is it you're trying to prove/that's no way to do it - the camera panned over the crowd's heads to the back of the room where a live band was playing. And there, dressed in tight nurses outfits, was Susan on bass, and Chris on drums, with a female rhythm guitarist/lead vocalist, also dressed in a nurses outfit, and a male lead guitarist, who was dressed in a hospital gown.

'Oh my God. There she is,' Adam thought. 'She looks…' at which point the video cut back to the kids at the party, and then to a flash as the gun went off, then a dizzying amount of quick shots of pandemonium, and the band, who were nurses, pushing through the crowd to start administering to one of the party attendees, a young guy, who was accidentally shot. The rest of the video were shots of the band in the ambulance taking care of the guy who was shot, and who miraculously got better. The lead guitarist somehow ended up driving the ambulance, which begged the question, 'How did the ambulance get there in the first place?' All of that was intercut with shots of the police arresting 'Jonny' at the party. It was a good rock song, and a useless, over-indulgent video. But Chris had done it. She was a professional drummer who was on tour with a major rock band, and her video was on MTV. Adam went right to the drumstick case he had randomly put Chris's sticks in, took them out, and put them into the pocket that held his most important sticks; Buddy, Ringo, who he had seen just a few months before at The Garden, with his All-Star band, where Adam waited until he was the last person in the entire arena, except the crew, who were so sick of him asking for a Ringo stick, that someone finally went over to Ringo's kit, which was in the process of being broken down, and gave him a pair. The sticks vibrated magic in his hands, where they remained until they were safely inside the pocket. Adam never minded making a pain in the ass out of himself in pursuit of getting a drumstick. If that's what it took to insure his success, so be it.

'She doesn't really belong in there,' he second-thought, realizing just how important that pocket of sticks was. It also included the last of the model of sticks Adam had learned to play on, a broken ProMark Fatso 5A, which were discontinued many years before, requiring Adam to change to a different model. He always felt fortunate that he, somehow, saved one of those sticks. Holding it was like holding an important relic. 'Fuck it. Yes she does,' and he left Chris's sticks in there.

'Do you remember the girl I met when I hitchhiked out west?' Adam asked his mother over the phone the next time he spoke to her, a day or two after seeing Chris on TV.

'What, do I have Alzheimer's?' Doris said. 'Chris, who you didn't write back to...'

'But who I did redeem myself with when I went...'

'Oh, that's right.'

'I just saw her on TV last night. On a video on MTV.'

'She was a drummer...'

'She was a really good drummer. I jammed with her band. Not the one I saw last night, although she was playing with the same bass player. They're touring...'

'Good for her. I don't know how you watch that crap. It makes me dizzy...

'Me too.'

'Speaking of which... This must be old girlfriends day. Do you remember my cousin Stan?'

'Of course.'

'Guess who his son Michael is marrying.'

These were people Adam hadn't seen in over twenty years. And, he could only remember interacting with them once.

'How would I possibly know that?'

'Molly Jupiter.'

Immediate bring-down. Molly, a member of his family, however extended or removed. He wished he was in love, to buffer the news. But he wasn't. He just had to deal with it. Try to shut down the questions about why he wasn't where he wanted to be, while others were getting there. He recognized he was on his own unique journey through life, and that only persistence and determination, like the inspirational poster hanging outside his Middle School gymnasium read, can insure success, sometimes not even then. He knew to keep quality of life comparisons to a minimum. He also knew he was doing okay, especially compared to half the planet. But there was no solace to be found in counting life's blessings at the expense of the less fortunate. He didn't think not having a painful disease was a blessing. It was just fate passing over him, like Elijah over the marked doors. There was just riding out the bouts of self and existence questioning, usually by practicing until he was too exhausted to think about it, which he kind of was – he had practiced like a demon that evening. After the initial shock of finding out that Molly was marrying Michael Pensky wore off, what remained was a feeling similar to trying to remember a word that was on the tip of his tongue, with wishes for her well-being somewhere in there. Michael, a little less so. He didn't really know him. He remembered vising his home in Brooklyn when he was eight or nine. They threw a football around in the front yard of a temple. Adam had no idea how strongly his jealousy would manifest. He'd never been hit with it so cleanly.

'Not too bad,' he evaluated. A little. Definitely a little.

'Oysh...' he said. 'That's too small a world. Michael Pensky.'

In his mind, Adam had the immediate realization that, not only had any possibility of future intimacy with Molly vanished, but also how immature it had been to think there might ever have been any possibility. It was a fait accompli. He had to concentrate on his own life, not waste time on things he had no control over. Relegate them to just another thing.

'How'd you...' he asked his mother.

'I got an invitation to their wedding, and I know my sister Min still keeps in contact with Stan. So I called her, and she just called me back right before you called... From Bayonne, went to Cortland, they know you had been 'friends' with Molly, so there was no surprises there.'

Friends. 'A lot more than friends,' Adam thought.

'They met down in Florida at a hospital they both worked at.'

'Please don't tell me he's a doctor.'

'No, although Aunt Min told me Stan was trying to make it out like he was... Something in hospital administration. And she's a nurse...'

'Come on...'

Adam couldn't believe it was all becoming so relative. Rather than allow jealousy to turn his evening into a neurotic shit-storm, he employed the old diversionary tactic of settling down in from of the TV and being swept away by a great movie, *Saboteur*, by Alfred Hitchcock, which the guy at the video store told him was one of the unsung Hitchcock classics, which it was. One of the greatest train scenes of all time.

There were no answers to a lot of the Adam's questions; why he had spent another New Years Eve alone, walking around a bar until it was late enough to justify going home, which he judged to be around twelve-fifty. Or why, in the middle of two million people watching the 4th of July fireworks at the South Street Seaport did he feel like the sole survivor, until he went home and watched *Dracula*, with Bela Lugosi, the perfect choice to redirect his energy, after which his mind was free to wander until sleep overtook him. 'All I can do is be in the present,' he thought, drifting. 'follow my instincts, want a little less, keep working, practice... It's like Vincent said, 'It's all a rum-go...'

Vincent Van Gogh had written that to his brother Theo, in 1897, something Adam had learned while doing research for a piece he was determined to write on Van Gogh.

One day, in a moment of clarity, Adam thought about a project to write rhythmic poems that he would recite over completed drum and rhythm tracks he had recorded. Start there. Multi-track himself. Get a tight, moving three to six minute drum track that doesn't have too many imperfections, and write and record the words into the contours of the rhythms; hybrid beat poetry/rap.

The idea for the project started with a jazz drum track Adam had recorded, that went from swing to tribal and back again, that reminded him of Charlie Parker. So he read a few biographies of Bird, and wrote the song of the same name. He felt he had created something real and beautiful. He remembered writing the poem on Lord Byron after reading a biography, and applied those same principles.

He had gotten into portable multi-track recording because he knew it was a smart thing for him to do; the next step in his musical evolution. It felt so essential to his development that, lunch-hour of the day after his epiphany about how important recording himself was, he went to Sam Ash Music, asked the right questions, and was set up and recording in his studio in the music building that night. The Yamaha MT8X recorded onto regular cassettes, which, Adam found out had up to eight tracks. Because the board only had four mike inputs, he had to use a y-splitter for the bass drums, a mike on the snare, one between the ride and the smaller tom, and the other between the hi-hat and the other tom. That left four tracks for the vocals, and anything else Adam could add. No sooner had he learned the fundamentals of multi-track recording - by the second night - than was he recording everything he did. Why not? It was only cassettes. Recording quickly became an integral part of his nightly ritual, track after track of full-on fluid drumming. Maybe for posterity. Definitely as the basis for Energy, which was the name of the overall project Adam had begun to conceive. The idea was just there, out of the ether, almost fully formed; make his own music, write to the drum tracks, research and write about every subject he could think of that had an impact on humanity. All the big ones; artists, scientists, religions, philosophers, cultures... Put together a huge overview of the nature of humanity. It started with Charlie Parker, then Picasso, then James Joyce and Van Gogh. He already had the Byron poem, which he was able to adapt rhythmically to a very Bill Ward-sounding drum track. The whole process felt right - recording a usable drum track, researching a specific subject, then writing the words in rhythm. It was a process both constraining and challenging, being limited by the number of syllables in the measure, trying to get the essence of the subject fully drawn within those limitations, rapping or reciting the words, Adam recording himself over himself. It felt very organic. Some of it even sounded organic, at least to Adam, which meant he was on the right track, even if the pieces were very limited sonically; just drums and words. But they were Adam's rhythms, so the energy was there, which was why the whole thing felt like it should be called Energy. That's what Adam knew it had. He felt it. Hopefully, the rhythmic poems about a vast array of universal subjects did the drumming justice. From Beethoven to Bushido. He knew it was a unique artform that could tap into the deepest part of his artistic expression. He also knew it was an acquired taste. He was under no illusion that what he was recording wasn't meant for anybody's ears but his, maybe a few others. Drumming and words do not a song make. But the whole idea of putting all the different subjects together, however long it took - and as the list that was circulating in Adam's mind began to take shape, he was looking well beyond the horizon, all with perfectly recorded drum tracks that stood on their own and were sturdy enough for a bass player and a guitarist to build upon - that was something Adam sensed was the first step of something bigger. He had heard brilliant rap. And he had heard bad rap. He knew he could do better than bad. He made his own rhythms. After feeling his way through *Bird*, he began to understand there were no limits.

Bird

Feel just like a two-dollar whore waiting for my final call
Down to beggin' pennies for drinks… the high life wasn't so high after all
Tried to live once, and to the limit… found the cool world, man
There was wind to spare, and new ways to make changes… All blending
into a single sound
The armless man, years ago, beat time with his spoons
Old man Virgil on the street, singin' and cryin' the blues
The old horn that Addie bought, with her sweat and vision
I could go wherever I wanted in this life
Like a bird across the Kansas City night

But then I found the dark glow
The wild ideas began to flow
A whole new system of sound and time
Shaped to provide its own design
Harmonies Lester hadn't heard
Borne along a lavender hazy world
Learn to play the blues in all twelve keys
A young Amadeus of the ghetto blowing out bop melodies… hearing
with a third ear the explosions of pure energy

A stereotype, a con man, a New York City nigger
A natural born gangster genius not afraid to pull the trigger
A monkey on my back kept the outside world off it

Somehow sprung fully gone from the brow of a modern Jupiter
A prophet who took the wrong course and wound up in a new world
Black pariah who brought the fire to the enemy
Dug in on the front lines blowing blue harmonic schemes
A self-contained nocturnal man no jazz hypes could redeem
The saxophone cried love and rage… the raw notes of a junkie sage
    running out of plays
In the fire of spring… what new songs to sing… bird on the wing… the
    scenery is shifting

They tell you there's limits, but man there's no limits... just forces...
   through my green age... and I am unable to shout at the devil... the
   child and dream remain deep within... but I done gone back to my
   kick again... to live without tomorrow...
Just live from day to day and try to play the blues a new kind of way...
   the beat behind the music pushing forward and against it
In hothouse halls and on the street, like a black cat landing on his feet...
   bursts of notes fired into space, cryptic and disjointed
Like a preacher shouting sermons in the desert
Like thunder in the distance
A place to sleep, something to eat, pussy, drugs, and a fifth of gin...
   don't care what I look like man, 'cause the game I play don't nobody
   win... don't believe the thunder, or the hype that music breaks down
   walls, when I'm sleepin' in the ghetto after freein' time in the concert
   halls... and I am unable to find my way through this languid fever...
   and I am unable to control the force that is my destroyer... I proclaim
   to the night my naked soul!
Ah, to hell with it man... how about a shot o' whiskey before the next
   set... Better make it a double

Energy. That was the word that kept floating to the surface. His
work may not have been ready for popular consumption, but there was
definitely an electricity, a flow, the drumming and words, capturing the
essence of the subject. Because Adam didn't play any other instruments,
he supplemented the rhythm and spoken word tracks with chanting and
vocal rhythm tracks, karnatic singing, making the overall pieces sound
fuller - still not ready to play for the masses, but definitely legitimate
art, part of something bigger. If he couldn't find people to play with,
at least he could do his own thing. Energy was such a big project, it
took away any pressure there might have been about what Adam was
going to do with that integral side of his personality, the one he felt
gave him greater purpose, his creativity. He believed he had stumbled
onto something he was meant to do, not only from a creative place, but
from a self-improvement place; like a course of study in college, akin to
a major, in this case the study of a broad cross-section of human thought
and application.

After a few weeks of thinking about it, and writing down all the names of all the subjects he could think of that added to the history of our collective conscience, using as a resource the New York Times biographies list and The Strand Bookstore's labyrinth of shelves, Adam knew Energy needed to be created, not contemplated as an abstract concept. It was too big to fully conceptualize. Research and write. That was how it would get created. Read books, take notes, work on the train, wherever. Only then would its full scope and meaning be revealed. When Adam looked at the list he had written, it seemed like a pretty big cross-section of everything.

The list:
Charlie Parker
Picasso
James Joyce
Jimi Hendrix
Van Gogh
Lord Byron
Charles Mingus
Tolstoy
Stoic philosophy
Charles Dickens
I Ching
Herman Melville
Louis Armstrong
Da Vinci
Beethoven
Mayans
Jack Kerouac
Shinto
Georgia O'Keefe
Mozart
Einstein
Miles Davis
Kaballah
Lenny Bruce

Mohammed Ali
Vikings
Eskimos
Plato
Sufism
Druids
Native Americans
Diego Rivera
Sikhs
Pygmies
Hermetica
Lincoln
Bob Dylan
Eleanor Roosevelt
Gnostics
Babe Ruth
Bruce Lee
Gandhi
Mark Twain
Mother Theresa
Zora Neal Hurston
Freud
Ancient Egypt
Benjamin Franklin
Talmud
Sumarians
Ramakrishna
Bushido
Sir Isaac Newton
The Mormons
Mao
Darwin
Yoga
Nietzsche
Rastafari
Elizabeth Cady Stanton & Susan B. Anthony

Aborigines
John Lennon
Shakespeare
Voodoo
Dr. Seuss
Che Guevara
Jerry Garcia
Karl Marx
Edgar Allen Poe
Saint Thomas
Scientology
The Golden Dawn
The Tao of physics
Carl Jung
William Blake
George Washington
Zen
Gertrude Stein
Catherine the Great
The Inca
Thomas Edison
Jean Paul Sartre
Napoleon
Genghis Khan
Buckminster Fuller
Thomas Jefferson
Sri Aurobindo
Martin Luther
Wittgenstein
The Lotus Sutra

After that, it was anybody's guess. Adam had no idea if he would get anywhere near the end of something whose end he couldn't imagine. It seemed a long way off. Each piece was its own project, the ones he had already completed taking between one and two months from start to finish. He knew it was just about going for it. Find out what he could find out. Maybe it would develop into its own presentable form; rhythmic knowledge. Maybe there were ways to make it more musical, more presentable. He'd work out the structure, rhythm and story; the skeleton and organs. The rest, he had no idea about. If nothing happened, there wasn't too much down-side; time spent learning something, writing, recording. In the back of his mind was always the outside chance for his artistic pursuits to succeed, although he tried not to have unrealistic expectations. For Adam it was more about guiding his energy. Keep ahead of the bring-down. The fact that his first shot out of the box, *Bird*, lead to an evening of unexpected pleasure showed his idea had great potential.

He was on a blind date he had arranged through the *New York Magazine* personals. Since nothing else was working - bars, museums, referrals, work - and there were just so many hours on a weekend he could practice, he decided not to stand on ceremony and throw a line into the random world of media dating; see if he got any bites. Her ad said 'petite' and Adam thought that sounded appropriate. 'Petite, cosmopolitan woman looking to meet intelligent, creative man to explore the best of what The City has to offer.' He arranged to meet her, Andrea, Andy, at Trader Vic's in the Plaza Hotel. Not only did Trader Vic's have an exotic, fun vibe, but after one of their specialty drinks you were seriously buzzed – two, and all bets were off.

'I'd love to hear it,' Andy said, at one point in the evening, after Adam told her about Energy. If Chris's theory of mutuality was correct, then Andy wasn't really attracted to Adam. She got the sense that they weren't destined to span the ages together. They weren't even destined to spend more than a few hours together. But the Goombay Smashes were delicious, and potent, and apparently, after taking a cab down to his studio, she really enjoyed Adam reciting *Bird* over the recorded drum track, like karaoke, the lights off, the rhythm immediately getting her attention, Adam taking his performance seriously – it was the first time anyone had heard his work, even though it was an audience of one. He felt the flow, the jazz of it. It felt like real Beat poetry. It was. It moved Andy to walk over to him when he finished, put her arms around his neck, lean in, and start making out with him, losing themselves in the drunken velvety Manhattan night... Until he felt her pull down on his neck, and he opened his eyes and looked down onto the top of Andy's head.

'Did she fall?' Adam wondered, still very buzzed. 'Is she on her knees?'

Andy had kicked off one of her shoes, which turned out to be more of a platform, or a stilt, nine or ten inches tall, putting Andy at just over four feet. She was a little person.

Adam arched back his neck just enough for Andy to understand that he wanted to stand up straight for a moment.

Her ad said petite. He didn't see through the thin veil of interpretation.

'Shit,' he thought. Just when it had started heating up. Seeing her at her natural height, Adam understood the disparity he thought he had sensed at her physical presence. Not that she wasn't proportioned for her size. She was. Just not for someone almost a foot taller. Instead of being on a blind date with a woman who was small, but not abnormally so, Adam was on a blind date with a little person. The difference was far greater than race or religion. He didn't want to be a dick, but he needed a moment to collect himself. Two Goombay Smashes and a misunderstanding had compromised his wits.

'Here we go,' Andy said, as if she was used to the shock of recognition. She wasn't angry. It was almost as if she was waiting to see how Adam was going to deal with the facts at hand. 'Your piece was very cool. I wasn't planning on doing that. I'm pretty wasted.'

'Me too.'

Adam felt empathy for Andy. Her cross to bear couldn't have been easy. Not that she was unattractive; short cropped blonde hair, small, sharp facial features, pretty smile, nice cleavage. He was just having a hard time breaking through the social stigma, being on a date with a little person. Not even recalling the orgiastic scenes from the movie Caligula was enough to rekindle the passion he had felt before Andy kicked off her stilts.

'So, you just gonna stand there looking... I don't know... abstract,' she asked, 'or are you gonna play for me?'

Adam was impressed with how together she was. She tried her best not to let her physical handicap define her.

'Absolutely.' He was in his studio on a Saturday night. Of course he was going to play his drums.

'Do you get stoned?' Andy asked.

'I do.'

'Can we get stoned in here?'

'I don't have...'

Andy had already taken a joint out of her bag.

'Okay, Mr. Drummer,' Andy said, after they were primed, 'let's see what you got.'

Adam rarely drank before he played. Alcohol slowed his reaction time. It made him feel less inside the rhythm, more like he was going through the motion, almost as if he was hollow. Except that night. Even though he was still very buzzed, he took it slow, feeling the tribal rhythm off of the tom-toms, like he was laying down the clave for an African percussion troupe. How quickly he was back in his element, the humming blue twilight of his studio, the rhythms that always seem to be running through him, eyes closed, letting his body follow its natural course, like dancing... 'I wonder if she's into it?' Adam wondered, opening his eyes to see if Andy.... 'Oh my God. That's fuckin' awesome...'

Andy had slipped out of her jeans, and was sitting on the drum stool of one of the other drum-sets set up in Adam's studio, eyes closed, facing Adam, a transported look of sensual pleasure on her face as she masturbated to his rhythms. It was one of the most erotic things Adam had ever seen; the fulfillment of a fantasy he had had for as long as he'd been in that studio. From across the room, her size was irrelevant. All that mattered was what Adam was watching, how deeply lyrical and erotic it was.

'All right,' he said to himself. 'Keep it steady.' He was the soundtrack of her erotic interlude, slowly building the rhythm in intensity, bringing her along, her bringing him along, losing himself inside the rhythm, letting go, going, at one point locking eyes, her's half-closed, the rhythm pulling him back in, until the final crescendo, a moment of attainment, until the cymbal overtones faded back into the ambient sounds of Eight Avenue after midnight, and the sounds of the street prevailed.

'Oh my God,' Andy said, reality slowly reclaiming them. 'I can't believe I did that... I'm so wasted. You... No, I know,' walking over to him. 'Why don't you move your stool out a little,' which Adam gladly obliged, allowing Andy to slip between his snare drum and him. 'Your turn,' she said.

It took him less than twenty seconds to cum in her mouth, him spread-eagle on his drum-throne, her between his legs, leaning over his crotch, holding herself steady with her two little hands on his thighs. He loved feeling what it was like watching the top of her head bobbing up and down, the primal immediacy of it. It was one of the moments that made life worth living.

Sitting down, he was almost the same height as her standing up, which he realized when she leaned back up and in to start making out again.

'Not too bad,' he thought, loamy, like blood mixed with something a little sweeter, the semen taste still on her tongue. He was all in - still inside his rock and roll fantasy... until they got dressed, and she asked if there was a bathroom she could use.

'Down the hall, and to the right,' he said. As he watched her walk out of the studio, the voice inside his head reminded him that he had just gotten a blow-job from a little person. Not that it diminished the moment, which he had to smile at. He just didn't see it going anywhere beyond dropping her off.

CHAPTER 17

Trying to keep it real

Finish one piece, move onto the next. When Adam was close to the end of the stack of research books he bought, one or two books per subject, sometimes three, in advance of the next three or four subjects he intended to write about; biographies, religious texts, cultural studies, it was time to go to the bookstore and buy the next round. He had completed forty-three pieces over the four years he had been composing Energy; everything from Sartre to the Eskimos. The Eskimo piece was called *Stillness*, and had seven tracks of chanting weaving through the three rhythm tracks; kit, conga, and an African drum of indeterminate age Adam bought at Drum Inn, the cave-like store on Bleecker Street in Greenwich Village, that had been there since 1921 – drums and percussion from every corner of the globe. Adam went there to get an authentic pair of claves the Aborigines played, made out of the hardest wood on earth, almost bell-like in tone, which Adam used in his piece on the Aborigines. Those sticks, also, could easily have been a hundred years old. When Adam was at Drum Inn and saw the hollowed-out tree-trunk with a flawless impala skin, he knew it was his drum. Even in the store it sounded like it should be played under an open sky, calling out beyond the horizon, where the paint is mixed that colors the world.

Stillness

The hunter awoke before dawn and prepared for another day of survival
The drifting snow of the eternal night whipping across the frozen sea
The shadow of death reaches out like an old man whose glory has faded
The open sea awaits like the first specter of eternity

Strong snow-slide roll past my weak house
There sleep my dear ones in the world
Let them sleep until the spring
Let their nights be calm

All songs are borne in man out in the great wilderness
The song of the seal whose soul we pray for
The caribou, whose skin keeps us warm through the frozen winter
The songs of the great raven, who planted the seeds of life

May these songs take flight across the hunting-grounds
May they be heard by the Great Spirit that I might drift upon calm
　　waters
The great sea moves me... the great sea sets me adrift... and I tremble
　　with joy

Alone through the canyons of stillness
The vault of heaven frees my spirit to wander to the other world
It moves me like the running waters
Through the seasons and the suffering

The hunter glides through the darkness
Listening for the breath of life
The narwhale breaches the surface
The gentle breeze whispers his name

How to endure the struggles until my brother's soul is laid to rest
To respect his sacrifice... to give no pause for revenge
Just as nature's personal reign
Will deliver me across the frozen sea

You earth... our great earth... see, oh see all those heaps of bleached
　　bones
Oh cycles of tide and time... see us through another season of acceptance

And when my legs are not strong enough to dance the ancient dances
And when my arms are too weak to chase the narwhale across the
　　open sea
I'll sit upon the rock in quiet meditation
And unburden myself of the memories of youth
As the great raven carries my soul back home

　　For the last many months Adam had been concentrating on the
more religious subjects on the list; Talmud, Gnostics gospels, Kaballah,
Sufism, the Lotus Sutra, The Tao. Once he had started reading about
Talmud, he got the sense there was a lot more to the nature of religious

belief than that. Judaism only represented a small part of humanity. An important and beautiful part. But many more weren't Jewish than were. Might as well see what everyone else believed.

'You know, my father studied Talmud in Russia,' his mother told him over the phone one evening. 'He was thinking of becoming a rabbi. But then they all left. Can you imagine, coming over here without a pot to piss in.'

'He didn't do so bad.'

Adam's grandfather owned a millenary business at a time when almost everyone wore hats.

'No he didn't. He would have love to talk to you about what you're doing.' Doris had taken an interest in Energy. She felt it was a constructive way for her son to spend his time. As an educator, she would rather see him apply himself to something more meaningful than climbing the corporate ladder and being a couch potato. She knew, especially for Adam, it was about channeling his creative energy. She had always felt that if Charles had found a more creative outlet, he might have had an easier time through life. Her youngest son, Barry, seemed to be more grounded than his two older brothers.

'By the way,' she continued, 'Aunt Min told me Michael and your old girlfriend Molly got divorced. How about that.'

'She's free,' Adam immediate thought. 'I gotta get in touch with her.'

An entire unformed scenario swept through his imagination – something about rediscovering one another. His last girlfriend and he had broken up over a year before, after having gone out for a little over a year. She had been the last *New York Magazine* personal he had answered; 'attractive thirty-something, into the arts, travel, strolls through Central Park, looking for love, honesty, and laughter'. Although it wasn't love at first sight, Adam and Nancy, Nancy Schulman, enjoyed each other's company, usually on a Friday or Saturday night, sleeping over one or the other's apartment, going about their separate ways after breakfast, Adam always to his studio, and speaking once or twice a week over the phone, usually to talk about what they would do when they saw each other at the end of the week. Both hoped it would develop into love. And both were disappointed it didn't, although when Adam told her he thought it was time they stopped seeing each other, she did get pissed off at him, accusing him of using her. He reminded her that he had recommended they stop seeing each other about six months earlier so they could both try to find what they were looking for. At that time, Nancy had told him she understood, and that they would see how it went. Adam had done his best not to lead her on. He never told her he loved her, nor did he speak about a future that included them as a couple, which was why he had brought up breaking up six months earlier. She was a dear friend he enjoyed spending time with; going out to dinner, movies, concerts, having really good sex. It was perfect, until it wasn't anymore. He had started to feel like he was using her, at which point it was time to cut her loose, come what may. He felt like a dick telling her he was breaking up with her, but felt relief an hour or two later. He had done what he knew needed to be done. Hearing that Molly was a free agent was the first time since breaking up with Nancy that he felt excited about pursuing a woman, as abstract as that pursuit, in his mind, was at the time. He did have the sense that it could be weird trying to go after her after she had already been a member of his family, but his relationship with that side of his mother's extended family was removed enough that he didn't think it would matter.

'Listen, I wanted to ask you something,' Doris said, while Adam was still formulating the idea of getting in touch with Molly. 'Have you heard anything from your brother?' a weird question. She knew he hadn't.

'Ma, after our last wonderful conversation, I'm pretty sure he's not gonna be calling me.'

The last few checks she sent Charles on his birthday were neither cashed nor returned. And the few phone messages she left had gone unanswered.

'Well, if you hear anything, let me know.'

'Why? What's going on?'

'Nothing's going on.'

'When's the last time you've heard from him?'

'It's been a while.'

'How long?'

'Long,' during which time a number of professional athletes, who they knew Charles had been associated with, started getting sick and dying from steroid abuse. Adam knew his parents were concerned, on a lot of fronts. So, Barry and he hired a private investigator to verify that their brother was still alive. Nothing major. Just a piece of video. The private investigator, who they found in the Yellow Pages, and did a reference check on, set up a fake hypnosis session with their brother. How weird it was to see Charles walk onto the television screen in the grainy black and white video the PI shot. He was resolute as he entered the frame, and very out of shape. Watching the video was like watching a memory that hadn't been made yet. It was strange, for both Adam and Barry, to see Charles becoming a middle-aged man. He had lost a lot more hair. At least he was alive, knocking repeatedly on the door, then kicking it when he started to realize no one was home. He didn't wait around too long. He was pissed. Adam felt guilty they had deceived him. But a little inconvenience on Charles's part was worth the piece of mind their parents felt when Adam and Barry re-versioned the truth and told them their old neighbor Kenny Sackler, who they knew Charles sporadically kept in touch with, had called Adam to tell him he had recently seen Charles on a sports hypnotherapy segment on a cable news show, and had called him to say hello. Telling their parents about the private investigator, and that they had video of Charles seemed a little over-the-top. Adam didn't want to get into it with them. He thought seeing grainy, undercover video of Charles, especially of him getting really irritated when he realized he'd been stood-up, would have bummed them out, as opposed to bringing them joy. He felt it was better to keep things out of sight, out of mind. It was enough that they knew he was alive. Adam literally saw the agony of the unknown leave his mother's body when he told her. How little she needed in order to not succumb to the weight of such despair; just to know he was alive.

While that little bit of espionage was being set up, Adam was also waiting for a response to the invitation he had sent to Molly, inviting her to travel with him anywhere in the world she wanted to go. It was an obvious gesture to dive right back into intimacy, as well as one, if she were so inclined, that could be, at worst, interesting, and at best, who knew. A week in India, Paris. Put it out there, see if it came back, make his intentions clear. That was the form his reintroduction took; take her away on a once-in-a-lifetime trip. At the request of her sister Doris,

Aunt Min did some digging, and was able to procure Molly's address and phone number in Florida. Adam felt cautiously optimistic he was making an offer Molly would accept.

Two weeks later, still no response.

'Maybe it was the wrong address,' Adam thought. 'Maybe I should call her. Nah, I don't wanna seem too presumptuous or desperate... But maybe she didn't even get it. Fuck it. I'm calling.'

'Hello?' Molly, whose voice was instantly recognizable, said over the phone.

'Wow, listen to you...'

'Who's this?' she asked, a little cautious. Not exactly how Adam had hoped it would go. It took him off his rhythm. He was hoping to start from a balanced place.

'It's Adam Stru...'

'Oh, Adam. Wow. I got your letter.'

'And?'

If she was going right in, so was he, although he knew he was dead in the water. She sounded about as happy to hear from him as he felt when he got the letters from Chris looking forward to visiting him in college. Thanks, but no thanks.

'Yeah, I...' she hesitated.

He was as uncomfortable as she was. It was a bad idea. The best thing to do was put the invitation behind him as quickly and understatedly as he could. Let the past remain there. He would gladly have taken the phone call and the invitation back if he could.

'Listen, don't worry about it,' he said. 'I gave it a shot. I don't regret it.'

'No, I thought it was very... nice. I didn't mean to... you know, anyway... So, I was a member of your clan there for a while.'

'My mother was at your wedding. She said it was beautiful. And she said you were... very beautiful. That's just what I wanted to hear. No. I'm kidding. I was actually really happy for you, although I didn't really know Michael or his parents. I think we hung out once like a quarter of a century ago.'

'They told me. All they had heard was that you were doing well. They didn't have a lot of details.'

'I got a little low-down on you, other than your marital status, statuses, and the state you live in. I heard you became a nurse. That's very cool.'

'I'm actually going for my PhD.'

'A doctor of nursing. Sound like you're the one who teaches it.'

'That's what it is. Very good. I was glad to get outta the ER. What about you?'

'I was glad to get outta the ER too. It's always too bright in there.' No response. 'I'm a Production Manager for an independent production company, and I'm still drumming. And I've been doing some song writing, although not for popular consumption yet. But I'm workin' on it.

'Still drumming… You were crazy on that ledge. Wait, wasn't I with you when you bought your first pad and sticks.'

If there was one thing that would pull Adam back to a beloved past, it was the beginning of him knowing he was becoming a drummer. He remembered buying that pad and sticks, which, sadly, were long gone. But he knew the past could not be reclaimed, and there was nothing to be gained by trying.

'Yeah, I've put in a few hours since then,' he said. 'And it's really good talking with you. But I'm sure you got other things, so I'll let you go. But my invitation stands. Take care of yourself, okay?'

He didn't want to overstay his welcome. There was a reason she hadn't responded to his invitation. He needed to respect that. One more unsolicited contact by him would constitute stalking.

'Oh, sure. Yes. You too.' She was right with him. 'Strange how things work out, right? It must have been a little weird, but I never expected things to turn out the way it did. Not that I'm complaining. After eight years at Broward General, let me tell you, it changes the way you look at things. Right now, I'm just trying to keep it real, you know?'

Adam wasn't sure what she meant by that, other than she was going to be honest with herself and the world, and within that was the reason for her shutting down his proposal, which she was hesitant to even speak about, that's how not into it she was.

'I understand,' he said.

'I'm glad. Okay, take it easy Adam.'

'Yeah.'

Every once in a while, over the course of the next several hours, he would feel the slight spasm of embarrassment – lower chest, upper abdomen - about having misjudged, in so personal a way, the potential of a situation. And then the next minute he was glad he did it. Don't be a pussy. You gotta go for it. No risk, no reward.

'Maybe,' he thought. Maybe at one point in the future she would accept his invitation. 'Not a chance. Fuck. That couldn't 'a gone any worse.'

The next night he drummed so hard that when he put his sticks down, his arms levitated on their own, like when you push hard, when your arm is at your side, against a wall, for seven or eight seconds. Move away from the wall. Up the arm goes.

CHAPTER 18

Fifteen steps from the end of the walkway

Adam's father passed away without reconciling with his oldest son. He hadn't seen or spoken to him since the one visit Charles made after he had moved to California, almost twenty years before. His own son. How did he not do everything he could to make sure his son knew he was there for him? It was kind of like the opposite. He just let him go, being soul-shaken by the loss, but never showing it, rarely even mentioning it, compartmentalizing his son in his own mind to the point of almost complete denial. The need to keep things mellow or avoid conflict dictated everything Adam's father had control over. Adam didn't think his father was necessarily afraid of what a struggle every day can be, but he certainly wasn't going to invite conflict, which his brother most certainly represented. So his father wrote him off, as he had done with his parents, brother and sisters. Adam knew his mother did almost everything she could to let his brother know she was there for him if he ever wanted to rejoin his family, even if that meant him berating her for it. But his father did nothing, just like his father never called him or got in contact with him other than when he visited them every few months. Not that it affected Adam day to day. His dad was his dad, he was there, relatively mellow, loving, good sense of humor, working in the City. He just didn't get involved in anything long-term or very deep, like promoting self or family interest. He worked, came home, had a martini or two, had dinner, watched TV, and then got into bed and went to sleep. And on the weekends he'd go wherever Adam's mother wanted to go, mostly shopping, except during the summer, when they rented a cabana at The Sands, one of the beach clubs in Long Beach Long Island, where he'd sit for hours, reading the paper, dozing in the sun, or striking up a conversation with one of the other dads who had a cabana near theirs. Adam knew it could have been a lot worse. But he wasn't sure that was the best or most useful basis of comparison. He was also relatively sure that life was much more complex than someone's ability to define it for someone else, and that most guys have issues with their dads; the whole competition thing, wanting your dad to be Superman, but at some point realizing he's just a man whose psychology is not exactly heroic.

Adam believed his father came to terms with his life as he got older, mid to late 70's and after, still schlepping into the City, the last few years with a geriatric cane. It was always comforting to see him finally mellow out. It centered Adam. His father smoked four packs of cigarettes a day for over forty years and stopped with hypnosis cold turkey because he was starting to get emphysema. Lived another twenty years. Definitely old-world stock. There were still horse-drawn carriages in the city streets when he was growing up. How Adam was growing up, an on-going process, was a reflection of his father; not the total man, and not Adam's total make-up. There were many other factors, but parents are definitely up there. Adam tended to have more good days than bad days, so there you go.

Adam's mother passed away five years after his father, also without being able to bring her oldest son back into her life. She had been a life-long smoker who had no problem lighting up while wearing a nasal-cannula attached to her oxygen, which she needed for the last two or three years of her life. COPD and subsequent hospital visits couldn't break her addiction. She had quit for about a year right before Adam's father died, but saw no reason not to take it up again once he was gone, although she knew better than to smoke in front of Adam or Barry. That wouldn't have gone over well. But, considering she had lost her husband, and, to all intents and purposes her oldest son, if she wanted to smoke in private, they didn't give her too much of a hard time. The fact that she was alive, had her wits about her, and wasn't in any pain after almost forty years of subsisting on coffee, cigarettes, cottage cheese, and chicken every now and again, was enough. They let her live the way she wanted to live, until her last hospital stay – she was seventy-seven – when it was obvious there was no way she could continue to live alone in her house anymore. It wasn't even advisable for her to live there with full-time help – too many steps, no ramps. By that time she was, more or less, wheelchair-dependent. She didn't have the strength or sureness of foot to walk with the oxygen attached to her walker. Both Adam and Barry insisted she could live with them, and that, not only wouldn't she be a burden, which was why she wouldn't do it, but that it would be their families' pleasure to take care of her. She wouldn't hear of it. So they agreed that, as soon as she was well enough, they would transfer her to an assisted living facility twenty minutes away from where Adam lived, and not much more than that from Barry. Because she was so sick, she wasn't able to check out the facility before she moved in. She would have to be transferred by ambulance directly to her new apartment when she was well enough to be released from the hospital. But Adam and Barry brought her all the brochures, and assured her it was a new, high-end complex with excellent medical care. She knew her health had deteriorated to the point where she didn't have many options, and accepted her fate. She knew her lifestyle had brought her to where she was. She wasn't complaining or in denial. Nor did she have many regrets, other than the big one, her oldest son. She was fighting to keep her dignity. The fact that she still had her two sons loving her and looking after her kept her spirit from sinking too low. Adam knew a lot of her up-beat spirit on the phone was not wanting inflict her sorrow onto her children, but better that than giving in. She was fighting for her piece of mind. Although she loved her grandchildren more than anything in the world, she had been hesitant to have them visit her after she got sick because she was afraid they'd be scared of how she looked. She didn't want her grandchildren remembering her as an old, frail, drawn woman with tubes in her nose who shuffled along dragging her oxygen behind her. When she moved into the assisted living facility, and her life normalized a bit, her grandchildren visited her more often, and it was always beautiful to see her gather her strength to be the loving grandma she had always been. When the time came to discuss selling her house, she accepted that transition with humility. She knew she wasn't ever moving back there.

She lived relatively happily at the assisted living facility for about eight months before her final trip back to the hospital. She had made friends there, and her family visited her more often than they did when she was still living at home. Then, one of the nurse's aids at the facility dropped an oxygen canister on her foot, causing an infection that lead to other circulatory complications, ultimately landing her in the ICU.

Visiting her at the hospital one day, Adam told her they had spoken to a real estate agent, a friend of hers from Baldwin, who highly recommended they put her house on the market as soon as possible. Housing prices in Baldwin were still good, and there weren't a lot of homes for sale. That was due to change in the foreseeable future.

'You gotta get the gun outta there,' Doris said, through her morphine haze. As soon as she said it, Adam knew what she was talking about. She never threw Charles's hand-gun in the creek. That was the first thing that came to her mind when he told her they were finally going to sell her house.

'Where is it?' Adam asked, smiling. He couldn't believe she kept his brother's gun in her house all those years.

'In the top draw in my dresser, in the back.' She was slurring and metabolically compromised, but the gun she was very clear about.

'Okay. Did daddy know you kept it?'

'Are you kidding,' meaning, 'No way'. 'Promise me you'll get rid of it.'

'What am I gonna do with it. Of course I'm gonna get rid of it.'

As soon as Adam finished his visit, he drove to Baldwin, went up to his mother's bedroom, opened her sock and underwear draw, reached in the back, and there it was, stuffed inside an old pair of pantyhose, the silver, thirty-two caliber Rossi pistol his brother had pointed at him and threatened to shoot him with roughly thirty-two years before. It was like an ancient artifact, only it wasn't ancient. Or an artifact. It was a fully functional deadly weapon. It felt so bizarre to hold that gun in his hand, so violent, so outside every other experience he'd ever had.

'What the fuck am I gonna do with this?' he thought. He was going to walk to the creek at the end of his block and throw it in, close the circle, bury that shit at the bottom of the sea. Before he did anything, he checked to see if the gun was loaded. It wasn't. 'Maybe I should keep it,' he thought. Kind of like a piece of psychotic family history. 'No, fuck that.' That was all he needed, his daughter to find a gun in the house.

How strange it was to walk down the block he had grown up on with a handgun concealed in his pocket. It made him feel hyper self-conscious. Almost everyone who had lived there when he had was long gone. His mother had been one of the last original families in the neighborhood. He was a stranger on his own block. A stranger with a gun in his pocket. Luckily, there weren't a lot of people around. He walked to a very secluded area of the creek – he didn't want anybody seeing what he was doing – took the gun out of his pocket, looked at it dispassionately for a second, and tossed it into the middle of the creek. It was very anti-climactic, like getting rid of a useless piece of garbage.

The walk back to his mother's house was not lost on him. He knew it was the last time he would ever walk the full distance from the creek to his parent's house, a walk he had done well over a thousand times.

That was his newspaper route forty years before. He used to know every family on that block – who tipped and who didn't, who had dogs, whose house smelled weird. It was a nostalgia trip he hadn't expected to take, but one he felt deeply.

When he got back to his mother's house, even that felt like a thing of the past. Some of her furniture had been brought over to the assisted living facility, so the vibe of the house had changed, diminished. And, it had been unoccupied for over half a year. He felt its emptiness, its loss of life within. He looked forward to someone buying it and restoring its soul.

'Did you get rid of it?' his mother asked on his next visit a day or two later. It was the first and only thing she said. She was nearly comatose, but had enough energy to rouse herself to make sure Adam had done what she had needed done.

'I did. I threw it in the creek.'

She looked at him like he was fucking around with her.

'I really did. I promise.'

She nodded, closed her eyes, and slipped right back into her far-away place. The next day she was unhooked from life-support. Nine minutes after that, Barry and Adam watched her take her last breath. They were glad they were there for her all the way through. It felt right to be there. It was all part of it. Acceptance. Facing death. Both Barry and Adam fathers. One generation passing away, another being born. They were both thankful for the love they shared.

Three weeks after Adam's mother passed away Adam got a call from a Sergeant Benson from the LAPD. Adam had just turned fifty, and was married, for eight years, to the head of the Physics department at Queens University. Dr. Susan Paik, granddaughter of Hyun Ki Paik, renowned artist, political activist and writer, daughter of Dr. Kyubok Paik, an MD/PhD doing stem cell research as it related to curing certain neurological diseases and cancers, and Dr. Myung-He 'Mary' Paik, a pediatrician at Columbia Presbyterian. Susan and Adam were set up on a blind date by one of the producers he was working with, who was producing a segment on Hyun Ki Paik. He interviewed all three Dr.'s Paik, and had a feeling about Susan; she and Adam should meet. As diplomatically and professionally as he could, he steered the off-camera conversation toward that aim. Adam had set him up with a sexy six-foot-one friend of a friend, and they fell in love. He hoped he could return the favor.

It wasn't really happening on their first date - no sparks flying, very different personalities – she was a little put off that he took a piece of lamb, which she said was perfectly cooked, from her plate; an unintentional invasion of her personal space, and an infraction of first-date etiquette. A second date was highly unlikely, until their cab-ride to drop each of them home, cruising along the FDR on a beautiful autumn evening, the jewel-like lights draping the cables of the three bridges, the picturesque expanse of the East River, the very essence of New York freedom and grace. Somehow Adam got to talking about the most prized episodes of The Twilight Zone; the 'Leg of Lamb' episode, the 'Nightmare At 20,000 Feet' episode, where a young William Shatner sees the gremlin on the wing of the airplane, and 'The Hitchhiker', where a woman was driving along a desolate road and picks up a hitchhiker and drops him off a few miles ahead. A short time later, without any cars having passed her, she sees the same guy hitching along the same road. She picks him up and drops him off again. And then again. By the time Adam explained that the hitchhiker represented death, and that the woman suddenly realized she had passed away, Susan was so spooked, in a fun, horror-movie way, that their inability to connect throughout dinner quickly evolved into something tangible, something that would only be revealed by exploring it together. Nine years later they had a five year old daughter, and were living in a hundred year old Victorian home in Glen Cove, Long Island.

'Does anyone at the residence know of a Charles Strulovitz from Los Angeles?' Sergeant Benson asked, over the phone.

'He's my brother,' Adam said, thinking, 'What a weird call.' Then he knew. 'Did he die?' he asked. Something about the officer's tone, and the randomness of the call. Adam felt a paradigm shift, a softness of focus infused in the conversation. Time's winged ship was carrying another member of his family away. It had just taken his mother.

'Can you verify your name for me?'

'Adam Strulovitz.'

'And your address?'

'17 Palen Street, Glen…'

'Do you have another… What street did you grow up on?'

'Lexington Ave.'

'That's it. Yes, I'm sorry to inform you that your brother passed away on Monday. No, correction. That's when we found him. He may have passed away several days before that. We're still waiting for the report.'

Officer Benson informed Adam that the preliminary investigation indicated Charles had died of a heart attack. He explained that the reason he got the date of Charles's passing wrong was because Charles might have been dead for a while before the police were called. They found him because a neighbor smelled something terrible coming from his apartment. That neighbor had knocked on his door, over a series of days, to complain, or at least find out what was going on, but there was no answer. Finally, the neighbor called the police, who let themselves in. Officer Benson also told Adam how difficult it was to find someone to report his brother's passing to. He had tried calling the number listed for a Doris Strulovitz on Lexington Avenue, but there was no answer. Adam told him why.

'Sorry to hear that,' Officer Benson said. 'At least she…' He was able to convey how it could have been worse if the sequence of their deaths had been reversed. 'Anyway, seems like your brother kept very much to himself.'

Charles had no one. Adam didn't know much about his brother's life, other than what he'd seen on his hypnotherapy website, which Adam went on once or twice just to check it out. He thought some of his brother's motivational methodology was very compelling. He was also aware of some of Charles's professional clientele, whose testimonials proved his potential. But at the time of his passing, there wasn't one person close enough to him to mourn his loss. Not that that's an important judge of character, or even a necessary element in some peoples' lives. But, not one person knew Charles well enough to really miss him. No friends, no lovers, no family. He died alone, on the toilet, in a one-bedroom apartment in a lower middle-class suburb of L.A., with a few thousand dollars in the bank, the sum total of his worldly assets. He was fifty-one years old. The apartment manager, who Adam had spoken to prior to

Barry and him going out to California to sign all the paperwork and take possession of their brother and his estate, told him that Charles had been in terrible shape prior to his passing – very overweight, unable to climb the few steps up to his apartment without stopping to take a few sweat-soaked, hunched-over deep breaths. That image, together with the pictures of Charles from his website, older, overweight, bald, brought it all the way home for Adam. He didn't know his brother, who he became as a man. He didn't even look like his brother. If Adam had passed the man who was pictured on his website on the street, he might have done a double-take, but then said, 'No. No way. Couldn't be.' But he was. His brother. And now he was gone. Thank God their mother didn't have to know.

At that point, all Adam's anger and unresolved emotions melted away. That circle was forever closed. Charles would always be a part of him, a part of his life. His death reflected Adam's mortality. He was so sorry he died alone, without love or friendship, or family. What he was left with was a prayer for Charles's eternal peace, made much less sad by twenty-five years of estrangement. There might have been some kind of Shakespearean justice in there somewhere. Adam didn't force his emotions nor did he hold them back. He didn't grieve, but he was moved. It was a weird perspective. But it kept coming back to love. Adam wished they could have loved like brothers. He realized when it came to life and relationships and matters of the heart, most people were going to lose big every once in a while. It was rarely a Hollywood ending. All anyone can do is try their best to let misfortune go and grasp whatever good lies within their reach.

When his father died, they buried his ashes in the sand in front of the cabana his father and mother rented at The Sands Beach Club in Long Beach for almost fifty years – by far his father's favorite place away from home. Right on the ocean. Where else would he rather spend eternity? They didn't scatter his ashes because it wasn't appropriate for beach patrons, when the summer came, to have to walk through the ashes of someone's cremated father, or have those ashes blow onto their lunch while they were enjoying the sunshine. It was a heart-felt little ceremony with just Adam and Barry's families, and their mother in attendance. Because it was during the off-season, there wasn't another soul around.

Just the gulls and the piping plovers. They dug the hole, about a foot down, poured the ashes in, and covered it back up. Their mother held her emotions in check, only because she wanted to be strong for them. Adam admired her depth of reflection. He knew she was thinking about her whole life, her sisters, both adored, one, the oldest, Aunt Min having died from bone cancer a little less than a year before, now her husband, her beloved parents, years before but never far away, always in her heart. There wasn't much to say. There wasn't much that needed to be said. The cycles of life and death would continue to be reenacted long after they, too, turned to dust. This was their time. And that, too, would pass.

'I love you,' their mother whispered, saying good-bye to her husband of fifty years. She was at the beach, her home away from home. She'd be back at the end of June. Adam knew she was thinking, 'I'll see you soon.'

They buried their mother's ashes in the same hole five years later – fifteen steps from the end of the walkway into the middle of the two rows. They might have been a little off with the exact location of their father's ashes, but it didn't matter. It was close enough. Their parents were where they wanted to be.

When Adam got Charles's ashes, sent UPS from California, Barry and he drove down to The Sands Beach Club and walked those coordinates for the last time. Just them. Not their families. Two brothers coming to terms with the death of an older brother who had made the decision to want nothing to do with them. Yet there they were, all together.

'You should say something,' Barry said before they cut open the plastic bag containing their brother's ashes. He was sad about his brother dying, but because Charles had so little respect for him throughout his life, he didn't feel he needed to say anything. It was enough to bury the past, or at least try.

'All right,' Adam said. 'Well, I hope you're finally at peace. And I'm so glad you're here with mommy and daddy. May God watch over you and keep you.' He got choked up. Not too much, but it was definitely deep. 'All right, let's do this.'

CHAPTER 19

So who's a better poet?

There's an allegory in the Talmud about a fox who tried to get through a fence surrounding a vineyard so he could eat all of the grapes. But the one hole in the fence was too small for him to squeeze through because he was big and strong, hunting and surviving, thriving, since he was turned out of the den. But he was a persistent fox and kept trying to squeeze through the hole, like he was possessed. Eventually, he managed to climb through the hole because he had been so committed to getting the grapes that he neglected to eat for a few days and lost the requisite weight. Once inside he feasted... ate enough to almost get him through the winter.

'Wait 'til my friends see what I did,' he thought with pride. 'I better get out of here before that human with the boom-stick sees what I did.'

But when he got to the hole he couldn't fit through. He was too fat from eating all those grapes.

'Like shootin' fish in a barrel,' the farmer thought later that afternoon, as he leveled his shotgun at the fat fox who had somehow managed to breech his fence.

Adam didn't want to lament what he didn't have; recognition, validation. He wanted to celebrate what he did - over two hundred songs, more than a hundred beyond Energy, all starting with a drum track, and then Adam singing a bass-line over it, and then playing that bass-line on the Roland XP 30 multi-voice keyboard he bought to give his music greater depth, something he figured out how to do out of necessity and the inherent understanding of rhythm as it applies to bass and drums - the interplay, the essential rhythm. Especially his rhythms, which he was able to play off of at the most organic level. He felt how a real bass play would interpret the track, and recorded his vocal interpretation of that bass-line. Because his Roland XP 30 had many different bass settings; acoustic, fretless, fender jazz, slap, classic rock, heavy metal, he was able to choose the most appropriate bass sound for the type of song he wanted to write. Then it was just a matter of taking the time to replace his vocal notes with bass notes, one or two notes at a time, a process which usually took a week or two. Once the bass-line was done and the rhythm section more or less composed, he would either sing a melody line over the rhythm section, feeling out how the lyrics he would write would be sung; notes, phrasing, tempo, cadence, or he would scat a rhythm that would approximate how the poem he would write would be recited or rapped. Adam loved getting into a hard 'Rage Against The Machine' rap. He understood the power, the fullness of expression. Then he would write and record the words, the lyrics, writing on the LIRR into Manhattan in the morning and out again in the evening, and more writing and recording at night and on the weekends. He had even met a local guitar legend, Tommy Vincent, who played with everyone from Bo Diddley to Brittany Spears, who charged him three hundred dollars per song to chart and then record one or two guitar tracks. Sometimes Adam would sing and record how he thought the basic rhythm guitar track should go, and email it to Tommy, along with all the other tracks, and sometimes Tommy would do his thing, generally following the bass-line for the rhythm guitar track, and then overdubbing the lead guitar track over that.

It had gotten to the point in Adam's creative process where he felt he had to – there was no rhyme or reason not to, reach out to other musicians, a guitarist, to make his songs come alive. Maybe it was because, after Charles's passing, Adam felt how uncertain the continuity of life was, how unknowable. He started feeling it was time to go for it. Fill the void, the lack of artistic sharing and collaborating. Not that Adam grieved for his brother – one or two moments of sadness that passed as quickly as a cloud across the sun. Apparently, any emotional connection had been erased by their years of estrangement. It was more a feeling of not wasting the time he had. Even with the full life he was living; family and work and creativity - the disappointment of not doing anything with his music was becoming deeper. He had written real rock, rap and jazz, and no one knew or heard; the old, 'If a tree falls in a forest and no one hears it, did it make a sound?' No one was going to answer that question but the one steering the ship across the indefinable cosmic sea. Keep it on course. Try to seize the moments when they arise. Create his own. Maybe he got to where he wanted to go, maybe he didn't, maybe he never really knew what that was to begin with. But the ship's gotta stay on course. Adam would listen to the song he had just completed; drums, bass, vocals, and knew he couldn't be imagining how real and wild it was, could be, if he could get a well-crafted guitar track on it, something his musical knowledge was too limited to enable him to figure out how to do on his keyboard. That was all the songs needed to breathe life into them. Without guitar they were incomplete, performance art. With guitar, they were ready. He knew a lot of local guitarists, really good guitarists. He had seen Tommy Vincent several times at local venues, and each time he had wished he could sit in, jam with him. Tommy was the real deal, a true guitar-slinger outlaw virtuoso, who happened to live a few blocks away from Adam.

'Fuck it. I'm calling him,' Adam decided. Break through the fear of rejection. What's the worst that could happen? That Tommy would say no? At least Adam was trying to move forward. If not Tommy, then someone else. But first Tommy, whose phone number was listed in the local directory.

'Hey man. My name's Adam,' Adam said over the phone. Tommy was the same generation as Adam, give or take a few years. It looked like Tommy had lived a pretty full life. Not old, but not young. But when he closed his eyes and took off, holy shit. All you could do was let it rock you; his deeper understanding of how to tap into the universal energy. It flowed through him.

'I'm a local musician, drummer mostly, and songwriter,' Adam continued, 'and I was wondering if... you'd be interested in laying down some guitar tracks on some of my songs. They're mostly progressive rock... some with a blues base. And some are more fusiony. I'm also pretty into swingin', but that's for another time. I have a home ProTools rig in my studio, and I'm only a few blocks away. So...'

'Okay, cool. Why don't you send me a song or two you want me to play on and I'll check it out...'

The door was open. It wasn't an 'I'd love to,' but Adam felt his songs had a good shot at tipping the balance.

'Definitely. By the way, I was at your gig a few weeks ago at JB's.'

'What'd ya think? What'd you think of the drummer? It was the first time we played with him.'

Adam thought the drummer was the weakest member of the band, and had wondered why he wasn't playing with Tommy instead. He knew he could have brought a lot more energy.

'He was great, man,' Adam said.

'I know. Really good pocket. Glad you were there. So, send me your stuff and I'll get back to you.'

Adam wondered if Tommy was just being nice, if he got the same request from every wannabe songwriter in the area. No way to tell. Adam had to be patient. He couldn't expect Tommy to listen to his music on his timetable. Give it a week, maybe a little more, and then, if he didn't call, accept defeat and move on. Call another guitarist. Don't give up the quest to validate the songs with a clear musical identity, the way only a guitar can. The songs sounded too intense to Adam to leave them unfinished. It was all part of the progression, the evolution of artistic expression. Adam still felt he was just at the beginning, thirty years on. But he knew getting his songs fully composed would be a milestone. He felt he was closer than farther away.

Two days later Tommy emailed Adam back.

'Very cool,' he wrote. 'Would love to play on them. I'll chart the rhythm track, and we'll see where that takes us. $300 per song. I'm free Monday evenings. Let me know if that works. T.'

'How's next Monday at 8,' Adam emailed.

'8. Email me your address. It'll be fun.'

'Yes it will.'

It was. Because Adam did everything in the studio himself, everyday, for hours a day, for years, he was a proficient engineer - not necessarily sonically versatile, but quick and efficient, and could capture a clean level that a better engineer could easily mix and master. Tommy was free to concentrate on his musicianship, which, Adam saw, was immense. Tommy had written out, chord for chord, the entire rhythm guitar part (which, when the session was over he gave to Adam, who loved knowing that his song existed as a written work). The chart was so accurate that Tommy played through whole sections in one take, and it was exactly what Adam was hoping to hear; crunching rock power-chords propelling the song forward.

'That felt pretty good,' Tommy said, after the rhythm guitar track was laid down. 'What do you think?'

'I think you did it,' Adam said. 'I can't wait to hear what you're gonna lay down over this.'

'Okay, just play it through a few times, lemme...'

'Okay, you ready?'

'Yeah. Just gimme a second... Okay...'

Adam knew exactly what Tommy needed, to jam along with the song and get a feel for how he wanted to lay down the lead track...

'Okay, stop there,' Tommy would say. 'Bring it back a few measures.' And Adam was able to give Tommy what he needed almost as fast as he could think it.

'Okay, let it just play,' Tommy said, after feeling his way through the song a second time.

He did it in one take, at a level Adam could only have dreamed of; like Clapton or Hendrix had played on his song. He felt a sense of validation he had rarely felt; watching a world-class musician digging deep to give his music its fullest expression... the fact that his music commanded that level of musical energy, as he could only have suspected. You can't fully know a sculpture until the last piece of stone is chipped away.

'Why don't you play it through one time to make sure you got everything you want,' Tommy suggested.

It was all there. Deep, fluid, melodic. Adam knew how into it Tommy was by his facial expressions, and the fact the he would touch Adam on the elbow and silently indicate he wanted him to listen to a specific riff that was coming up.

'Well all right... Sounds good, man,' Tommy said, packing up, slipping the three hundred dollars into his pocket, like that was the necessary evil of an otherwise collaborative artistic endeavor.

'So, do I get to get you on more songs?' Adam asked, hopeful.

'I'm around next Monday, then I'm going on a mini-tour with Neil for a few weeks, but I'll be around after that. I've already started the chart for the other song you sent me.'

Neil Young. All Adam could think was, 'This guy is playing with Neil Young, and he's in my studio playing guitar on my songs.'

'So let's do that one next Monday,' Adam said, inwardly joyous, 'and we'll see what happens after that.'

Even though Adam was jumping out of his skin to get Tommy to play on as many songs as he could, as quickly as he could, he didn't want to scare him away with his over-zealousness. He knew he had to keep it easy, keep it fun. The money was not what would keep Tommy coming back.

'I'm down with that. Send me the track once you've mixed it. Don't forget a little extra volume and reverb on the solo sections.'

'You'll be duly represented, I promise. I really appreciate you doing this. It's kinda like a dream come true.'

'It was fun.'

As was their next session, and the one after that, all the way through twelve songs, at which point Tommy had to leave for a four month tour of South America with Shakira. Twelve songs, all sounding to Adam like they could be played in concert. It was an amazingly intensive six months of musical creativity; playing, recording, mixing, listening. Even though the final versions were less dynamic than a professional recording – not only was Adam not a professional engineer, he didn't have the high-end equipment professional studios have - they never failed to blow Adam away.

But as had been the pattern of Adam's life, most lives Adam suspected, there were highs and lows, the highs of having his songs fully realized giving way, by the fifth or sixth listen, a few months after the last time Adam had recorded Tommy, to Adam feeling like he was back inside his world of isolation, bummed out that the whirlwind of colorful electro–magnetic melody and vibration was fading into the past, that Tommy was just a phase, of limited consequence, the songs he was on no more than more evolved versions of all the other songs on Adam's hard-drives, to be catalogued and heard by very few. It felt like buying a lottery ticket and dreaming about how his life would change if he won, and then learning he only got one out of the seven numbers, and he was right back to the life he had maligned during his dreams of fortune. But how could he complain after listening to *Like Leonard Said* and *Three Photographs*. He felt blessed to have been given the talent to write those songs. What he needed was a little luck, the unexpected receiving of good fortune. Adam's was a life of small gains over long distances, the evolution of his music his life's work. He'd never thought of himself as lucky. Or perhaps luck had saved itself up for the only time Adam ever really needed it, the culmination of all the staying away from walking under ladders and shiny heads-up pennies ever collected.

Adam's daughter was in fifth grade. On the south side of her elementary school was a little street, little even by home-town standards. Across the street was the school's playground - nicely wooded, very peaceful and 'after-school play-time' raucous at the same time, but safe. Usually the kids ran across that street after school because there was rarely any traffic during school hours. And if there was, people from the neighborhood knew to take it easy. And there were always a lot of parents around waiting to pick up their children, which was what Adam was doing when he saw his daughter coming out of the side door of the school, and all she knew was that all of her friends were already on the monkey-bars, and that was where she was going. And if Adam hadn't been right there and seen the car out of his periphery fly through the stop-sign on the corner and come barreling down that street... And if he had missed grabbing enough of a hold of his daughter's Girls Rock!, with a picture of a diamond on it tee-shirt, to stop her momentum, life would have taken an unthinkable turn. The right place at the right time. A rare but fundamental stroke of luck. Adam made a deal with God right there. He would take care of everything in his life on his own, not even a hint of divine or cosmic intervention, except when it came to keeping his daughter safe in an unpredictable world. All chips and karma credit were to be redeemed on that. Adam looked at his daughter, who was looking at him not knowing why he had grabbed her shirt from behind. She seemed perplexed.

'Can't I play?" she asked.

Adam looked around, saw that it was safe... 'Of course. But then you have piano.'

'K.'

The day after that happened, they closed off the street with steel posts and chain, because the day it happened Adam went right to the Principal and started freaking out, along with a few other parents who were there, one of whom had had a similar experience earlier in the year, and had lodged a formal complaint then. She got much louder than Adam, who had given her the floor.

Adam knew grabbing onto his daughter's shirt at the last possible second was very lucky. He also felt lucky that he always knew he was a drummer, since he was eight years old, even if those dreams were deferred until Charles went to college. As soon as he could he followed that instinct without ever questioning if he was doing the right thing. A very real impulse was revealed to him, and he knew to go for it regardless of discouragement or distraction. He was sure many people had similar revelations, but something prohibited them from following it, whether it was from within or without. And he was certain many people were still looking for the right path to follow.

But over the course of Adam's life, luck had rarely played a part. Mostly it was a daily grind - finding happiness and fulfillment in those moments revealed to him as happy and fulfilling, where he breathed a little easier, and knew he was, essentially, on the right path. Even then, doubt wasn't more than a thought away. He could listen to one of the songs he had recorded with Tommy and be uplifted by how real and intense it was, how blessed he felt to be able to do what he did. And two seconds after the song was over, he would be bummed out that he had no way of sharing what he had done with anyone, like the song was a library book on a shelf in a library that only existed in Adam's world.

'I gotta figure this out,' Adam thought. 'I can't let these songs die on the vine.'

But more months passed since he had recorded with Tommy. He was back to his old process of singing a bass-line over a drum track, that would eventually become an incomplete song no one would hear. He started to feel like the Colonel in the Gabriel Garcia Marquez masterpiece *One Hundred Years Of Solitude*, who, in his time of absolute power, was so isolated that he would mold beautiful small fish out of gold, only to melt them down again when they were finished, and remold them into the exact same shape, more passing the time than the fruit of labor. But for Adam, the seeds of progress had been planted; ideas about performing the songs. Because he knew putting a band together was not going to happen - as a suburban dad without the access to players who would drop what they were doing to do his thing - maybe he could front his own music with his tracks behind him, like karaoke...

'Do it like a show,' he continued formulating, the idea of a 'Storytellers' type of experience hovering around the place of inception; stories, into the songs, maybe some other performance elements. He could envision it, mixed tracks of the song, minus vocals, on play-back, another musician, Tommy, maybe, hopefully, breathing more life into the musical experience. If it was all mixed properly live, the energy of the songs should come across, even though half of it was pre-recorded. It wasn't as if Adam hadn't felt the need to express his creativity to a live audience before.

Over the years since his artistic impulses became stronger and identity defining - beginning with writing and recording Energy - Adam had jumped into the unknown of live performance, both musical and theatrical several times - home-grown and unpolished performances he always came away from more enriched than when he went in, never a regret about having done what he did, as infrequently as he did it. He had put his shit out there hoping it would lead to something. But those performances never built upon themselves. They were more like a high peak on an EKG that immediately settled back to the rhythm of daily life. But he knew he had to start somewhere, begin to pay the dues that would eventually yield dividends.

Paying his dues. That was exactly what was going through Adam's mind, almost a generation before recording with Tommy Vincent, as he sat alone, scanning the poorly attended poetry reading he was slated to perform at, yet another solo Saturday night right after the Reagan era trying to push his artistry forward bit by bit. At least he was doing it, putting his words where his hopes were. Because the first songs he had written, starting with *Bird*, felt so much like beat poetry, he had read at a few poetry readings, eventually, one night, becoming one of the featured poets at one of Greenwich Village's last coffee shop and late night bars popularized by The Beats in the mid-to-late fifties and early sixties. The only problem was how weird the poetry sub-culture in New York City had become since its heyday. Not the poetry slams, which had more of a hip, musical vibe – but the hard-core poets who bore their naked souls to rooms of three or four audience members: like the Russian guy who performed right before Adam, who chain-smoked and chain-drank black coffee, performing his poetry in the most serious adjustment he could embody.

'I bleed to death from my soul,' he recited, in a thick Russian accent. 'You bleed from your cunt. We bleed together.'

And the crazy thing was, he was there with his wife or girlfriend, who seemed to be completely mesmerized by this guy's bullshit. He was literally talking about fucking this woman, who was very attractive, in the gutter and on a mountain, and her begging him for it. And Adam was going home alone and jerking-off onto an old tee shirt.

'So who's the better poet?' Adam wondered.

At the last poetry reading Adam attended, a woman roughly his age at the time, early thirties, with a shaved head and hairy legs shoved yams up her ass, and while she recited a poem about the joys of indulgence, shit the yams out, for which she got a standing ovation. Adam had to admit, it was pretty awesome.

After his stint as a poet, still in his early thirties, the idea of performing; conceiving and writing a show, some vehicle that got Adam back on stage expressing, sharing his creativity with an audience had taken root. Too much time alone in the studio. Not enough balance. What were all those thousands of hours of practicing, writing, recording without sharing it with an audience? Adam's evolution as an artist was slow, with ideas for big projects few and far between, but deep, real. He knew when a good idea had come to him, one he would devote a great deal of time and energy to, like Energy. When he thought about writing and performing his own show, he felt something settle within him. The undeniable touch of grace, a subtle epiphany, evolving, being influenced by, inspired by other artists he had seen; Eric Bogosian, Lori Anderson, Bruce Springsteen. Bruce made Adam want to be a better man. Achieve his potential. Share the beauty of creativity, of self-expression. If only to know he did it because Bruce Springsteen inspired him to do it. Make Bruce proud, in the abstract. Lay it on the line. Jump and the net will appear.

Four months after Adam saw Bruce Springsteen and the E Street Band at Madison Square Garden, less than a year after his last poetry reading, he had completed the first draft of a one-man show that included character monologues - a Jewish deli owner, a transvestite hooker from the meat-packing district, an Indian cabbie - the story of when he was in Alaska visiting an ex-coworker from his Telecom days, and they were camping in Danali, and the pit bulls his ex-coworker and her future ex-husband bred started freaking out because a grizzly bear and her cub could be seen in the distance, and how, when he got out of his tent to seek shelter in the cab of the flatbed they were traveling in, a swarm of mosquitos the size of dragon-flies descended on his naked body, and then he got stung in the ass by angry bee he somehow sat on. There was also a physical humor section; seeing how many marshmallow he could shove in his mouth and still say 'pudgie bunnies', holding matches in place in his furrowed brow, lighting them, and doing his impression of a truck at night. He also included a quasi stand-up section about when his brother Barry and he got the giggles in inappropriate places; the General Assembly of the UN... When Barry saw Adam's fly was open he exploded in laughter, sending Adam over the edge with him; The Metropolitan Opera House during a performance of the Grand Kabuki when silence was assumed. They had to get up and leave; At temple on Yom Kippur listening to a woman tell about her suffering - spouse and child dead, a cancer survivor, her beloved sister dying of leukemia – they had to get up and leave from there as well.

Everything seemed to work. There was a good vibe in the small theater on 18th Street, with friends and family and coworkers in attendance. Adam's performance felt, for the most part, fluid. It all felt natural. He knew, as he was performing, that some of his material was better than other, which meant some was worse; like the story of when a pigeon flew onto his face-shield when he was on I95. He had just finished a motorcycle trip through New England and was on the way home when the pigeon got caught in the updraft of an eighteen-wheeler right in front of him doing about eighty, and was thrown onto Adam's face spread-winged, right outside of Boston, some of the densest and most challenging Interstate in the country, no place you want a freaked-out pigeon blocking your vision. But overall he held his own as a first-time performer.

And that accomplishment, through some magic alignment of time, space, and prayer led to him having sex with two lesbians, one who he had worked with on a few productions, who he saw on the street and they got to talking, and he mentioned he was almost done writing a show, and she said she knew someone who ran a small theater on 18th Street, and one thing lead to another, and there they were, after the show, Brenda, a big Irish girl, very attractive, great spirit - you could leave your kids with her for a month and they'd be better behaved and happier than when you dropped them off, and her partner Terry, the more sultry of the two. The three of them were cleaning up the theater, putting everything back the way they found it.

'Talent is so sexy, don't you think so,' Brenda said to Terry.

'You should keep at this. That was really good. Did that really happen at the kabuki?'

'It did.'

'Let's go get some cocktails.'

Three margaritas in, beautifully buzzed, the fact that he had just performed his one-man show settling in, Brenda on one side of him, Terry on the other, the thee of them sitting at a classic, old style New York City bar; dark wood, low lights, comfortable stools, both of them pressing into him – he felt their warmth, their rhythm. Still he didn't think he had a shot. He was of the wrong persuasion, and they were, like, married. He was just thankful to be hanging out on such a fulfilling night with friends, who happened to be women, who happened to be pressing against him without inhibition, Brenda's large boobs constantly butting up against his shoulder. He already owed her a favor for helping him with his show. He didn't want to be disrespectful in any way by bringing attention to how nice her boobs felt against him, which he was thinking of doing, by way of suggesting how much more he would like to do with her boobs.

'Talent is so sexy,' Brenda said a second time, actually jiggling her chest against his shoulder and upper arm.

'That's gotta be something,' Adam thought. 'Once, I could see. But twice? Nah. No way. She's just being super friendly.'

'You can't do that to me," he said, half-joking. 'I'm too fragile right now. You're gonna make me have to go to the bathroom and play with my little friend.'

'What's the matter, you've never been with two women before?'

'Only in my mind.'

'Sweetie, why don't you settle up the tab,' Brenda said to Terry, a look passing between them. 'And then we'll get outta here.'

'Easy come, easy go,' thought Adam, a little bummed that one of the great nights of his life was coming to an end, with him, ultimately, going him alone. Same as it ever was, regardless of how cool he thought he was performing his own one-man show.

Outside the bar, Brenda hailed a cab that was passing by, opening the door for Terry, who got in. 'Come on, Mr. Sexy Pants. Let's continue this party uptown.'

The party started in the cab, all three of them making out with each other, Brenda and Terry's right hands rubbing Adam's crotch over his pants, him screaming for joy on the inside. At one point Adam looked up and saw, in the rear-view mirror the cabbie's chagrin at what was going on in the back of his cab. Boy, did Adam not give a shit. He was thankful it was happening, all the way to Hells Kitchen. Their behavior was a little more appropriate once out of the cab and on the street, but heated up again three seconds after the apartment door closed behind them, which was how long it took them to get naked. Instinct lead Adam to Terry's clit. She sat in the corner of their plush couch, leaning back in cobbler's pose, very receptive to Adam's tongue. He was extremely comfortable on his knees on the thick, padded carpet, her lap a perfect height off the floor. The whole thing felt like its own comfortable yoga pose; cunning linguist's pose, kneeling bear at a honey-pool pose, Brenda next to Terry on the couch, making out with her, sucking her tits, holding the back of Adam's head in her palm while he ate her wife out.

'Hold on Adam,' Brenda said. He was on-task, lit. For a billionth of a second he thought something went wrong, that it was over and could get weird.

'Thank God,' he speed-thought after the moment passed. They were just changing position, Terry roll-sliding over face down into Brenda's lap, Terry on her knees, back arched, whole butt calling Adam over like the holy grail, him going for it, the dream tableaux for a horny heterosexual thirty-something man who hadn't gotten laid in longer than he would care to admit. Adam let himself absorb the beauty of what was going on, the shared sexual energy, the intimacy, on his knees as well, banging Terry from behind, watching her going down on Brenda, who was fondling her own breasts.

'I wanna watch you come,' Brenda said. 'I always like to see that.'

'I'm glad I'm gonna get to show you,' he thought, riding her partner like it was a samba.

'I'm gonna come soon,' Brenda whispered.

'I'm gonna come with ya,' Adam said, pulling out of Terry.

'Let's all come together,' Terry said. 'Stand in front of us.'

'I told you talent was sexy,' Brenda said, going to town on her vagina. 'You can come on me Adam. Just don't get any on the couch.'

And that was the way the scene climaxed, Adam standing in front of Brenda and Terry, straddling Brenda's left leg, his penis in his right hand, his balls in his left, wanking it for all he was worth, Brenda and Terry spread-eagle side by side melted into each other on the couch rubbing one out watching Adam watching them.

'I'm gonna...' a second later shooting all over Brenda.

'Oh my God. Look at that,' Brenda said, almost giggling – no one had ever been that fascinated watching Adam come, her right hand continuing to work herself into an orgasm.

'I'm gonna... Oh fuck yeah,' Terry climaxed.

'I'm almost there honey...' rubbing it out, Adam and Terry watching, Adam wishing his dick was hard again so he could be jerking off to what he was seeing, a scene he would be recalling in the future.

'Okay Mr. Sexy Pants, I think it's time to call it a night.' It was late. Everyone had their lives to lead. Adam got dressed quietly, not wanting to upset the delicate balance of so extraordinary an evening, an inner calm pervading his essence it was a joy to experience.

'Good night,' Adam bid, kissing each of them softly on the lips. 'What an epic fuckin' night. Because of you,' referring to Brenda.

'Let us know when your next performance is,' Terry said, in her bathrobe.

'You better,' Brenda said. 'I wanna be able to say we discovered you.'

'I want you to be able to say that too.'

But to be discovered he had to perform, and he had no plans for that. The high after the show, which lasted for days, began to fade into the realization that another show wasn't magically going to happen again. It would require the same dedication and determination the first one did, and something about that, at that point, drained him, the thought of writing another one. He couldn't do the one he did again because his audience was built in and they had already seen it. Not only would he have to write a new show, but he'd have to go through the whole process of memorizing eighty-ninety minutes worth of stuff, and getting everything together with the theater.

'Ups and downs,' Adam thought. That was how his life was evolving, more ups than downs, but certainly plenty of those too, which, fortunately, didn't last long enough on a consistent basis to be a major concern. He was learning how to mitigate long-term negative impulses and self doubt; 'shut up and practice', don't wonder why he wasn't where he thought he wanted to be. Spend the time to get there, direct the energy there banging it out on the drums. Keep the insecurities at bay. Creative ideas that weren't there yesterday would, hopefully, as had happened, float to the surface, in their time, inspiration to be written down and worked on. Perhaps at end of that process another night to remember involving lesbians and margaritas. If not that, a continuation of the creative process as applied to self-expression and performance. Adam didn't want to dwell on his lack of accomplishment, his return to life in the studio - shut up and practice, try to rise above the echoes. Something good will work its way into the rhythm of life. It couldn't all be a slow descent into misery. But Adam took nothing for granted. He knew about the bell-curve of life. He just hoped he was somewhere forward of center, closer to the tip than farther away. He was cautiously optimistic.

Sometimes it was as simple as a sign on the Music Building bulletin board: 'Gotham City Improv... Go For It... You Know You Always Wanted To... Improv and Sketch Comedy classes... Auditions this Thursday and Friday.'

At the audition, the teacher asked if anyone wanted to volunteer to be first to improv a scene where the student worked at a Macdonald's counter. No one did, so Adam did. See if he could do it. That's what he was there for.

He decided, as soon as the teacher placed her improv order, to get everything wrong.

'Okay, that's a big map and a side of thighs,' Adam improvised.

'No. I ordered a Big Mac and a side of fries.'

'Okay, sorry. That's two gentlemen walking their pet schnauzer, and a sign from Fridays. The restaurant Fridays or the actual day of the week?'

'No I want a Big Map and a side of flies.' The teacher didn't miss a beat

'Oh. Got it. A Big Mac and a side of fries. Why didn't you say so? It'll be right up. Please stand off the line. Thank you. Next…'

'Okay, thank you. Who's next?' the teacher said. 'That was good.'

After that everyone volunteered. The ice was broken.

The best thing about New York City extra–curricula performing arts classes was collaborating with some of the country's most talented performance neophytes. You have to start somewhere, and Gotham City was a fertile breeding-ground. Proven techniques. Complete artistic freedom; within specific confines in improv, without restriction with written material; skits, sketches, monologues, very much connected to New York theater culture. Five month semesters, classes once a week for three hours, writing at home and on the subway, Gotham City gave Adam structure and goals, and was a great way to continue to develop his writing and performing. The entire semester was focused on self-improvement; both writing and performing, scene development, improvisation, culminating in a final live performance in an off-Broadway theater on 42nd Street, for which everyone in the class, fourteen freaks, geeks, and wanna-be Saturday Night Live cast members had to write or conceive two original pieces. Even though it was called Gotham City Improv, the final theatrical performance, since it reflected the quality of the curriculum, had to be worthy of an off-Broadway theater, which meant less improv and more developed material. Improv at its best, at that level, was hit or miss.

For the show Adam, and a talented writer, singer, comedian had written an ensemble piece about a marriage-counseling Indian sexual mystic who had his clients say and do outrageous things. And he wrote a monologue, in a gay stoner accent – he introduced it that he couldn't decide which one, so he combined them - about the character's iowasca trip lead by a voodoo priest, that developed into and ended with dancing and Adam's interpretation of karnatic singing. If he hooked in and went full on, he knew it would be okay, fully commit to going off. Also, because he volunteered, he improvised a scene, asking the audience for three characters and a location, and ended up with Katherine Hepburn, Joseph Stalin, and Donald Duck at an S&M club.

For obvious reasons, Adam invited Brenda and Terry as his guests. If there was any shot of reviving their fantasy night, he was going to take it. He knew they would have a good time. He was confident his pieces were good. And there were people in class more advanced and much funnier than him, guaranteeing a legitimate night of theater. In fact, because there were such talented people in the class, it allowed, it forced Adam to be honest with himself about his strengths and weaknesses. He was not a stand-up comedian or a potential cast-member on Saturday Night Live. He was a musician who could develop a character or a story, and convey the essence. But he wasn't Steve Martin or Billy Crystal. He didn't need to be. He needed to work at learning what his potential was. He needed to just put it out there. He knew he wasn't going to make a fool out of himself. It was just a matter of being in the moment on stage and committing to the performance.

'Those were great vagina references,' Brenda said, meeting Adam in the theater lobby after the show. 'From now on, Terry's gonna refer to my… you know, as my enchanted garden.'

'I liked moonlit cove,' Terry added.

'I know you did, honey,' Brenda said.

'I hope you liked it enough that I get to visit it again,' Adam thought.

They didn't. They were at a west-side dive after the show, doing shots of tequila, talking about some of the other skits; an interview between a crazy interviewer and a belligerent Mickey Rourke, a game of Family Feud between cereal characters; Tony the Tiger, Count Chocula, and Serial Killers, Charles Manson, Ted Bundy. Brenda and Terry were sitting next to each other, their backs to the bar, twirling their stirrers in their cocktails and smiling.

'Just so you don't get your hopes up, you're not getting lucky tonight,' Brenda said. She picked up on Adam's vibe; casting a net upon invisible rivers. The fact that she was smiling so warmly and conveying empathy when she said it went a long way in cushioning the disappointment. 'We don't want you to think we don't love you, 'cause we do. But going that way's a whole bigger consideration, and we're trying to keep it a little smaller, at least right now. It seems to work better for us.'

Adam's guess was that Terry liked cock a lot more than Brenda did, to the point of threatening their relationship.

'We were like crazy for a week,' Brenda continued.

'You should'a called me,' Adam joked.

'Yeah, I don't think so,' Brenda said.

'Shit,' thought Adam.

Back on the street, saying good night, they both kissed him on the lips and gave him deep hugs. Then he put his helmet on, got on his Harley SuperGlide, and toured around Manhattan, a perfect thing to do on a warm spring night when he was alone and wanted to celebrate life; driving up the Hudson Parkway along the river, the lights of the George Washington Bridge, the whole span lined with light, against the night sky and Palisades shadows, long stretches of road where he could push eighty miles an hour, gun it in the middle lane. That was a big, beautiful road to be wild on, when traffic allowed, later at night and early in the morning. Adam got it to about ninety-one, just past The Cloisters, before something told him to slow it down, come back downtown at a comfortable sixty-five, seventy miles an hour and do a slow crawl through The Village, old Manhattan, the Lower East Side, through Chinatown, which was always surreal when seen from a motorcycle – a tangle of inner-inner-city streets that felt like the foreign land it was, yet part of the essence of New York; stop for soup-dumplings at that place on Pell Street. He had been onstage again, a lot shorter than his one-man show, but incredibly fun.

But as fun as it was, it wasn't nearly as compelling as writing and recording Energy. That was the undeniable pursuit that would weave the years together. There was a lot to get through. By the time of the live performance at the end of Adam's second semester at Gotham City Improv, he was completely committed to his music; song after song, every subject that touched humanity. Don't think about it. Just write it. Read it, write it, and rap it. It didn't leave much time for other creative writing. Instead of two original pieces for the end of the semester show, Adam went with one original piece; a monologue, a Chassidic rabbi, with a Yiddish accent, in the style of Professor Irwin Cory, talking about why his flock had to wear their long coats and dresses even when sunbathing or canoeing or horseback riding, 'Or when you're doing a zetz off'n de maidela'. Instead of a second original piece, he went with 'pudgie bunnies', knowing he had taken the easy way out. He hoped most people didn't know about the old camp gag, the way he didn't when he first learned about it not long before he performed it the first time.

Based on the audience reaction, most had never seen or heard of 'pudgie bunnies'. He was on solid comedic ground. Plus, he did write an intro to the skit. Alone on stage with his two-dollar prop, he asked the audience, 'How many angels can dance on the head of a pin? Who gives a shit. How many marshmallows can I shove in my mouth and still say pudgie bunnies?' Then it was just a matter of selling it. The fact that he was able to get the entire bag in his mouth – none of the marshmallows blocking his windpipe or falling out of his mouth or in any way inhibiting the insertion of the next marshmallow, which he brought to his mouth with theatrical flourish – added to the general over–the–top silliness of his less-than-composed second skit. Others had written elaborate comedy sketches involving many cast members. And Adam shoved marshmallows in his mouth.

It all centered on music after Gotham City Improv; writing and playing, jamming with friends of some of the people from Gotham City, and with other musicians from the Music Building, a six-month stint with a progressive rock band, Before The Brave, which culminated in several live shows around Manhattan, the biggest at Webster Hall opening for Danger Zone, although the show at CBGB's felt tighter. Unfortunately, the bass player moved to Barcelona soon after that show, bringing to an end the band's career. It was all about writing and recording songs after that, not getting too discouraged that no one was hearing them, just keep going, sailing into the future upon time's winged ships, being sustained by the work itself. It was always there, always present, one song into the next, the seasons and rhythms changing, the spark never dimming, not even a little, actually burning brighter. The music just kept coming out of him, his life's work, over two hundred songs and another three hundred drum tracks waiting to be written to, until even the songs with Tommy Vincent started to become digital files stored on hard-drives that represented a certain period in his life. Even that was becoming the past. He was getting older, too old to wait any longer. There was the reality of age and the marketplace, especially if you're not already established. He hadn't really even started. And that made him evaluate his whole life because he thought of himself as a performing artist, and he hadn't made it happen. He had made many attempts, to no avail.

'Maybe I'm just a fuckin' loser who's so unaware of himself that I can't see what everyone else sees,' he thought. Talk about a rude awakening. But he'd been there before, questioning himself, and knew not to let discouragement overshadow his artistic accomplishments. All he had to do was listen to one of his songs to revive his belief in the choices he had made, to keep going. How could he be so misguided, with Tommy Vincent wailing on *Desperation Angel*, a song that rocked as hard as any Adam had ever heard.

And then a spark of inspiration. Want conspired with need and determination to forge a viable concept. Present the song and the story behind the song, especially if it was a story that could be written and dramatically or comedically performed, like *Desperation Angel*, which was about the guy who pulled a gun on Adam at a party. And that immediately lead to the song *Powermind*, which Tommy had also slayed, which was about his brother, who was the only other person to ever threaten him with a gun.

'I gotta write this down,' Adam thought. 'Okay, what other songs should I do?'

Ideas for a show were taking shape. Start with the songs as the basis. If the songs were great, how bad could the show be? Good stories, presented naturally, and then rock the shit out of them. He had nothing to lose by going for it. Even if it was another one-off. Better another one-off then another none-off. The only question was, could he do it? Could he put it together; writing, memorizing, technically integrate the music? That was the big question. How was he going to present his music without a band? He knew it had to involve him fronting himself on playback, mixing his vocal tracks out, blast the other tracks through a great PA, with a huge sub-woofer. If he couldn't get the players, at least he could get the sound.

'If I could get Tommy to play live,' he considered. In his mind's eye he saw Tommy on stage with him, Tommy doing his thing, and then his spotlight fades during the non-musical parts, integrating the flow as seamlessly as possible. 'I wonder if he'll do it.'

He emailed Tommy that night. 'Hope all is well,' he typed. 'I'm writing a show with songs and stories. Hopefully get a little theater. Mostly our songs. I would love to do it with you. No band. Just us to track with a great sound system. You'll dig the stories. You already know some. I promise to buy you a shot and a beer after.'

'When,' Tommy wrote back.

'Around three months. I gotta finish writing it. And then I gotta learn it and get everything set up.'

'I'm around for a few weeks at the end of March. You just want me to jam over what we did?'

'Eggsackly.'

'$500. Two rehearsals. A shot and a beer.'

'Deal.' Ask, and thou shall receive.

It was on. The only question was could he pull it off? Could he actually command an audience, a question that couldn't be answered in the abstract. The only way to find out was to do it.

'Okay, I gotta get *The Horizon Off Canvas* in there,' he decided, putting all the elements of the show together at the same time as he was writing the specific stories. If he could get through *Horizon*, a long, deep, Sufi-inspired poem that was one continuous stream of ideas weaving through a mystical landscape, the audience would have seen something unique... intricate tribal drumming, 7 tracks of chanting and 7 tracks of interwoven karnatic rhythms... Adam alone in the spotlight willing himself to get in the center of the energy so he can keep the flow going.

But how to start the show? Music? A story?

'Shock and awe,' Adam decided. Start with *Balance*, a complex hard rap piece integrating a number of concepts Adam learned about researching and writing Energy, with an extended solo section that Tommy played some of the wildest guitar Adam had ever heard on. Bring the audience in right off the bat - let them know why the show was called Energy, which Adam knew it was going to be called almost from the beginning, which meant he knew he was going to make it happen almost from the beginning. If Tommy could shred live like he did on the recording, he knew the show would be worth the price of admission, even though he wouldn't even think of charging anyone anything to see him. He was grateful if they came.

'Maybe I'll check out that theater in Glenville,' he thought. He had passed The Sunshine Theater a million times, and had always wondered what type of productions they put on there.

His recon mission was a success; a fifty-four seat theater – he felt the sanctity of performance as soon as he walked in - a simple lighting grid, ample power, a small, comfortable back-stage area, all for a hundred-fifty dollars for the night, two-fifty if he wanted someone to work the lighting board, which he did. And it was available on one of the Saturday nights Tommy would be around. Ten minutes after talking to the theater manager, he had his theater. Everything was falling into place. The last production element was sound equipment, which he planned on renting from LI Sound Concepts, a company he had used on a number of Long Island productions. He knew their prices were competitive, and fully expected the owner of the company to give him a discount when he told him this was a personal gig, not a professional one.

'How about you just pay for transportation and setup,' the owner offered. 'I'll even throw my guy in to run the board. You've been good to us over the years.'

'I really appreciate that. I hope you're gonna be able to come.'

As soon as Adam had booked the theater, he was conscious about making sure he didn't perform to an empty house. It was a little early to start a concerted effort to invite people; sending or handing out fliers, emailing. The show was still too far away. But anyone he ran into who he knew he wouldn't be running into again he invited. Altogether the night would cost around a thousand dollars, not an insignificant amount of money, enough for him to take the undertaking very seriously. He was producing a show, an industry he had been involved in most of his professional career. The fact that he was performing it made it that much more important that all the elements came together.

'I better start rehearsing,' he told himself. He had eleven weeks 'til blast-off, and he wasn't even done writing. Almost, but he had one more section between two songs that he wanted to fill with something other than another story. He thought about 'pudgie bunnies' and other physical humor, but that seemed too far afield from the tenor of the show.

'The improv scene,' Adam decided. He had done a quick sketch of an improv where the character he asked the audience to come up with doesn't want the scene to end and gets belligerent. He hadn't fully developed the skit because he wasn't sure if it belonged. But when he finished writing it that night, and laughed when he read what he had written, he knew it did.

'Done,' he said to himself. Step one: write it. Step two: rehearse and memorize it. Step three: do it.

He spent the next night remixing the nine songs which comprised the show to remove his vocal tracks and Tommy's lead tracks, downloading those mix-minus tracks onto his iTouch as individual playlists. That was how he was going to coordinate the music live; finish the story, casually walk over to the supplemental mixing board he would set up on stage, that plugged into the main mixing board, pick up the iTouch, which would be plugged into the supplemental board, choose the song, press play, and go for it, let the sound guy from LI Sound mix everything on the fly. Hopefully, the lighting guy would remember that, as soon as the music started to play, he had to turn Tommy's spot-light on.

That was how Adam rehearsed it every night in his studio, running through the entire show, first from the script, to using it only when he got stuck, until he had memorized the whole thing. There were no shortcuts in the process, just persistence and determination, and the realization that every day he was referring to the script a little less. He also realized that his singing was getting better as he rehearsed the songs over and over. Of the nine songs, only two were rapped or recited. The rest were sung. Adam knew his audience was much less hip-hop than it was old-school rock and roll. He was under no illusion that he was a great singer, or even a good one. To him it was about the feel, the energy, the ability of the engineer to put the right amount of EQ and reverb so that his vocals sat comfortably in the mix. He was able to do that on his mixes, and he was confident the engineer from LI Sound knew a lot more than he did.

By the time Tommy and he had their first rehearsal, Adam had the flow in hand. Their rehearsal went so well they decided not to do another one; keep it as spontaneous and on the edge as what they had just done.

'Any shot you wanna jam?' Adam asked. They had run through the show in almost real time, and Adam wasn't ready to pack it up. Although Tommy had been to his studio many times, it had only been to record his parts over songs that were already recorded. Adam was the engineer, Tommy the player. They had never played together, with Adam on drums. 'I can use these sticks,' Adam offered, Hot Rods, bound, very thin dowels that were originally designed to cut the volume off the drums, like Dave Grohl used in the Nirvana Unplugged session. Adam had developed a certain technique with the Hot Rods that enabled him to control the flutter, allowing for a very unique, high-speed approach. Usually just drums and guitar together sounded somewhat hollow. But with the Hot Rods, it was more like hand-drumming, more organic and round-sounding.

'Go for it,' Tommy agreed. 'Why don't you start it off.'

It was sick. It sounded like a cross between Mahavishnu Orchestra and Coltrane, with a little flamenco thrown in.

'We should do that live,' Tommy said. 'That was pretty crazy, man.'

Adam had thought about setting up his drums, maybe doing a drum solo between two of the stories, but decided the hassle of load-in, set-up, and load-out didn't justify it. He felt it might be seen as him trying too hard to impress the audience, throwing in a singular, tangential element just to show he could. But if he could play with Tommy Vincent live, it wasn't self-aggrandizing. It would elevate the overall performance. And he knew exactly where it belonged.

'I'm there if you are.'

'You'll play with those sticks, right?'

'Of course, man. I'm gonna go as far and straight-ahead wild as I can, I'm telling you right now.'

'Go fot it. Oh yeah, any suggestions for wardrobe?' Tommy asked, as he was packing up.

Adam hadn't considered what Tommy should wear. He was going to wear a pair of black jeans, black suede boots, and his favorite jeans shirt that was cut in a western style.

'I don't know,' Adam said. 'I guess hip,' images of Hendrix and Stevie Ray and Keith coming to mind.

'What are you gonna wear?'

'Jeans and kind of a western shirt.'

'Okay, cool.'

They met at the theater about two hours before show-time to get set up and do a quick sound-check. Tommy looked like the rock-star he was; black leather pants, black boots, black western shirt, round-brimmed,

Stevie Ray Vaughn-style hat with a colorful silk scarf around the head-piece.

'Just gimme a clean feed out,' he told the sound guy. 'I'll do everything from the pedal-board. Just EQ me a little on the high end.'

'And make it loud,' Adam added. 'I want to try to make it as much of a real band sound as we can.'

'Dude, you have a massive sub-woofer I'm gonna pump the bottom through,' the sound guy said. 'I promise the audience will feel it in their soul.'

That's what Adam was hoping for. If he could make the audience physically feel the music, as he often does at his favorite concerts, he knew he'd be all right. Not overwhelmingly loud, but not for the faint of heart.

The sound-check allowed Adam to work out some of his abundant nervousness. He hadn't done what he was about to do in decades –trying to entertain an audience with all original material. It wasn't just the remembering of all of the lines, of which there was about an hour and a half's worth, some of it, most notably *The Horizon Off Canvas* requiring intense concentration. More importantly, was what he had written any good? Was it professional? Would the audience appreciate it, the way they would any night of legitimate theater. Although it was just the lighting guy, the sound guy, and the owner of LI Sound Concepts, who was there to make sure that Tommy Vincent, who he had seen play many times, including the time he sat in with Deep Purple, had everything he needed, Adam was still on stage doing his thing, feeling his way through the performance for people who had never seen him perform. He was so glad to just go for it, a slight weight lifting off his shoulders the deeper into the sound-check they got. The more experience the better, anything he could latch onto when he was in the spotlight and there was no going back.

'All right,' he said to himself, 'I think I got this,' after running through the beginning of *Horizon* and *Against the Day*, a song he included in the show because it was one of his favorites. Not much of a story behind it. Just a serious funk-fusion groove with a solo section that Tommy burned through on the original recording. It was the only song Tommy asked about when they originally spoke about the concept for the show.

After the sound-check there was nothing to do but hang backstage with Tommy and hope that, out of all the fliers he had handed out and all the emails he had sent, people would be good to their word and come to see him.

At one point, the pressure of anticipation too great, he stuck his head out from behind the stage to check out what was happening. He had heard the murmurs of the audience loading in. It looked like the theater was almost completely full.

'What, do you think we don't see you?' his brother Barry said. 'Come out here and gimme a hug,' which Adam did, and a kiss, to the applause and greetings of those assembled.

'Look who I brought,' Adam's dearest friend Robert, who was sitting two seats away from Barry, and who gave Adam a big hug and a kiss said. Sitting next to Robert was Adam's old friend Stevie Schecter, who lived a few towns away from Robert in Westchester, and who Robert had told Adam he had seen and spoken to on occasion. They had all gone to high school together, and Robert knew all about their trip out west after they graduated. Apparently, they had run into each other a few weeks prior to the show, and Robert told Stevie what Adam was doing.

'How could I miss this,' Stevie said, bending down to give Adam a kiss on the cheek. He was even taller than Adam remembered. 'I don't know if you remember, but I was there the first time you played drums.'

'I think about it all the time, man. Your silver sparkle Ludwig. I was hooked from the first minute I played. Are you gonna be able to hang after?'

'Of course.' They hadn't spoken to each other in about twenty years. It was amazing to see Stevie as a middle-aged man, closer to old than young. Adam realized Stevie must be seeing him the same way. Yet there they were, sharing a bond that time and space couldn't completely erase.

'Okay,' Adam announced to the assemblage of friends, family and neighbors, not wanting to leave Tommy alone backstage too long, 'lemme piss for the hundredth time. And then we'll come out and rock your asses. Wait 'til you see who I got playing with me.' He couldn't resist the build-up.

'Tommy Vincent,' the father of someone Adam's daughter went to school with yelled. Adam quickly scanned the audience and saw that was who had, for the most part, come to see him; neighbors, people he had handed out his fliers to, many of whom told him they'd love to come if only as an excuse to get a babysitter for a night out. Then someone started to chant 'Tommy, Tommy.' Then everyone joined in. Most people in Adam's home-town knew of the rock star in their midst.

Adam felt that was the natural queue to get the show started. He gave his wife, who was sitting next to Barry and his wife a final kiss, gave the lighting guy the hand signal to bring the house-lights down, went backstage, took a quick piss, and said to Tommy, 'You ready?'

'I'm always ready,' Tommy said.

CHAPTER 20

Energy

They came out front and took their places on stage to cheers, love and anticipation. Adam walked over to his little iStation, picked up his iTouch, chose *Balance*, pressed play, and waited for the first notes of the intro to settle his erratic spirit. It was fuckin' on.

First, the intro, which gave Tommy a chance to weave a bluesy solo through a very driving hard-rock rhythm, which he did like it was as natural as breathing. Then it was Adam's turn.

'All right. Here we go,' he said to himself. Then the adrenaline took over:

Balance

Looking for the rapture in a world defined by opposite extremes… and
    broken signals in between
The song, the law, the lies, a thousand words to write and memorize…
All of the attention like some gospel choir quick-fire jamboree… eve of
    judgment day
One time down the center, next one with more balanced energy… like
    the poet used to say:
Desire without balance is incomplete… want begetting want
Mercy without balance is weakness… the will burning down into darkness
Ambition without balance is selfishness… goals forever unattained
Reason without balance is madness… the faithless depth of the soul
Because the falling star never made it home
Because the narrow death has widened the world
Because the city is what we will it to be
Because we can live in a past that never was

I was riding on the 1 train one afternoon
Heard this guy talking about the left hand of the arc
Who was the left hand of the arc
Wasn't he the one who prepared the way to the celestial light
Set the balance in dreamtime and then tripped the wire
Be my mind open to the higher
Be my heart the center of the light
Be my soul of equal measure

Perfected by the four orders of nature
Be my body the temple of the inner plane
Prayers so loud you can hear them on the far side of the horizon
But the poet warned about living upon hope... you can die of hunger
And that ain't satyagraha... nothing higher about it

Who am I to pass judgment
The way I feel is the way you feel
Projecting hope and insecurity
All I see is my reflection
Less looking and more doing
Looking didn't build the pyramids
Looking can't offer guarantees
The only guarantees are the changes

Rapture finds me singing out of tune in an absorbing landscape... on a
     Saturday night
The words had all been written without measuring the endless road
Road leading back to the take me to the river jamboree... in the pale
     moonlight
One by one our present days come looking for that balanced energy
Prayer without balance is fear... all hope denied
Love without balance is confusion... a broken mirror
Nature without balance fails... a prelude to war
Faith without balance is blindness... the game of false prophets

Back on the 1 Train later that day
Same guy shouting sermons to the faithless... like Seneca under the
     bridge of piles
Poverty is no disaster, he said, as long as you haven't succumbed to the
     madness of greed
What can be taken from us... there is nothing to lose
Nothing...working...trying to set the night on fire
March... and then what... every day a stage for life
Questions... answers... the sight of stars made Vincent dream
The twists of fate we translate into our destiny

Nothing left to do except continue writing Balance to the end... start
   all over again
Keep above the echoes until the wind beneath me changes direction
Before the falcon flies across the east gate of heaven... preparing the way
   for the raven
But first things first, the way the universe has always been...

   The music fades. Tommy's spotlight fades. The audience is cheering.
   'Whoah,' Adam thought, knowing Tommy killed it, hit everything.
'Okay, here we go. Nice and natural.' Time to put the mike back on the
stand, come out front and start the theatrical part of the show.
   A deep breath... He felt the connection...
   'That song is called *Balance*... And it's basically me working my shit
out in an abstract way... sitting in my studio in front of the computer with
a drum track recorded on pro-tools software and seeing what ideas rise to
the surface of the rhythmic flow. Clearly that day I was thinking about
Kenneth Patchen. He's the poet I referred to, who wrote about, among
other things, the ying-yang nature of existence and the brotherhood of
man. There's a little bit about the Filipino missionary that was preaching
on the subway in a dirty pith helmet and old safari fatigues who said
one of the most brilliant things I ever heard. I'm telling you, this crazy
guy comes walking through the 1 train, talking to himself a mile a
minute, and everyone, including myself, is trying to shut him out and
get on with their day, and in the middle of this heavily accented white
noise he's laying on us I heard him say, 'Moses brought the law. Jesus
brought the blessing.' A wild-eyed Filipino missionary in a pith helmet
on a New York City subway just defined western religion in eight words.
It was amazing. I also included the social theory an old friend of mine
discovered. The Theory of Mutuality, which simply says that the way
you feel about a person you have an interpersonal relationship with is
probably the way they feel about you. Feelings tend to be mutual, which
is why I wrote the words, 'Who am I to pass judgment. The way I feel is
the way you feel. Projecting hope and insecurity, all I see is my reflection'.
If you wonder what your friends or family or co-workers feel about you,
think about what you honestly feel about them. And honesty is crucial.
You have to really understand how you feel about someone, and then

you'll know how they feel about you. For instance, I once dated a woman, and I was wondering what she felt about me, and I realized there were a number of things about her I didn't really like, and then she broke up with me because she told me there were a number of thing about me she didn't really like. I got it. Not that the Theory of Mutuality is gonna change the world. It's just a handy tool in the game of life. It let's you know where you stand with others. And if you know where you stand you can move forward with a little more confidence and vision. And that lets you feel more grounded. And when you're more grounded, you won't be so compelled to think about how you're going to feel about something if and when it happens, because you really don't know how you're gonna feel until you're there. So why waste time thinking about it. That's neurotic by definition, something I know a little something about...

'This next song is my version of a Sufi poem... and for those who don't know, Sufism is the mystical sect of Islam... and any mystical aspects of any religion, Kabbala for example, are just a way to commune with God now, not through prayer or ritual, but through more direct means... like the Whirling Dervishes, who go into a religious trance through their spinning... or Buddhist monks who chant the universal vibration... or Kabbalists who navigate the sphiroth... this is 'The Horizon Off Canvas'.

Adam slowly walked over to his iStation, willing himself to forget about everything around him. He needed total concentration to get through the six-minute almost-stream-of-consciousness poem. One screw-up, one lost word or thought and he'd fuck the whole thing up. That's how tight the piece was constructed. Also, he would be on his own out there. *Horizon* was the only piece of music Tommy didn't play on. It was just drums and voice, as organic as anything Adam had ever written. Luckily, there was a thirty second meditative intro that allowed him to just breathe, to settle into the center of the music...

The Horizon Off Canvas

'Imam, they found the body of the merchant in the desert crushed under the weight of the gold he stole from his neighbors, who trusted the words of a liar and the promise of a future where nothing existed absolutely but ignorant assumptions and primitive patterns of emotions and reactions to the stabbing summons to a misguided life filled wheels within wheels that keep spinning around for the rest of time among the fallen buildings laid to waste by everyone seeking their own advantage, without knowledge of the horizon off canvas where the paint is mixed that colors the world with the capacity to perceive truth and deception and the music of the grieving reed flute telling stories of its separations with songs of the spheres sung by eternal voices who became perfect reflections of the beloved light that shatters heaven's roof illuminating the path for the falcon returning to the celestial hunter, who translated the wind into a thousand metaphors each a reality without a name, like an inaccessible pearl laying at the bottom of the meeting place of the seven river by the lotus of the farthest edge, where the tall cypress echoes the commanding stature of the infinite will extending without end through the inner reality behind the illusion of the lovers, who curse the thief thought so often to be their friend, who jumped into the river to get away from the rain because he loved the water more and the pitcher less than the inner light of truth that shines through the pillars of the world that support those who inhabit the height of the universe, where various transformations and combinations of the letters and the names constitute a mysterious knowledge of the inwardness of creation and the absolute perfection in which there is no distinction between the messenger and the message blown by the whispering wind through the valley of the seeker, who knows if the dust was not there his shoes would not raise it as he searched for the unity revealed by the prophet during the 92 seasons of enlightenment that divided the twin divine attributes of grace and wrath into the world of unification and the world of separation where the names of vengeance infect the stranger's heart as truth reaches him from the imperial sphere floating behind the mirror of creation reflecting the essential identity of the will and thoughts of a lost soul whose struggles cling to him like the flames that enshroud the cypress trees burning in the garden since the day after the world was created until the night of the seven secrets, when those kneeling at the door of the beloved – owned by nothing, owning nothing – walk with the spirit of the saints along the path of the inner approach of the hall of the patriarch, through the seasons of the inner mounting flame, when the warrior embraces the children of the jihad, who must lean to serve themselves best by not trying things out of right harmony causing discord throughout the radiant universe, where Buddha climbs the tree of life to see the view of Shiva dancing slowly as the planets revolve around the blessing brought by the falcon prophet, noble, giver, whose love is a spring whose waters never fail as it flows with the static equilibrium of a crystal through eternity now, returning to the source of the true faith on the wings of the ministering angels withdrawn from involvement in the world where the wayward mystic believes haste is speed as he travels from premature action to wild assumption, from despair to insufficient remedy, from carelessness to derision, from obedience to humility to the knowledge that he must always think about the end before beginning to harmonize thought with faith, as though faith was a simple garment of course wool to be worn by the impatient and then sold for a few gold coins to the fallen prince dressed as a wandering rustic offering today for tomorrow with a supplicant's humility......... The goal of all is one... The moon receives its light from the sun... We are all composed of the two lights.... We are in the world, are we not?'

'I did it,' Adam thought, standing there, eyes closed, not letting the audience see his inner glee, as the final meditative chanting and karnatic rhythms filled the theater. He had lost himself inside the poem, and came out the other side almost purified, as if the poem, or the performing of the poem, was a refiner's fire. It was a moment of bliss.

The music faded, and there was silence. Then a few people clapped. Then the theater erupted. Adam couldn't believe he got through it without even thinking about it. He looked over to Tommy, who smiled and nodded.

A deep breath, and then back into the performance:

'This next song was inspired by one of the most immediate and perfect applications of karma I've ever seen. And when I say inspired, I mean the lyrics aren't a direct translation of the story. I used the emotions the experience evoked and free associated them in abstract form, which is the way a lot of my songs get written. The actual story is pretty crazy though. I was at a dinner party at my friend Robert's

apartment many years ago during one of my prolonged single periods…
'That's Robert over there.' Adam pointed to Robert, who waved. 'And
I met the woman Robert's girlfriend, who's now his wife, who's sitting
next to him, told me she was gonna hook me up with, whose name
was Stephanie, by the way. And after a few margaritas the sparks were
definitely flying. We were on the couch, our shoulders were melting into
each other. I was doing my best to be cool and keep it light and funny
because I had learned over the years that fear and desperation were not
the best first impressions. But this time the stars definitely seemed to be
in alignment. Then there was a knock at the front door, and Stephanie
and I happened to be sitting right near it, so we answered it, and this
guy who looked like he was wearing what he slept in, and who didn't
look too happy, asked if we could speak with him in the hallway for a
second. And I really didn't think anything of it. I figured he was an
unhappy neighbor, and he was gonna ask us to keep it down a little. So
we stepped outside, and the door automatically closed behind us. And
as soon as it did, this motherfucker pulls out a gun. I hadn't noticed
that his right hand had been behind his back the whole time. And
Stephanie screamed and hid behind me, but no one inside heard her
because the music was playing. And this guy is saying things like he's
sick of all the noise, and this time he's gonna do something about it,
and Stephanie's nails were digging into my arms, and the crazy thing
was, I wasn't scared. I was actually pissed off that this jerk-off was such
an asshole. So I just told him to put the gun away and I'll go inside and
lower the music. Then he tells me it's too late for that. It's too late for
that. And that was a crazy moment 'cause I didn't know what was going
to happen, but I knew I had to get the fuck out of there. So I turned
around as fast as I could, and thank God the door was unlocked, and
I pushed Stephanie through and prayed that this guy didn't shoot me
in the back, which thank God he didn't. Then I went over to the stereo
and turned it off, and told Robert what just happened. And Stephanie
was on the couch, really upset, and Robert couldn't believe it, and told
everybody what an asshole that guy was and that he hears him and his
wife fight all the time, and he beats the shit out of her, and this time
he's calling the cops. And that was kind of the end of the dinner party.
Everybody started to leave except Robert's girlfriend and I 'cause I

had to make the formal complaint. And we put Stephanie, who was still very upset, in a cab, and she promised me that we would see each other again, and then the cops came and they were really being weird about the whole thing. They were telling me that pressing charges was a waste of time and taxpayer money, and that once I go through with this I could be a target for getting more parking tickets. It was just really bazaar. But I didn't give a shit. This guy pulled a gun on me and he was gonna pay for that. So they wrote out the complaint, and I asked them if they were gonna arrest the guy, whose name is Bruce, by the way, and they told me to shut the fuck up and mind my own business, and then they left, and that was that. But I called the following day to make sure the complaint was filed, and it was, and they told me that I would be contacted about appearing in court and formal charges. And the woman I spoke to also told me that some cops moonlit as security at Bruce's father's lumber-yard, the largest in Queens, so there that was. But since there was nothing I could do about it at that point, I just let it go and called Stephanie to make sure she was all right and that I still had a shot with her, which I definitely did. She kept telling me how brave I was and she couldn't wait to see me again, and she accepted my invitation to make her dinner later that week. And the shrimp scampi was perfect, and the wine, and we ended up in my bedroom, and I was like the happiest guy in the world. Her shirt was off. I hadn't been with a woman in over a year... And then the doorbell rang, which was really unusual. Usually people call before they stop by. So I get up and look through the peep-hole, and it's Bruce and the same two cops. And they tell me they have a warrant for my arrest, that I'm to open the door immediately, which I did. And they tell me I'm being charged with the exact same thing that I charged Bruce with. Apparently that's the law, something about reciprocity. And while they're telling me this shit, Stephanie comes out of the bedroom with her shirt back on, and she's really upset. She heard what was going on and she was indignant and scared, and she started to tell the cops that this was bullshit. And one of the cops told her that if she said another word, he'd arrest her for obstruction, and I knew the best thing to do was to get her out of there and deal with what was going on. I really wasn't in any position to be Mr. Hero again. So I asked the cops if I could go downstairs and put her in a cab, which they said was fine, and Bruce had this dick-bag smirk on his face which I would have loved to smack the fuck off. But then wasn't the time. And I could tell Stephanie hated his fuckin' guts. He ruined another perfect evening. Two in a row. I got a tense kiss on the cheek when I put her in the cab. And she didn't say anything when I told her I'd call her later that evening, but I couldn't deal with that at that moment. I was about to be arrested for something I didn't do. So I go back upstairs and the cops lay it out for me; if I dropped the charges against Bruce, he'd drop the charges against me. If I don't, they're gonna arrest me right there, and take me to the 15th precinct and keep me there until somebody posted bail. And all I could think about, other than the fact that not seven minutes before, I had a woman's breasts in my mouth for the first time in like a year, and they tasted like heaven, and now I got two corrupt cops and the devil, and they're gonna win, and they knew it as well as I did. So I dropped the charges, but I didn't sign the piece of paper they told me to sign, and they didn't push it, and they left with a threat that I better not do anything stupid, like recant my decision. And all I could do, besides hope that I still had a shot with Stephanie, was hope that Bruce paid for all the shit he had done… Which was why it was insane that later that evening Robert called me and told me that he heard Bruce and his wife have a really bad fight, and it got physical, and then he heard a gunshot, and he called the police, and ten minutes later he looked out the window and saw the EMT guys wheeling Bruce out on a stretcher, alive and screaming in pain. Talk about karma. This one's called Desperation Angel.'

Adam looked over to Tommy to make sure he was ready. Tommy nodded, and turned up the volume on his guitar.

Desperation Angel

Throw away the ballast of the soul
Illusion of the selfish, baby
Beauty by mistake
Sunset of nostalgia and control
No one lives there anymore

Looking for some leverage in the silhouette of night
Litany of a liar on the stand about to break
Words are getting heavy and are dropping out of sight
Time to write your epitaph
Caged bird standing on the grave of dreams
Before the brave go underground and sleepers awake
Distant lighthouse spark ain't what it seems
The sword of Damocles

Thought you were a better man
Thought your friends would understand
One calling… one demand
Now you got no one
All that possibility
Echoes in your memory
Promises not meant to be
Nowhere left to run
Blind man without second sight
Darkness at the edge of night
Standing naked in the light
Reason with no name
Pressure bearing down on you
Tell me what you're gonna do
All the lies you thought were true
Only you to blame
Always what the preacher would say
Reeds in the rushing water
Don't abide you fade away
And so it goes

Full effect of the infinite cause and a five dollar bill
Dreamtime bum's rush through the past but you never will
Tried to buy redemption with a bag of stolen prayers
Falling down the neon night and no one really cares

Desperation angel
Threw it all away

Broken signal and a weary soul
New York City skyline getting farther out of sight
How far down the winding road
Many roads becoming one
One is where the muses set the balance long ago
Last one sometime later to complete the cabal
Crystal prism sunshine through a stained-glass window
Getting to the other side
Zeno at the painted porch one night
Something to consider as you're running toward the wall
Missionaries reborn as they fight
Fill your soul with love

Tommy's spotlight fades. Adam took a few deep breaths and collected himself after rocking out as hard as he could. It was the first time he had ever sung his songs live. It was a revelation, a full-on release, like screaming with joy.

As soon as the applause died down, he placed the mike back in the stand, took another deep breath, looked out to the audience and continued:

'Stephanie and I ended up seeing each other a few times over the next couple of months until she told me she wanted to see if she couldn't take the relationship with her female lover to the next level. Talk about a bummer and an erotic fantasy all at the same time. At least that explained the occasional weirdness about making plans, and the need and appreciation for incredibly long foreplay and cuddling. And there was one night the three of us were together and I thought I was going to fulfill my fantasy, until her lover got pissed off at me for not hating Ronald Reagan enough and not knowing who Andrea Dworkin was, so there went Stephanie and my fantasy in one fell swoop. I learned later that Andrea Dworkin was a hard-core feminist who believed that all sex between a man and a woman was rape, so I'm thinkin' a better man than I would have had to walk that tightrope to get to the Promised Land.

'The only other person who pulled a gun on me was my brother. I had spent the summer after graduating high school hitchhiking across country, and my family had no idea when I was coming home. I wanted to surprise them because it had been a few months since we'd seen each other, and it was the first time I'd ever been away. So I get back to my house and all of the doors are locked, and I knocked, and apparently no one was home. So I figured I'd go around to the back of the house, climb onto the roof of the shed like I'd done growing up many times before, and climb through my brother's window. But before I opened the window, I decided to knock on it just to make sure my brother wasn't home. What I didn't know was that my brother had seen The Exorcist the night before, which had just come out, and had given him nightmares, something that he suffered from. And there I was knocking on his window and saying 'Charles... Charles... Let me in...' in kind of a whisper. And he had no idea it was me 'cause he thought I was still out west. And the next thing I know the shade rips off the window from the inside, and there's my brother in his underwear with the most terrified look on anyone's face I'd ever seen. And, thank God, a split second before he pulled the trigger of the shotgun he had bought that year, he realized it was me. I literally thought I was gonna die; not exactly the happy homecoming I was expecting. And not only had my brother gotten into hunting that year, but he also became obsessed with bodybuilding, and all the steroids that went with it. And not only did he get a shotgun, but he also got a handgun, and we never had a good relationship. I was kind of like the bane of his existence, mostly because I was only 16 months younger than him, and in his mind I had deprived him of our parents' undivided affection. He also suffered from depression, which my parents never dealt with, because that wasn't something you did back then, or at least they didn't. And that combination of depression and steroids was toxic in terms of his mental and social stability. I'll never forget the time our neighbor, who was my brother's only friend at the time, had to find out where I was so he could get in touch with me to tell me not to come home because my brother was threatening to shoot me for real this time. And I took that threat seriously. Then my brother moved out to California after he graduated from college, and that was kind of the last time I saw or spoke to him. And one night, just a few years ago, I got a call from LAPD that he died of a heart attack, and apparently nobody really missed him. They found him because a neighbor had smelled something terrible coming from his apartment, which meant he had been there for a while. And at that point all the anger and unresolved emotions melted away. I learned it's never good to lose your brother. All I was left with was a prayer for his eternal peace made much less sad by 25 years of estrangement. I guess there's some kind of universal justice in there somewhere. I don't know. What I do know is that when it comes to relationships and matters of the heart, we're gonna lose big every once in a while. It ain't all a Hollywood ending. All we can do is try our best to let misfortune go and grasp whatever good lies within our reach. Maybe take the pain and turn it into art. This next one's about my brother. It's called *Powermind*...

Powermind

empty room off sunset... back of the beyond
ocean dreams against the jagged edge
distant voices long denied... still longing
and he passed away
two in a row
ashes in the sand
times winged ship sailing on

thirty years of silent reproach without a reason why
younger brother on the line and you said good bye
the illusion of a trinity never meant to be more than a store on thirty-
    seventh street

lying
crying
powermind was dying
blood and stone
refused to atone
to live and die alone

today I pray
today I embrace
today I remain determined
today I am
today I will
today I see the light

energy leading the power astray
who you are not what you say
struggle converting to suffering, not knowing
the need
determination strong
lift yourself up off the paper
no more running away
may you rest in peace

believed you were forever giving
the power of manifestation
the secret was you were living without a family
days of tangled expectation
hope like a snowdrift through spring
tears behind the motivation
never heard

lift yourself up
keep hope alive
honor your right to deserve
the back of your mind
the love left behind
the angels that you're gonna serve
it's all in the past
the falcon has flown
horizons beyond your control
coming back home where you belong
God watching over your soul

seas have become peaceful
balance has been set
destiny fulfilled in ways beyond imagination

trust
choose
hope
today I stand
today I strive
today I share
yesterday and forever

'A footnote to that last story: My mother had always maintained that she made my brother give her that handgun which, she said, she threw in the canal at the end of our block. But when she was in the hospital right before she passed away, just a few weeks before my brother did, she told me I needed to get it out of her underwear drawer before anyone else found it. And there it was, the gun my brother had threatened to shoot me with decades before. And not long after that I ended up working for Eldridge Johns, one of the world's most famous and gifted psychic mediums. And we're in one of our regular meetings, and, I swear to God, he looks right at me and says, 'Hold on. Your, brother's here…' And coming from El, I knew exactly what that meant. And the first thing he says to me, after he tells me that my brother is knocking down the door to get to me is, 'What's the story with the gun?' We had never had that discussion. He didn't even know I had a brother who passed away. He even knew the gun was underwater. It was shocking, unexplainable. Sometimes it's just about acceptance.'

Adam walked over to his drumset as Tommy's spotlight faded up. He picked up his Hot Rods and started laying down a fast, funk-fusion rhythm that Tommy immediately hooked into, letting the jam take him where it would. At one point Adam decided to push it as hard as he could, and was amazed to hear Tommy running through his rhythm like electricity through a coiled wire. Adam sensed that if he could just get through the rest of the show in the same, natural presentation, keep it going, he'd have done it, whatever it was.

After the jam, the audience cheering, Adam came back out front, Tommy's spotlight fading. Everyone got quiet, waiting for him to begin again, and so he did.

'I'm guilty of denying the truth,' Adam continued. 'I knew my cholesterol was sky high, but because I didn't want to start taking medication everyday like my parents used to have to do, I had a heart attack a few years ago while I was on vacation with my family in Jamaica. I was doing the Macarena with my four year old daughter on my shoulders with the rest of the resort at the nightly show performed by the resort staff, and I felt something like bronchitis in my chest, only I never had bronchitis so I wasn't sure what it was. But at that point it wasn't so bad, so I kept on doing the Macarena, and we were leaving the next day so I figured I'd be fine. But on the bus from the resort to the airport the next morning I was feeling really crappy. I had this weird pain that stretched from one arm all the way across my chest to the other arm. And not only that but I was sure I had a fever. And this shit was getting worse every minute. And I'm lugging our luggage through the airport, and I know something is very wrong 'cause I never felt anything like this before. And all I could do, once I was on the plane, was hug myself and rock in fetal position and pray that everything was all right and if this shit didn't get better by the time I got home I was going right to the hospital. I'm telling you, this was the worst I ever felt. And when I got home I was in bad shape, so I drove myself to the hospital, and they did some tests, and it was definitely weird when the doctor told me I had a heart attack and they were going to transfer me to another hospital to do more tests, which they did and, thank God nothing life-threatening or requiring any type of surgery was happening. A secondary blood vessel at the back of my heart had burst, but apparently I can live without it as long as I take the right medication, eat better, which I thought I was doing, and exercise, which I did, two days on, one day off for the last thirty years. But hey, if I have to eat boiled chicken, take Lipitor, and do a hundred push-ups everyday for the rest of my life, it beats dying... Oh yeah, and the fever I thought I had, I did. It was pneumonia. A heart attack and pneumonia, all at the same time. What a great vacation. This one's called *A Jamaican Tale*.

A Jamaican Tale

Sanctuary about the size of yesterday
Never thought, but I'm not surprised it turned out this way... it's the
    only way
Never saw eight rivers or the fire burn down into darkness
Both sides of my life on a beach in paradise and it's serious
Could have been an angel laying tells upon my history
Could have been my last breath in a reggae tragedy
Now I'm back in New York with a twist of fate behind me
Another turn of fortune to accept 'cause it was meant to be

Not too far until the time is right
A deeper level where darkness turns to light
Remember what the great Lalane had to say
The runner too but in a different way

Now they're gone
The word lives on
So do I
Gonna get to where I'm going
I can't deny
Or wonder why
Or get too high
That's just asking for trouble

Too many hours with a heart of shattered glass
Whisper prayers of memory but it doesn't pass
Wake up tangled in wires and still far gone
Try to get myself together and go on
And I got the old woman laid to waste
Time and nature's calling and demons that we faced
Even what this thing was all about
Or that right off Northern that almost took me out

The shades of night fall fast
The future becomes the past
As all rivers run
Many becoming one
And in the end we're back where we began
Tomorrow wait for me

It felt great to Adam to play a slower bluesy jazz. The flow of the show felt natural, with Tommy's playing on *A Jamaican Tale* sounding like a cross between Joe Pass and John Scofield.

'Tommy Vincent, everyone,' Adam introduced, as if Tommy needed any introduction, especially to the locals. As the applause died down, and Tommy's spotlight began to fade, Adam put his mike back in the stand, came back out front and continued:

'A few times, not often...' Here, Adam fake coughed, and while he was fake coughing mumbled, 'Bullshit,' under it, 'but a few times, I've read a situation completely wrong. Or maybe in my heart I knew it was wishful thinking, but not without some tangible reason, however small, for optimism. I'm too insecure to start thinking that a beautiful model, who was an on-camera host on one of the TV shows I helped produce, would be into me without her giving me some kind of indication that maybe she was. As surprising as it may seem, I'm not the kind of guy that models tend to gravitate toward. I know I made her laugh every chance I could. But still. And she was the one who asked me if I wanted to hang out. And, believe me, I completely understood that the first time she asked was just as friends. I had no expectations, other than to have fun, and maybe impress her enough that maybe she would give me a second look. And it was really fun. I picked her up on my motorcycle at her apartment and we drove all around the city for hours. She was totally into it. We hit a few bars and laughed all night. And we gave each other a big hug when I dropped her off. It was really a fun night. Then she asked me if I wanted to hang out the next Friday night. And the next. And the next. And every time we hung out it was really fun, going out to dinner and bars and galleries and clubs. We were really getting close as friends. And I never overstepped my bounds because I wanted her to see how cool I was, even though I lusted after her like a death-row inmate his freedom. But

I was biding my time, hoping that the right opportunity would present itself. And one night I got us tickets to see The Rolling Stones at Giant Stadium in the rain and I was smart enough to bring a huge umbrella. And we were laughing and rocking out and everything was in perfect harmony underneath the umbrella, and I asked her if I could kiss her, and she looked at me with unbelievable disappointment and a little anger in her eyes and said, 'No.' And I, with my heart sinking faster than a kick in the balls asked, 'Why?' And she said because then I'd want more, and I said, 'Of course I want more. But that doesn't mean I'm coming after it. I'm just asking to make out with you.' And she turned to stone, and we didn't speak on the limo-ride that I paid for home. Or for the next few weeks, until she came to my office and told me she missed hanging out with me, and couldn't we try being friends again. And, I'm telling you, this girl was like the most beautiful girl I'd ever seen, like a cross between Selma Hyack and Marilyn Monroe, so I said 'Sure', and invited her over to my apartment to see the film I had just finished of me doing all these character monologues on location, and drum solos and comedy bits... And when I picked her up on my bike, I noticed that her eyes were all fucked up. She had pink-eye. Anyway, we watched my film, and she told me she had no idea I was that kind of artist, even though I had been doing that kinda shit with her for months. And she gave me a hug. And that hug turned into a kiss; a long deep kiss. And I didn't push it beyond that because I couldn't believe I had just kissed the most beautiful girl I'd ever seen. And then we went out and had a great night, and I dropped her off and had another deep hug and a perfect kiss, and the next day I woke up with a raging case of pink-eye. And since it was the weekend, I couldn't get to a doctor, so I went to work on Monday with pink-eye. And she came to my office and saw that I had pink-eye and she started to laugh hysterically that she gave me pink-eye. And I kind of understood that kind of warped humor, laughing at other people's inconveniences that you were the unintentional cause of. I started to laugh too. And while we were laughing she told me the reason she came to my office was to tell me that, even though she had a great time the other night, she didn't want me to get the wrong idea about her intentions, and that it was probably a better idea if we were just 'friends'. And as she's telling me this she can't stop looking at my pink-eye and laughing. But I did. From happiness to loneliness in the blink of an eye. And all I could think to say, trying not to let her see how bummed out I was, and trying to put up a humorous front, was something like, 'If this happened from kissing you, I can't imagine what I'd catch if we made love.' She kinda stopped laughing after that, but we remained friends until she moved out to California to pursue a career I haven't heard anything about since. But I wish her well. Pink-eye and blue balls on a white dude. Now that's patriotism. This next one was inspired by the book 'Against The Day' by Thomas Pynchon:

Against the Day

And the rhythm of the riders... of the borderline
The voice of benediction... red blood, pure mind
Legends were foretold... and forgotten
Children of the darkness become the wind
God across the table laying tells with a mighty hand
A trembling apparition casting his net upon invisible rivers
Protected by the natural order
Every thought a declaration
Down the road to perdition... listen
Listen to the silver laughter
Looking at a broken mirror
And the flow of time... elevated into grace

Eternally
Returning to
Continually reborn
Ourselves alone

What of a city known to abandon its poor
Sunshine, you're on your own
Then come the riders of the borderline
The white riders
From the fire
Gesture us toward our fate
Like the dim blessed coming home

A secret history
Wrapped in the nature of time
Against the day of judgment
Heaven and earth are reserved unto fire
Thus the riders
Ascending in a long departure of light
As they pass through the prophets gate
Seeking shelter under sacramental skies
Valor forged by desperation
The white riders call the fallen to arise

Red blood pure mind
Allegiance to their limits
All the incarnation and the slaughter... in the silence

Reenact the cycles of betrayal
The riders' ungrateful ghost passing judgment
God has turned a blind eye
Toward the pale phantoms vanishing behind the mirror

'That was wild,' Adam thought, everyone cheering, Tommy's spotlight fading. 'Keep it going. Let 'em know I'm feeling it with 'em.'

He placed the mike in the stand, turned to face the audience and continued:

'The next song is about me getting caught on the George Washington Bridge on my motorcycle in a hurricane, all because a friend of mine, who lived in Paramus New Jersey, told me I should come over because she had a friend she thought I might like, and at that point in my life I would have gone anywhere in any condition if someone told me they had a friend they thought I might like. It wasn't exactly my best couple of decades in terms of my social and sexual life. So it was out to Paramus for the scariest experience of my life, and I'm not talking about the blind date, who ended up being the grand-daughter of a friend of my grandmother, Gussie Sedlack, which wasn't necessarily a bad thing. It was the fact that she looked like Gussie, who I had thought was an effeminate man, mostly because I was very young and she looked like a man, and sounded like a man.'

Faking smoking, in a deeper drag-queen voice, Adam said, 'Hi sweetheart. It's good to see you again. Look how big ya getting.' Then he continued with the story: 'Until I inadvertently walked in on Gussie when she was going to the bathroom, and she didn't have a penis, which meant that I saw Gussie Sedlack's vagina, something her grand-daughter found very funny, but not enough to create any chemistry between us. So, as soon as it was socially acceptable to do so, I said goodnight and made my way to the George Washington Bridge, where all hell broke loose. I thought I had outrun the storm, but as soon as I got onto the bottom level of the bridge, the wind started to blow so hard that it's pushing me over to the side of the bridge. I swear to God, I thought there was a real possibility that I was going to have to lay my bike down or get blown over the side of the bridge. But as I got closer to the guard-rail the wind decreased because of the barriers on the side of the bridge, which shielded the wind a little, and I was able to stabilize enough to hug the guard-rail and go, like, five miles an hour. And in the middle of this carnage of rain and wind, there was Mother Theresa in my mind's eye. I mean, I really never thought about her that much, but there she was, even when the eighteen-wheeler out of nowhere comes whizzing by me and I get caught in its vortex and get spun around. So now I'm facing the wrong way on the George Washington Bridge on my motorcycle in a hurricane. It was literally a scene out of a nightmare. But luckily, once the eighteen-wheeler passed me, there was very little traffic, so I was able to turn my bike around, hug the guard-rail, and get my ass off the bridge. This one's called *Sometimes...*

'Good setup,' Adam thought. Flow right into it. Into the grunge of it. He pressed *Sometimes* on the iTouch screen and nothing happened. He pressed it again. Nothing. He immediately went to the next song, and that launched. It seemed to be just a problem with *Sometimes*. 'Okay, close out of this, and relaunch...' he said to himself. He needed to buy a little space and time. Keep the audience engaged, the energy flowing.

'I got ghosts in the machine,' he announced. 'Gimme two seconds.' He pressed it again and it was still frozen. 'Fuck. Okay...'

He walked over to Tommy, who saw exactly what was going on and asked, 'Can we do this like unplugged?' Just guitar and vocals, singer songwriter style.

'We can give it a shot,' and Tommy starts finger-picking a slower, bluesier version of the song, which Adam hooked into within the first few measures. Everything was slowed down, more internal. He gave Tommy the universal 'one more time' signal around the intro so he could recalibrate his soul to the new groove. This was uncharted territory, a stripped-down version of a song. He needed to feel it.

Ultimately, it wasn't as good as it needed to be to keep the show at a certain level. If it was part of a film or video, the performance would have been left on the cutting-room floor - except live he couldn't do that. Live was warts and all. Because he was used to humming the bassline intro to get the note he started the song on, and there was no bassline, he was a little shaky through the first verse, singing 'Times and times and sometimes/Outside the perfect circle/Racing with the devil through wind and rain/Into the unknown, completely out of tune.

By the second part of the verse he had made a few tonal corrections and felt like it went okay through most of the middle part and the solo, which Tommy wisely abridged because of circumstance, more entropy than creativity, until Adam had to come in on the second verse and had the same problem he had on the first verse; no bassline to hum to. 'Fuck,' he thought, trying to steer his singing back on key.

As Tommy finger-picked a soulful ending, Adam knew he had exposed his lack of experience. He wasn't at the unplugged level. That was the first time he was ever plugged. Hopefully, he could redeem the energy as the show progressed. Right then, it wasn't about falling. It was about getting up.

'And for our next selection,' he delivered to the audience in his best Lawrence Welk, just to be silly. 'Aren't the girls wonderful... Listen,' he continued, back to himself, 'I need to take a break from myself for a little bit. Can we do something together? Like, how about an improv? You guys define a character for me, and then we'll set up a scenario, like, I lost something, and then I found it in a weird place. All right? Okay, give me a nationality.'

Adam's brother Barry yelled out, 'Serbo-Croatian.'

'Serbo-Croatian?' Adam said with fake incredulity. 'How about Eastern European?'

'Sorry my friend,' his friend Robert insisted, with a big smile, 'you asked. You gotta go with Serbo-Croatian.'

'Serbo-Croatian,' Barry said.

'Okay, Serbo-Croatian,' Adam agreed, intending to do an Eastern European accent regardless, since that was where he believed Serbo-Croatia was. 'All right,' he continued, 'now what did I lose?'

'Your testicles,' Adam's next-door neighbor, who was a contemporary of Adam's said. Mike and Adam drank many beers together over the years.

'Okay, thanks Mike. My testicles. Let's see how much farther this thing can devolve. And what's the weird place I found my testicles?'

'In a lion's mouth,' Stevie Schecter said.

'Of course. I wouldn't have expected anywhere else. Thanks Stevie. All right, so I'm a Serbo-Croatian who lost his balls and found them in a lion's mouth... And scene:

"Okay," Adam said, in an Eastern European accent, thinking where he needed to take the scene in order to get all the improv elements, while at the same time performing it. "Wot I want to do today? See movie? New 'Fest and Furious' is out. No, last two suck. Maybe I go to cheap whorehouse, get hum-job from Olga. No. Since she got new teeth she bite too much. I know. Maybe I eat pot brownie and go to zoo. Should be fun..." Adam mimes walking to the zoo and looking at the animals. "Oh, look at lion. Veddy beautiful enimal. Pot brownie veddy strong. Too strong. I think I need to lie down..."

Adam mimes someone walking up to, and speaking quietly yet decisively to someone sleeping. "Don't move."

"Who? Wot?"

"I am zoo-keeper. You fell asleep right in front of lion cage. Lion was licking your balls, so we had to tranquilize him. Somehow, he has your whole, you know, shvants in his mouth. As soon as we open his mouth, please to remove yourself."

"Oh shit. This much worse than Olga."

"Who is Olga?"

"Not important right now."

"Okay, on three. Wahn, two, three... Okay... You are lucky man. You almost lost your testisi in lion's mouth. Next time, don't come to zoo so fuzzy-headed."

"You are right. Long live Milosevic."

"Long dead, that piece shit. I piss on his grave.'

'And, end scene,' in Adam's voice.

"Hey tough guy," Adam said in the character's voice, "who said to end scene?"

Adam:	It's just over, that's all.
Character:	So you think you just throw me away like I'm some garbage or something?
Adam:	No, it's just an improv scene.
Character:	Improv scene. I get it. You think I'm you.
Adam:	You are me.
Character:	You flatter yourself.
Adam:	Whatever. End scene.
Character:	No! Fuck you.
Adam:	No, fuck you.
Character:	No, fuck you.
Adam:	Listen, we can do this all night, but I gotta get going with the show.
Character:	Your show sucks. Your singing sounds like dying mule.
Adam:	Yeah, I know. I was just hoping that the songs, you know, and the energy...
Character:	Is better when you talk songs. What's next song?
Adam:	It's called *To Know To Dare*.
Character:	You talk it?
Adam:	No, I sing it.
Character:	Talk it, I'm telling you.
Adam:	No man, it's a song. I'm gonna sing it.
Character:	Okay, your funeral. But I'm not sticking around. Maybe they are, but I'm not.
Adam:	What a shame. Do me a favor though. Before you go, turn on the music.
Character:	Sure... Dick.
Adam:	What'd you say?
Character:	Nothing. Nothing. End scene... Dick.

Still in character, Adam walked over to the iStation, chose *To Know To Dare*, walked back to center-stage, as Tommy's spotlight faded up. It was comforting to hear the loud bottom rumble of the sub-woofer. It allowed him to get inside the song.

To Know To Dare

Nothing should be different
Half the battle letting go
What else do I need to know
Still less to conceal
Realize… Chaos can be organized
Harmony
Memory
Signs that light the way
Fragile prayer
To know to dare
To keep silent
One must learn to fall if one would fly
I'm still falling
Some days rising
Some days just getting by

Maybe what I'm saying
Lose the battle win the war
Lesser angels keeping score
'cause the greater don't care

Fighting from the center
After fighting bring it back
Ready for the next attack
The way of the world
Moving… like the moon beneath the waves
Energy
What will be
Symbols marking time

Almost there
To know to dare
To keep silent
Learning to obey and then command
The challenge standing
First light commanding
Love and the tides flowing from inside

Through all the changes, should the king have known
You'd think so
But you never can tell
The king was all alone

Looking toward the future
I know shadows fall

Learning to surrender
Letting go... letting go
Unbroken echo
In the silence
Listen

'One more story and song,' Adam thought, looking at Tommy and smiling. 'Tommy. Beautiful... I hope they dug it.'

Facing the audience, feeling energized, fulfilled, he continued:

'Gujar nomads sliced my tent open with a razor blade while I was on a trekking expedition in the Himalayas about twenty-five years ago, and stole everything I brought with me, except my drumsticks, which I had in my sleeping-bag. But they took everything else - left me as naked as the day I was born. I had gone to India on a quest for a little spiritual enlightenment, a little immersion into deep nature, some musical education, because I had always been into Indian music, and I was hoping to find a very special set of tabla drums that somebody, hopefully, would show me how to play, maybe even jam with the locals. So one night, after a day of trekking through one of the oldest and most extreme and breathtaking landscapes on Earth, we set up camp, and everything was beautiful. The sky was so clear you could see the Milky Way all the way around. And because everyone else on the expedition was part of a group of friends who had just graduated from NYU Law School and had come on this trip to celebrate life before starting to work in the real world, I was the only one in the group who slept alone in a tent.

'So I retire for the evening... And the next thing I know, I wake up with the most sever headache I ever had... And 'what are those flashlights right above me? Who is... Wait, I'm in my tent. How the fuck?' In that instant I thought something terrible was happening: I'm in the process of getting ripped off, and they must have crushed my head in. And all I could think about was how sad my mother was going to be when she hears that I was killed. It was terrible. And then the people with the flashlights, who, it turned out were our guides, were calling my name and telling me not to move because they wanted to check to see if I was okay. 'My head. It's killing me.' They told me that's probably the ether the Gujars used to knock me out, because they could still smell it in the air. And they asked me if I could get up. And after tensing and loosening the muscles in my arms and legs to make sure they were still attached to my body, I told them I probably could, except that I didn't have any clothes on. I was in the habit of sleeping naked. 'Let me just get something on.' Then they told me they'd probably have to get me something 'cause it looked like the Gujars stole everything in my tent. But they also told me how lucky I was because the Gujars are also in the habit of cutting people's throats, and it looked like all I got was ripped off. But then I realized that if they stole everything, they got my passport and travelers check receipts, and being in India without a passport or money is like being homeless in, like, the worst city in America. How was I gonna get home? But the guides had already dispatched the guys who took care of the trekking ponies into the surrounding area to see if they could find out anything. And, like finding a needle in a haystack, one of the pony-boys comes back less than an hour later with the book I had brought with me, *Sometimes A Great Notion* by Ken Keesey, inside of which I had stuffed my passport and travelers check receipts. I mean, there is no way you could tell me that the pony-boys were not in on this. In the entire Himalayan expanse, these fuckin' guys come back with the one thing I needed to make everything else a relatively minor inconvenience; the one thing that would be the most incriminating piece of evidence for any thief if they were caught. But I wasn't going to argue with good fortune. So someone lent me some clothes so I could make my way to the nearest town to get the police report I needed to get a refund on my traveler's checks. Now, keep in mind, this is a deeply Muslim part of India, and Americans are the enemy, and an American coming into their town accusing some of their townsfolk of stealing pissed the police chief off so much that he threatened to put me in jail for some bullshit charge. And our guides, who didn't have money to pay this guy off, were only making matters worse. And I finally realized that this was no joke, that I had better do something or I was fucked. And the crazy thing was I had finished a comparative religion study not long before my India trip, and part of that study was reading the Koran. Yes, I'm one of the few Jews who's read the Koran. So, I interrupted my guide, who was telling the police chief that his company would gladly make a contribution to the town civic association as soon as he got back to Srinagar, and said to the police chief, "As Allah is my witness, everything we've told you is the truth." And when the police chief realized what I had just said, I thought the guy's head would explode."

In an Indian accent, Adam continued, "Who are you to invoke the name of Allah. How dare you!"

"Sir, I mean no disrespect. But I just finished reading the Koran, and was so deeply moved by Allah's mercy and compassion that I felt it would be wrong not to do everything I could to make you believe me." And the edge came off. He was still deeply suspicious, but he wasn't freaking out.

"And why did you read Koran?"

"Because I wanted to get the full story, both eastern and western. I read the Bible, the Vedas, the Upanishads, Buddhist scripture, the Koran. Most people don't know Allah is the God of Abraham. Same as mine. It's the same God..."

'And how about this... This guy's son was a comparative religion student at the University in New Delhi. Talk about providence. He took a piece of paper out of his army surplus desk and hand-wrote the report himself. He even had his assistant bring in a pot of tea and a plate of macaroons. And he told me that he'd look into the theft, but that I needed to realize that the value of the things that were stolen would probably feed a number of people for quite a while, and that the clothes that were stolen would probably be worn by any number of children for years to come, and I understood. He was making the Gujars out to be like Robin Hood, even though they're cold-blooded murderers. And I was the bloated American. But I wasn't about to argue. And as it turned out, one of the guide's wives made me a pheran and poot, the traditional Kashmiri suit with the knee-length blouse and loose fitting pants. And I was able to redeem my travelers check receipts, and I got my tabla and spent my last night in India sitting in with an Indian band in my pheran and poot. And because I was so tan from trekking in the mountains, and had a pretty full beard, no one who didn't know me wouldn't have known that I wasn't a local tabla player jamming like I'd done a thousand times before. This last one expresses that type of equilibrium. It's called *Thundering Silence*...

THUNDERING SILENCE

When the moment became lost in time
When the wind blew through the autumn sky
When all that remained return to the earth
And the three rays like the moon and the tides

Let us transcend the limitations
Let us dance the eternal dance
Where the rhythm is heard above the echoing
Outside the thundering silence

What is gained if the spirit is lost
Surrender to the fate of the forsaken
Listen to the music in the breathing darkness
Sounds like twilight in a minor key

'Wow. That's it,' Adam said to himself, taking it all in, blown away how he grooved with Tommy, inside the music, his rhythms holding their own. He always felt that if he was into it, the audience would be into it. It all felt fun, good, his less than stellar singing abilities notwithstanding.

He wasn't under any illusion of where he stood in the pantheon of great performances. He had seen The Who, Bogart in Casablanca, Nureyev dance Romeo and Juliet at The Met. But for what it was, a suburban dad who, after decades decided to get off his ass and see if he could write it and perform it, it was pretty good, a night made more professional because Tommy Vincent made it so. Adam knew how fortunate he was to have had someone of Tommy's experience and ability perform with him. It upped his game. The synergy he hoped would be created was. A lightness, a purity of the soul. The soul's willing deed, however fleeting. It was all about being in the moment, appreciating it for what it was, not lamenting it wasn't more. It reminded him of climbing a mountain, how peaceful and settling it is when you make it to the summit, knowing how difficult the descent always is. Whatever it took to get there, he was glad he stuck with it. He gestured Tommy over so they could say goodnight together.

'That was fun, man,' Tommy said, giving Adam a quick hug.

'You were ridiculous.' Then he turned to the audience, his friends and family. 'All right, that just about does it,' Adam said to everyone. 'First round's on me next door. I love you all.'

Walking backstage, the sense that time's winged ship continues to sail on, that there was still a long way to go, some high, some low. Adam thought of a line he had written for a blues monologue he performed at one of the Gotham City Improv shows, that he thought about from time to time. The character, Sonny Rhodes, was recounting some of the crazy experiences he'd had over the years, like the time at a juke joint in Clarksdale – he had heard Robert Johnson had just passed through. He thought that must have been the reason, the spirit of Robert Johnson still around, that he blew his harp so hard during his rendition of *Hellhound On My Trail* that his glass eye popped clean out of his head and landed in the woman's drink in the first row. Neither of them knew it until, at the end of the song, the woman took a swig and felt something in her mouth, that wasn't ice. There she was, screaming, looking at a glass eye in her hand looking back at her, and Sonny laughing so hard at what he was seeing, his eye in her hand, and she's looking at it and screaming. He couldn't catch his breath enough to tell her it was his and please be gentle with it, and that he certainly owed her another of what she was drinking, and plenty more if she was so inclined. Later on, after May-Ann got dressed and went home, he thought about what had happened and had another good laugh.

"Ain't no tellin' which way the wind's gonna blow,' Sonny thought, 'as long as you hold onto your hat when it does."

Printed in the United States
By Bookmasters